Destiny's Crucible

Book 1

Cast Under an Alien Sun

Olan Thorensen

Olan Thorensen

copyright © 2016 Olan Thorensen

The is an original work of fiction. Any resemblance to people and places is coincidental.

All rights reserved.

Cast Under an Alien Sun

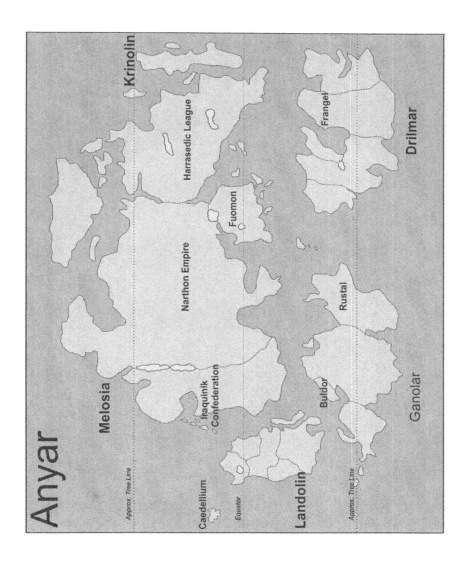

Olan Thorensen

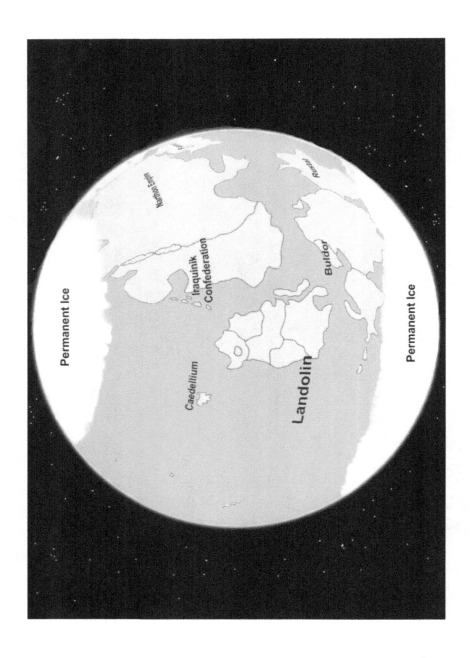

Caedellium

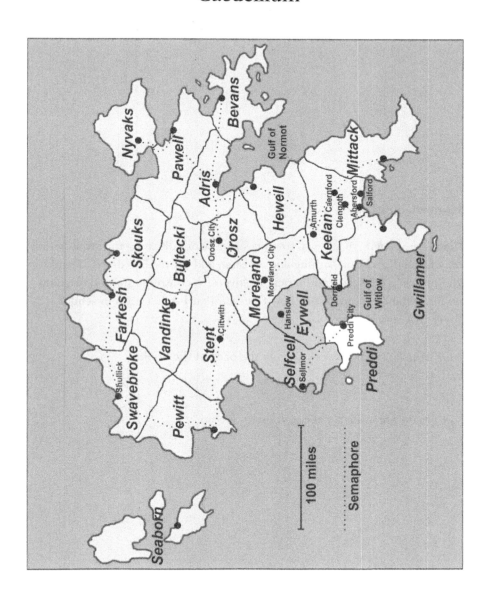

Olan Thorensen

Acknowledgments

Thanks to my wife, Kathleen, for encouragement, tolerating my sequestering away for endless hours writing and revising, and for reading drafts. Thanks to editors Felicia Sullivan and Patricia Waldygo for contributions and teaching me those things about writing and grammar that I didn't learn in school. Cover by Damonza.com.

A list of major characters is given in the back of the book.

Color maps are available at olanthorensen.com.

CONTENTS

1	A Change in Destination	1
2	Alive	8
3	Planet Anyar	23
4	Recovery	31
5	A Gathering Storm	38
6	Acceptance	56
7	Caedellium Life	66
8	Thorns	73
9	Interview with the Abbot	77
10	Buldorian Mercenaries	87
11	Yozef Learns About the Narthani	92
12	What to Do?	101
13	Great Hall of the Keelans	104
14	The Snarling Graeko	116
15	Chemistry	122
16	Guinea Pigs	132
17	Impact	141
18	Supplicant to Tycoon	148
19	A House of His Own	157
20	Maera	164
21	Keelan Justice	177
22	The Buldorians	190
23	Earth Fades	199
24	A World Beyond Abersford	212
25	Ignition	220
26	Fertilizer	229
27	A Close Encounter	237
28	Not to Be	243
29	Could Be Worse	251
30	The Raid	265
31	Panic and Preparation	277
32	The Battle of St. Sidryn's	288
33	Aftermath	299
34	Not Over	311
Major Characters		322

Crucible (a.t. Merriam-Webster)

- : a container in which metals or other substances are heated to a very high temperature or melted
- **: a difficult test or challenge**
- **: a place or situation that forces people to change or make difficult decisions**

"It is not in the stars to hold our destiny but in ourselves."
— William Shakespeare

"One meets his destiny often on the road he takes to avoid it."
— French Proverb

"It is a mistake to try to look too far ahead. The chain of destiny can only be grasped one link at a time."
— Winston Churchill

"Only in the crucible of strife does God burn away the impurities to reveal the essence of a person, an inner core that might otherwise have remained hidden for an entire life."

— Rhaedri Brison, Caedellium, Planet Anyar.

CHAPTER 1

A CHANGE IN DESTINATION

The plane lurched, hitting the first pocket of air shear. He cinched his seatbelt tighter, and his grip on the armrests ratcheted up two notches. He wanted to close his eyes but instead looked out the window at the last of the mountains. A dot in the sky appeared above the distant horizon, then zoomed larger, expanding as if to engulf the plane!

Before his brain reacted, he catapulted forward. The seatbelt cut into his abdomen, his view whirled, and he slammed back in the seat as the Boeing 737 disintegrated.

The belt held him to the seat as his torso, arms, and legs gyrated. Something hammered against his legs, turning him toward the girl in the seat beside him. Her eyes wide, she opened her mouth, but her scream was lost among other noises assaulting his ears. The man on the aisle was—gone. The spot where he'd been sitting had turned into blue sky, brown and green earth, and . . . pieces.

He tumbled, wind tearing at his face. He had glimpses of open sky, felt freezing cold, and gasped for breath. Intense pain accompanied impressions of people, baggage, seats, metal sections, and the shock of contact with something, and then . . .

***

Three Hours Earlier, Flight 4382

"We continue with boarding of United Flight 4382, direct from San Francisco to Chicago. Group 3 may now board."

What Joe Colsco heard was something closer to, "Wek you board tid ight flity-ate-and-tuh, wrecked farm saloforsco shillack. Grope eemaywo ord."

He wondered if they deliberately trained the announcers to sound like they had a mouth full of mush. It took inquiries to a nearby elderly woman with gray hair and a man in a cowboy hat and boots for the three of them to come up with a plausible translation. Reasonably confident their group was called to board, all three joined the queue. They shuffled forward, presented their boarding passes, and snaked down the gangway.

As the line of passengers reached the aircraft door, Joe looked up at blue sky and fluffy clouds, then back at the aluminum cylinder where he would spend the next four hours. The plane looked so small against the vast sky. Sweat beaded his forehead and plastered the shirt to his skin.

Why am I so nervous about flying?

It certainly wasn't because of the conference in Chicago. While it was his first presentation at a major scientific meeting, he knew his results were impressive, and once he started the talk, he could ignore an audience of any size.

Inside the plane, passengers jostled for space. Joe's apprehension persisted. The elderly woman took her seat, then Joe went to his row. He had a window seat. He shoved his bag into the overhead bin and sat his 5 foot, 10 inch, 175 pounds into 28A, slid his laptop and a folder into the seat pocket in front of him, and crammed his knees against the back of the seat in front.

His attention drifted to Chicago and the huge annual weeklong American Chemical Society (ACS) gathering. Scores of simultaneous presentations would be held in rooms that varied in size from hardly more than a large bedroom to an auditorium holding several thousand.

He'd based his presentation on a paper that one of the better chemistry journals had accepted for publication, contingent on what the editor considered minor revisions. He had resubmitted those revisions to the journal two days ago. The title of his talk, "A New Approach to Synthesizing Derivatives of the Thiopyran Class of Heterocyclic Rings," might be nap-inducing, according to his girlfriend Julie, but Dr. Ellsworth, his graduate school advisor, thought the title and focus appropriate for the setting. Joe had developed a novel method of synthesizing cyclic bases, a class of compounds that included both the information-carrying parts of DNA and RNA and other compounds with important industrial and medical applications. Joe and Ellsworth had submitted a patent application and expected significant interest from chemical companies.

In two months, Joe would give another talk, this one at the Western Chapter of the American Association for the Advancement of Science (AAAS) conference in Sacramento. At this catch-all meeting for every branch of science and for any social and political issues impinged on by science, many presentations would be less about hard science results and more about implications and speculations.

Ellsworth referred to them as "pseudoscience," but Joseph didn't care. The meeting gave him a chance to relate his research to a topic he found more interesting than his ACS talk. His AAAS talk, "Alternatives to Standard Heterocyclic Bases in DNA of Exobiosystems," would address one of the basic questions in biochemistry and exobiology: whether the four bases of Earth DNA (adenine [A], thymine [T], guanosine [G], and cytosine [C]) were required or the result of randomness in the first organisms that evolved on Earth. Could life have settled on other heterocyclic bases? A, T, G, and X? Or even X, X, X, and X, where each X was a different base from Earth's ATGC?

Joe's novel path to base synthesis used conditions both relevant to efficient commercial production and similar to the environment theorized to have existed on Earth as life developed. He had already prepared presentations for both meetings, but his focus this day was the ACS gathering in Chicago.

Getting his advisor's agreement to reveal their latest data at the Chicago meeting hadn't been automatic.

"Joe, you know what can happen if you reveal results before publication. I know the good reviews are encouraging and the requested changes minor, but you can never tell for sure. It's always best to wait for formal acceptance before talking at a meeting."

While Joe had pretended to take everything Ellsworth said seriously, he knew Ellsworth always drummed into everyone in his lab horror stories of people being scooped by trolls at meetings who hurried home and published preliminary results to claim priority of publication. Joe understood the concern. Revealing approaches, much less results, before publication had a checkered history in science.

Joe's reasoning and his insistence the conference was a chance for him to impress the academic community assuaged Ellsworth, and the title and summary were submitted to the meeting's organizers. Joe only felt minor guilt at his lapse in honesty. It was not the attendees from academia he was interested in impressing, but those from industry—particularly, chemical companies. Joe's ambitions were limited to an interesting job that paid well, a secure future, and marriage in suburbia with two kids. He had seen enough of the rat race of grant applications and the politics of academia and was even less interested in teaching the same classes to cookie-cutter students, year after year. Neither Ellsworth, whose lab he worked in, nor the Berkeley Chemistry

Department would be pleased if he left early. Their goal consisted of churning out PhDs after years of benefiting from cheap graduate student labor.

But that's their problem, Joe thought, comfortable in his small subterfuge.

In theory, only the journal editor and the three reviewers knew details of the paper. In practice, word of the paper was already circulating. Joe had been contacted by two chemical company recruiters with job offers, each at a salary comparable to that of a full professor with twenty years' experience, plus generous benefits—information he had not shared with Ellsworth. He and Julie anticipated a further increase in interest once he publicly revealed the latest results in his meeting presentation. They would have to do some hard thinking if they got an offer they couldn't refuse.

"Then you wouldn't get your PhD," Julie pointed out when he told her of the first offer.

"No, but a doctor of philosophy degree is less important in industry than at universities, where they wouldn't even look at your application if you weren't Dr. Somebody. I've asked around, and there's not much difference between a master's degree and a PhD for companies unless you aim to become head of a division or even of the whole company, neither of which I have any interest in.

"If we decided to bail on the PhD, all I have to do is withdraw from the doctoral program, and a master's degree is automatically granted, based on my first two years' work. Is sticking out two to three more years as a graduate student worth adding three letters behind my name?"

"You know my feelings, Joe. I'm ready to nest and move on. And there's the other little item to consider."

They had been living together for three years, with a wedding scheduled in two months, soon after Joe's AAAS presentation. Julie and her family were in full wedding-planning mode, something Joe was happy to leave to them. Then, a week before Joe left for Chicago, a complication appeared when a pregnancy kit came up positive. They had been careless. Having a family was something they wanted "someday" in the nebulous future. Now, whether "someday" would come in seven months or whether Julie would end the pregnancy was under discussion. The option of Joe having a well-paid job would factor into their decision.

From his seat, Joe saw his vague reflection in the plane's window. What stared back was the face of a man twenty-six years old, of average appearance, fine, mousy brown hair, and unusually light blue eyes. He accepted himself as a classic science nerd. He loved watching sports but was not athletic, being too slow, too uncoordinated, too unmuscular, too lazy, and from an early age too reluctant for the physicality of team sports. Occasional hiking and jogging, spurred on by Julie's nagging, were his only vigorous activities.

While Flight 4382 continued loading, Joe reviewed the notes for his talk. He lost his concentration when the occupants of the other two seats in his row appeared. A tall man of about forty-five and dressed in a suit nodded a greeting as he sank into the aisle seat. The man rose again a moment later for the occupant of the middle seat—a teenage Hispanic girl. She said hello to Joe with a friendly smile and took her seat. They all settled with minimal elbow joggling as the plane finished loading. Joe smelled perfume on the girl, and when she bumped his elbow and apologized, he responded politely, then promptly forgot about both of his row-mates and resumed mentally practicing his talk.

"Sir, please buckle up," said a flight attendant.

"Oh, sorry." He tussled with the seatbelt, then loosened it to accommodate his girth. He really needed to lay off pizza so often. Never one to mince words, his fiancée called him *pudgy*.

The plane taxied to the runway and waited in a queue. When cleared for departure, the engines roared as the plane picked up speed and lifted off. Joe clamped his hands on both armrests. They rose to cruising altitude, and the engine noise settled to a steady drone.

Three hours fifty-five minutes before they touched down in Chicago. Joe's stomach churned. He took a deep breath and closed his eyes.

"You okay?"

Joe turned to the girl. "What?" He pulled out a handkerchief and mopped his brow, then laughed. "Guess I'm a little nervous."

"Do you fly often?"

"Nope, only my third time."

"Then this isn't the best route." She smiled sympathetically. "It's normally bumpy when we cross the Rockies. But don't worry. We'll bounce around for a bit, and then it'll be okay. They seldom lose a wing." A mischievous grin played on her full lips.

"Thanks for nothing," he muttered.

"It's quite exciting when we go through turbulence."

Joe's mouth twitched, and he glanced at her. She couldn't be more than sixteen. "My need for an adrenaline rush is limited to computer games." He tightened the seatbelt. "Even roller coasters are more than I can handle, and they're only a few hundred feet off the ground."

"Then you haven't lived. I can't wait to try skydiving."

Not for him. Nor bungee jumping, rock climbing, or any other inconceivable activities. Video games and watching sports were plenty of action for him. He pulled out his laptop and opened it, hoping she'd get the message he wasn't interested in conversation, and especially not the sort that involved aircraft wings falling off.

"What do you do?"

Joe sighed. To work, he needed to escape this chatty teenager. "I'm a scientist." He opened his presentation and turned the screen so she could see his slides. "Sorry, I need to work."

She shrugged and pulled out a book.

Joe worked on his presentation, which helped calm his nerves. Two hours into the flight the plane jolted, and his stomach spasmed.

The girl giggled. "Turbulence. Guess we're over the Rockies."

His belly tightened, and beads of sweat reappeared on his forehead. He put the laptop away, cinched the seatbelt tighter, and clutched the armrests.

The plane lurched. Joe's seatbelt squeezed his stomach. Gasps and squeals reverberated through the cabin; somewhere a child cried.

The captain's controlled voice drifted from the address system. "Please return to your seats and fasten your seatbelts. We'll have rough air for the next few minutes."

His anxiety mounting, Joe's grip tightened. He opened his eyes and stared down at mountains far below. A wave of vertigo swept over him, and he raised his eyes to the horizon. A dot appeared in the distance and drew Joe from his thoughts. He frowned. A plane? His eyes widened in panic as the dot expanded to fill the window.

The plane lurched sideways, and an explosion rocked the aircraft. High-pitched wails filled the air, and a flight attendant and a drink trolley careened down the aisle. Baggage compartments burst open, and bags became missiles.

A second explosion sent shards of metal flying. A ball of burning fuel burst in through an exit door several rows to the front, incinerating passengers close to it. The inhalation of smoke stopped the scream in Joe's throat.

The plane tilted, nose down, and the seatbelt bit into his midriff, then the aircraft swung nose up. The seat in front jerked back violently, slamming into his knees. Joe stared at his legs. A femur jutted through torn flesh, and blood pumped from the wound in thick ribbons, but he felt nothing. He looked at the girl next to him. Her eyes were wide, mouth open in a scream that was lost in the noise of grinding metal and chaos.

The plane cartwheeled. The wall across the aisle peeled open, and seats vacuumed out. The suited man disappeared through the hole in the fuselage. Other passengers followed, including the cowboy and the teenage girl.

Still strapped to his seat, Joe hurtled through the gaping hole, jagged metal slicing into him. Arms and legs spiraling like a puppet, he twisted helplessly as icy air engulfed him.

I'm dying!

He tumbled, caught glimpses of open sky, felt freezing cold, and gasped for breath. Intense pain accompanied impressions of people, baggage, seats, metal sections, and the shock of contact with something, and then . . .

CHAPTER 2

ALIVE

He awoke. Not the instant awareness of being jolted by an alarm or the gentle rising from dozing in and out, but a gradual recognition of existence.

All he heard was his breathing. Wherever he was, the air was odorless and still. When he tried opening his eyes, they ached. His whole body ached.

Finally, Joe's eyes opened, and he stared up at a ceiling so white it hurt his eyes. He turned his head to the left, then to the right. He was in a room with walls of the same featureless white, with no hint of seams, tiles, windows, doors, or lights.

He tried to talk, to ask questions, but a croak came out.

"You can get water from the tube to the right of your mouth," said a voice.

Joe turned his head, and something touched his cheek. He opened his mouth and a tube entered. He sucked cool water into his mouth. While it felt good, when he swallowed, it was as if the water fought its way over rocks. After several more swallows, it became easier. Finally, he pushed the tube out with his tongue.

"W . . . what happened? Where am I?"

"You were in an accident and were injured. Everything should be fully functional."

Accident? What accident?

He couldn't remember an accident. He was on a plane going to the meeting when . . . the plane. Sitting. The man and the Hispanic girl. Looking out the window. The dot. The dot getting bigger! The impact? Everything turning to pieces! His heart rate shot up as he remembered.

"Do not be alarmed. Everything is fine. We believe you are functioning within normal parameters."

The voice sounded hollow. Recorded.

Functioning within normal parameters? Who the hell talks like that? I must be in a hospital. Where's the staff?

He tried to move something besides his head: legs, arms, fingers. Nothing responded.

Why can't I move? Am I paralyzed!?

"Everything is fine. You cannot move yet because I need to speak with you first. Do you understand?"

"No, I don't understand," he rasped. "Where am I?"

The voice ignored his question. "What is your name?"

Joe said nothing, his mind racing, groping for solid ground.

"Please answer. What is your name?"

"Joe," he mumbled. "Joe."

"Your name is Joe? Is that your entire name?"

"Joseph. Joseph Colsco. Joseph William Colsco."

"You have given three different names. Are they all equally correct, or is one more correct?"

"My full name is Joseph William Colsco, but people call me Joe." The rasp in his voice was fading.

"Thank you, Joe."

"Who are you?" he demanded, his tone hardening.

"You may think of me as your doctor."

"Think" of you as—? What the hell is going on?

His mouth went dry again. He returned to the tube for more water and a moment to think.

"All right. You're a doctor, and I was in an accident. Why can't I move?"

"To keep you calm until we can talk," said the voice with its odd flatness. It had an accent, though he couldn't place it. That was unusual, because people from all over the world attended Berkeley, and he could easily identify most accents. This voice strangely lacked intonations.

"I will allow a little movement so you can be reassured. Test your fingers and toes."

Joe clenched his hands, then splayed his fingers. He wiggled his toes. He wasn't paralyzed.

He tried to sound calmer. "Yes, I can move a little. Why can't I get up?"

"In time. Please answer more questions. This is to check your memory. Where do you live?"

"Berkeley, California."

"What is your occupation?"

"I'm a chemistry graduate student at the University of California."

"Where were you born?"

"La Mesa, near San Diego."

"What is the name of the San Diego football team?"

"Huh? Who cares?"

"The name please."

"The Chargers. Well, used to be before moving to Los Angeles."

"Now I will ask questions to test your mental responses. What is two plus five?"

"Seven."

"The square root of twenty-five?"

"Five."

"The cube root of 4,913?"

"Gimme a break!"

"Please recite back the following numbers, three, five, two, two, seven, six, eight."

Joe complied.

"Three, five, two, two, seven, six, eight."

He repeated the string of numbers again—barely.

"Five, eight, one, eight, three, six, two, seven, four, five, seven, five, nine."

"Who the fuck can remember that many?!"

The questions continued, alternating from the trivial to the ridiculous. Joe was about to call an exhausted and angry halt when the questions stopped.

"Thank you, Joe. Your mental functioning seems to be satisfactory."

Joe was too tired to respond.

"You will rest now, and we will talk more later."

"Wait! What about some answ—"

Joe descended into a black void.

***

Then . . . awake again. This time suddenly, still looking at the same white ceiling. Joe opened his mouth to call out and realized he could move his arms. He drew them up in front of his face to look at his hands, rotated the wrists to view both sides, and flexed his fingers. While everything worked, the pallid flesh and his thin arms startled him.

"You may sit up," the voice droned. "Be careful. You may feel dizzy."

When Joe tried to sit up, it was as if his abdominal muscles had forgotten how to contract. He grunted and pushed against the surface with his right arm, struggling into a sitting position. He was on a platform two feet off a floor. The voice was right. He was so dizzy he thought he might faint. He sat, head hanging, hands gripping the edge of the platform, eyes closed until his head cleared.

The ceiling, walls, floor, and platform were all the same white. He was inside a ten-foot white cube, empty except for the low platform on which he sat.

He looked down. He was naked. His genitals were there but shriveled. His legs were pale, thin, and unmarred.

The accident! My leg!

He remembered the bone sticking out. Ribbons of blood. Now, there wasn't a mark. What kind of hospital was this?

"Joe, can you catch this ball?"

"Ball? What ball?" Something thudded off his forehead. A blue ball about two inches in diameter bounced across the floor, hit a wall, and continued to ricochet around the room. It wasn't the blueness that caught his attention, but the slowness with which the ball bounced and the height of the bounces. It was like he was watching a slow-motion film. That possibility was eliminated when the ball came within reach, and Joe reached out and grabbed it with his left hand. Another ball appeared—red this time. He caught it in his right hand.

"Good reflexes. Thank you, Joe."

He stared at the two balls in his hands, then his fingers curled into fists. He opened his hands and gaped. The balls were gone!

A chill washed over him, and his breathing turned quick and shallow. A knot formed in his stomach.

"There is no reason to be frightened, Joe. You are fine. You were injured, but everything seems to be sufficiently repaired."

Repaired? Like a toaster? And sufficiently? Sufficiently for what?

He drew several deep breaths, trying to slow his racing heart. "Please answer my questions. Who are you, and where am I?"

"Joe, I am a simulation of a human being, designed to communicate with you."

"Yeah," Joe snorted, "and I'm Jim Thorpe, the greatest athlete ever."

There was silence for a few seconds, then, "I'm sorry. You told me earlier your name was Joseph William Colsco. Did I misunderstand?"

"All right! Enough of this shit! Who the fuck are you, and where am I?"

"Joe, do you see the bar next to you?"

"What?"

"The bar, Joe," insisted the voice.

"There's no bar—" Joe glanced to his side and scowled at a two-inch-thick bar about eight inches above the end of the platform and curving to connect to the two corners. It hadn't been there a moment ago. "Where . . . ?"

"Please hold onto the bar."

Joe placed his right hand lightly on the bar.

"Do not be alarmed. Please hold onto the bar to avoid injury."

"Injury from wha—" His feet left the floor. Joe gasped and clutched the bar with both hands as he floated, attached only by his death grip on the bar, his mind blank of any thought except holding on.

The sensation of weight slowly returned, and he settled back onto the platform, keeping a firm grip on the bar with his right hand and his left hand gripping the edge of the platform. His mind was frozen, waiting for an explanation.

Finally, he croaked, "What happened?"

"The gravity in your room was adjusted to zero to prove you are no longer on your planet. You are in a vessel at a Lagrange point."

"Lagrange point?" The part of his mind still reasoning drew from a classroom memory. *One of the points in space relative to the Earth where an object stays in a stable position with respect to the Earth while they both orbit the Sun.* He remembered the balance between gravity and orbital motion caused the stability. He thought there were several such points, but all he could remember were the ones where the Sun, the Earth, and the Lagrange point were in a line, Sun-point-Earth, Earth-Sun-point, point-Earth-Sun, and point-Sun-Earth.

"That's not possible," Joe whispered, another chill raising the hairs on his back and arms. "How can I be at a Lagrange point?"

"How do *you* think it would be possible?"

Joe froze. To answer would make the impossible possible.

"Joe, how might you be at a Lagrange point?"

Joe's brain seized, trapped in a vortex. The voice repeated the question at thirty-second intervals until Joe swallowed and choked out, "A spacecraft?"

"Very good, Joe. Yes, you are on a spacecraft."

"How did I get into space and whose ship is this? Ours? Russians'? Chinese?"

"What do you think, Joe? Which of them could have adjusted the gravity in this room?"

Joe's mind raced, rummaging frantically for plausible answers. He was on Earth, and they faked the floating? No. No way to do that on Earth. And what about the slowness of the bouncing balls? Some secret NASA, military, Russian, whomever or whatever? Nothing fit. But it had to be one of these, didn't it?

Joe's grip on the bar tightened even more, as he eliminated all possibilities except one. The blood drained from his face.

"Can you think of an answer, Joe?"

"No," he said in a small voice.

"Then what is left?"

He was silent for a full minute. Joe was cold and sweating at the same time, his throat constricted, his heart pounding. "A spaceship not made on Earth?"

"That is correct, Joe. This craft did not originate on your planet."

I'm insane, dreaming, or hallucinating.

Joe scrambled for an explanation he could understand. Acceptance came only after more demonstrations of gravity manipulation, and when one wall turned transparent and he could see the Earth in full view. At first, it was a small orb of blues, browns, and greens. Then it grew closer—magnified, he assumed—until it filled the wall. He stared for some time, long enough to notice the view had the Earth's surface in total sunlight. The only way the surface could be in complete sunlight was if the vessel was positioned between the Sun and the Earth.

This must be the L1 Lagrange Point, his mind dredged up. *So the Sun must be behind us to get this view. The Sun-point-Earth Lagrange arrangement.* Only when the wall changed back to white, and his heart rate returned closer to normal did his mind accept as possible the option that couldn't be true. The voice was silent, waiting for him to initiate. He didn't know what to say or ask, as his mind tried to gather itself.

"Do you need more evidence, Joe?"

"No. It must be true, or I'm insane." After a moment, he said, "Hey, wait a minute! If you're supposed to be some kind of alien, how do you speak English and how do you know about Lagrange points?"

"All languages can be understood with sufficient samples, such as the broadcasts emanating from your planet. I assumed your language was English, based on the position of your aircraft. As for knowing the name for the Lagrange points, among the electromagnetic emanations from Earth are education programs. Joe, you are on a vessel near your planet, both orbiting your Sun."

Joe's mind whirled, unable to settle on a single thought for more than a fraction of a second before careening off in other directions.

When Joe didn't speak, the voice repeated, "Joe, do you understand you are on a vessel orbiting your Sun?"

"You mean an alien spaceship?"

"A vessel not of your planet. Yes. An alien spaceship."

"Who are you?" Joe whispered.

"I am a simulation of a human being, designed to communicate with you." The same statement, word for word, the voice had used when Joe first asked the same question.

"Simulated? Designed? You mean you're a computer program or AI?"

"You may think of me as an AI, an artificial intelligence, as the closest analogy to your species' technical level."

"Who made you? Who made this vessel?"

"That information is not important for you to know, and I am not authorized to give an answer."

"Why am I here? What do you want of me?"

"A malfunction of the systems of this vessel caused it to accidently destroy your craft. There was a temporary single sub-atomic systems fault that would normally have been corrected by redundant subroutines, except for coinciding with a routine reboot of a process whose role was monitoring the reliability of subroutines. Unable to confirm reliability, blocks of subroutines shut down or paused, affecting both the vessel's cloaking technology, making it momentarily visible, and stopping the processing of external sensor data."

"A computer crash? You're saying you crashed into my plane because your systems glitched?"

"A crude but accurate assessment. It took two seconds to recognize the faults from the initial quantum error and make the necessary corrections. Unfortunately, in those two seconds, our vessel transited thirty-eight miles and, for a brief instance, attempted to occupy the same volume of space as your airplane. Not unexpectedly, the attempt failed."

"Well, no shit."

"There were negligible effects on our vessel, but consequences for your aircraft were substantial. Our systems resumed normal function too late to avoid the collision. However, we managed to hold onto pieces of the plane, the baggage, and the passengers. Most of the humans died instantly, but a few survived the seconds it took the ship's systems to recover and attempt to save the plane. You are one of the survivors."

"Was I injured?"

"Yes."

"How badly?" Joe steeled himself.

"It is not necessary for you to have that information."

That doesn't sound good.

"How many survived?"

"I cannot give you that information."

"Why not?"

"I cannot give you that information."

"You can't tell me how many survived, or you can't tell me why you can't tell me?"

"Yes to both questions."

"Why am I here? You didn't answer when I asked before. Why rescue anyone?"

"There is an obligation," said the voice in the same flat tone, "an obligation to be acknowledged and mitigated as much as possible."

"Why is there an obligation and to whom?"

"You would likely not understand if I tried to explain. Also, it is unnecessary for you to know the reasons."

"I must be dreaming this, or else I'm going crazy. If this is all true, why do I feel so calm? I should be climbing the walls."

"Why would you climb the walls? You have no physical attributes that would assist this action, and climbing would lead nowhere except the ceiling."

"I mean, I should be screaming and running around, scared shitless!"

"I do not see any logical connection to feces. However, if I understand your meaning, you are wondering why you do not have more severe reactions to your situation. Part of the answer is that we are suppressing the portions of your nervous system that respond to agitation."

Joe was quiet for a moment. "You mean, dampen the fight-or-flight response?"

"Yes. The hormones and neural pathways that energize your physiology to either flee from danger or attack an enemy are being suppressed to allow you to rationally accept events."

"What comes next?" Joe asked. "Do you keep me here, take me to your planet, return me to Earth, or what?" At the edge of his consciousness were other options, ones he didn't care to consider.

"None of those three options are possible. For reasons unnecessary for you to understand, you cannot remain on this vessel or be taken to my creators' home. Neither can you be returned to your planet. You have knowledge of our existence. You may choose one of two options. For you to understand the options, it is necessary you be given limited knowledge. I will not answer additional questions."

The voice paused a moment, while Joe sat waiting to hear his options. Fear curled over raw nerve endings, in spite of the alien's attempts to keep him calm.

"This vessel observes Earth and its civilization," the voice intoned, "because there are other planets in this region of the galaxy inhabited by humans. Earth is evidently the origin of humans, though both humans and some animals and plants were taken from Earth in the past and transplanted to other planets. Who did the transplantation is not known. Humans did not then, nor do you now, have such technology. Our purpose is to gather information to explain who is responsible and why this was done."

"Humans on other planets! How many such planets and where are they?"

"I cannot give you that information."

"You don't know, or you won't tell?"

"I cannot give you that information."

Joe ground his teeth. He wasn't in the best frame of mind for sophisticated reasoning, which was fortunate, since there seemed to be only one option.

"Let me guess. If I can't stay on this ship, I can't return to Earth, there are other planets with humans, and since you're interested in my survival, the only option would be to take me to one of these planets inhabited by humans."

"Partly correct. That is one of the two options. The other one is you can choose to terminate your existence."

Joe sat transfixed. "You mean, like, be killed?"

"You would cease to be. There would be no discomfort, I assure you."

"Well, thanks. I appreciate the shit out of that."

"I am sorry, Joe, but I am still not clear on the relevance to feces."

"It's an obscure English language reference. I cannot give you the information to explain it."

Two can play at this silly game.

"Wait a minute," Joe said then. "I thought you couldn't give me information, but you just did, about other planets having humans."

"As I said before, you need this information to recognize your two options and to make an informed decision. Will you need time to decide?"

"If you return me to Earth, I would swear not to tell anyone about what happened here—so your secret would be safe."

"I believe if you considered this logically, you would see the fallacy in this assurance."

While Joe wanted to argue, he couldn't give any assurances that they—whoever *they* were—would have any reason to trust.

"Besides, it is unlikely that anyone would believe you."

Joe bit his lip, eyes darting about. It was time to grasp at straws. "If no one believes me, why not let me return to Earth?"

"There is the low probability you would be believed or your account would be on a permanent record that someday could correlate with additional information."

"I'll never see my family or friends again," Joe said in desperation, "never have my life back!"

"That is unfortunate."

He blinked back tears. "Please, I beg you, take me home."

"That is not an opt—"

"I promise to keep this to myself!"

"There is no point in continuing this exchange. There will be no more discussion. You are required to choose one of the two options."

As if about to fall into a pit, Joe grasped for reasons to delay the decision. "You haven't given me enough details. This limited information would contradict the obligation for my survival. I need to know more about the planet to decide whether I prefer that over termination."

The silence encouraged Joe to think they were considering his complaint—he hoped. Then the voice returned.

"I will answer relevant and allowed questions."

For several days, as Joe considered his sleep/wake cycle, he asked questions, and the voice mainly wouldn't answer. Joe soon became tired of thinking of whatever he was communicating with as "the voice." He debated within himself, aloud at times, about what name to bestow, and he settled on

Harlie—the friendly AI of a science fiction novel by author David Gerrod. For the alien whatever they were, it was more difficult, because he knew nothing about them, neither their appearance, type of environment, origin, nor intentions. Harlie claimed his creators were only observing humans. That's what Joe would call them. Watchers who were benignly studying humans. He hoped.

Talking to Harlie kept Joe's mind temporarily occupied. Whenever the voice didn't respond, or Joe didn't want to talk, he fell into despondent moods, even though he suspected that they continued to dampen his emotions.

Periodically, a slot would open to a cavity containing cream-colored food cubes. They might be keeping him alive, but otherwise the fare reminded him of papier-mâché in early grade school. Cups of metallic-tasting water were available on request from the same slot, and with instructions from the voice on the functions of several levers, Joe used a corner of the room for "waste disposal."

While Joe's efforts to wheedle more information out of Harlie about the Watchers failed, he had more success with the proposed destination.

"Joe, I am allowed to show you an image of the planet."

A white wall instantly displayed a planet against a black background. After a few seconds, the orb rotated to show the entire surface, and superimposed lines indicated the equator. Resolution was sharp, though no fine details were discernible. In the first view, major land masses covered 40-50 percent of the surface, with a large continent in the northern hemisphere, three smaller in the southern, and islands were scattered around the larger masses. However, once the planet rotated, Joe could see the opposite side was devoid of land except for scattered islands. Ice and snow extended farther toward the equator than on Earth, and he couldn't see if the white covered land or water.

When the view returned to the planet half with most land, and stopped, Joe could see mountain ranges and the largest rivers and lakes. The land was shades of brown and a darker green than on Earth. Cloud cover was similar to that shown on satellite views of Earth, and several low-pressure whorls suggested the planet's version of hurricanes.

There was no sign of human artifacts. Then again, would he have seen anything on Earth from space before megacities arose? He remembered the astronauts said the only single structure they could identify was the Great Wall. Wait . . . were there some pinpricks of light just inside the night portion? Several of them on the coast near the equator. Cities?

While Joseph studied the image, Harlie droned a commentary.

"There are significant human populations on all the major land masses and larger islands. The social and political systems are unknown at present, other than there seem to be a variety. The level of technology resembles Earth at approximately the years 1650 to 1750."

Joe flashed on images of Stone Age humans, tribal societies, the Roman Empire, medieval Europe, Mongol hordes, and other times and places on Earth he wouldn't have wanted to find himself. However, by around 1700 there were reasonable civilizations.

His positive attitude dissipated when he remembered that in 1700 on Earth, plenty of Stone Age and tribal places still existed, along with more advanced cultures in which he wouldn't have lasted long.

"Where would you leave me on this planet? Is there any way for me to know more about the local conditions and have a choice where I end up?"

"No to both of your questions," said Harlie. "However, I am allowed to give you basic information about the planet itself. The planet is cooler than Earth, has a 329-day year, a day equivalent to 23 hours, and gravity 1.18 times Earth's, due to the planet's larger diameter and mass."

Making a rough calculation, Joe figured a year on this planet would be almost nine-tenths of an Earth year, 20 years equivalent to nearly 18 on Earth, and so on. More disturbing was gravity. His 175 pounds on Earth would translate into 206 on this planet.

"It's hard enough that I'll be dumped into a foreign society where I'll know absolutely nothing, not even languages, but to make matters worse, I'll weigh more and be more physically stressed. I admit to not being much of an athletic specimen, but this'll decrease my chances of survival."

"Do not be concerned. We made minor adjustments to your body to account for the increased mass."

"Adjustments?" Joe frowned. "What kind of 'minor' adjustments?"

"We altered your physiology by increasing the efficiency of your cells' energy-producing organelles."

"Energy organelles? You mean the mitochondria?"

"Yes, the mitochondria. The increase in efficiency should result in more muscle mass and faster reflexes."

"I'm not sure I'm reassured by the 'should' part. How does it work?"

"Basic Earth physiology is relatively simple, and it only required replacing a few genes."

"You mean, like, actually *replacing* genes? Everywhere?"

"In most of your cells. Not every cell had the relevant genes replaced, but enough of them to have the same effect as a total replacement. The nuclear genome was too complex to modify in the short time available. Fortunately, the smaller DNA content of your energy-producing sub-cellular organelles was easier to change."

Joe didn't like the sound of this. Humans had nowhere near this technology, so how confident should he be that some alien race could do it in such a short time?

Which brought forth another question. "Say, just how long has it been since you crashed into my airliner?"

"Two of your years," Harlie replied.

"Jesus! Two *years*!"

"Yes. It took time to fully analyze your biochemistry, physiology, and genome structure. Since you were our first physical specimen of Earth biology, the repairs to your injuries were carried out with caution. The actual gene replacement took only a few hours."

Two years. *Two years!* Everyone he knew believed he'd been dead for two whole years. As far as they were concerned, time had passed and they'd moved on without him. Julie? Where was she? What about the baby? Was there even a baby?

One shock after another, and Joe stayed surprised at how he continued to accept everything with relative equanimity. But after the previous revelations, what were a few more? *It must be the drugs or whatever they're doing to me that keeps me semi-sane.*

"All right, so let's say I'll be strong enough to compensate for the increased gravity. What about diseases to which my immune system won't have any resistance?" He rubbed the back of his neck. "And what about me giving them diseases? I may have latent viruses and bacteria that will find a virgin field—a whole population without resistance. I could accidently kill most of the people on the planet!" Joe thought about the devastation of the American Indians by diseases brought in by the first Europeans.

"That is not a problem. As part of repairing your body, it was necessary to preserve your parts from external contamination. Microscopic elements were designed for your basic physiology and biochemistry to exclude foreign entities and were injected into you. You will neither transmit any microorganisms to other humans nor be subject to external microorganisms."

Two simultaneous concerns intertwined in Joe's mind. He wasn't sure if he wanted more details of his "parts" that they had to preserve, because they invoked scenes from grotesque movies. Then there were these "elements" they'd put into him.

"Are these like the predicted nanomachines—microscopic machines that could be put into a person to remove arterial plaques?"

"I know nothing of your species' predictions. Such elements, or nanomachines, as you call them, are a normal step in technological development."

"What exactly do these elements do?"

"They recognize and destroy anything not belonging to your body. This includes bacteria, viruses, fungi, or any other organism types, as well as any cells of your body that escape the normal limits on proliferation. The only negative aspect is that you cannot receive transplants from other humans or animals."

"So," Joe said cautiously, "if I understand correctly, I will not get sick, will not get cancer, but cannot have organ transplants?"

"Correct."

Well, he thought, *it wasn't like there would be any heart transplants with the level of medical technology on the planet, so it was a pretty good trade-off. No illness and no cancer.* Joe hated to admit it, but given what had happened, they seemed to be making a genuine effort to do right by him, apart from his never seeing Earth again.

"So maybe I'll have a chance to survive. What about the humans on this planet? Am I correct that whoever made you doesn't want it known that they exist and are observing humans as you do Earth? If that's the case, won't putting me there risk revealing your existence?"

"It is estimated that the probability you will impact the civilizations is close enough to zero to be considered nonexistent. It would be like adding a drop of water to an ocean."

Bastards! I just disappear, and whatever obligation they feel is satisfied.

Over the next days—sleep cycles—he and the Harlie danced around the topic of where Joe might be "dumped." Joe's questions became more and more repetitious, and in one session he was about to ask another question when Harlie announced, "It is time for your decision. Do you wish to be terminated or be put on the other planet?"

"Wait a minute! I have more questions I need answered."

"There are no more questions for which you *need* answers, only questions to which you *want* answers."

"What if I'm not ready to make the decision?"

"It is estimated that there is a ninety-three percent probability your decision will not change by any amount of additional information. Nor would additional information increase your survival probability. Therefore, it is necessary for you to decide."

"And if I don't decide?"

"Then our obligation to you is ended. If you refuse to decide, the decision will be made by a random procedure."

"Meaning you'll flip a coin to see if I live or die?"

"If I understand the reference—yes."

Christ!

"Then I choose the planet. How long will it be before we—" Joe slipped into unconsciousness.

CHAPTER 3

PLANET ANYAR

Preddi City, Island of Caedellium

Lieutenant Bortor Nestor stopped at the office door of General Okan Akuyun, commander of all Narthani forces and civilians on the island of Caedellium. The young officer ran one hand over his uniform to check buttons and smooth wrinkles. Satisfied, he raised a hand to knock, gauged the appropriate firmness expected by General Akuyun, and executed three firm raps.

"Come in," said a baritone voice.

Nestor opened the door and walked to attention in front of the general's desk. On first impression, Okan Akuyun appeared stern and humorless—a carefully crafted facade. As a young officer, he determined that a serious demeanor served well in rising through the Narthani hierarchy. He was uncertain whether it had helped, but it was an ingrained part of his public persona.

"A message from Admiral Kalcan, General," said the young officer, holding out a folded and sealed single sheet.

"Thank you, Lieutenant," said Akuyun. He took the message, broke the seal, and his eyes scanned the sheet. "That'll be all, Lieutenant. There's no return message."

Nestor slapped a right fist to his left shoulder, spun, and exited.

Akuyun read the sheet again, slower this time, absentmindedly running a hand from scalp to chin. Of average height and with a lean frame and face, he wore his hair cropped. Just noticeable were the patches of gray appropriate for his fifty-two years.

Although he was smooth shaven himself, many Narthani men sported mustaches, though nothing resembling a beard. No Narthani remembered that their distant nomadic ancestors had suffered facial fungal infections when they came roaring out of the harsh northern wastelands and mountains of the

Melosian continent to capture more hospitable lands from weaker tribes. The beards, practical in their cold ancestral homelands, became breeding grounds for germs when the Narthani reached the warmer and more humid central latitudes. Shaving the beards solved the problem. Now, the Narthani considered beards a feature of lesser peoples; it was typical of their arrogance to ignore a history not fitting their self-image of inherent superiority.

Okan Akuyun rose and walked to his office window. In the glass, he saw two faint reflections: his own face, and the six-foot-square wall map hanging behind his desk. He knew every detail of the map. The Caedellium Archipelago consisted of one large island, two smaller islands to the northwest, and several islets off the main island's coasts. That large island, Caedellium, measured five hundred by four hundred miles and was politically divided among twenty-one provinces ruled by clans steadfast in guarding their independence. A total island population estimated at 800,000 seemed to the Narthani ridiculously underpopulated for the richness of the land.

Through the window glass and past the reflections, Akuyun surveyed parts of Preddi City, the original capitol of Preddi Province, and the main trading port for Caedellium. The city's population of 35,000 was 9,000 more than when the Narthani first arrived and when the majority of the population were members of the Preddi Clan. Now, only 3,000 to 4,000 clansmen remained. The replacements were Narthani civilian settlers and tradesmen and their families, members of the military accompanied by a few families of the higher ranks, and slaves from conquered lands.

His eyes moved past the busy square and street in front of his headquarters and on to the main object of his attention: the harbor of Preddi City. He drew a deep breath, suppressing the excitement surging through him. Troop transports and cargo ships filled the harbor. A row of protective frigates anchored farther offshore, their sails furled, the closed gun ports for their single deck of 30-pounder cannon visible from his office. No larger escorts were deemed necessary because Caedellium had no warships and was not allied with any major power.

Akuyun's mission was to bring the isolation of this resource-rich land to an end. He watched with satisfaction as the first two of the newly arrived troop transports disembarked lines of men down gangplanks to form units on the dock, their dark blue pants and maroon coats identifying them as Narthani infantry. Even from this distance and through his closed window, he could faintly hear officers shouting at their men, boots drumming against wood, the clanking of weapons against metal canteens. All of these sounds rose above the background of thousands of men whispering, cursing, grunting, complaining, and talking with the next men in line. Cannons, ammunition, tools, more settlers, slaves, general supplies, and the heavy cavalry's horses waited offshore in cargo freighters.

He again perused Admiral Kalcan's listing of the men and materials carried by the ships. His forces were now complete. He drew more deep breaths, satisfaction warming his face. Everything was in place for the next phase of the subjugation of Caedellium.

Caernford, Capitol of Keelan Province, Caedellium

For Hetman Culich Keelan, hereditary leader of the Keelan Clan and Province, the morning brought no satisfaction. His forehead furrowed and his jaw clenched as he read the semaphore message. Another contingent of Narthani ships sailed toward Preddi City. A Keelan Clan fishing boat straying closer to the Preddi Province coast than advisable had made a good count of the number of Narthani ships before the fishermen beat a hasty retreat into safer waters.

The fishermen reported their sighting to the mayor of the port town of Dornfeld, the only Keelan town on the Gulf of Witlow, and opposite Preddi Province. Word of the new Narthani convoy reached Culich by riders from Dornfeld inland to the nearest semaphore station in Keelan Province, then on to Caernford. Dornfeld lay on the border with Gwillamer Province, an ally of Keelan, and along with the eastern province, Mittack, the three made up the Tri-Clan Alliance. The only semaphore lines connecting Gwillamer and Mittack to the rest of the island ran first to Caernford, then north and northeast to reach all of the other clans except Seaborn, the clan inhabiting the smaller islands off the northwest Caedellium coast.

"Will there be an answer, Hetman?"

Culich's eyes rose from the sheet. The semaphore messenger stood five feet away, waiting.

"Yes," Culich mumbled, his gaze returning to the disheartening news, then raising to judge the height of the sun. If he got a message off to the other hetmen, most should receive it by sundown. Not that there was anything immediate they could do.

The semaphore flag towers stood an average of five miles apart, depending on the terrain, and were manned during daylight hours as long as signals were visible. The system had begun operating ten years earlier, and only in the last six months had it connected to the last mainland clan. Rearranging the large panels took time and limited the complexity of messages, but a short communication starting at any clan capitol, except the island province of Seaborn, could reach all of the other clans within ten daylight hours.

If past experience were repeated, most of the hetmen would acknowledge receipt but would not respond further. Too many clan leaders considered the Keelan hetman an alarmist, and in the view of too many hetmen, the Narthani were far from their own provinces, so why should they care? Culich's innermost thoughts, those that prudence prevented him from sharing overtly with all of the other hetmen, were that failing to understand the looming Narthani threat was as dangerous as the Narthani themselves.

Culich hurried into the front entrance of Keelan Manor and to his office. There, he composed a two-part message: the number and type of Narthani ships, and a statement that the ships signaled another sign of future danger from the Narthani. He folded the paper, sealed it with wax, stamped it with the Keelan emblem, and strode back to the waiting messenger holding his horse outside.

"Take this to the Caernford semaphore station quickly. It's to go out to all other clan hetmen."

"Immediately, Hetman." The man jumped into his saddle, pulled on the reins to spin his horse, throwing fine gravel onto his hetman's boots, and spurred his mount toward Caernford.

Though Culich's eyes followed the rider down the manor lane and out onto the road, his real attention was inward. How many Narthani were now on Caedellium? And how many of those were Narthani soldiers? Thousands? Tens of thousands? He could only estimate, since the Narthani had cut off all contact with the rest of Caedellium. Whatever the exact number, every piece of news of more Narthani arriving felt like a noose cinching tighter around his people's necks.

As hetman, he feared the future. He saw no reason to hope the Narthani intentions were limited to the three lost provinces: Preddi, which they controlled, and the neighboring Selfcell and Eywell provinces and clans, who were now de facto allies of the Narthani.

"Why would the Narthani bother with Caedellium at all unless they intended to absorb the entire island?" he once asked his advisors, hoping they would argue. They hadn't.

This fear stalked Culich every waking hour, along with frustration at his inability to convince more of the other seventeen clans' hetmen of the danger. The clans of Caedellium had never faced such a threat, and Culich feared their stubborn independence and distrust of one another might be their epitaphs.

He sighed and returned to reviewing the quarterly reports from his district leaders. There was nothing more he could do today about the Narthani. He'd sent the news on to the other clans. Whatever the future held for them all, normal life went on in Keelan Province.

Even Culich Keelan, the presumed alarmist, had no idea how wrong he was.

Beach Outside the Village of Abersford, Keelan Province

Brisk morning sea air moved onshore. The sun peeking above the eastern horizon had not yet warmed the air, its light just hitting the tops of sand dunes. Gulls and murvors cruised the shoreline, the calls of the former and the whistles of the latter creating a strange counterpoint.

Yonkel Miron ran as hard as his seven-year-old legs would take him up the sand dunes from the surf's edge and onto the Abersford-Gwillamer dirt road paralleling the shore. He then headed inland through the village of Abersford. As he passed adults and other children, they yelled out, "Why are you running so hard? Is something wrong?" He ignored them, his lungs too committed to running for him to answer.

He raced past the school his father made him attend three days a week and past the well-tended outer grain and flax fields of the abbey complex. When he reached the eight-foot-high stone wall surrounding the grounds of the Abbey of St. Sidryn, he sprinted up to the twenty-foot-wide main gate. The double doors opened with the first chimes from the cathedral and remained open until sunset. The chimes had not yet struck, and the gate was closed and barred.

Yonkel went straight to the foot-traffic door built into the leftmost main door. Gulping lungfuls of air from his mile run, he reached up to the metal ring knocker on the center of the door and clanged it against the underlying plate.

By the twentieth clang, the upper half of the foot-traffic door opened, and a cassocked, bearded figure appeared.

"Yes, yes . . . I'm here, you can quit banging now," said Brother Alber in an irritated voice.

"Brother Alber!" Yonkel gasped, still out of breath. "My father said to get Brother Willer to come to the beach. Some kind of dead man or demon washed up! He's all pale and skinny and ugly! I thought he was dead when I found him. We were fishing when I saw him on the sand. I—"

Brother Alber shushed him with waves of both hands. "Slow down, slow down, Yonkel. Brother Willer is attending to a childbirth, but I'll come with you."

Yonkel looked doubtful. "Well . . . Father said to bring . . . I suppose it's all right if you come."

"Thank you, Yonkel," Alber said dryly. "I'm glad I'm acceptable."

"Can we go now?" Yonkel urged, bouncing on his toes like a hyperactive racer eager for the starting gong.

"Let me get my medical bag and some better shoes." Alber closed the door, and within two minutes he returned wearing walking shoes and a cloak for the morning dampness. His brown leather medical bag hung by a diagonal strap over his right shoulder and rested on his left hip.

Yonkel ran ahead, stopped for Alber to catch up, and repeated this pattern until they reached the cliff above the beach. Below, Alber saw a cluster of people gathered around something lying on the sand. They took the winding trail down to the beach and slogged through the soft sand about a hundred yards until they reached the firmer sand where waves washed up. They approached the cluster of men. There, splayed out on the sand, was a naked man on his stomach. At first, Alber thought the man dead. His body appeared emaciated, and his pale skin had a grayish cast. Alber bent down for a closer look, then jerked back as the dead body twitched.

"Here!" he yelled to the others. "Help me turn him over! He's still alive."

The watching men hesitated until Alber barked at them again. As they turned the man onto his stomach, he gasped, but no water trickled from his mouth as Alber expected if the man had been in the sea and nearly drowned. The man coughed, spasmed, and breathed. He wasn't dead.

"Quick! Gather driftwood and use your cloaks and coats to make a stretcher. We have to carry him to the abbey."

The men scattered, and within minutes, four of them carried the man from the beach toward the abbey. Yonkel and two other children alternated running ahead and circling the procession.

Word raced ahead, and when they arrived at the abbey, two medicant acolytes met them at the main gate. They transferred the man to a real stretcher and took him into one of the examination rooms where the medicants on duty waited. Alber watched the examination, talking with other medicants and Abbot Sistian Beynom, who appeared after getting word of the strange man found on the beach.

"Any idea who he is or where he's from?" asked the abbot.

"Nothing so far," said Alber.

After finishing the initial evaluation, Brother Elton Bolwyn wore a puzzled expression. "Physically, he's in unusual condition. I know you say he was found on the beach, but I see no signs of that. If he had been in water even a short time and gotten washed up, his condition would be very different. There's no seawater in his lungs, his skin is unblemished—no bruises anywhere on his body, no cuts or lacerations. That part of the coast has so many rocks that if he'd washed ashore, he should have abrasions from hitting rocks on the way in. If I had to, I would say he was *placed* on the beach, instead of being washed up on it."

Alber shook his head. "The men who found him say there were no tracks near him when they arrived. The tide was just coming in, so any tracks wouldn't have been erased yet by the surf."

Abbot Beynom wrinkled his eyebrows. "But if there were no tracks and no sign of his being in the water, how did he get there?"

Bolwyn shrugged. "I'm just telling you my evaluation of his condition. How he got there, I wouldn't know."

"What about the man himself?" asked Alber. "What can you tell about his physical condition? He looked near death."

Bolwyn shook his head. "He may look near death, but his heart and lungs seem fine. What's strange is his muscles. They're atrophied as if they haven't been used much for a long time. When we don't use muscles, they shrink in size. This can happen with people paralyzed, in comas, or confined for a long period. When I tested his reflexes to see if the muscles were functional, everything seemed normal."

"So," said Abbot Beynom wryly, looking at Alber and Bolwyn, "what we have is a man who by magic appears on the beach and has been in a coma, or confined, for months or years?"

"We're only medicants," Alber quipped. "You're the wise theophist who knows all and sees into the hearts of men." The two had been friends for many years, and the banter between caregivers of body and soul was an integral part of their friendship.

"Oh, pardon. I'd forgotten for a moment. Thank you for reminding me," said the abbot, patting Alber on the shoulder before addressing the other brother. "Bolwyn, you believe he's in no immediate danger?"

"While his body is obviously weak, if he wakes up, and if we can get nourishment into him, then maybe he'll survive."

"I know I can always look forward to your confident diagnoses," the abbot chuckled. "Let me know if his condition changes."

Abbot Beynom took a last view at the pale body lying on the table. *Well, well,* he thought. *Today, God had granted us a surprise outside our normal routine. We'll have to see what comes from this addition to our community.*

CHAPTER 4

RECOVERY

Abbey of St. Sidryn, Keelan Province

He awoke suddenly, staring at a white ceiling—again. Confused—again. His first coherent thought was of home. Had it all been a dream? The voice, Harlie, the plane crash, the story about other worlds and being taken to one of them. Would he look around and see everything back to normal? What if it wasn't a dream? What if he was still in the small white room with Harlie?

He looked closer at the ceiling. In the "dream," it was smooth, pure white. The ceiling at home was smooth but off-white. This ceiling was painted dull white, with visible brush strokes. Gathering his courage, he turned his head. He wasn't in Harlie's room. A momentary sense of relief was replaced by confusion. Neither was he at home. Sunlight came through a window, the rays filtered through green foliage with leaves moving in the wind. Something flew by the window. Not quite a bird, but too big and fast for a butterfly.

He heard voices. More than one. Perhaps a man and a woman. Human voices! Voices with tones, cadences, and hints of emotion! Multiple voices and not Harlie's cold, disembodied one. He couldn't quite make out the words, even when he concentrated. He listened harder but still couldn't understand. He gathered his energy and courage, turning his head in the direction of the voices.

The first thing he registered was a matronly middle-aged woman with gray-streaked dark brown hair pulled into a bun, her clothing a plain brown smock. A man stood next to the woman. He was younger, with a trimmed and frosted dark beard, medium-length dark hair, wearing trousers and a tunic of the same brown cloth as the woman. Their mouths moved and sound came out. Occasionally, he thought he could pick out a word, but it was fleeting, quickly lost in the otherwise unintelligible stream.

Oh, God! It hit Joe like a blow to his chest. *Oh, God—it wasn't a dream?!*

The man glanced in his direction. Their eyes met, and the man turned to speak to the woman. The two came to the side of the bed. She put a warm hand on Joe's forehead, while the man checked Joe's pulse and stroked his palm.

Joe's fingers closed reflexively. It was too overwhelming, and Joe drifted off . . . or fainted.

He slept through the night and the next day, moving in and out of awareness.

"His reflexes seem good," said Brother Bolwyn the next morning. "Same with the eye focus. It's too early to be sure, but I believe he's come through whatever happened to him in reasonable condition."

Abbess Diera Beynom nodded. "Yes, but as you say, still too early to be sure. I did get the impression he was confused."

"Hardly unexpected, given how we found him, but that's something *you'll* have to deal with. I think I've done about all I can. Let me know if there's anything else you need. I'll be getting back to my other patients."

"Thanks, Elton, I can take it from here."

Nodding, the medicant brother left Diera with the strange man. She was also a medicant, a member of the Medicant Order of the Caedellium service society. While both she and Bolwyn were trained in general medicines, she was also the abbey's chief medicant, although in this abbey it was more a light touch of authority based on respect. Not that anyone didn't know who was medicant-in-charge. Diera's title as abbess was due to her husband and not because she led the abbey. Sistian Beynom was chief theophist and the abbot in charge of the three orders represented in the abbey: medicants such as Diera, Alber, Willer, and Bolwyn; theophists like Sistian, who tended to worship and ceremonies honoring God; and scholastics, brothers and sisters who focused on understanding the workings of God's world. The fourth order, militants, focused on meditation, self-discipline, and martial arts but were not represented at St. Sidryn's, the Abbey of St. Sidryn. Militants had never been numerous on the island, with only a few in the northern clans. According to lore, however, they were more prominent elsewhere in the world.

St. Sidryn's was one of the larger abbeys and had members from three orders. Smaller abbeys tended to have staff from only one or two orders. At St. Sidryn's, the Medicant Order was more represented than the other two orders because the abbey was the main medicant treatment and training facility for the district, an area twenty miles across.

The Theophist Order at the abbey ministered to people in the nearby town of Abersford. In addition, Abbot Sistian Beynom was a prominent figure in the district and active in administering to the religious and societal issues within and beyond Abersford.

Brothers and sisters of the Scholastic Order completed Sidryn's staff and were in larger numbers than in most mixed-order abbeys. Abbeys where scholastics gathered to study separately from other orders were also called scholasticums. Sistian had started his training in one until he became dissatisfied with the scholastics' tendency to interact within their own order and not perform service to God's role in the world. He switched to the Theophist Order, and when he became the abbot at St. Sidryn's, he encouraged select scholastics to join them. He was eager to bring the different orders closer. St. Sidryn's was also unusual in that a few brothers and sisters performed duties across orders, another example of the abbot's reluctance to compartmentalize service to the people and God.

The strange man had created a minor sensation, both in town and among members of the three orders in the abbey. Medicants regarded him as a patient. To theophists, he was one of God's children to minister to, assuming he wasn't a demon. And to scholastics, he was a puzzle, and what was more fun than a puzzle?

Diera touched the stubble on the sleeping man's chin. He had been clean-shaven when found. Whatever happened must have occurred recently, because the stubble couldn't be more than two or three days old. Who was he? A slave escaped from the Narthani? The Narthani slaves were beardless, though she hadn't heard of a Narthani slave without bruises or scars. He obviously wasn't a eunuch. Rumors were that some Narthani male slaves were castrated as children to make them more docile. So, was this mysterious guest a demon? Sent by the Evil One to tempt them, or an agent of God sent to test them?

Diera returned to her duties, musing on how the daily routine had changed this day and wondering whether there was any higher meaning to it. She and Sistian would have an interesting conversation over the evening meal.

Responsive

The next morning the stranger was still asleep when Diera visited him.

"He did wake several times during the night," the night attendant told Diera, "and then drifted back to sleep. At mid-morning he awoke again."

They tried feeding him broth, but he turned away when the spoon came under his nose. By afternoon, he'd swallowed a small cup of phila juice. While it was too sweet for Diera's taste, and she didn't care for the musty flavor, it was heavy in sugar and other nutrients. By the third day, he kept down a small portion of barley and beef soup. By the fifth day, he consumed large helpings, and on the eighth day, the stranger sat up and ate solid foods by himself.

He was still weak, but the change astounded the medicants. The pallor that had made them afraid he was near death had transformed into a healthy complexion, though lighter in tone than most Caedelli.

They also confirmed he didn't speak any of the languages known to them—Caedelli or any of the major mainland dialects of the same language group, several dialects of Collardium of the Iraquinik continent, Frangelese, or High Landolin, the learned language of the Landolin continent and the accepted scholastic language of most of Anyar.

Diera felt trepidations when they brought in an escaped Narthani slave working on a farm near Abersford to try the Narthani language, fearing the stranger was either a Narthani or one of their agents. She was relieved when he was as oblivious to the Narthani language as any of the others they tried.

Five days later, an impromptu staff gathering was called to discuss the next step for the stranger.

A senior theophist, Callwin Wye, sat hunched over, lines of discontent scoring his dour face. "Where is he from, then?"

Diera sighed. Wye was a difficult, conservative man. "We have no idea, Brother Callwin. I sense he hasn't been deceptive, at least as far as language is concerned. Although he might be suffering from a mental impairment, my instinct tells me he's from a distant part of Anyar, where the language is completely unknown to us."

Brother Bolwyn nodded. "That's possible. It's not as if Caedellium is on the main travel routes or widely known on Anyar. He could be from an island population even smaller than ours or some geographically isolated language enclave. All we know about him is his name. Yozef Kolsko, if we are pronouncing it correctly."

"Yozef Kolsko," Diera drew out the sounds. "I don't recall ever hearing either name."

"Me, neither," Bolwyn said. "Which gives more credence to his origin being somewhere unknown to us here on Caedellium."

"We should have serious reservations about leaving him unguarded," groused Wye. "The speed of his recovery should be a warning that he could be an agent of the Evil One."

The others looked at Wye with resignation. The stubby brother never faltered in his search for signs of demons and malefactors. While they usually tolerated his fixation, it was tiring.

Bolwyn waved a dismissive hand. "Let's get back to the purpose of this meeting and our next step with the stranger. For the last few days, he's visited the relief room in the ward and sponged himself off." He smiled. "I didn't think he was up to it, but I suspect having people help him with voiding and washing his body makes him uncomfortable. His people may have stronger privacy customs than us. Since he is able to care for himself, I recommend he be moved to a room in the visitor's building. He needs fresh air and sunshine."

"And you think he . . . ," Diera paused. "I suppose we should quit calling him 'he' or 'the stranger' and use his name." She glanced at Bolwyn. "You think this Yozef Kolsko is ready to be moved?"

Bolwyn shrugged. "I see no reason not to."

Into a New World

That afternoon, two brothers helped Joe to quarters in a nearby building. The simple room contained a narrow bed and bedding, a plain chest with three drawers, a small mirror on the wall, and a window looking out at a garden and the abbey's main wall. There was one painting in the room, one that Joe suspected was a depiction of God bringing the first man to life. A flask of water sat on the table, along with a drying cloth, a sphere of soap, a comb, and a tooth cleaner, all of which the staff hoped he knew how to use.

Because he had no clothes when found and had worn nothing but a patient's gown during his recovery, they had laid out two sets of clothing on the narrow bed: a pair of sandals, a pair of sturdy shoes, two trousers, two pull-over shirts of the same brown cloth he'd seen worn by the people caring for him, and a brimmed straw hat. Joe had been nervous when two men walked him to a different building, wondering what was in store. When he saw the clothing, he took it as a sign they expected him to stay for a time.

Well, at least they aren't turning me out on my own, imprisoning me for being an illegal alien, or burning me at the stake. Yet, anyway.

They left him, after pantomiming he should rest. At evening mealtime, an elderly brother, Fitham by name, if Joe understood, came to Joe's room and guided him to a large dining hall with about forty tables made from light, grainy wood, some with four chairs and others with eight. The floors were foot-wide planks worn smooth. A variety of tapestries, patterned cloths, and paintings hung on the stone walls, among them, a larger version of the painting in his room.

He later learned the permanent staff lived in their own quarters, which had meal-preparation facilities. The abbey also operated the central dining hall for ambulatory patients, patients' family members, visitors to the abbey, and any abbey staff who either preferred not to prepare their own meals or wanted to join the others on occasion.

When Fitham led Joe into the hall, the buzz of conversation died. Talk picked up again as the brother sat Joe at a table. He ignored the covert glances from the diners. The move to new quarters and the walk to the hall were the most exertion and excitement he'd had since his arrival. He focused on eating hunks of meat in thick gravy over starchy chunks of greenish vegetables and generous slices of heavy, dark bread. Thankfully, the bread was familiar enough, although the starch and the vegetables were too much in the "some kind of" category for him to be comfortable. It didn't matter. His appetite had blossomed. He ate the portion Fitham brought to him in a round wooden bowl, and after he'd devoured the contents, Fitham, without hesitation, took the bowl back and returned with an even larger portion. Joe ate it, slower this time. He thought his stomach might have room for even more food, but by now he was aware of the other diners' attention.

Brother Fitham waited for him to finish eating and then led him back to his room. Already, he seemed steadier on his feet. They stopped off at the large communal outhouse. Joe thought that "an out-chalet" would be more descriptive of the elaborate facility. Back in his room, Joe undressed, lay on the bed, and pulled the covers up to his chin.

I'm alive. They're feeding me, giving me clothes, and a place to stay. What's next? What am I going to do here?

With no answers forthcoming, he drifted off to sleep.

CHAPTER 5

A GATHERING STORM

Narthani HQ, Preddi City

Five men stood in General Okan Akuyun's office. Two stood at the window overlooking the Preddi City harbor: Admiral Morfred Kalcan, commander of all Narthani naval forces in Caedellium waters, and Nizam Tuzere, head administrator of Narthani non-military personnel. Three men faced the wall map of Caedellium: General Akuyun; Colonel Aivacs Zulfa, in command of all Narthani ground forces; and Sadek Hizer, who carried the title of Assessor and reported directly to the Narthani High Command.

Zulfa waved a hand across the map. "General, information shows the mountains of this island contain sources of minerals the Caedelli haven't exploited, either because they don't realize what's under their ground, or because they lack markets. And that's on top of the agricultural potential here."

"All the better for us." Hizer shrugged and tugged an ear. "Otherwise, some other realm might have gotten here ahead of us, like one of the Iraquinik states or even the Fuomi."

"I'm surprised they haven't, given the strategic location of the island," Zulfa commented.

"It may be considered strategic for us, but not anyone else—yet," said Akuyun. "The High Command is looking for options on how to break out of our current stalemate. The coalitions on our western and eastern borders have successfully stalled us for many years. Caedellium has the potential to serve as a staging site for direct action against the rears of the Landolin continent and the Iraquinik Confederation. So far, they haven't become aware of our interest in Caedellium, and we want to be firmly in control of the entire island before our enemies realize our control of Caedellium puts a dagger pointed at their backs."

The other four men continued talking, but Akuyun only pretended to pay attention. He asked questions, but his mind was elsewhere. This was the traditional day of rest and worship of the god Narth: Narthday, Godsday to the Caedelli. It was Akuyun's custom to schedule an afternoon meeting with his senior commanders the day before beginning the five workdays of every sixday. However, today's meeting was not routine.

"All right, gentlemen, let's start." Akuyun turned from the map and took his seat. The other four men followed and sat at the round table, shuffling papers, adjusting chairs, and clearing throats.

Akuyun waited, his right hand on the tabletop, thumb lightly tapping the surface until the other four were ready. These men were among the best the Empire had produced, yet only Akuyun knew their selection by the High Command was deliberate compensation for the poor quality of troops they commanded and the limited resources assigned to achieve their objective.

"Gentlemen, as you're aware, there's only one item to discuss today." His eyes went from one man to the next. "To consider the formal decision of whether it's time to move into the next phase of our ultimate goal here on Caedellium—bringing it into the Empire." Akuyun's hand lay on his notes, though he didn't need to consult them. While he wouldn't be saying anything they didn't already know, he believed in formalities and clarity of purpose.

The silence of the four men belied their anticipation.

"None of us at this table were here for Phase One, establishing a Narthani presence on the island. Granted, we've all studied the reports, but I'll review how we've gotten to this point. It began six years ago with the establishment of a Narthani trading presence in Preddi City, the largest city on Caedellium and capital of the Preddi Clan and Province. The city had an original population around twenty-six thousand and was the center of external trade for the entire island—the source of the Preddi Clan's wealth. Our agents, acting as trading companies, established themselves in the city with the cooperation of the clan's leadership and traders."

Akuyun allowed himself a small smile. "This part of the plan went so easily as to be absurd. The Preddi leaders, eager for our gold, either ignored or didn't recognize our agents as arms of the Narthon Empire. After all, money was money, and the cheap goods we supplied, along with contributions to Preddi infrastructure and bribes to all sectors of the province, greased the acceptance of our growing presence. The Preddi also sold us land adjoining the city for a Narthani enclave. By the end of the third year of Phase One, the locals were accustomed to having Narthani around. Though our people weren't liked, they were scrupulously honest in business dealings and took care not to offend Preddi laws or customs. And that, gentlemen, is when it was determined Phase One was complete, and we moved on to Phase Two." Akuyun raised an eyebrow and gestured with his left hand to solicit comments.

"This was a critical stage," offered Tuzere, shaking his head. "The Preddi could have rejected our opening ploys and made things much harder for us. However, I think the Preddi leaders became addicted to Narthani gold, and it numbed their reasoning powers."

"Now, now, Nizam." Zulfa smiled. "Let's not be too critical. They did some of the hard work for us."

"Whatever motivated the Preddi," Akuyun said, "our people moved on to Phase Two, undermining the Preddi and the adjacent clans, Selfcell and Eywell. Despite being the richest of the Caedéllium districts, Preddi had one of the smallest land areas, the result of being on the losing end of a series of border disputes with the Eywell and Selfcell clans." Akuyun used a wooden pointer to touch clan territories on the wall map. "By judiciously manipulating trade and playing on Preddi resentment, we stoked tensions among the three clans, leading to a series of clashes.

"This gave us the excuse to claim we needed to provide security for our enclave." A sardonic smile graced his face. "We argued that since the best Preddi fighting men were concentrated on the borders, then our trade center was at risk if there was a raid on the city. The Preddi Hetman was so focused on the other clans, he allowed us to bring in several hundred soldiers to ensure the *security* of our trading houses. Our numbers grew until the enclave included more than three thousand traders, craftsmen, and their families, and security forces."

Tuzere grinned. "Still, hard to believe they accepted our story."

Akuyun nodded. "Indeed, and by orchestrating a chain of events, we arranged for Selfcell and Eywell to attack the Preddi in a series of major raids and inconclusive minor battles, with casualties on all sides, thus weakening the Preddi Clan. In a gesture of support, the leader of our mission at that time offered to help the Preddi by bringing in more troops." His smile broadened. "Troops, on their way to another destination, that just *happened* to come to Caedellium to replenish stores. The Preddi leaders, afraid of being dismembered by the other two clans, agreed, and two thousand more of our troops disembarked."

Kalcan put his hands behind his head and stretched expansively. "They really were dim-witted."

"Maybe so," Akuyun said, "but it was at this point two years ago that the five of us came to Caedellium. The threat of our backing the Preddi cooled the fervor of the other two clans, and a three-way truce was well brokered by Administrator Tuzere."

"Thank you for the compliment, General Akuyun, but it wasn't all that difficult. Neither of the other two clans resisted once their hetmen got a look at our men in formation and the artillery demonstrations."

"Thank Narth, they didn't know the condition of our men." Zulfa slapped the tabletop. "Besides being the dregs of our army, they could hardly stand on their feet after months of being crammed in troop ships."

"Then maybe Administrator Tuzere does deserve credit for brokering a cessation of fighting based on a bluff," Akuyun said.

The other three nodded in agreement.

Tuzere opened both palms, accepting the praise.

Akuyun cleared his throat. "Naturally, the Preddi expected most of our troops to withdraw. The hetman wasn't happy when I informed him there was still too much uncertainty, and the troops would remain to protect Narthani citizens. Without bothering to inform the Preddi hetman, we then filtered additional military and civilian personnel into our enclave. Once the Preddi realized what we were doing and protested, we gave up any pretense and brought our totals up to four thousand troops and three thousand civilians."

Zulfa shook his head. "I'm just glad they didn't come to their senses earlier."

Akuyun raised his eyebrows. "Don't forget, Colonel, that during these months, although you mercilessly worked our men into better physical and fighting condition, it was mainly out of sight of the Preddi. Finally, the Preddi Hetman and other clan leaders realized they were losing control. After increasing acrimony in our meetings and small clashes between our men and the Preddi, the hetmen led an attack on our enclave, one we were prepared for. The Preddi ineptitude at organization and security, along with our paid Caedelli agents, combined to keep us apprised of their every move. When they attacked, we stayed in our enclave until they amassed their fighting men outside our defenses, then we landed another two thousand men behind the Preddi. In the ensuing battle, we crushed them between our two forces and took control of the Preddi Province. Any leaders who survived the initial fighting were hunted down and killed, and their families shipped off as slaves to Narthon. Fighting erupted within Preddi City and some of the smaller towns, but we put an end to any significant resistance within a month."

"An amazing result in so short a time," Admiral Kalcan remarked. "I remember wondering back then why we didn't move on to the rest of the island if taking down the Preddi Clan was so easy."

Zulfa frowned. "But—"

Kalcan raised a hand. "No, no, Zulfa. I don't mean to pass judgment on army strategies. I was just thinking from the deck of my flagship offshore and not on the ground. It was a fleeting thought."

Zulfa grunted. "It wasn't that the Preddi weren't brave enough, at least at first. In several fights, they continued even after losing over half their men. They simply had no concept of coordination, tactics, picking their ground, of strategic withdrawal. It was charge straight in. By the time we'd killed enough of their older leaders and younger, more flexible-thinking leaders emerged, it was too late."

"Zulfa's right." Akuyun steepled his fingers. "It wasn't so much their fighting spirit as inexperience in warfare. However, the result gave us our foothold on Caedellium. Narthani casualties were less than two hundred dead, compared with destroying the Preddi Clan and almost a thousand dead each for Eywell and Selfcell during previous years of fighting. At a minimal cost, we absorbed one of the Caedellium clan provinces, and two other clans were about to be co-opted as allies.

"The Selfcell and Eywell clans were shocked at the suddenness of the Preddi destruction and belatedly understood their own danger. At separate meetings with the two clan hetmen, I explained that although we had 'inadvertently' gotten involved in Caedellium affairs, the die was cast. The trade had proven lucrative to us, and we intended a further increase. However, to justify the investment, we required confidence that our trade center, which now comprised the entire Preddi Province, would never again be threatened. Yet even an entire province did not provide enough 'security,' and we needed assurances of the friendly status of their two clans by means of formal alliances with them.

"As an inducement, we offered to aid them in eventually annexing major territory of their immediate neighbors, lands belonging to the Gwillamer and Moreland clans for Eywell, and more of Moreland and the Stent Clan for Selfcell. We'd already reached an agreement with the Eywell hetman, unbeknownst to Selfcell. Administrator Tuzere had identified the Eywell leader as the more gullible hetman and also dangled the possibility of adding half of Caedellium to Eywell control, but only if they were our ally.

"The Selfcell hetman was less interested, evidently having no inherent desire to carve up neighboring clans. However, he saw his province enclosed by our navy on one side, our army that he couldn't defeat to his south, and the Eywellese to his west. We know he appealed to the other clans for help and was refused. He decided he had no option but to agree to our terms."

Akuyun's summary passed over the calamitous details for the Preddi Clan. In the two years after crushing the Preddi, the Narthani undertook a massive settlement and development program. All living Preddi males who were part of the Preddi fighting forces or were deemed potentially part of any resistance were deported as slaves back to Narthon—more than 4,000 men between the ages of fourteen and fifty. Another 12,000 clan noncombatants had died as collateral damage during the fighting or the following chaos; 10,000 more fled to other clan provinces; and 16,000 older men, women, and children were eventually shipped off to slave markets. The remaining 20,000 Preddi were spared for their specific skills after convincing their new Narthani masters they had switched loyalties, or they were converted to slaves when they could fill specific needs on Caedellium. This latter included 900 Preddi women taken as concubines by Narthani officers and officials or used to fill troop brothels.

The Preddi, as a clan, ceased to exist. Narthani immigrants slid into existing farms, mines, fishing, and trade shops, then expanded the cultivated acreage and established new farms on lands the Caedelli had not yet developed. On the day of the present meeting to formally initiate Phase Three, the sixth anniversary of the first Narthani trading house establishment, there were 12,000 Narthani troops and 100,000 civilians on Caedellium. Of the civilians, two-thirds were Narthani officials, craftsmen, farmers, overseers, and their families. The other third were slaves or indentured servants from conquered peoples within the Narthon Empire.

Akuyun cleared his throat after concluding the history summary. "Up to this point, we've scrupulously confined military action to the three original provinces. We now need to decide if it's time for that to change." He looked at each man in turn. "You've all been asked to give a formal report on your areas of responsibility. Colonel Zulfa, start off with the status of our troops."

Colonel Zulfa straightened in his chair. "The newest troops are still getting their land legs back after the voyage from Narthon." Zulfa's tenor conveyed satisfaction, as did the smile on his dark, handsome face. "It will take several sixdays before I can start whipping them into shape." He settled his tall frame back in the chair and ran a finger and thumb over his dashing mustache. "As expected, these men include both new recruits and a fair number of trash and troublemakers that commanders in Narthon wanted to be rid of."

Akuyun rubbed his chin as he listened. People often misjudged the thirty-eight-year-old Zulfa because of his impressive appearance. He was a gifted tactician, fearless but not reckless, and decisive at critical moments. For these reasons, Akuyun had chosen him as his second in command.

"How long will it take to train them?"

"I plan on treating them as if they had no previous military training. It'll take most of a year before they'll be in decent shape for a campaign. Once ready, the new arrivals will be integrated into existing units. I believe mixing the new arrivals with troops who've been on Caedellium for some time will make our units more uniform. Otherwise, we'd have two sets of units with different experiences and backgrounds."

Akuyun approved. "A sound plan."

Zulfa frowned. "Some of the officers who arrived with the new men are disgruntled about breaking up units organized in Narthon. According to my evaluation, and how we all know these things work, some of these officers got their positions based either on their family's status or on bribes. Most have little practical experience or ability."

Assessor Hizer leaned forward. "And you're satisfied with how those disgruntled officers are adjusting?"

Zulfa smiled, his eyes expressionless. "The problems diminished after I demoted a more vocal officer down a rank and sent him to command a guard unit attached to improving the main road to Selfcell."

Hizer sighed. "Please try not to alienate *too* many great families of Narthon, Colonel Zulfa."

Zulfa scowled. "You did agree with my action."

"Oh, I did, but fortunately, the officer in question already had numerous official and unofficial marks against his record. However, actions such as you took might accumulate negative consequences. If possible, next time please try to find *other* solutions for problematic officers."

They all knew his meaning: find an assignment with maximum chances of death or disappearance, preferably to allow a plausible report on the individual's bravery and noble service to the Empire.

"And our Caedellium allies?" prompted Akuyun.

Zulfa shrugged. "Brave enough, and will be useful as buffers between us and the rest of the Caedelli when we start raids into neighboring provinces, and then later as light cavalry screens for our troops. The Eywellese continue to be more enthused about the alliance than the Selfcellese. We'll need to stay aware that on occasion we may have to prod Selfcell and restrain Eywell."

"But you believe we're on track?"

"Yes, General. If necessary, we should be ready to take the field in a year, although I'd prefer a few more months."

Akuyun turned to Administrator Tuzere. "And you believe the civilian area is also going according to plan?"

The other man next to Zulfa and across from Akuyun was Nizam Tuzere, fifty-four, the administrative overseer of the non-military population, which included the civilian Narthani transportees to Caedellium and native Caedelli. Tuzere's portfolio also included maintaining order, watching for dissidents, and counter-espionage. Tuzere dressed in his usual dapper manner, and while his graying mustache, baggy eyes, and verging on portly figure made him appear older, his energy was unmatched among the five, and his mind was encyclopedic about the hundred thousand non-military Narthani and slaves on the island.

The civil authority's voice was like mellow oil flowing over his vocal cords. "All aspects are satisfactory, General. Within Preddi Province, our people have replaced most of the original Caedelli. Farms are producing well with new Narthani farmers and herders. As new settlers arrive, we're expanding total acreage under cultivation as fast as possible. The land here is among the most fertile I've ever seen, and we're more than self-sufficient, at least in grain and meat production. I project we can begin exporting back to Narthon this year."

Tuzere's animated eyes exuded pleasure at the last assessment. "Until now, the ships from Narthon brought troops, settlers, food, and everything needed for an enterprise of this magnitude, then sailed home empty after delivering their cargos. The ability to return laden with food and other products of the island will pay for the operation's expenses and reinforce the progress of the mission to higher authorities.

"As expected, setting up sufficient crafts and industry bases will take longer." Tuzere ran a plump, manicured hand over his embroidered waistcoat. "While we'll still need to import finished goods for a period of time, the situation will improve as we expand and bring in more of our people."

Akuyun shifted his weight in his chair. "And the Caedelli? Those within the former Preddi territory?"

"No problems there. I think we've eliminated any major potential resistance. The few remaining Preddi are well incorporated or subdued." Tuzere plucked at the skin fold under his chin and spoke next as if carefully crafting the words. "Ah . . . the only ongoing problem is converting the ex-Preddi to worship Narth. There have been a number of minor incidents, but they've decreased once the Caedelli learned our low tolerance for disturbances."

Noticeably absent at the meeting was the mission's chief Narth prelate, Mamduk Balcan. Balcan's absence was mainly due to his lack of interest in administrative and military matters, except when they interfered with converting the native Caedelli to the *true* religion, worshipping Narth, god of war and dominance. Although Balcan was not an acknowledged part of the Narthani command-and-reporting structure, Akuyun was obliged to give the prelate reasonable respect, though he didn't have to invite him to every meeting. Akuyun publicly and privately assured Balcan that he understood the prelate's concerns, but it was Akuyun's higher duty not to permit fervent conversion efforts to interfere with political and military affairs. Those had first priority before universal worship of Narth was possible. Balcan had chafed but acquiesced.

Akuyun only confessed to his wife, Rabia, his desire that Balcan suffer some unfortunate fatal accident. Akuyun believed that among his subordinates, at least Zulfa and Hizer had the same unspoken wish. However, thus far Balcan had not interfered enough to warrant such a calamity. At times, Akuyun wished the prelate would overstep.

"Of course, conversion is a priority," Tuzere avowed for formality, "and we cooperate with Prelate Balcan as much as possible."

Though none of the five men were devout followers of Narth or any other God, lip service was required.

"Outside of Preddi, it's as Zulfa says from the military side. On one hand, the Eywellese will integrate the smoothest. Within another generation, two at the most, they'll quit thinking of themselves as Eywellese. To help that along, we've encouraged teaching Narthani in their schools, arguing it will help them interact with our people. We know from experience that switching to our language as soon as possible is a key to assimilation. Once the entire island is under our control, we'll mandate all islanders learn Narthani. For now, I believe we can be confident about the Eywellese.

"On the other hand, Selfcell is still problematic. I've seen no signs of active resistance, but there's no doubt they're warier than the Eywellese, at least as far as the leadership is concerned. The Eywellese Hetman is about as venal and dense as we could hope, but Hetman Langor of Selfcell is shrewd and sees the reality of making the best of a bad situation."

Zulfa leaned forward, his eyes on Tuzere. "But you still think the Selfcell situation is stable enough not to consider taking firmer steps before we advance to the next phase?"

"We've been through this before," answered Akuyun before Tuzere could reply. "While they may drag their asses, the Selfcellese haven't given us sufficient reason to act, particularly since we want to convince other clans not to resist. It's one thing to do what we did to the Preddi clan when they openly attacked us. If we're too severe just because a clan isn't enthusiastic, it will only make the other clans more resistant and more likely to unite too soon—something we definitely don't want."

Zulfa sat back. "I know. I only bring it up because I'm looking at the military side of it. I'm still not comfortable with the local auxiliaries I'll need to include once we get to Phase Four."

Tuzere nodded. "I appreciate your concerns, and as the general says, we've been careful not to press the Selfcell and the Eywell too hard. Neither clan is happy with our stationing one thousand strong permanent Narthani garrisons in their provinces. Those garrisons cause the usual resentments, but much of that is ameliorated by our generous expenditures into the local economies. We've also restricted troop movements to minimize conflict, at least for now. Once we expand and control other provinces, we'll tighten control over the Selfcell and Eywell clans. I believe those clans' leaderships know we could interfere much more. For example, the Selfcellese may disapprove of our using Preddi women in our troop brothels, but it serves as another warning of what can happen to our opponents."

"I'm just reiterating we need to keep a close eye on the Selfcellese and not depend on them too much, yet," said Zulfa.

"Duly noted," acknowledged Akuyun. He turned to Admiral Kalcan seated on his left. The fifty-two-year-old commander of Narthani naval forces in Caedellium waters had a constant twinkle in eyes set in a round, smooth-shaven face. Kalcan's habitual cheerfulness contrasted with the more severe countenances of the other four men, but his casual demeanor belied his fierce dedication to the Empire. The admiral was one of the few men to whom Akuyun showed his more whimsical side when they were alone, and the one who might be regarded as a friend, if Akuyun had had that luxury.

"Admiral Kalcan, we've read your report on naval readiness and scouting and mapping of the Caedellium coasts. To confirm, is it your assessment that we're ready to proceed?"

"Oh, we'll continue with those activities." Kalcan clasped his hands on the table. "Mainly refining our charts. We've still seen no sign of navies from other realms, and our ships and men are in good condition." He smiled and rapped his chest lightly with a fist. "Our naval forces are ready to proceed."

Akuyun turned to Hizer. "Assessor Hizer, any comments or observations?"

The final man at the table had listened attentively to the discussion. At being addressed, he absentmindedly rolled his shoulders in a manner reminiscent of a predator shifting weight, confident in itself. Sadik Hizer was fifty, of stocky frame, and dressed in plain dark trousers, a shirt, and a light coat. He might pass for a well-dressed but common tradesman until he looked at you. Behind penetrating dark eyes resided a sharp intellect refined by years of experience and education beyond most Narthani. Hizer was an assessor, a member of a small corps of men who served as the direct eyes and ears of the Narthani leadership's highest levels. He had no formal authority and instead was charged with providing two types of information: general advice, if solicited by the mission's leaders, and independent evaluations of the mission's progress and leadership.

"I think you've covered all the necessary grounds, General. As we all know, there are always adjustments to any plan, though I'm satisfied everything is proceeding through the major milestones. I see no reason to hesitate in moving on to the next phase."

"Thank you, Assessor. We appreciate your input." Akuyun kept a smile off his face. While Akuyun and Hizer had gone over the same material two days earlier, this was the official support statement for the benefit of the record and the other leaders.

Assessors were often thought of as spies for the Narthani High Command, which they were, but one of Akuyun's talents was to meld assigned assessors into his overall leadership structure, even if informally. In Hizer, Akuyun knew he was fortunate to be assigned an assessor with whom he worked well. He would never understand those commanders who resented the presence of the assessors and kept them at arm's length—not when it risked friction between the two, and that friction possibly affecting the assessor's reports. Also, you lost the ability and insights the better assessors could provide.

The five men spent another hour discussing details of the current status of Phase Two. Then Akuyun spoke the words for which the previous hours had been a prelude.

"I think we can all agree that we're established enough to move into Phase Three against the other eighteen clans. Any disagreements or qualifications?"

They shook their heads, and all four leaned forward in their seats, eyes alert, anticipating the mission commander's next words.

"Then, as of today we'll begin Phase Three—direct action against the other clans. The plan has three interconnected parts. First, the Eywellese and the Selfcellese will increase low-level forays into neighboring clan provinces, gradually ramping up into raids. Second, I will finalize our arrangement with Buldorian mercenaries to carry out raids on coastal villages, abbeys, and other selected targets. These raids should create turmoil within the coastal clans and force them to concentrate their fighting men to protect their own coasts, as well as minimize their ability to aid other clans."

Hizer's smile was that of a serpent. "These non-Narthani Seaborn raiders will sow uncertainty and give us a degree of deniability."

Kalcan laced his fingers, elbows on the table, and cautioned, "Yes, the Buldorians are notorious pirates and raiders, but it won't fool the brighter Caedelli for long."

Akuyun pursed his lips. "We don't require fooling *all* of them or for *too* long. Just long enough to sow confusion and force them to focus on their own security and not on helping other clans, as we move into direct efforts to destabilize the clans and any existing allegiances. We'll attempt to provoke inherent Caedellium clan conflicts to stir up old resentments. The methods will vary, depending on the clan and circumstances, but include using bribes and veiled threats to be sure a clan fully understands the implications of being on the wrong side of the inevitable Narthani supremacy.

"We're following the basic strategy that has worked well for the Empire. When the time is right, we'll move to Phase Four and commit our troops and compel either a centrally located clan or that clan and its allies to fight large-scale battles so we can deliver decisive defeats. At that point, we expect some of the clans to concede Empire control of Caedellium and ally with us. The remaining clans will then surrender or be systematically destroyed."

"Invasion on the cheap," Zulfa growled. "It would have been faster to bring in enough troops to crush them all in one season's campaign, then move on." It was not the first time Zulfa had expressed this opinion.

Akuyun nodded, keeping his tone even, hiding his impatience. This ground had been covered many times, in many meetings. "Faster, yes, but not as efficient."

Hizer drummed fingers on the tabletop and shifted his weight. "We all know the arguments. High Command plans carefully. Though we're not averse to using overwhelming force, we can obtain our objectives at less cost if time is not a critical factor. Incorporating Caedellium is part of our long-term plans for expansion of the Empire, but with other ongoing conflicts bordering Narthon, our mission here is important, though not particularly urgent."

"Efficiency is always an important factor," Akuyun reiterated. "The Empire's forces are engaged in many places worldwide, limiting the number of troops they can commit to Caedellium if it can be avoided. As Zulfa has said, the new men assigned to us are not the best. Even the original units sent here had poor performance ratings. High command didn't think first-line units would be needed." He smiled at Zulfa. "You did a good job of working those men into shape, and I'm sure you'll do the same with the new arrivals."

Zulfa snorted. "It's unlikely they'll ever be more than mediocre. We wouldn't want to pit them against a real opponent."

Akuyun pushed aside his unused notes on their mission through Phase Two. "Even so, they only need to be *good enough* to handle the Caedelli."

Akuyun rubbed his cheek. "What we don't want is for the clans to retreat to the mountains. It would take years to root them out. If High Command's plan works, we'll get most of the Caedelli to either cooperate or surrender with a minimum amount of our resources expended. Taking over the Preddi Province as we did was necessary but wasteful." He eyed Zulfa. "Too much was destroyed and too many clansmen killed. We want to preserve as much as possible as we incorporate the islanders in the Empire. Living people are more useful than dead or enslaved ones. If possible."

The decision formally made, Akuyun ended the meeting with a final reiteration of assignments. He didn't believe a fundamental purpose could be drummed in too many times or subordinates reminded too often of their roles.

The meeting also served to ensure that all of the senior commanders understood how their interrelated tasks fit together.

"Let's keep our eyes on the details, gentlemen. Colonel Zulfa, the Eywellese and the Selfcellese are to slowly ratchet up their incursions into neighboring clan territories, but not so quickly as to cause the other clans to unite too soon. Keep on top of them, especially the Eywellese.

"Admiral Kalcan will handle the Buldorians and work with Assessor Hizer on general intelligence gathering and planning Seaborn raids. Administrator Tuzere will also assist Assessor Hizer in overseeing our overtures to selected clans, directing intelligence gathering, maintaining existing agents within Caedellium, and recruiting more agents as needed."

The summary complete, Akuyun ended the meeting. "Gentlemen, we all know our assignments. Let's get to it and bring the entire island into the Empire."

Okan Akuyun and Wife

"Busy day, Okan?" Rabia Akuyun set a plate of food in front of her husband, then sat and picked up her fork. "I arranged for the children to spend the evening with Major Nubar's family. I thought it would be nice to eat alone, in case you wanted to talk. Just the two of us."

"Thank you," Okan smiled. "From the aromas when I walked in, I assume you cooked this evening. Another clue is the smudge of flour on your elbow."

"Well, the servants never quite get the seasoning right for braised beef the way you like it. And, as long as I was cooking, I figured I might as well bake fresh bread. Anyway, you know I like to lend a hand with preparing and serving the evening meal, and it's been a while since I had a chance. It reminds me of the importance of family and that we're not so far above other Narthani."

He shook his head. "And because you enjoy it?"

"And because I like it. Even if cooking and serving are low-class, it's sometimes relaxing."

Rabia's impish grin always brought a catch to his throat. He chuckled and filled her cup with Melosian tea, then poured himself a goblet of imported wine. "Well, you certainly don't admit that to others."

"That's between us." She sipped her drink. "Just like you only show me you're not always the . . . ," she lowered her voice and took on a dramatic tone, "totally assured commander of men." Rabia touched his hand tenderly. Okan projected himself to others as confident and only allowed uncertainties to show with her, which was one of the reasons she loved him.

She canted her head. "How *did* the meeting go today?"

"Good." He buttered a thick slice of bread. "We all agreed that we're ready to move to the next phase." He sopped up gravy with a wad of bread. "I'm relieved that none of the leaders brought up problems I hadn't thought of."

"And you expected there was something you hadn't thought of?"

Okan grunted through a mouth full of beef and gravy, then swallowed. "Not really," he admitted, "but you never know, and I try never to assume too much."

He was cutting another piece of meat when he stopped, set both hands on the table, and looked fondly at his wife. "Thank you for this evening, dearest. I'm forever glad I have you and our two youngest children with me on this Caedellium mission." He set down his knife, took her right hand, and kissed her fingers.

She felt a faint blush of pleasure at the gesture. "I'm glad, too. I'd have missed you terribly. I know we've always accompanied you, but this was to be so far from home and for so long, I wondered if this time might be different."

Okan shook his head, released her hand, and resumed eating. "It's not so far I wanted to be without you."

While some of the Narthani officers brought their wives, others left their families back in Narthon or wherever in the Empire they originated. Some looked at this as an opportunity to "sample" the local women, and they took concubines or slaves. Akuyun had never felt the urge. Rabia came from a prominent Narthani family. She had seen great promise in the young Narthani officer serving under her father. Her family had not been pleased with her intention to marry Akuyun, his being from a subjugated tribe, albeit two centuries earlier. Only dim records remained of his original people. So thoroughly had they been absorbed that his family never considered themselves anything but authentic Narthani.

Rabia set down her cup and brushed back a strand of hair. "I know it's a relief for you to finally move forward. We've been here two years, and we both would like to get back to Narthon."

"It's coming, dearest. Another year, two at the most."

Okan drank from his wine goblet, then sighed. "Besides the meeting with my staff, there was the usual endless paperwork—annual evaluations of my immediate subordinates, and reviewing those of all the other officers. Then more paperwork and meeting with Tuzere and the other civilian leaders to review settlement progress and future expansions. Then *more* paperwork for the quarterly report due to be sent to Narthon. It's still a month away, but I want it completed in a timely manner."

Rabia raised her napkin to hide a smile. Her husband's meticulous work habits, along with his native intelligence and force of personality, had been the three pillars that justified her evaluation of him those many years ago, as well as the basis of his fast rise in service to the Empire. "I'm sure you'll finish on time and with your usual thoroughness," she gently remonstrated. It had not only been his future potential that had attracted her, for theirs was a love match not usual in the upper reaches of Narthani society.

Okan smiled fondly. "Thank you, my dear, for the endorsement. I may include it in the report summary." The interchange was part of a routine evolved over their twenty-seven years of marriage. Her hair showed gray strands, and the lines around her eyes had deepened with the years, but he still saw the young woman who once seemed out of reach to a junior officer. A beauty she might not be, but the lively eyes, the mischievous smile, when directed at him, and the trim figure hadn't changed, in addition to the indescribable something that made them belong together.

He had never been tempted by other women once he and Rabia wed. Narthani society mandated there be only one wife to avoid inheritance and dynastic conflicts that had been the bane of early Narthani history. Not that there was prohibition against a man having multiple women in his household, but there was only one wife, and her children would inherit. Any other women in the household, be they free concubines or slaves, were subordinate to the wife. Promising children of other women were formally recognized as the wife's, and such children might inherit under some circumstances. In Akuyun's case, the issues never arose. Rabia satisfied all of his needs—emotional, political, and sexual, and she was cognizant of all three roles.

"Narth forbid you mention a mere woman was consulted on anything of importance," she teased. It was another part of their interplay. Narthani society excluded women in any role outside the home. To her, it was a never-healing sore, and to him a stupidity that lost valuable contributions from women such as his wife. Not that they voiced such opinions except to each other.

"Don't forget, you promised Lufta and Ozem you would be home tomorrow night for their eleventh birthday." Okan and Rabia had decided that the fraternal twins were skilled riders and old enough to graduate from ponies to trained, docile horses for birthday presents. Ozem, the boy, had failed in his campaign to be allowed to choose his own horse, while Lufta was indifferent to horses and would be content with whatever her parents chose.

Okan sighed. "You're right, I had forgotten. Thank Narth, you're here as my memory for such things." His smiled, taking years off his face. "I promise, dearest. Home in time for the birthday dinner."

"Oh, Okan, before I forget, the mail packet included letters from Bilfor and Morzak. They're on your desk."

Their two oldest sons were twenty-five and twenty-three years old. The twins had come much later, after he and his wife thought there would be no more children. Bilfor and Morzak were junior officers in the Narthani army and had families of their own. Bilfor, the oldest, was steady and thorough. Akuyun thought he would rise to be a respected major or colonel, but likely no higher.

Morzak, however, seemed to have inherited the intellect and astuteness of his parents. Rabia suspected he was the brightest in the entire family, and Okan once told her he could see Morzak going far, possibly at least as high as his father. As for the twins, they were still too young to be sure, though Okan thought Ozem had potential, while Lufta's mind flittered in all directions. Half the time, Akuyun thought she might turn into another version of her mother; the rest of the time he wondered if she would end up an empty-headed twit.

Through the rest of the evening, Okan and Rabia talked of family, of matters weighty and trivial, and of whatever their futures might bring.

Okan Akuyun finished eating, his belly full, a slight buzz from the wine, his eyes always coming back to Rabia. Life was good. He'd risen high and might go higher, the mission was progressing well, and he was more than pleased with his family. And then there was Rabia. Always Rabia. Life was good.

CHAPTER 6

ACCEPTANCE

Catharsis

Joe had no sense of time, only that days blurred together. He gained strength and needed less help getting to and from the dining hall and the voiding house. Finally, the day came when he no longer needed assistance and could walk the abbey grounds. The staff acted friendly. At least, he assumed and hoped so, since their speech remained unintelligible. He lived in a semi-mute world, seeing mouths move and hearing sounds, but not communicating. The pattern of his life was to wake, eat in the dining hall, walk the grounds, sit in his room, and fall asleep hours after dark.

In his explorations of the abbey grounds, he found places to avoid seeing another person. In the southeast corner of the abbey complex, where a fruit orchard abutted the eight-foot main outer wall, sat an old wooden chair. He would lean the weathered back against the wall and face a mixed row of lemon and a local fruit tree—foilamon, he later learned—which produced plum-shaped yellow fruit evocative of tomatoes and almonds. Though the taste combination was foreign to his palate the first time they served slices at evening meal, he came to appreciate the subtleties of the flavor mix.

On other days, he rested within formal gardens behind the cathedral: several acres of small trees, bushes, grassy plants, and flowerbeds accessed by a maze of paths. A wicker bench sat tucked away on a short, seldom-used side loop off a wider path. It was there, on this day, he sat contemplating his existence. The midday meal had been a combination of foods from both Earth and this planet: wheat for the bread, a stew of beef (he had seen cattle grazing in pastures outside the complex walls), and a mixture of unrecognized vegetables. For dessert, he'd eaten foilamon and a brown banana-like fruit with purplish flesh that tasted of raspberry and licorice.

That he could eat foods from plants and animal evolved on this planet told him the biochemistries of Earth and the local ecosystem were compatible, since he hadn't been poisoned and his strength improved daily. The local organic molecules—proteins, carbohydrates, fats, and DNAs—must have similar basic structures as those on Earth. He thought it ironic that to one question posed by his planned presentation at the AAAS conference, "Alternatives to Standard Heterocyclic Bases in DNA of Exobiosystems," he now knew the answer. Earth's biochemistry was not unique. It was knowledge worthy of a Nobel Prize, except he was the only human in existence, now or perhaps ever, to possess it. Even worse, he had no one to share it with. He and the knowledge were locked away as surely as if both served life sentences in solitary confinement.

Gray clouds hid the sun, but an initial drizzle passed. Despite the cloak draped over his shoulders, he shivered in the chill air. The bench in the alcove allowed views of lovingly designed and tended pebble paths winding among a mélange of plants, perhaps a quarter of which he recognized or suspected of originating on Earth. The rest he assumed were indigenous. He studied the juxtaposition of striking foliage, bloom successions, and colors. Wherever his eyes turned, he saw variety. To the left grew a shrub covered in blue, bell-shaped flowers. To the right, yellow and red flowers rose from a bed of foot-high foliage. Across the path, a grass-like plant bore small white flowers on thin, nearly invisible stems. A breath of wind moved the grass, and the flowers seemed free-floating, dancing like a swarm of small white insects.

Joe followed the undulating passage of a butterfly with yellow and black markings. It fluttered past and settled on the blue flowers, sucking nectar from a blossom. It looked like a tiger swallowtail. Just like at home. For an instant, his imagination transported him back to Earth and let him pretend he *was* home.

The butterfly veered away as dragonfly-like creatures appeared. Their red-and-green striped wings flashed iridescent in the sunlight as they settled on the flowers. One unfurled a proboscis and probed for nectar.

Joe leaned closer and studied one of the strange insects. They had six wings, stood on four legs, and used two more appendages with small pincers to manipulate the flower petals.

It was not a terrestrial life form.

The illusion of being on Earth evaporated. He trembled, slumped, and covered his face with his hands. Tears ran through Joe's fingers. Lost, alone, and desolate, he rocked, shoulders jerking as he sobbed.

The bench shifted, then moved again. Someone's leg and body brushed against him. An arm draped over Joe's back, and a hand gripped his right shoulder. The warmth of the person's body seeped into his consciousness. The nearness of another human being, any human, anchored him. His sense of absolute loneliness faded, along with his sobs. A soft breeze caressed his face. Overhead, birds twittered, and in the distance a dog barked. Murmurs of workers in the vegetable garden filtered through the trees. The even breathing of the person brought Joe calm. He drew a shuddering breath, his emotions spent.

The tears and sobs simply stopped as if a faucet had turned off. He still felt the loneliness but not the same sense of despair as before.

I'm alive. I'll never see Earth again or any of the people I knew. Not my friends, family, Julie, our unborn child. I'll never know whether it was a boy or a girl, or if it even existed.

He closed his eyes and turned his face to the sun uncovering behind clouds. His skin warmed to the touch of brightness.

And everything else he knew. Every little thing. No Giants' games. His lips curled into a wry smile at the hint of humor seeping into his list of losses. No *Call of Duty* video game sessions with friends, no summer days in the California wine country, no grousing whether the Democrats were more venal than the Republicans. No more wondering why anyone would care about the Kardashian family. No M&Ms. No single large moon, instead of the two small ones he'd seen here, or wondering why he liked some Country and Western music. It was all gone. He opened his eyes and stared across the garden. The soft wind dried the remaining tears on his cheeks.

To look at some bright sides, if Harlie had told the truth, he'd be immune to everything on the planet. He'd never have a cold again or any other disease. Also, no tooth decay, since it was caused by bacteria. Those had to be major pluses. Having cavities here had to be grim. No cancer. Fortunate, since there'd be no treatments. Harlie also said his physiology would be more efficient. Whatever that meant, he had no idea but hoped it was a good thing.

He gazed at the garden now bathed in sunlight, the last clouds clearing and the sun warming the air. Once more the bench shifted, and the person's hand still gripped his shoulder. He turned, expecting to see Fitham, the older, kindly brother, or perhaps the woman called Diera or one of the others who helped care for him when he first arrived.

Joe's eyes slowly traveled from a massive chest to a broad face. It was the hulk of a man Joe had seen working around the abbey. He'd noticed the man on occasion, but he always seemed alone, as if the other staff avoided him. They had walked past each other once, the man never indicating that he noticed Joe, who was awed by the man's size. He was enormous—a good six-foot, seven or eight inches, and a solid 300 or more pounds of bone and muscle. A perpetual scowl framed his wild red hair and beard, but as Joe inspected the man's face, he realized the scowl was only an impression given by the prominent brows and lines in the weathered face. Joe was drawn deeper. The eyes. Were they filled with concern . . . and compassion?

Joe smiled tentatively and nodded, patting one of the man's massive legs. "Thank you."

The man inclined his head, rose, and flipped his hand.

He wants me to follow him?

Rising unsteadily, Joe walked beside the man. Joe wasn't short, but he barely reached over the man's broad shoulders. They walked slowly, side by side, through the garden and into the rear of the dining hall, where staff members prepared for the evening meal.

Joe stood in the entrance, confused. What was the man up to?

The giant approached a middle-aged woman with flour smudges on her arms and spoke in a deep, rumbling voice. She glared at him and shook her head, barking something at him.

He took it calmly and again spoke quietly.

Still frowning, she glanced at Joe and back at the giant. She nodded, wiped her hands on an expansive apron, and strode away.

Turning, the giant walked back to Joe and took his arm, leading him to a table outside. He sat and waved at an opposite bench.

Overhanging vines festooned with red flowers brushed Joe's head as he sat, then studied the man.

The woman reappeared and slapped down two large metal steins, spilling liquid on the rough wooden table. Joe jerked his arms away from the spill. Foam covered the contents of the stein, and a strong aroma of hops hit his nose.

Beer?

She clomped away, and his fingers curled around the stein. It was icy cold. How did they keep it so cold? Even a cellar would only keep it cool at best. He took a sample sip, and then a long draft and wiped his mouth with the back of his hand. It was beer, strong and good. He smiled at the giant and lifted his stein.

"To you, whoever you are. I needed this."

Setting down his half-finished beer, the man-mountain pointed at himself. "Carnigan." He tapped his own chest. "Carnigan. Carnigan."

Carnigan poked Joe's chest with a large forefinger and said something.

"Joseph," Joe responded. "I'm Joseph."

Carnigan's lips formed over the name. "Yohhzzeefff. Yohzeff." Then quicker. "Yozef!"

"Close enough." Joe grinned. It was the same with the hospital staff. They didn't seem to have the "j" sound, and they turned the middle "s" of Joseph into a "z." "Yozef" was as close as they could pronounce. Looks like he was Yozef now.

Carnigan pointed to himself again. "Carnigan Puvey."

"Joe, Joseph, ah . . . " He bit his lip. "Yozef." *Might as well get used to my new name.* "Yozef Colsco."

"Yozef Kolzko, Yozef Kolzko," Carnigan echoed with a broad smile.

They quaffed the steins in amicable silence. Whether it was the alcohol, the catharsis of weeping, or the personal contact, Yozef didn't know, but he felt . . . different. The loneliness remained, as did nagging thoughts about what he was supposed to do next. He relaxed, however, at least for the moment. The woman from the kitchen reappeared, checked the status of the steins, took them away, and returned minutes later with two more and a plate of bread and cheese.

Yozef and Carnigan spent the rest of the afternoon at the table talking, neither having any idea what the other said, but it didn't seem to matter. Their occasional laughter drew puzzled attention from staff members. Finally, the light faded as the workday ended, and other staff members headed into the dining hall. Carnigan rose and motioned for Yozef to come. They walked in and sat together, eating in silence. Yozef didn't think he was hungry after the beers, bread, and cheeses, but he ate the meal without hesitation. He tried to ignore questioning stares and the conversation buzz aimed at the two of them.

Yozef yawned and rose. He could have slept where he sat, head on the table.

Carnigan also stood and walked with him to his room.

"Thank you, Carnigan." Yozef held out an open hand. "I know you don't understand anything I'm saying, but thank you." Then it occurred to him that an offered hand could be an insult in this culture. Thankfully, Carnigan understood the gesture. Yozef's hand disappeared in Carnigan's massive paw. He had a brief scare that local customs might mandate a firm handshake, which, when delivered by Carnigan, might require last rites for his hand. Fortunately, the grip was just firm.

With a final smile and nod, Carnigan walked away, and Yozef entered his room, lay on the bed, and feel asleep without undressing.

Carnigan's Debriefing

Though Sistian and Diera Beynom could have lived in generous quarters in the abbey complex, they preferred a house a few hundred yards from the outer abbey grounds. The distance allowed them time and space away from responsibilities and provided a normal family life for them and two children still living at home.

As they walked home that evening, their shoes disturbed dust on the wide path, her skirt and his pants brushing against bordering grass. Diera linked her arm in Sistian's. "Brother Fitham called me to witness a rather strange thing today involving Yozef."

Sistian glanced at her. "Yozef? What did he do?"

She chuckled. "It isn't what he did. Brother Fitham took me to the area behind the kitchen where I saw an amazing sight. Yozef and Carnigan were drinking beer while talking and laughing."

Sistian's eyebrows rose. "Carnigan! Laughing?"

"Yes! Laughing, although I can't imagine at what, since he wouldn't understand Yozef. According to Brother Fitham, Yozef was weeping in the main garden. Fitham was about to go to him when Carnigan stopped working and sat next to Yozef. Soon they were acting like old friends. Sister Mollywin was taken aback when Carnigan showed up at the dining hall and spoke to her. I think it flustered her so much, she didn't even argue the way she usually does about a break in routine, at least not too much."

Sistian shook his head. "Carnigan and Yozef? Who would have thought?"

"Maybe it's simply a matter of two lost souls finding each other at a chance moment." Diera pressed a finger to her lips. "Almost like God put them together to help them both."

"Whatever it was, it's good for them." The abbot stroked his beard, then glanced at his wife. "I think I'd like to hear Carnigan's view about what happened. Let's bring him in tomorrow morning."

Diera shook her head. "You're assuming we can get more than two words out of him."

The next morning, the rising sun touched peaks of the western hills when the two Beynoms arrived at the abbey and went directly to the abbot's office. Sistian spoke to an aide, who then hurried off.

"Brother Elbern will ask Carnigan to join us." Sistian walked to his chair and sat. Diera moved beside him and laid a hand on his shoulder.

She looked down and smiled. "And am I correct that from Brother Elbern's face, he was hesitant?"

Sistian sighed. "Carnigan intimidates everyone. I've counseled him to be friendlier, but he looks at me like I'm speaking Narthani."

"I think it's also that he's had little experience with people being friendly to *him*." Diera smoothed her dress's folds. "He's certainly calmer than when he first came, but it's as if he's always sad. Like he's accepted the status of being apart from others, or perhaps *resigned* might be a better word."

A few minutes later there was a knock. Brother Elbern opened the door and stepped in. "Abbess, Abbot, Brother Carnigan is here."

"Thank you, Elbern," Diera said. "Please ask him to come in."

Elbern stepped away, and Carnigan filled the doorway. It wasn't a small doorway, but only narrow gaps separated the man and the door jambs.

Diera stared, folding her arms, tucking her hands into her sleeves. There was the rumor that Carnigan had once killed a steer with a single blow. She'd always assumed it was one of those snide comments people made about someone different who made them uneasy. It was probably just a silly rumor. Probably.

Carnigan stood motionless, his face stoic. If he was surprised at being asked to come to the abbot's office so early in the morning, he didn't show it. He and the abbot usually spoke once or twice a month; the abbot would inquire how Carnigan was doing and offer advice. Such counseling was not an option for Carnigan, as it was for other staff, but it would be more effective if it involved two-way conversations, which were seldom forthcoming.

Carnigan's summons to the abbot's office was the second unusual event he'd experienced in two days. As he followed Brother Elbern, Carnigan reasoned the two events were connected.

He didn't know *why* he had gone to the stranger he had heard other staff members talking about. He'd seen the man walking the grounds and sitting on benches, as many staff, visitors, and Carnigan himself had similarly done.

He had been on his hands and knees, weeding a flowerbed, taking care his bulk didn't disturb the flowers. Halfway through the bed, he heard weeping on the other side of the bushes. He stopped weeding, rose to his knees, and listened. The sounds were of bone-deep emotional pain. He stood and walked around the parallel path to a junction and to the sounds. It was the stranger, elbows on his thighs, body shaking, head bowed in his hands, tears running between his fingers. Carnigan had stood for several moments, first simply observing, inclined to return to weeding; then he felt he *should* do something. He sat next to the man, moved closer, put an arm over the man's back, and gripped a shoulder, saying nothing but sensing the man needed someone *there* at the moment.

"Thank you for coming, Carnigan," Diera said. "Please sit." She motioned to the sturdier of two empty chairs. Diera could see her husband hold his breath as the man eased himself down. The chair survived, although its strained joints audibly complained.

She studied Carnigan's expressionless face. Whatever went on inside the big man's mind stayed there. As far as Diera and Sistian knew, there was no one Carnigan spoke with regularly on anything other than work assignments. Neither did he socialize with anyone at the abbey or in Abersford. Several nights a week, Carnigan would walk to a pub in the village. No matter how busy the evening, he sat in a corner table alone, sipping steins of beer. He attended Godsday morning service every week. As far as she knew, that was the sum of Carnigan's life in his two years at the abbey.

Sistian steepled his fingers. "I understand you met Yozef yesterday."

Carnigan grunted and gave a brief nod.

"He was troubled, and you sat with him."

Another grunt.

"Perhaps you could tell us a little about what happened," Diera said gently, as she sat in the other seat.

"He was just lost for the moment," Carnigan said in his deep, emotionless voice.

"Carnigan," Diera said, shifting forward in her seat, hands folded on her lap, "we've worried about Yozef since he recovered from whatever happened to him. We can't communicate with him, and we're concerned about how to help him."

"He's fine."

So much for in-depth diagnoses. Diera pressed on. "This could be important for Yozef, Carnigan. He was crying, then later he seemed in a better mood."

"As I said," Carnigan rumbled, "he was lost for the moment. Once he stopped crying, he was fine."

Sistian rubbed his cheek. "I think the beers may have helped there."

"Maybe," Diera said, "but it might have been just what it seemed. It's not unusual for someone who suffered a bad experience to get relief by crying. There has even been speculation in medicant circles that crying is God's gift to help us overcome what might otherwise seem overwhelming."

Sistian's expression was one she recognized to signify his doubt, but she knew he would defer to her on this. While she might study people's behavior with more of a medical slant than his theological one, they both served those in need.

Diera sat back and smoothed her tunic. "Would it be acceptable if we asked you to keep an eye on Yozef for the next few sixdays? Don't press him if he wants to be alone, but be available for whatever contact he wants."

"Of course, Abbess," Carnigan said in a flat tone.

"And try not to let him drink too much, Carnigan," Diera added, "if for no other reason than he's still recovering. Remember, his capacity won't be the same as yours, even when he's fully recovered."

Carnigan frowned. It was the first expression Diera saw on his face, as if he was offended at the suggestion he might consume an inordinate amount of alcohol.

"I'll see he doesn't drink too much," Carnigan grated, then rose and left without a by-your-leave or dismissal.

Diera held her laughter until Carnigan left. "Oh, Sistian, even those few words are more than I've heard from Carnigan the whole time he's been here."

"Loquacious he's not, though I'm encouraged by even *this* little of what passes for a conversation with Carnigan. I think you're right. Maybe he and Yozef can somehow touch each other in ways the rest of us don't understand. I'll give extra prayers today for the two of them."

Diera tapped a finger against her cheek. "That Yozef and Carnigan talked so long without knowing what each was saying makes me think Yozef is ready to start learning to speak Caedelli. I wouldn't rush him quite yet, but as soon as he's ready, we should encourage it. We'll never know more of who he is and how he got here until that happens. Whatever his story is, it's *bound* to be fascinating."

CHAPTER 7

CAEDELLIUM LIFE

Adjusting

Yozef awoke with sunlight flooding his bed through a window. He stretched his limbs and noticed he ... felt *good*. A warm lassitude faded, as his surroundings jolted him fully awake, but he still felt more alive since waking on this planet. How many hours had he slept? Ten, twelve hours? Hours? However they measured time here, the day was well along.

His bladder's urgent signals interrupted his wondering about time. He pulled on clothes and hustled to the voiding house he had first thought of as an outhouse. The building was more formal than the classic shed with the crescent moon on the wooden door on Earth. This one was the size of a house, with common areas for washing and two classes of closable compartments, one for showers and sponge-baths and another for the activities that gave the building its name. The facility was unisex, with the compartments providing privacy. He was consternated the first time he defecated by himself and intuited the purpose of baskets of moss-like material next to the hole in the floor. Then, surprise and momentary embarrassment resulted when he exited his compartment at the same moment a woman entered a neighboring one.

This morning, his bladder satisfied, his stomach announced food as the next priority. He had missed the morning meal.

"So, what are the rules here?" he spoke aloud to himself. If you missed the mealtime, were you shit out of luck until the next one? Only one way to find out—go over to the dining hall and look hungry.

As he walked the gravel paths, he noticed he "hustled," as he had on the way to the voiding house. That he *could* hustle was notable. Not running or even what anyone would call quick, but with movements faster than days before.

He lifted the latch on the dining hall main door, leaned in to open the door, and walked in. As expected, no one sat and ate at the tables. He stood for perhaps a minute, wondering what to do next, when a girl carrying a box came out of the kitchen area, saw him, and started jabbering.

He assumed she said something notable, like, *"Dining Hall is closed until midday meal,"* or *"You missed breakfast, dumb-ass,"* or some such. Of course, she could be reciting local poetry or asking him to come by her room this evening, and he wouldn't know the difference.

After more vocalizations, the woman either recognized him as the strange man or got tired of getting no response. She huffed, set the box on one table, pulled out a chair at another table, and motioned for him to sit. He did, and she went into the kitchen area, returning with a bowl, a large slice of the standard heavy, dark bread, and a steaming mug of something.

He gave her his best smile. "Thank you. Sorry I'm late."

She scowled and stomped away.

The bowl held a porridge resembling dark oatmeal, supplemented with small chunks that appeared to be nuts and berries. The bread was split down the middle with a hunk of yellowish cheese stuck in the crevice. The contents of the mug looked like coffee but smelled like moist earth. He had drunk the brownish liquid before, though didn't recall the taste. He sipped gingerly, blowing to cool off the surface.

It definitely wasn't coffee and had a faint root beer flavor to go along with the pungent aroma. Probably some kind of extract from a local plant root. After another sip, his head cleared of sleep's residues, and he eyed the mug with respect. Maybe not from a bean like coffee, but wherever it came from it must have similar alkaloids to caffeine, by the way it hit him.

The mug's contents, the bowl's, and the bread and cheese disappeared, while he mused over the botanical origin of the drink. He took the empty dishes and the spoon to the kitchen door, called out, "Hello," and the same young woman appeared. She took the dishes from him, he thanked her, and she jabbered back.

He expected she said, *"Okay, get out of here and stop bothering us."* He somehow doubted it was, *"You're more than welcome and come in anytime for anything you want to eat."* Also probably not, *"My room, 8 o'clock, be there."*

He smiled, chuckled, and bustled out the main door.

Yozef Learns Caedelli

Once outside, he stood in the light and felt warmth against his face. He looked up and, for the first time since his arrival, consciously noticed the sun. That he *could* look at the sun for a few seconds without having to avert his eyes was one more clue he wasn't on Earth. The orb was larger than Sol, and the color had more of an orange tint than the yellow of Earth's sun.

If he remembered his astronomy, this must still be a Class G sun, like Sol, though a little smaller and cooler. It probably looked larger because this planet's orbit must be closer to its sun than Earth. Whatever the sun's characteristics, the colors he saw around him appeared "normal": the sky was robin's egg blue, the nearby flowers red and yellow, the foliage a mix of familiar greens plus darker-hues he assumed were native to this planet.

He walked the paths of the formal garden behind the cathedral, his mind clearer than since arriving to this place. He'd shit and eaten. Normally, he'd say he needed a shower and a shave to finish out the morning rituals, although perhaps in a different order. Shaving didn't seem to be in the cards here. Every man Yozef had seen since he'd awakened here sported a beard. The lengths, shapes, and degree of grooming seemed left to individual preferences, and the only smooth-faced males were boys still too young to have developed fuzz. Even if he *had* a razor, to fit in he would have to get accustomed to a beard. He had had one in college as an undergrad, back in his "Look at me, I'm adult and an intellectual," phase. He hadn't cared much for the beard then, and the one he was currently growing felt scruffy after a couple of weeks' growth. He was just going to have to get used to it.

As for the last of the four rituals—bathing remained. His nose had already noted that daily showers or baths were not the norm here. Although the BO levels were much higher than he was accustomed to, it surprised him it wasn't worse. Maybe it was the clothing, constructed from some natural fibers like wool, cotton, flax, or bandersnatchi. He already knew he got more odoriferous if wearing shirts made of synthetics, compared to cotton. Still, it got pretty earthy at evening mealtimes when the dining hall filled with bodies who had been working all day.

He sniffed his left armpit and grimaced. He needed a shower, but not now. Later, before evening meal. For now, he needed to think.

He continued a slow walk around the gardens and the grounds. An occasional local passed him, giving what he assumed to be a greeting, although for all he knew they were incantations to ward off the weird stranger who might be a demon. He only partly noticed them. He was deep into thoughts about where he was, how he got here, and most important . . . what was he going to do?

The same thoughts dominated his mind all day and the next. He was here. Not wanting to be *here* was meaningless. He *was* here. Simply sleeping in the small room they provided, eating three meals, shitting, and walking around agonizing over what had happened wouldn't work. What was he actually going to *do*?

The immediate answer was obvious. He didn't know.

Though he didn't have a long-term plan, he needed to act on the proverbial advice "Don't just stand there, do something!" Since he didn't know what he was going to do long term, at least he needed to do *something*, if only to get ready for when he did have a plan.

He stopped in the middle of a garden path and spoke aloud, oblivious to his surroundings and an approaching man.

"Language. No question. It's the unavoidable priority. Nothing long term is going to happen or be decided until I know enough of the language to communicate."

The man passed, eyeing him carefully and stepping aside to avoid contact with the stranger conversing with the air. Yozef didn't notice.

"Yes. Language. That's what I have to do first."

Having a clear, immediate goal both reassured and intimidated him. To know what he needed to do, even if short term, was a rock to stand on. However, it could also be shifting sand. He had had two years each of Spanish in high school and German in college—the latter a chemistry degree requirement left over from the days when much of the world's best chemistry work was published in German. That those days were many decades past by the time he got to college was evidently irrelevant to the Berkeley chemistry department. Neither language stuck with him, leaving him enough to pronounce the menu items at a Mexican restaurant and stumble through German chemistry publications.

This was going to be ugly and grueling. But he had no choice. He had to understand and speak the language.

Having an action plan, he sought out Carnigan at the next morning's meal and found him eating by himself as usual. Yozef plopped himself down at the same table, facing Carnigan, who appeared a little taken aback at the effrontery of someone sitting with him until he recognized Yozef. The initial frown changed to a twinkle, as Yozef started talking to him in English.

"Well, Carnigan. Congratulations on being appointed my first tutor in whatever you people call your language. Hope you appreciate the honor."

Carnigan grunted, his usual response to bursts of English, and continued eating. Yozef picked up the two-pronged local version of a fork, held it up with one hand, pointed to the utensil with the other hand, and said, "Fork . . . fork . . . fork."

Carnigan looked at him speculatively, then raised his eyebrows and said back, "Sonktie . . . sonktie . . . sonktie."

They moved on from there: head, eyes, hand, foot, chair, bowl, and knife. Once they finished eating and went outdoors, the lesson continued: tree, sun, clouds, path, wood, rock, on and on. Yozef forgot many of the words immediately, but repetition encouraged him that the overall task wasn't hopeless.

The lesson ended when Carnigan shook his head and made pushing and chopping motions with his arms.

"Work. You're saying you need to get to work. Thanks, Carnigan for picking up so quickly what I was trying to do." Yozef patted his shoulder and watched him turn and stride toward the barns.

It was a start, but he needed to write down what he heard. He needed a pen and paper. Or a quill and papyrus, or whatever the equivalent was here. Brother Fitham. He was the one to check with.

It took an hour to find the elderly brother who had helped him in his first weeks. Fitham was hanging laundry on lines behind the guest quarters. After exchanging unintelligible comments to each other, Yozef mimed for writing materials. Later that evening, when Yozef got back to his room, on his table sat a stack of blank pale-brown paper, several sharpened quills, and a stoppered vial of ink. Thus began the first, and certainly the only ever, English dictionary to the local language. He wrote down everything he could remember from Carnigan, perhaps twenty nouns in English and how he transcribed the equivalent local word.

He grimaced at the results. It looked pathetic. *Oh well, the longest trip starts with one step*, he recited.

The next morning, he brought paper, quill, and ink to the morning meal. Carnigan filled in nouns Yozef forgot from the day before, then left for work without further contributions to the dictionary. However, word had spread, whether by Carnigan, the abbot and the abbess, or the general observation the stranger was learning their language, and other staff took up the lessons. Whenever a staff member served a meal, he or she would point to each item and pronounce its name. When walking on the grounds, men and women pointed to buildings, doors, hoes, rocks—on and on. As he passed people, they greeted him with phrases whose exact meaning he didn't understand but assumed were versions of "Hello," "Good-bye," "Good-day," or whatever were common greetings.

After a few hundred nouns, he moved on to verbs. By the end of the first sixday, Abbot Sistian approached him with a boy about thirteen years old. The boy carried several thin, bound books and additional writing materials. Sistian and Yozef managed to communicate enough for Yozef to understand the boy would provide lessons in the local language, both spoken and written.

Thus began Yozef's serious study of Caedelli, as his young tutor gave him the name of the language and the people. He came to suspect Caedelli was an ancient ancestor of Indo-European, which, if correct, put the transplantation from Earth probably no later than 5,000 years BC. As he had noticed while bedridden, about one word in three or four seemed related to one or more of the Earth languages he was familiar with: English, Spanish, and German. He remembered from an anthropology course that among diverse Indo-European languages, some of the most common and important words had similarities—words such as *mother*, *father*, *water*, and occasional other nouns, although the similarities varied. While Caedelli words for *mother* and *father* sounded familiar, *sister* and *brother* didn't. The color blue sounded like "blue," and "red" and "black" were familiar, but no other color sounded similar enough to stretch credulity of ancestry. "Cold" sounded like *cold*, but "hot" sounded closest to a local animal, and "warm" was a female body part whose specificity he didn't explore further.

As his vocabulary and knowledge of Caedelli grammar increased, he learned details of his environment. The enclosed cluster of buildings he found himself in was a center of medicine, religion, and learning, and he conferred to the complex the title of "abbey," which he translated as making Sistian and Diera the abbot and the abbess, respectively. The abbey was formally named the Abbey of Saint Sidryn, commonly referred to as St. Sidryn's—Sidryn being the name of some past religious figure. The nearby town was Abersford, the Province Keelan, the land a large island named Caedellium, and the planet was

Anyar. From observing activity around the complex, Yozef had already figured out the cycle of days was by sixes, a sixday—five days of work and one day of rest and worship services in the large cathedral-like building. He learned the seasons (four), the months (nine, plus a five-day start-of-year festival), and a thumb pointed upward from a fist meant the equivalent of a raised middle finger and not approval, a good thing to know.

Language by total immersion. His brain often felt fried by the end of a day spent memorizing words, practicing phrases and pronunciation, and a gradual increase in the morning reading/writing lesson with the boy assigned to him by the abbot from two to four hours each day. By the end of two sixdays, Yozef had enough words to try asking questions and understand answers. He learned that his tutor was Selmar Beynom, the youngest son of Abbot Sistian and Abbess Diera Beynom. Another son, Cadwulf, was about eighteen years old and studying at the abbey. There were also two Beynom daughters, older, married, and living with their families elsewhere. Selmar was diligent and tireless, so much so that several nights Yozef dreamed of being back in the fifth grade and drilled by a relentless Mrs. MacMurty.

"God, what I wouldn't give to talk to someone in English for just a few minutes!" he mumbled to himself after one language lesson on past and future tense. "Someone other than myself."

He found himself singing softly just to hear the lyrics, which got him more than a few stares. Singing and humming to yourself seemed common here, but his tunes were not any the locals had ever heard. He got smiles at the obvious gaiety of "Yellow Submarine," "Jingle Bells," and "I Get Around." More mixed looks accompanied hearing him whistling or singing "Everything Is Beautiful," "Imagine," "I Walk the Line," and various Bruce Springsteen numbers. He was surprised he could remember most of the lyrics to so many songs. Maybe whatever the Watchers did had improved his memory. An alternative explanation was more melancholy: Maybe the lack of English made his brain work harder to remember what it could before losing details of Earth forever.

CHAPTER 8

THORNS

Even with Yozef's commitment to master Caedelli, there was a limit to what his brain would tolerate. As a counterbalance, a few days after he started language lessons he began helping Carnigan in the big man's daily assignments. The weather was warm that day, with a breeze coming off the ocean, and increasing cloud cover suggesting rain later in the day. He had been on one of his slow walks around the grounds after morning lessons and came upon Carnigan hoeing weeds in a vegetable field outside the complex's main wall.

Damn if this isn't a scene that might go viral on YouTube. The hoe looked like a toothpick when handled by someone who looked like he could carry a horse.

Yozef stood watching, then, without a conscious decision, went to a shed he had seen workers taking tools from and picked out another hoe. He went out to where Carnigan worked and started hoeing in the next row. Carnigan looked up from his work, nodded to Yozef, and went back to the weeds. Yozef kept up with the hoeing for almost an hour the first day before lagging. Even hoeing weeds was a major exertion, given his condition. When he had dropped several yards behind and audibly puffed, Carnigan took the hoe from his hands, turned him around, and pushed him gently but firmly toward the buildings. He rumbled something to Yozef, who without understanding a word, knew Carnigan said, "Nice work, but that's enough for today." On subsequent days, Yozef met Carnigan either at morning meal or at the main abbey entrance and followed him to the day's assignment.

Thus, Yozef learned more than just weeding. Within a month, six sixdays, or thirty-six total days to a month by local custom, he experienced cleaning stables, brushing horses, milking cows, chasing ducks for the evening meal, pruning in the formal gardens and orchards, loading and unloading wagons and, less to his liking, moving voiding vats to refuse pits, rinsing out the vats with buckets of water, and putting the vats back under the commode platforms of the voiding house. Fortunately, Carnigan's turn for that task came only once a month.

Working with Carnigan gave Yozef's brain a break, and his body strained with physical work unlike any previous experience. The rest of the hours into the evenings were absorbed with further language study. By the end of the first month, Yozef had learned enough Caedelli to pick up stray pieces of conversations and even carry on limited exchanges.

One morning Carnigan came to the morning meal, but instead of his usual loose trousers and pullover shirt, he wore heavier, tighter clothing and an over-vest of thick leather, like a version of a jerkin—a type of leather clothing worn on Earth in the 1500–1700s. Yozef scanned the room. Several other men in the hall wore similar clothing.

Yozef mimed and used his limited Caedelli vocabulary to question the different dress. After several minutes of stumbling through words and gestures, Yozef thought he understood Carnigan and other men would be gone for two sixdays for some unclear obligation.

After eating, Yozef followed Carnigan and watched the men saddle horses and secure packs to other animals. By the time they left, the jerkins were added to with helmet-like protective headgear of thicker leather with inlaid metal bands. Aside from those general features, there was uniformity in neither their gear nor the weapons. Each man carried an assortment of swords, lances, muskets, pistols, and a few large crossbows.

The number and array of weapons mesmerized Yozef. "Christ, man, what the fuck are you guys getting ready for?" He had previously noticed men from the village carrying knives, yet nothing more deadly.

Similar to clothing and weapons, the horses and the tack ranged in quality, sizes, and colors. Carnigan rode what resembled a grayish Percheron with a dark mane and tail, a horse suited to pulling large wagons or plows or as a mount of a very large rider. Two huge flintlock pistols hung from Carnigan's saddle, he carried a lance two feet longer than other men, and a battleax hung across his back.

Yozef eyed the wicked-looking double blade. *My God!* he thought. *That thing must have belonged to Paul Bunyan. I doubt I could swing it with both hands, but I'll bet Carnigan twirls it like a baton.* Yozef swallowed, and a taste of bile touched the back of his throat at an unbidden image of damage those blades could inflict.

A grizzled man shouted to the others, and the men followed him out the main gate. Carnigan nodded in passing. Yozef climbed a ladder to the rampart inside the complex main wall and watched the men ride toward the village a half-mile away. Other single men and small groups joined them on the ride. By the time they reached Abersford, the group had grown to perhaps twenty riders. They disappeared into the village, then reappeared several minutes later, and forty to fifty riders headed inland on the main road. Yozef couldn't make out details, but they rode in a mass, reminding him more of a Western movie posse than a military unit.

"Well," Yozef spoke aloud, "so things aren't all idyllic here. This isn't some Amish village. The people may live the simpler life, but something out there required guns and blades. Bandits? Rival clans? Predators? Whatever it is, it's serious."

When the last rider dipped behind a hill a mile away, Yozef climbed down from the rampart and walked back to the complex.

Carnigan had indicated he would be gone two sixdays, but it was four sixdays before Yozef saw the big man again. Then, one morning, Carnigan and the other absent men sat at morning meal. Yozef didn't press where they had been, as he sat and ate with Carnigan. He hadn't realized how much he'd miss the gruff man.

Maybe it was only because Carnigan was the first person Yozef connected with, but, even so, Yozef *liked* him. He might look menacing, and Yozef could believe it wouldn't be a person's smartest move to get on Carnigan's bad side, but there was more to him. And Yozef had a hunch Carnigan was brighter than he looked, yet with a more common sense of the world smarts than book learning. He was also kinder than others might think.

With the men back, Yozef returned to the routine of following Carnigan in his daily duties, yet Yozef's awareness had changed. Seeing Carnigan ride off with other men armed to the teeth, by the standards of this world, meant there were physical threats to warrant having armed groups of men.

He'd been so focused on learning Caedelli and getting through each day that his universe was limited to his room and the abbey complex. Obviously, there was more he needed to know to survive and build a life here.

The recognition of dangers outside the abbey walls brought back other questions that had temporarily retreated. Questions about the Watchers. Their unknown physical appearance was not as important a question as their intentions. Yozef inferred that the Watchers had been around this part of the galaxy for a long time, at least some thousands of years. He believed Harlie when the voice said the Watchers didn't know who had transplanted humans, both here and on the other planets; Harlie said there had been multiple translocations. Why had he ended up on Anyar? Simply a convenient place to dump him, or was there some rationale? Why Caedellium? Was the island a deliberate or a random choice? Were there other survivors of the collision dumped on Anyar? He doubted he would ever know the answers.

A more fundamental question and one for which even the Watchers didn't have the answer was why had that other alien race transplanted humans, along with terrestrial plants and animals? Was it a benign act to let humans spread and evolve on more than one planet? A safety measure to assure humans survived in case something happened to their original planet? A malign act? A reason only understandable to an alien species?

On one starry evening, he sat in the complex gardens and gazed at the stars with no constellations he recognized.

He was likely the only human, on Earth or Anyar, who knew about the Watchers and the other human worlds, and there was nothing he could do with the information. He knew what would happen if in 1700 Earth he tried to describe television and aircraft. Depending on the country and perhaps even the locals, he could end up in an insane asylum or burned at the stake. So forget about telling anyone. Ever. It was knowledge he'd hold close and in isolation. That wasn't all he knew. Even if he couldn't share how he got here, he had scientific knowledge that would push Anyar civilizations ahead centuries. But what to do with that knowledge?

For sixdays, he thought about how he might introduce knowledge or whether he dared at all.

CHAPTER 9

INTERVIEW WITH THE ABBOT

"Yozef! Wait a moment."

Yozef stopped and turned to face Brother Fitham. The kindly older brother smiled as he always did.

Fitham laid an arthritic hand on Yozef's forearm. "Abbot Sistian requests you meet with him in his office tomorrow after morning meal."

Yozef's breath skipped at the words. He had been expecting this. "Did the abbot say what he wanted to meet about?"

"No, but I assume he's interested in how you're progressing."

Yozef's gut tightened. "I'm sure. Tell the abbot I'll come as soon as I finish eating."

"Fine, fine." Fitham patted him on the shoulder, turned, and retraced his steps.

So. It's that *time. I've been wondering when the abbot would get around to this. I expected it to happen soon. The fact that I can carry on conversations with Brother Fitham is proof I'm ready to answer questions. The abbot has to be curious in the extreme about who the hell I am and how I got here. His manner is friendly enough, but this is likely to be a serious interrogation all the same. I'd better be on my toes.*

He ambled back to his room as he reviewed the past months. The language studies had progressed faster than his initial concerns, based on his experience with high school Spanish and chemical German. He was a sponge, soaking up Caedelli. He knew part of the reason was total immersion. There was nothing to fall back on, to clarify uncertainties in lessons, to socialize, or to retreat into English. Caedelli was *it*—unless he wanted to talk to himself, which he often did. Even granted the incentives, the speed at which he went from stumbling over a few words to freely conversing was unanticipated. New words keep cropping up, though once he heard them two or three times, he *didn't* forget.

Then there was the sheer necessity. He couldn't communicate for any purpose without the language. In spite of that incentive, the speed with which he was picking it up gave him pause. He knew he was smart. Science, mathematics, yes. Languages, no. Yet here, fewer than three months into intensive study, and he could carry on conversations and read simple texts.

At first, two-way verbal communication was a multi-stage process with a mental English-Caedelli dictionary. A local would say something, he would mentally translate, assemble the suspected correct Caedelli words, and pronounce them back. As time went on, mentally leaning on English faded. He still thought to himself and dreamed in English, but talking in Caedelli became easier day by day.

He thanked God, or whomever, for the simple grammar. The rules were reasonably straightforward, with limited irregularities, compared to the declensions, cases, and genders of Spanish and German.

He wondered whether his progress was only because of necessity or from effects of whatever the Watchers did when they fiddled with his physiology to help him survive? Was he now smarter, or was his memory enhanced? He suspected memory, since he didn't feel smarter.

"Thank you for coming, Yozef," said the avuncular-sounding abbot as he welcomed Yozef. "Selmar and Brother Fitham tell me you've made amazing progress in learning Caedelli. Enough so that I'm anxious to learn more about you and your people." The abbot waved to a pair of chairs facing each other, and they both sat. "And the medicants say you're fully recovered from your ordeal."

The abbot continued inquiring into Yozef's condition and was oh so friendly and supportive sounding. However, Yozef never lost the feeling that the agenda was to determine whether he was a victim or a danger, a lost human, an enemy spy, or a demon of whatever pantheon of gods they had here.

"Tell me, Yozef, where is your home? The name of your people?"

Best stick as close to the truth as possible—without telling the whole truth. The closer to the truth he stayed, the fewer inconsistencies would crop up later. Lying forced him to remember what story he told.

"My people are Americans, and our country is called America."

"America," said Sistian, letting the syllables roll off his tongue. "America. I don't believe I have ever heard of America. Of course, I'm not well traveled throughout the world. What continent is America on, or is it more of an island like Caedellium?"

"It's on a continent, but we've had little contact with neighboring peoples. Though I don't understand why, I know I'd never met any other peoples of Anyar before I awoke here on Caedellium."

Well, thought Sistian, *the world is wide.* There were many lands he was sure he'd never heard of. Still, it was unusual the man had never met anyone from outside his own people.

Sistian reached behind himself and pulled a folded paper off a shelf. He laid it on the small table separating them and unfolded it several times to reveal a world map.

"This is a map of Anyar. Can you show me where your land is?"

Yozef looked at the map, his eyes roving over the features of the planet. He'd seen Anyar from images of the globe Harlie had shared with him, but the projection map made clearer the relationships of the major landmasses concentrated on half the globe.

To the left side of the map was an island with more prominent labeling than the other lands. Yozef's Caedelli reading lessons let him recognize the name of the island, Caedellium. It was about half the size of Texas or Madagascar, maybe some hundreds of miles across. Selmar hadn't shown him any of this, so he wondered where Keelan lay.

"I'm afraid I can't show you where my land is, Abbot. To be honest, this is the first complete map of Anyar I've ever seen." Which was true, though, of course, it was the *only* map of the planet he'd ever seen—he didn't count the images of Anyar Harlie had shown him.

"I don't know why, but for some reason my people don't interact much with the other lands. All I can say is that the voyage here was long. I wasn't always fully conscious, so even that might be faulty memory. The climate also seemed similar to Caedellium, yet that could include much of the world."

"Do you remember how you got here? On what ship and of what people?"

"No. I never saw those who took me from my homeland." *True.* "They fed me, but I never left a small compartment or saw anyone." *True.* "I don't understand why they took me or how I got from their ship to the beach near Abersford and the abbey." *True . . . or close enough.*

The abbot shook his head. "Too bad. We would all like to know more about you, how this happened to you. What about your family? What is their place among your people?"

Yozef paused. Was the abbot trying to pigeonhole him into a societal class? If he said the wrong thing, would it change how they treated him? Maybe they'd been so supportive of him out of being uncertain whether he belonged to a powerful family or clan. Yozef decided to take a chance and continue saying things were different where he came from . . . yet not *too* different.

"My father's a scholastic, one who studies the heavens and the stars."

"Ah, an astrologer. One who predicts the future."

"Not exactly. He studies the heavens, only by observing the moons, the planets, and the stars. It's called astronomy, and my father is an astronomer. In my land, we don't depend on predictions based on the heavens. Although they can sometimes come true, we believe such auguries are often too vague to serve as guidelines for our daily lives." That was as close as Yozef thought he could come without debunking astrology.

Sistian nodded. "Something I agree with, although a few of my more conservative colleagues are not so sure. Astrology was important to our people in the past, though not so much anymore, except for perhaps the common, less educated people. It's a belief not given credence by most of my brothers and sisters, so I find it interesting your people have come to the same conclusion."

Yozef saw an opening to both establish a rapport with the more educated locals and cover himself for the future. "Yes, it makes one consider that no matter where we are in the world, our peoples are coming to common understandings of God's realm."

Sistian frowned a little. "Well, now we're getting into theological areas we can discuss later."

Whoops, thought Yozef. *Maybe I reached a little too far on that one. Be careful.*

"And the rest of your family? Are they all scholastics?"

"Not all. Many found different goals to their lives. Some soldiers (*at least in Grandfather's generation*), some theophists (*I think Aunt Marcie's minister diploma from that mail-order outfit qualifies—at least as far as the Caedelli are concerned*), some leaders of our peoples (*Uncle Fred was mayor of Castleton for one term before they realized he was spending more time bonking constituent wives than running the town—and Mom and Dad had stints as chairs of PTA chapters*), and merchants and skilled tradesmen (*well, a butcher at Safeway and cousin Bill's marijuana dispensary in San Francisco have to count*). My people believe that God's plan for us is to do what each is best at and not be tied to a particular position or trade."

Sistian frowned, more puzzled than disapproving, "Then how does your family know its proper place? It sounds chaotic. Does the family have no role?"

Yozef formulated his next words carefully. From what he'd gathered so far in speaking with Carnigan and other staff, the family, the village, and the clan took care of its members and normally provided a role for them. This naturally meant limiting options. If you were the son of a blacksmith, chances were you'd also be a blacksmith, since by the age of twelve a boy would be helping his father. If a daughter, you'd learn the skills of being a mother and caring for a family and in some circumstances work in a family trade. Stepping out of those boundaries would be difficult. If your family members were tradesmen and you decided to be a farmer, you'd have to save enough money to buy your own farm. Your family would help if they were affluent enough, or you'd marry the daughter of a sonless farmer. And forget about moving to a different village or town. It was always a balance between limiting options and providing for livelihood.

Yozef thought there were advantages to knowing your place. He wondered whether the United States was overall better. Yes, the options there were infinitely greater, but the downside was less family and community support. But how to answer the abbot?

"My people put great value on each person being responsible for his or her own success in life. While sometimes this means people don't have as much help from family and clan as you have here, they have more options for what to do with their lives. Now that I've seen the people of Caedellium, I'm not wise enough to say which is better, your system here or ours at my home."

"Interesting. I'd like to speak with you more about this. As for your feeling your own lack of wisdom, the *Word* tells us that a path to wisdom is knowing you don't have it."

Yozef frowned. "The Word?"

"The *Word of God*," Sistian stated. "Our main religious writing. It's usually shortened to the *Word* in everyday speech."

Yozef nodded. "My people say a wise man knows he doesn't know, while a fool knows what isn't true."

Okay, maybe he couldn't remember the exact quote, but who here would know?

Sistian smiled and nodded appreciatively. "Very true and interestingly stated. I may even use those words someday in a Godsday message.

"And yourself, Yozef? You mentioned you were a student. Forgive me, but for us, someone of your age who was still a student would be unusual or the student not particularly bright. Certainly, the latter doesn't apply to you. By your age, they would have finished their schooling and have a position based on their learnings."

He'd been waiting for the question. It was his chance for an opening to explain why he seemed to have so much exotic knowledge. No matter how careful he tried to be, it was only a matter of time before he began dropping pieces of that knowledge. He had to find a way around this, or it could have catastrophic consequences for him.

"Our land is blessed by God to be extraordinarily bountiful. We've more than enough food for all, and we send much of our bounty to a trading center where it is exchanged with other lands for their goods. Also, our hills and mountains are rich in gold and silver. All of this allows our people to spend more time considering the wonder of God's world in all its aspects. Many of the fields of study would probably seem trivial and pointless in Caedellium. Your land is productive, at least the parts I've seen, but still requires much effort and sweat to yield. Imagine if suddenly your people only had to work half as much time as they do now. What would they do with the rest of the time?"

Sistian considered this novel idea for a few moments. "I think it'd depend on each person. Many would simply take the time to do nothing. Sit and talk, engage in games, perhaps consume more alcohol, if they had both the extra time and money you suggest. For myself, there are always people I wish I had more time to counsel, and I'd spend more time studying and considering the *Word*."

"What about your wife?"

"Diera? Ah . . . she'd spend more time with patients and studying medical books. She always worries she's forgotten some piece of knowledge or records of past treatments that she might find useful."

"What if Diera had access to ten times as many books and records?"

"I'm afraid she would try to drive herself to learn everything, no matter how much there was." Sistian smiled. "I might have to drag her from the library every day."

"What if it was a hundred times? A thousand?"

Sistian was silent, his eyes narrowing as he looked at Yozef. "A thousand times as much knowledge? How is that possible? I know we're remote from the rest of Anyar, but we're not *that* isolated!"

"Consider if your people spent half their time in study for a hundred years."

Sistian sighed and sat back farther in his chair. "I see where you're headed. I can't say I truly understand the consequences of what you imply, though I can see how the amount of knowledge could become huge. However, in your proposal, if there's that much knowledge, how does any one person learn it all?"

"They don't," said Yozef. "With this much knowledge, the best that can be done is that any one person can only study small parts of the total."

"Then they would be almost ignorant of the whole and all the interconnections of knowledge!"

"Not completely. All students study basic topics. This gives some knowledge common to everyone and takes perhaps the first fifteen years of study. Beyond that, we narrow our focus into specific topics and study those in more depth—a common knowledge base and then specializations. While it's not a satisfactory solution, it's the best resolution my people have come up with, and many have argued and struggled with the problem."

"I can see how that might be one solution," Sistian allowed, "although, as you say, not completely satisfactory. I suppose it's not that different from here, although your people spend many more years at study than we do. And that explains how someone of your age is still a student."

"Yes. I had the common fifteen years of study, followed by another four years narrowing to only a fraction of knowledge, and finally, another three years of even narrower specialization before whatever happened led me to be here on Caedellium."

"And yourself, what's the area of knowledge you specialized in?"

"We call it 'chemistry.' The study of how to take known substances and use them to make new ones."

"Chemistry," repeated Sistian slowly. "Chemistry. I've never heard this word. I assume it is in your language. What exactly does it involve?"

"Many aspects would be difficult for me to explain to you because you don't have the words or background knowledge. This one example may be instructive. You make beer out of barley and wheat. Do you know exactly what is happening during the process of beer-making?"

"No. I assume the brewers do, though."

"I doubt it. They probably are simply following steps they learned from past brewers. In contrast, our scholastics understand exactly what is happening. The same with winemaking. Although I have never made beer or wine myself, by 'chemistry,' I know that both drinks contain something we call 'alcohol,' the ingredient that makes you relax and feel good. This alcohol is converted from the ingredients of the grain or fruit—starch in grain for beer and sugar in fruit juices for wine."

Sistian put a hand to his chin. "So you know about beer and winemaking. Perhaps we could find you employment in Abersford or even the district center at Clengoth."

"Perhaps. Although the fact that I know more about the underlying mechanisms doesn't mean that I could make better beer or wine than your brewers or winemakers. However, I believe the basic knowledge would eventually be useful."

"Well," said Sistian, "still, it might be something to explore."

Yozef paused . . . then said, "I suddenly realized there may be something else useful for your brewers and winemakers. I also know some of the properties in your spirits that could allow them to produce a completely new form of drink, one much more potent than either wine or beer. Do you have something like 'ice-wine,' where you make wine more potent by freezing it and then removing ice forming before the entire liquid turns solid?"

Sistian nodded. "The northern clans do something as you describe. I've tasted it, and it's definitely more potent. I've seen men get drunk after only a small amount. There's also the stronger spirits that make one drunk even by drinking much smaller amounts. It's one of the few pieces of new knowledge that the Narthani brought to Caedellium. A shop in Abersford produces some of this with the help of an escaped Narthani slave. I've tried the drink; it tastes terrible."

Hmm . . . Yozef pondered. Maybe some kind of early pot distillation. Interesting. Maybe my example wasn't that good. And Narthani? I've heard this name before, often accompanied by curses. I should ask more about whoever they are.

"I'm sure if I talk with the shopkeeper in Abersford, I could show him how to make a stronger drink faster, unless you think introducing a stronger drink is not good."

"It might not necessarily be a good thing to make stronger spirits more readily available," the abbot said with a frown. "Some men already drink too much."

"Then how about another use for alcohol? As a disinfectant for your medicants?"

"What is this 'disinfectant?' Another of your 'English' words?"

"I've already seen the medicants rinse their hands and instruments with a solution of a thin acid and soap to reduce corruption. Alcohol can be used the same way and is more effective. I could show you how to purify alcohol in a form pure enough for use."

The abbot stroked his beard. "I would have to check with Diera, but I assume she'll be interested."

Yozef paused for a moment—it was another opening. "One thing I worry about is how would such knowledge be received by yourself, the other brothers and sisters, and the common people. In my country, this knowledge simply derives from our attempt to understand God's world, but here it could be considered as having an evil source. I wouldn't want to cause any discord among your people, and, to be honest, my own safety worries me. Would it be better for me to simply be silent?"

The abbot sat back in his chair, his eyes narrowed toward Yozef. "Not an easy question to answer, Yozef. The *Word* tells us to beware of the Evil One's temptations. In some lands of Anyar, I think your worries about safety would be well considered. Even on Caedellium, there are some of the more conservative who'd question new ideas. You may have been fortunate to have washed ashore in Keelan. I believe we're more tolerant than many other clans, at least with more willingness to listen to new ideas. While this doesn't mean we might not find something you say disturbing, we'd at least listen."

Sistian thought for a couple of minutes, stroking his beard with one hand and gazing out a window as he considered. "Here's what I suggest for the moment, Yozef. Whenever you have a piece of this knowledge you wish to share but are worried about how it would be understood, talk to either me or Diera before anyone else. At some point, I'd bring this to the attention of the entire senior staff at the abbey for a more thorough review, though for now let us keep this among the three of us."

"Thank you, Abbot. I'll do as you suggest." *Well, that should cover me for a while.*

The abbot's expression was pensive. "Yozef, I continue to sense no evil in you, although some have wondered when you appeared on our beach so mysteriously and looking half dead. Also, though I have a sense of excitement whenever I talk with you, I can't say exactly why this is. However, I also wonder if your coming is going to disturb our culture in ways I can't imagine or know whether it's good or bad. Change is good if it helps the people, yet it can lead to losing contact with the good aspects of the traditional. The *Word* says that God can put opportunity in front of us and won't give us what we don't work for. In such cases, it is up to us to seize those opportunities as part of our responsibilities to exercise free will. Time will tell."

Yozef smiled. "Our people have a saying that perhaps is another way to express the same thing. 'God helps those who help themselves.'"

Sistian laughed. "Nicely worded. I may use this one also in one of the coming Godsdays. Perhaps I should ask you for help in finding the right words for my messages."

He leaned forward in his chair, placing both hands on the arms as if he was about to stand. Yozef discerned the interrogation was about to end.

"So, Yozef, let us say that you will continue to stay with us for the time being until you can find a place for yourself here with our people. In addition, we can talk further on these topics and perhaps discuss some of your 'pieces' of exotic knowledge before they are loosed on the people of Caedellium."

Signaling the end to the interview, the abbot rose from his chair. He reached out a hand Yozef clasped with his own.

"Thank you for your advice, Abbot. I appreciate the care you've given me, and I'll look forward to further discussions."

Yozef walked out of a side door of the cathedral with a spring in his steps.

He thought the meeting went well. He didn't think he'd said anything he was liable to contradict in the future, and now he had the abbot primed in case he wanted to introduce new ideas. Now the questions were, *what* to introduce and *when?*

CHAPTER 10

BULDORIAN MERCENARIES

Musfar Adalan feigned patience as he waited for his meeting with the Narthani commander. He would have preferred to pace, though it was best to not give any indication of weakness, certainly not when dealing with Narthani. He often wondered if the day would come when the Narthani bothered to bite off the tiny, rugged, and isolated piece of Anyar where Buldor sat.

May the Gods grant that day come well past my lifetime or someone takes them down before then. I'm at least thankful Buldor is on the Ganolar continent, instead of Melosia with the Narthani, so we have the ocean separating us.

In any event, today was today, and there were spoils to be had, if he played the game properly.

Adalan was also irked that the cursed Narthani required him to come to Caedellium to finalize their agreement for his and his men's services. His seven ships had trolled waters off the Landolin continent, watching for stray merchant ships, when a Narthani sloop appeared flying parley flags. Adalan could have avoided a meeting, his ships being at least as swift as the Narthani vessel, but curiosity and his outnumbering the single Narthani led him to hear what the sloop's captain had to say. Since Adalan spoke the Narthani tongue but didn't read it, the Narthani captain read a letter from a Narthani commander, a General Akuyun, on the island of Caedellium. It was an invitation to raid the island under Narthani protection, but only after Adalan himself came to meet with General Akuyun, and with only one ship. A small chest holding 500 gold Narthani coins and the offer of leaving the sloop and crew as hostages persuaded Adalan to go to Caedellium. Six of Adalan's ships now sat idle in a remote cove off the northern Landolin coast, awaiting their commander's return. As for his flagship, *Warrior's Pride*, a Narthani cutter met them as they neared Preddi City and directed them to a deserted fishing village. Once anchored, Adalan rowed ashore and rode thirty miles by horse to meet with this General Akuyun. Developing saddle sores did nothing to improve a sailor's mood.

A Narthani junior officer interrupted his reflections. "Captain, please come this way. General Akuyun is ready to meet with you."

Adalan followed the young officer into a medium-sized room with a rectangular table and twelve chairs, four occupied by men. At first glance, the room gave the impression of being plain, though it took only a moment for a sharp eye to see that although the room lacked adornments on the walls and the furniture was simple in design, all of the woodwork was of the highest quality. Some imported woods he recognized, others he didn't and assumed were from the island's trees. He could sell this room itself back on mainland realms for enough to keep a Buldorian village well supplied for a year.

"Please sit here beside me, Captain," said a friendly voice from a lean man in his fifties, whom Adalan took to be Akuyun. Lean in both frame and manner, if Adalan was any judge of men.

Adalan sat at the indicated empty chair. He wondered whether the man's acting friendly was supposed to put him at ease. While he assumed it was deliberate, it wasn't convincing. He suspected being at ease around this one was comfortable until you crossed him, and then it would become exceedingly "uncomfortable."

Adalan's assessment of the Narthani general's initial demeanor was accurate. Akuyun had early in his career incorporated politeness into his dealings with non-Narthani. He understood and used on occasion the tried-and-true method of playing on fears, but he believed it never hurt to start off polite. He would never fully realize the tactic sometimes worked, though often had the opposite effect, with the object of his politeness waiting for the dagger or poison from a too-polite Narthani.

Akuyun introduced the other three men at the table. The Narthani troop commander was of little relevance to Adalan, but the other two men more notable: their naval admiral, and a man they titled Assessor, who ran their intelligence service. The former was important because Adalan and his men would be sailing in Narthani-controlled waters, and the latter because Adalan knew little about this isolated island.

"Welcome to Caedellium, Captain Adalan. I hear from Admiral Kalcan that your ship arrived in good shape, and he has arranged for your re-provisioning."

"Yes, thank you, General Akuyun. The Admiral's aides have been most efficient, and we should be ready to sail again in three days after some minor repairs."

"You don't feel your men need any more time ashore after the voyage here?"

"No," answered Adalan. "We're sailors, and being on land or at sea is all the same to us. Besides, I need to get back to my other ships off Landolin. I've already been gone from them for several sixdays. Plus, you would have us restricted to that fishing village. There's not much to do ashore, and I'd like to move quickly to bring the rest of my ships here and begin in accord with your proposal."

Akuyun consulted his notes. "Ah, yes, the village of Rocklyn. The original inhabitants are gone, but we'll provide support there for your ships and men. You're not to be seen anywhere else on Caedellium, except for the raids." The Narthani commander looked back at Musfar. "And you're aware of the reason for this restriction?"

"Of course. You want to minimize the knowledge you're supporting a Buldorian raiding party," Adalan answered.

Akuyun grinned, although there was no humor in it. "Correct, Captain. This is a case where we're helping each other. There's no need for you to know any more details of why we've invited you, only that you follow instructions. In return, we'll provide information on likely lucrative targets along the Caedellium coasts and assure that no other naval force interferes with your . . . activities. Whatever booty you get from these raids is yours to keep. You're to cause maximum damage, and you're not to let any of your people get captured or indicate Narthani involvement."

Adalan nodded his understanding, though his tone was cold. "Since we're men of honor and need to be clear with each other, while I understand the conditions we will operate under, I hope *you* understand we're not here to fight your fights. I cannot waste my ships and men for your objectives. We're here to raid vulnerable targets, not engage in warfare."

Akuyun wasn't offended by the Buldorian's statement and appreciated dealing with someone who, like himself, wanted all parties to understand the scope of their cooperation.

Men of honor? wondered Akuyun. Yes, he supposed they both were, but within their own kind. He certainly wouldn't trust any Buldorian enough to turn his back on them, and he doubted it would ever occur to them to trust any Narthani.

"That's understood, Captain. We'll provide information on likely targets, and it's up to *you* to carry out the raids. However, as you say, I don't expect you to engage in any pitched battles, since we'll choose targets carefully."

Akuyun studied the Buldorian leader as they spoke. He'd wanted this face-to-face meeting to assess who they would be employing. This Adalan fit the stereotype expected of a pirate—garish dress, braided hair, and, if his nose was being truthful, a good dose of Fuomi perfume. Akuyun was pleased. The man was imposing, taller than any of the four Narthani, with not an ounce of fat evident. Several visible scars established that he'd not gotten his position by nonviolent means, he spoke fluent Narthani, and, by Akuyun's judgment, he was both intelligent and controlled.

Yes, he will do quite nicely, thought Akuyun.

For the next hour, Adalan asked questions about the conditions on Caedellium, and the four Narthani assessed their mercenary hire. When questions lagged, Akuyun looked to his subordinates. "Any other questions for Captain Adalan or comments?"

There were none.

"Then you believe you'll be ready to leave in . . . as you said," Akuyun asked the Buldorian, "three days?"

"As I said," confirmed Adalan, "the only reason my men might have used more time ashore was to utilize brothels, but the women you provided are servicing quite well."

Akuyun turned to Tuzere and raised an eyebrow.

"We've given the Buldorians six Preddi women," offered Tuzere. "My, uh, understanding is that six women per ship would suffice for the Captain's men."

"And the women are from where?" Akuyun asked.

"Younger women from that group of Preddi that tried to escape via fishing boat across the Gulf of Witlow into Keelan or Gwillamer Provinces last week."

"Ah, yes. We'd not settled on their disposition, as I last recall. I'm sure I have your report of the outcome somewhere on my desk, and I just haven't gotten to read it yet."

Tuzere nodded. "Correct, General. Most of the Preddi were young, I assume those able to travel fast. The men were executed and the younger children given to Narthani families. The other women and older children were whipped and converted to slave status."

Akuyun turned back to the Buldorian. "Consider the women a gift of the Narthani. You may keep them, along with any other Caedelli you choose to capture in the raids. Be aware, you'll have to transport any slaves you keep yourselves, so be judicious in the numbers. We're not prepared to keep slaves from the other clans at this time, so any captives you take have to be taken off Caedellium."

"I think we can manage to do that, General." The implication in the Buldorian's tone left no doubt he didn't feel the need for a Narthani to tell him his business.

"All right then, Captain Adalan. I'll expect you and the rest of your ships back here in no more than five to six months. I assume you'll spend the intervening time doing whatever you do, but be sure to be back as we've agreed."

The mercenary leader nodded and, with cursory leave-taking, exited the room for the thirty-mile horse ride back to his ship.

Akuyun addressed the other three men. "Any thoughts about our erstwhile Buldorian employees?"

"Scum," snorted Zulfa, "but I think they'll do nicely for our purposes."

"I agree," said Admiral Kalcan. "Scum, as Aivacs says, but no question about their seamanship, and I think they'll do well with raiding civilian targets."

Akuyun sat back in his chair. "All right then. They'll be back within six months, and we'll turn up the heat on the Caedelli one more notch. I know we're all glad to move toward the next phases of our mission here and see a time to return to Narthon."

CHAPTER 11

YOZEF LEARNS ABOUT THE NARTHANI

In the sixday after the interview with Abbot Beynom, Yozef's ears repeatedly picked out the word *Narthani* in abbey staff conversations. Although he knew he must have heard the name before, it was only now registering with him, since the abbot had mentioned the Narthani and one of their ex-slaves. Who were these Narthani? Were they related to whatever reason Carnigan and the others went off for those sixdays, armed to the teeth?

Carnigan was the first person he thought to ask. At a morning meal, Yozef entered the dining hall and looked for the large, red-headed figure. Most of the tables were full with brothers and sisters in their brown clothing, individuals, and family groups he suspected were visitors and relatives of patients. Carnigan ate in a corner, alone as usual. Yozef walked among the tables and sat across from the red-headed man. A staff member had seen him come in and placed his own meal in front of him. This day the bowl held the usual thick porridge-like something, supplemented with pieces of a ham-like meat and fragments of a different nut than usual, this one deep black, with convolutions like a walnut. He knew the meat wasn't ham, since he hadn't seen any pigs, and how many different nuts did they have in this place? He swore he must have seen at least six or eight different kinds in these gruels.

Yozef picked up the spoon, scooped up and blew on the steaming porridge, taking the moment to look at Carnigan. *You know, I think of him more as a friend than anyone else I've ever known. Look at us. A gruff, red-headed giant and a castaway. Are we an odd pair or what?*

"Carnigan, don't let this go to your head, but I missed you when you were gone those sixdays."

"Go to my head? What does that mean?"

One of those phrases that doesn't translate. "Never mind. I missed your ugly face."

"You should talk. At least now you don't scare strong men like you did when they first found you, though I'd advise not looking in a mirror more than necessary. A pair of strange eyes might look back at you."

They both laughed. At first, Carnigan had been irritated and puzzled by Yozef's banter, but he quickly retaliated in kind, and the back-and-forth became part of their routine.

Yozef suspected others listening in on their interchanges wondered when Carnigan would pound him into the ground. He had noticed worried expressions and cautious movements away from their table by others in the dining hall the first month they'd sat together, talking and laughing. Not that talking had come easy, but, when the two were together, Carnigan's trademark grunts and minimal sentences evolved in concert with Yozef's improving Caedelli.

"I never asked at the time about the trip you and the other men took, and all armed. Was there some danger? Some enemy or wild animals to hunt? Maybe just training?"

"Training?" said Carnigan. "No, it was my turn to do patrolling against the Narthani and the damned Eywellese."

"Narthani? Who or what are the Narthani?"

Carnigan's face flushed and he hissed, "Narthani. The Evil One's offspring. We also have to be always on alert for Eywellese raids. The cursed Eywellese Clan is in league with the Narthani and does their bidding. We had a sighting of Eywellese riders to the northwest part of Keelan Province and needed to search for them."

Yozef didn't like the sound of this! He knew Eywell was the clan north of Keelan, but Carnigan tied them to the Narthani. What was going on?

"Did you find the Eywellese?"

"No," Carnigan said, shaking his head. "There were signs of a small party, but they either had gone home or hid too well. This makes us worry all the more. Why would they send groups to spy on us, unless planning to some day send large raiding parties?"

"Raids! Have there been raids into Keelan Province?"

"No. So far only Moreland Province has suffered serious Eywellese raids. They burn farms, steal crops and animals if the party is big enough, and kill all of the people they don't take away as slaves."

Yozef sat back, shocked. This didn't match the view he was developing of Caedellium as a version of an idyllic eighteenth-century New England.

"How often do these raids occur?"

"More often recently. The first one in Moreland was only two months ago. Nothing like this had ever happened before. Oh, there were the usual small raids and vendettas among clans and even families within Keelan. These reports are of scores or more Eywellese. Several small villages and hamlets were destroyed. In some, the people had warning enough so they could run or hide, but word is over fifty Morelanders were taken away and as many as a hundred killed."

"And you say these Narthani are behind the Eywellese?"

"Everyone assumes so. The Eywellese weren't so bold before allying themselves with the Narthani."

"Who exactly are these Narthani? Are they from Caedellium?"

"No. From somewhere else on Anyar. I don't know the details. You'd have to ask someone like the abbot."

"So you and the other men . . . you're part of the protective force against the Eywellese. Part of an . . . ?" Yozef struggled for the Caedellium word for "army," and nothing surfaced. "I don't know the Caedellium word. In my language, it would be *army*. A regular organization for large numbers of men that fight wars."

Carnigan laid his spoon down and wrinkled his brow. "I don't understand. What kind of organization?"

"Well, to fight efficiently, the men are organized into groups, starting with the smallest group, which are led by a leader, then several of these groups together with a higher leader over them all, and so on with larger groups. It's necessary to control and coordinate the fighting."

Yozef winced. *Words of wisdom from an armchair strategist and movie watcher.*

"I still don't understand. If we have to fight, we gather, find the enemy, and drive them away or kill them if we can."

It sounded more like a mob or a posse, similar to what he saw Carnigan riding off with.

Yozef thought for a moment. "Sorry, I'm probably not explaining myself clearly. My use of your language still needs work."

Carnigan grunted and finished his last bite. "I'm off to the stable this morning. Grooming horses and cleaning stalls. Then later helping the abbey blacksmith. It's a chance for you to learn something new."

"Not today, Carnigan. I have to do some thinking. I may take your advice and try to speak with the abbot about the Narthani."

Carnigan slapped Yozef's shoulder and left for his day's assignment.

Yozef emptied his own bowl, as he searched the dining hall for Brother Fitham. He spied the elderly man rising to leave, and he hurried over to him.

"Hello, Yozef! And how are you this fine God's day?"

"Fine, fine," Yozef responded absentmindedly and then rushed on. "There's something I'd like to talk with Abbot Sistian about. I was wondering if you could find out whether I could see him this morning?"

"I'll check, but the abbot might ask why you want to see him."

"Please just say it's something I need to speak with him about."

"Whatever you wish. I'll stop at his office and ask."

"Thank you, Brother Fitham. I'll be at my Caedelli language studies in the library."

The language session proved difficult. The tutoring by Selmar, the abbot's and abbess's younger son, had ended a month earlier, and Yozef studied on his own in the abbey library, in his room, or seeking out staff to practice Caedelli. Most days, the necessity of mastering Caedelli provided enough incentive to steel himself to study. But not this day. His mind wandered, fighting concentration while awaiting word from Fitham.

At mid-morning, Fitham appeared at Yozef's side. "The abbot can see you as soon as you're ready."

"Now is a good time." Yozef gathered up his papers and followed Fitham to the abbot's office.

Sistian Beynom sat at a desk full of stacks of paper, folders, and ledgers. He smiled when Yozef entered, laid down a quill, and sighed. "You would think a shepherd would spend time with his flock instead of reading and writing reports, planning sermons, and worrying about enough money to run everything. That's the life of an abbot, one aspect I'm suspicious my predecessor did *not* fully explain before I took this position."

Yozef smiled with sympathy, strangely reassured that some aspects of human civilization were the same, no matter what planet.

"Thank you for seeing me, Abbot. There's something you mentioned when we talked a few days ago. The Narthani. I wanted to find out more about them."

The abbot's genial mood vanished. His eyes narrowed, as did his lips. There was a noticeable tightening of the jaw. Something told Yozef the good abbot was not as charitable toward these Narthani as might be expected for someone in his position. However, maybe understanding and forgiveness were not the same here.

"The Narthani," the abbot spat. "A scourge straight from the Evil One, if there ever was."

It was the same response as Carnigan. Yozef was definitely getting a bad feeling about these people.

"Who are they?" asked Yozef. "And what do they mean for Caedellium?"

The abbot composed himself for a moment, leaning back in his chair and taking a few deep breaths. Yozef wondered whether he was praying for a more peaceful frame of mind or imagining shoving these Narthani at sword point into the pits of whatever hell the Caedelli believed in.

"They came to Caedellium six years ago. Their own land is on the large continent of Melosia. Though I don't know their complete history, about four hundred years ago they were one of the minor semi-nomadic peoples living in the cold, dry plains and mountains of north-central Melosia. After consolidating control over a number of other similar peoples, they invaded and took over more fertile lands to the south in a series of bloody wars lasting nearly fifty years. By the time the other peoples of Melosia awoke fully to the Narthani threat, they controlled almost a tenth of the whole continent. In the next hundred and fifty years, they expanded their control to a third of the continent."

Yozef remembered from the world map Sistian had shown him during their previous meeting that Melosia covered three-quarters of the planet's hemisphere containing the major land masses. A quick estimate by Yozef put the area controlled by the Narthani at something larger than the entire North American continent. Yozef whistled to himself. *Like Mongols?*

"Are they still expanding their territory, or were they stopped?"

"Slowed, but not stopped. The Narthani kept pushing on their neighbors, but there's been no further major loss of land to the Narthani in the last twenty years, at least according to reports we got before the Narthani stopped all communication between the clans and the rest of Anyar. Not that there aren't still battles, but the neighboring peoples had stopped them on Melosia."

"And elsewhere?"

"The news there is not so good. Those spawn of the Evil One found their way blocked to the west and the east, so decided to look for easier prey. They had been a land power, then they built a huge fleet of ships and invaded the

Kingdom of Rustal in the eastern part of the Ganolar continent. In less than two years, the Narthani subjugated the entire kingdom."

Yozef remembered the map again. Rustal, a realm about the size of Canada.

"Rumors are that resistance still exists in the mountains and colder, more southern parts of Rustal, but most of the population and all of the best lands are now part of the Narthon Empire. The only reason the Narthani didn't continue to conquer the entire continent is probably because they found the lands too poor to justify further conquest. In addition, immense mountain ranges block access to the western part of Ganolar, and there are easier victims elsewhere.

"About the same time this was happening, the Narthani trading ships came to Preddi Province. The capital city was the island's main port for trade with the rest of Anyar. All believe there were enormous bribes paid to the Preddi Hetman and other leading Preddi families. Whatever the reasons, the Preddi were fools and allowed the Narthani to build a separate Narthani compound near the city. The Narthani provided the trade goods at unreasonably low prices and gave the Preddi complete control over supplying these goods to the rest of Caedellium. As you can imagine, the Preddi became enormously rich, and I'm afraid the Preddi Hetman and his family dreamed of using this wealth to expand the Preddi Province at the expense of their two neighbors, the Selfcell and Eywell clans."

Yozef remembered enough Earth history to suspect where this was going: playing the clans against one another, if he was right.

The abbot shook his head. "Inter-clan fighting became more severe, and the Preddi overreached. A simultaneous attack by both Selfcell and Eywell put Preddi in danger of being dismembered by their two neighboring clans."

England and India! This history sounds like how the English and the East Indian Company manipulated the Indians to fight one another, and the English took over the continent with minimal military forces of their own.

"Let me guess," said Yozef. "The Narthani helped the Preddi."

Sistian eyed Yozef. "Yes, though at a cost. At first, the Narthani insisted this was an internal Caedellium matter, and they were just there for trade. Finally, the Narthani were 'convinced' by the Preddi that trade would suffer or even be eliminated if the fighting continued. We hear that the Narthani agreed to assist by providing troops to help defend the Preddi—"

"And in return," Yozef cut in, "they would be allowed to increase the size of the Narthani compound and permanently keep troops to assure the security of their compound?"

Sistian squinted at Yozef. "Why do I have the feeling you already know this story?"

"While I don't know the particular details of *this* story, something similar has happened elsewhere on Anyar, according to the histories my people are taught. Not to *us* directly, but what we know of from histories of other peoples. Let me guess what happened next. The Preddi agreed. The Narthani presence increased, and the fighting continued."

"Yes, and not only between Preddi and Selfcell or Eywell, but also between Selfcell and Eywell. All three clans slowly bled themselves for several more years, with the Narthani presence increased as the Preddi leaders saw their power slipping away. When the Preddi finally came to their senses, it was too late. As if 'magically'. . . ," the abbot shook his head, "a Narthani fleet appeared and landed thousands more soldiers. The Narthani crushed the Preddi clan. Though exact further details are clouded by lack of information or enough eyewitness testimony, within a year we believe there were fifty thousand Narthani in Preddi, including thousands of soldiers. The Selfcell and Eywell clans were so weakened by years of fighting, they evidently felt they had no choice when given ultimatums to ally themselves with the Narthani.

"It seems the Eywell clan was more enthusiastic about the alliance. Unfortunately, when Selfcell appealed to the other clans for aid in resisting the Narthani, no clan agreed to help. I'm friends since my youth with Culich Keelan, the Keelan hetman, and I know he'll never forgive himself or the other clans for not recognizing the danger at the time and coming to Selfcell's aid."

"So, what's the status at the present?"

"There followed a period of relative quiet. There was little reliable news out of Preddi or the other two clans. We believe many more Narthani were brought in—soldiers, tradesman, farmers, and slaves." The sour expression from Sistian accompanied the last category.

"We now believe there are at least a hundred thousand Narthani in Preddi, so there's no doubt they see their presence as permanent, and I am afraid, as does Hetman Keelan, that this is only the beginning."

The abbot looked at Yozef curiously. "How would you predict this story will continue, based on what you say has happened elsewhere on Anyar?"

Yozef rubbed the back of his left hand against his cheek. "If I had to speculate, I'd say the Narthani tightened their hold on the other two clans at the same time, pretending any conflicts between those two and their other clan neighbors are not their concern. They will claim to be interested only in protecting the territory they already have. I expect they have also sent envoys to many of the other clans, trying to convince them of their limited intentions and possibly offering more bribes. One purpose would be to discourage the other clans from uniting against them."

Sistian's hands clenched. "I see our separate histories do follow similar paths. Maybe it's the nature of people, which sometimes makes one wonder how much free will we have and how much is predestined."

Yozef offered, "Or maybe free will is the province of the individual and not the group?"

"I suppose that option should give me some succor, yet somehow it doesn't. Anyway, yes, you're correct. There were initially Narthani delegations visiting various clans openly, but that stopped a year ago, although there are rumors some coastal clans still have occasional Narthani visitors. Even *that* seems to have stopped in the last few months, and about the same time, small raids began into Moreland Province, along with Eywell riders seen in remote parts of northern Keelan. I know Culich is afraid this is only the beginning."

"And how does all this affect Keelan?"

"Keelan is committed to defending not only its own territory but also the two neighboring clans. Keelan, Gwillamer, and Mittack Provinces are part of a Tri-Clan Alliance. It was formed many generations ago to discourage aggression from neighboring clans. There was a time when Caedellium was plagued by territorial fighting and extended blood feuds across clan borders. Now we have an All-Clan Conclave yearly in Orosz City to settle such issues, but the alliance between Keelan and Gwillamer and Mittack is more obligatory. Keelan is required, by formal treaty and honor, to assist Gwillamer and Mittack should they be attacked. The original treaty didn't envision a foreign invader like the Narthani and their Caedelli allies, but I know our three hetmen are interpreting it that way. The immediate possible threat is from Eywell Province, which borders on northern Keelan and is not far from Gwillamer."

"Is there any sign all the clans may work together to resist the Narthani?"

"Hetman Keelan believes more clans are coming to understand the threat, though nothing yet is decided. I fear our hetman is trying to be more optimistic than is justified. The clans' history make them too accustomed to seeing the first threats as one another, rather than outsiders like the Narthani."

"Let me guess again. Those clans farthest away are the least worried, probably saying they shouldn't get involved, since the Narthani aren't threatening *them*."

The abbot stroked his beard with both hands. "As new as you are to the island, you seem to understand Caedellium politics."

The abbot looked down at the papers on his desk, shook his head, and looked back up at Yozef. "I hope I answered your question about the Narthani. There's not much else I can add, and I'm sorry, but I need to get back to all of this paper."

"Thank you, Abbot. I appreciate your taking the time to talk with me. I'm afraid I agree with your worry and the hetman's about the Narthani."

Yozef walked to his room, his mind replaying the abbot's words. The Narthani sounded like real pissers. He'd been so wrapped up in trying to adjust to here—to Abersford and the abbey complex—that he hadn't thought about what was happening on a larger stage. What this all meant for him personally could be bad, if he got caught up in a war of conquest for Caedellium. Could whatever future he had, be with these Narthani, instead of the Caedelli?

Christ! After what happened to me, is it too much to be able to live quietly? Well, there's nothing I can do about it. I only hope I don't get directly involved.

It was to be a forlorn hope.

CHAPTER 12

WHAT TO DO?

Yozef's daily routine gradually altered during the next two Anyar months. He switched to mornings to accompany Carnigan at his work assignments. Language study changed to expanding vocabulary, tackling more advanced readings, and exposing himself to social situations, including attending the Keelan version of evening bible lessons, musical evenings, or a discussion or a lecture by one of the scholastics, all at the abbey.

The religious lessons gave Yozef a grasp of the Caedellium theology—a single God, who made the world and watched and judged but seldom intervened.

Sort of a monotheistic lite, he first thought.

Later lectures and discussions showed a more complex, evolving theology. The theophists at St. Sidryn's saw a single God, who interacted with humans through three divine aspects: healing, wisdom, and discipline. From this view had developed the four Orders: theophists for humans' obligations to God, medicants to heal, scholastics to know God's creations, and militants to teach humans self-control. Details varied among and within clans, and more so elsewhere on Anyar, with variations on a single god, four separate gods, and hints of minor gods and entire pantheons.

The enemy of God was the Evil One, a version of Satan who tempted humans but who had no power over God. Yozef also read *The Word of God*, the holy book canonized a thousand years earlier, and *The Commentaries*, writings interpreting and extending the *Word* and which could still be added to. These writings were not universally accepted throughout Anyar, and there were allusions to past religious wars on the major continents.

The music evenings provided an interesting introduction to local music. None of the instruments had exact analogs on Earth, but some had similar tones, while others were weirdly novel for Yozef's ear.

The scholastic evenings provided an opportunity to understand more complex aspects of the Caedelli language and intellectual discourse, meaning half of the time he had no idea what was being discussed.

Same here as on Earth, he often reminded himself. Scholastics anywhere could talk up a storm without saying anything.

The only times he left the abbey vicinity was once or twice a sixday when he visited Abersford with Carnigan. The village had a central square with official-looking structures, two perpendicular main streets filled with shops, and houses of various sizes, enough to account for the village's population of nine hundred. The number of shops in Abersford surprised Yozef, until he realized the village drew business from ten or more miles away. The square, the main streets, and some side streets were cobblestone, with the rest of the streets covered by a mixture of gravel and crushed seashells. At the edge of the village, the roads turned to dirt—or mud, depending on the weather. The walls of the larger structures around the square and the more affluent-appearing houses were made of stone with slate roofs. Lesser structures were stone, wood, or a combination, with roofs of wood or thatch.

On those nights when Yozef accompanied Carnigan, they walked to the opposite side of the square, a block down the north-running main street, and turned a corner to Carnigan's favorite pub. While there were two other pubs in the village, Carnigan patronized only the one he considered the best. Yozef went along with the choice, since Carnigan was paying. Yozef had no "coin," as the locals referred to money, and he was obliged to agree with Carnigan's opinion.

A day when Yozef's life changed again came when he anticipated an evening with Carnigan at the pub. The first event of note that day occurred in the afternoon. He had taken time away from helping Carnigan to walk the gardens and the groves within the abbey complex, then exited the east gate to a nearby grove and came to *his* log. A major branch, some three feet in diameter, had split off a truly heroic tree whose canopy topped out at more than two hundred feet. The leaves seemed Earth-like, more rounded with serrated edges, instead of the slenderer leaves of Anyar trees, and of a familiar green, instead of the shadings from deep green to purple of most indigenous plants. He didn't think the tree oak—maybe elm or chestnut. The log was partially decayed, just enough to be soft, without splinters, and shaped in a curve that fit his body. He could lie on the curvature and stare upward through the leaf-filtered light to the sky. The sound of the wind through the branches and the dancing of the leaves sometimes lulled him to sleep, but on this day, he thought about the future, as he had many times previously.

He repeatedly asked himself the same question, because he still didn't have an answer. *What am I going to do?* The Caedelli at the abbey were gracious, understanding, and caring. However, there must be a limit to how long he could merely exist here. He might not be reading the signs correctly, but he got the feeling even the abbot was hinting about him finding a place in this society.

So. What could he do? He had no physical resources, none of the coins he saw others use, no experience or skills in trades or farming, and although he was communicating well, given everything, he was still far too ignorant of the culture and the histories of these people. This left . . . what?

"Knowledge," he blurted out, switching from internal dialogue to speaking aloud to the trees and sky. "The answer that keeps coming back is my knowledge of chemistry and the other sciences. Within my brain is more knowledge of the physical universe than this entire planet will possess for centuries. There has to be a way to tap into that knowledge. A way that will provide a living for me and still let me avoid getting in too much trouble with local beliefs and superstitions."

A problem was no infrastructure—the totality of knowledge, skills, and industry needed to use science from Earth. He knew the processes to make almost any, save the most complex, chemical compounds and molecules, but most required reaction ingredients, each of which might take a set of other ingredients to produce, and they in turn—on and on. Most would take decades or longer to develop, even under the best of circumstances.

Yet there must be simpler reactions and products he could start off with. He needed to speak with the abbey staff and troll the village shops for ideas. Between the two, he should be able to gauge the level of chemical knowledge and what chemicals were already available. There might also be books, even if not formal textbooks, in the abbey library that could at least give clues.

"Why haven't I thought of this before? Maybe the accident, the Watchers and Harlie, being dumped on Anyar never to see Earth or hear English again, all stunned my brain more than I realized."

CHAPTER 13

GREAT HALL OF THE KEELANS

Caernford, Keelan Province

Two structures dominated the twenty-acre brick-paved plaza of central Caernford, Capitol of Keelan Province—St. Tomo's Cathedral and the Great Hall of the Keelans. The walls of both buildings were made from two-ton stone blocks quarried from the craggy mountains of the Wycoff and Brums districts of northeast Keelan. The white stone with the yellow veins was unique to Caedellium, and the polished outer surfaces gave the illusion of sparkling gold in the early morning and late afternoon suns.

While the cathedral soared to signify glory to God, the Great Hall was an edifice with a different design, a single-story octagon with high multi-paned windows on its eight sides to let light enter from all directions of the province and serving as a symbol of clan unity and strength. The interior measured 220 feet diagonally from corner to corner, with 2-foot-diameter trimmed tree trunks supporting a ceiling peaking at 40 feet. The flooring consisted of slate slabs from the eastern slope of Mount Orlos in Shamir Province, the slate trimmed and fitted so carefully a finger could stroke the floor without detecting seams. Below that floor, a basement housed clan records and relics of the clan's history.

Although the Great Hall served the people of Caernford and nearby villages and farms for festivals and events requiring a large indoor space, the true purpose of the structure was for a "Gathering of the Clan." By tradition, every clan member could attend, and when the hall was built 130 years earlier, it *could* hold the entire clan. Now, with numbers having risen five-fold since that time, the hall was large enough to squeeze in only a fraction of the clan's people.

A yearly Gathering of the Clan opened the five-day festival marking the New Year and the transition from winter to spring. Each district sent proportional representatives, with clan members attending at least once every ten years, if possible. On such occasions, the hall held up to seven thousand standing clansmen and clanswomen surrounding the central platform and dais. There, the hetman, supported by the clan's leaders, would greet the clanspeople, followed by the scholastics' traditional recitation of the clan's history, and ended by the hetman's report on the condition of the clan. The entire ceremony seldom lasted more than two hours, there being only so long so many bodies could stand packed together into a single room.

The only other occasion for a formal Gathering of the Clan was under extraordinary circumstances, when the entire clan needed to be addressed. No such occasion had occurred in Culich Keelan's nineteen years as hetman or in his father's or grandfather's tenures, on back to the time the gathering was held in a natural amphitheater near Caernford.

On this day, three somber men stood at the base of steps leading to a meeting room attached to the south side of the Great Hall.

"Nothing new about the Narthani, Culich?" Pedr Kennrick addressed his hetman.

Culich Keelan shook his head. "Only what I passed on to you and Vortig two days ago. Although they've still made no major overt threat to the other clans, every instinct tells me it will happen. For myself, the only two questions are *when* and *where*? And that's what eats at my gut."

"I beg to disagree, Hetman," said Vortig Luwis, slamming a fist into his other palm. "I know all three of us think the Narthani are not yet finished expanding, and although I agree with your two questions, there's a *third* one that may be even more important—and that's *if* the other clans can somehow agree to cooperate when the Narthani do make their next move."

Culich didn't disagree. He and his two major advisors had chewed to exhaustion the possible Narthani intentions. Kennrick was Culich's age, a lifelong friend, and a shrewd mind atop a short, rotund form. With his ruddy complexion and red hair and beard, he always appeared to be escaping from something. The Kennrick family owned tracts of farmland, but Pedr's sons managed the family estate ten miles north of Caernford while their father advised and assisted Culich with clan affairs.

Vortig Luwis was a few years younger and not a close friend, but his loyalty to the clan and hetman was absolute. His family had timberland and mines in the Nylamir district, but as the Narthani threat increased, so did Luwis's role in overseeing clan security, organizing the clan's men of fighting age, and serving as liaison with counterparts in allied Gwillamer and Mittack clans. Luwis's height and bald head made him easily identified in any crowd, as did his habitual frown, hook nose, short-cropped, prematurely graying beard, and cold, dark blue eyes. His stern countenance and known fearlessness hid a sharp mind. Few knew, Culich being one of those, how much Luwis doted on his wife and three daughters and how, as a youth, Luwis had considered becoming a theophist. He was also blunt, honest, and honorable, sometimes to even Culich's annoyance.

Culich placed a hand on Luwis's shoulder. "All we can do is all we can do, Vortig. Along with praying for God's grace to guide and deliver us, should the worst happen. The three of us have critical tasks in front of us. *I* must try to convince more of the other clans to come around to my fears."

The hetman rested his other hand on the shorter man's shoulder. "*You*, Pedr, must see to increasing arms production and food stores, while *you*, Vortig, must see to the clan's fighting men and patrolling our borders. I've said to you two what I'll not yet say to the rest of our people. I fear the future. A storm is gathering that bodes disaster for all of Caedellium."

Neither of the other men had anything to add or counter.

Culich removed his hands from their shoulders, and his tone enlivened. "In the meantime, routine clan affairs continue, no matter what else."

"Speaking of routine affairs, I think the others are gathering," said Kennrick, looking through the glass-paned door into the meeting room.

A boyerman led each of Keelan Province's eleven districts. The semi-hereditary position normally passed through the current boyerman's lineage, unless altered either by lack of the district people's support or by hetman decree. Today was the quarterly meeting of Culich with his advisors and the eleven boyermen or their representatives.

Culich turned to the door. "Then, by all means, let's greet our boyermen."

Luwis climbed the three stairs, held open the back entrance door, and followed Culich and Kennrick inside. The meeting room was a twenty-five-foot square with a fifteen-foot-diameter round table and chairs dominating the room. Additional, less ornate chairs lined the walls, and a double door led into the Grand Hall. Small tapestries depicting events in clan history hung between windows along with objects of renown: a nicked sword, several banners, copies of documents encased in glass, a long lock of fiery red hair intertwined with another of deepest black, and a pair of aged leather shoes purportedly worn by the first ancestor of the clan to set foot on Caedellium. All other participants would enter through the Great Hall's north side main door and cross the empty hall to the meeting room.

Three men already occupied boyermen chairs, the men either looking at papers or talking to aides attending the meeting. One grizzled and harried face looked up as Culich entered from the outer door.

"Hetman!" said Boyerman Arwin. "We need to discuss the Mittackese fishing in our waters. It's getting worse, and my fishermen are tiring of waiting for this to stop. I'm afraid there may be clashes unless something is done."

Culich scowled. Fishing boundaries were loosely agreed to between and among clans, with details left to local leaders. Although Mittack was a neighboring clan and ally, formal agreements between hetman didn't always seep down to the local level. This particular issue had festered for several years, and it displeased Culich that the issue remained unresolved without the clan hetmen becoming involved.

"No, Belman," answered Culich, "it won't be on the agenda today. Stay after the meeting, and you and I can discuss how to proceed." The Arwin boyerman was Belman Kulvin. Custom allowed he could be addressed by his title, which Culich had nearly done. However, that would have signaled his level of displeasure. If the later individual discussion didn't go well, "Belman" could quickly change to "Boyerman Arwin."

He wished that either he could light a fire under Belman or the man would demonstrate enough incompetence so Culich could replace him. As hetman, it was Culich's right to remove any boyerman, though a right judiciously asserted and best resorted to only when the other boyermen recognized the necessity.

Moving on from Arwin, Culich greeted the other two boyermen, as he sat in the hetman's chair facing the open double doors through which he could see the cavernous hall. The boyermens' path to the meeting room was intentional. As they crossed the empty hall, each man's eyes invariably rose to the central platform and dais, the tapestries and the banners on the encircling walls. He would hopefully be humbled by the expanse, the emptiness reminding him of the hall packed with clanspeople on Gathering Day and of his responsibilities to the clan and its members. Culich knew the feeling himself ever since his father first took him at the age of twelve to the meetings.

One at a time or in clusters, the men attending this day came through the double doors, exchanged greetings and small talk, and found their places. Nine of the eleven boyermen were present. A tenth had broken a leg, and his eldest son represented the district. An eleventh boyerman was too old to travel and had written a formal request to step down from his position, in favor of a nephew who had served as proxy at several previous meetings. Culich would soon make the formal appointment.

When Culich Keelan greeted the last seating boyerman, he sat back in his chair and surveyed the other eleven men at the table. The general bustle died down, as everyone sensed the meeting was about to begin, and all eyes turned to their hetman. Naturally, Culich's chair was slightly larger and more ornate than the other eleven, appropriate for the hetman of the Keelan Clan and Province. The hereditary leader of the Keelan Clan was imposing. Not so much his actual size, which was of good height and still robust, in spite of his gray hair and beard, but more the aura of his personality, his ability to project the difficult-to-describe essence of a leader, his known history of fairness to those recognizing him as their liege, and his decisiveness in defense of the clan's interests.

The men representing the eleven districts of Keelan Province sat in seats randomly assigned yearly at the round table, the shape and assignments to avoid hints of favoritism toward any boyermen. The table and seating arrangement were traditional since the time of Culich's great, great grandfather, the precedent set to avoid squabbles about positioning and rank among the boyermen from provinces of differing populations, wealth, and shifting political aspirations. Still, there were always grumblings. The provinces in the best condition, at least in their own minds, thought they should sit closest to the hetman. Naturally, nothing was spoken. Tradition and the expected response from Culich eliminated overt complaints.

Behind the twelve men at the round table sat aides—sons, advisors, others of note, and occasionally church prelates, depending on the agenda. Behind Culich were three occupied chairs: Kennrick, Luwis, and one other.

All of those present were men, with the one exception. Maera Keelan was twenty-three Anyar years old—twenty Earth years—and the eldest daughter of Culich Keelan. She sat with serious demeanor, her green eyes shifting with moods from warm to impassive, to cold. Her hair coiled atop her head, and, as some in the room knew from experience, that head housed a tongue capable of flaying the purveyor of parochial interests or slovenly arguments. That she was in the room at all rested on Culich's simply *saying* so. For the last three years, Maera had attended all of the most important meetings, including those of the hetman and his eleven district boyermen, in the formal role as recorder, since Culich insisted he needed a written record to remind him of advice from the boyermen, as well as the necessity for a record of their deliberations for the clan history.

Though Maera spoke only when prompted by her father, her demure dress and manner fooled no one. On her lap lay a small wooden platform holding a vial of ink, a cup from which sprouted quills made of feathers from Caedellium seabirds, and a stack of blank paper. As the men conversed, the assiduous scratch of her quill point on paper became part of the ambient noise. Culich would occasionally ask her to repeat something said earlier that day or perhaps from a past meeting. In those latter cases, she would delve into bound ledgers on an adjacent chair to retrieve the appropriate transferred notes.

It was in these requests for reviewing past proceedings that Maera might interject dreaded comments such as, "I wrote down that Boyerman Arwin said earlier today that his district was short of wheat this year and needed a supplement from the central clan stores. Perhaps I misheard, since the boyerman reported sales of wheat to Mittack at the meeting last quarter." She would look up from her writings, give the target her attention, and wait while the boyerman explained to Culich how he failed to keep sufficient grain reserves.

However, Maera's less acknowledged role came later, when her father reviewed the meeting with her and other advisors. By not actively taking part, she could observe the proceedings and often caught subtleties Culich missed or wanted confirmed.

In addition to her intellect and insights, Maera was, in all but title, a scholastic of Caedellium history and customs. Ever since learning to read, she had voraciously consumed writings from all of the provinces, and Culich had indulged her by paying to have copies made at abbeys throughout Caedellium. Culich smiled to himself every time he remembered when she unearthed a two-hundred-year-old reference to a treaty between the Stent and Moreland clans that helped settle a dispute over clan boundaries in Stent's favor—an outcome that the Stent Hetman communicated a debt owed to Keelan. For the Keelan Hetman, it was an outcome to be savored, since he respected the Stent Hetman and despised Moreland's leader. Culich chastised himself for the guilty pleasure he felt at such a minor thwarting of Hetman Moreland, but still smiled.

Equally amusing, tinged with regret at his own actions, was the memory of another issue involving Moreland—a border disagreement involving a distant and unpopulated part of northern Keelan Province. A meandering stream used as part of their clans' boundary cut a new course southward. A square mile of land that had been south of the stream found itself north. The formality of the border was in doubt, and the Moreland Hetman claimed the square mile now part of Moreland and would bring up the issue at the next All-Clan Conclave in Orosz City. Culich's intention to dispute Moreland's claim was dissected calmly and cruelly by his eldest daughter.

***

"So, Father. You will dispute Moreland's claim to the shift in boundaries?"

"Of course, I will! It's Keelan land, and it's a point of honor."

"And you're not influenced by your feelings about Hetman Moreland?"

"He's a vile piece of animal excrement, a disgrace to all of Caedellium, a tyrant to this people, and no, my opinion of him doesn't change that I can't let him steal Keelan land."

"Correct me if I'm wrong, Father, but isn't the land a piece of swamp with no practical use? Would it *really* hurt the clan to lose so little land of so little value?"

"The value is irrelevant," snarled Culich. "It's the principle!"

"With all your worries about what's happening with the Narthani and the Selfcell and Eywell clans, is this issue with Moreland important enough to divert attention at the All-Clan Conclave next month? If the two of you get into a shouting match, what effect will this have when you try to convince the other hetmen of the Narthani danger?"

Culich flushed. "When I want your opinion on how to serve the clan, I'll ask you!" he ground out.

Maera didn't respond, sitting with hands folded in her lap, a serene face waiting. He glared back. Neither spoke for several minutes until Culich's ire faded, and he sat back with a deep breath. Another minute passed, along with longer breaths by Culich.

He cleared his throat. "Uh . . . I'm sorry I snapped at you, Maera. I shouldn't have said what I did. You know I value your thoughts. It's just that *damned* Gynfor Moreland and his two sons. The *Word* tells us not to judge, but I'm afraid I fail when it comes to them."

"*All* of the Moreland family?" Maera chided.

"All right, all right. *Most* of them. I make an exception for Anarynd Moreland."

A smile warmed Maera's face, both at the thought of Ana and at being right that bringing up Ana's name would soften her father's mood. It had taken him some time to accept that his daughter's best friend was a Moreland, albeit from a minor collateral branch of the Moreland Hetman's family, and longer still before he would admit that he actually *liked* the girl, even if she *was* a Moreland.

"And you're right to caution about arguing too much about a worthless piece of land when there are more urgent issues. Still . . . it would gall me to no end to agree to let Gynfor Moreland take even an inch of Keelan land."

Maera smiled again, the curl of her lips and lilt in her eyes alerting her father she had something devious to add. Which she did. "In looking at old records, I found the offending stream has changed course numerous times over the last century. In fact, it changes course about every ten to twenty years and usually runs two miles *north*."

"North?" Culich echoed, his thoughts churning over the new piece of information. "That . . . that means . . . " His face crinkled with a smile and a narrowing of eyes, as he looked at his daughter. "If I agree to cede this little piece of worthless land now, then the next time the stream shifts north, Moreland will face this precedent of taking the stream bed as the boundary."

The twinkle in Maera's eyes was unmistakable. "And unless I am wrong, the land to the north is good farmland."

The hetman sat back in his chair and roared with laughter. "Oh, Merciful God!" he choked out. "May I and Gynfor Moreland still be alive when it happens!"

***

Culich recollected that day and how much he depended on Maera. A secret Culich shared only with his wife, Breda, was that often Maera gave as many useful comments as all of his advisors and boyermen. Not always *better* advice, but from a different perspective and with broader views of many issues. Culich often rued she hadn't been born a son. *What a hetman she would have made!* he thought many a time. However, traditions were that the hetman was a man—not a hetwoman. That Culich and his wife, Breda, didn't have sons was a point of potential conflict within any clan. Ascendency struggles and even intra-clan feuds and savage fighting had happened too often in Caedellium history.

Clan Keelan avoided such problems by careful plans laying out paths of succession. No one doubted the four daughters of Culich and Breda Keelan would produce grandsons. From these, Culich would anoint a successor. Fortunately for Clan Keelan, their custom didn't follow strict primogeniture, as did some clans—a custom too often leading to mediocre hetmen, since being firstborn was no criterion for ability. For every truly qualified firstborn successor, there were those either incompetent or even disastrous. For Clan Keelan, Culich would see to the training of all of the grandsons and choose the one he believed most qualified to be the next hetman. Although the boyermen had to confirm the choice, only one recorded case of a rejection was quickly followed by acceptance of the hetman's second choice among fourteen grandsons.

Culich and everyone who knew Maera assumed one of her sons would become the next hetman. The flaw in this assumption was her not yet having married. Although frowned upon, children outside of formal marriage were not uncommon—but not for a hetman's family. The need to maintain security of succession lines and minimize clan and inter-clan political complications was paramount. Normally, the daughter of a hetman, particularly of a clan as prominent as Keelan, would have numerous suitor options with appropriate political advantages to the clan. Maera understood her duty and from an early age assumed her eventual marriage would be managed for the good of their people. Her father wouldn't force a marriage she objected to, but she knew and accepted her obligations . . . at least intellectually. What she felt in her heart of hearts not even her parents were sure of, since she held close her innermost feelings.

Whatever those feelings, Maera played her assigned role, to a degree. However, she herself was an impediment to finding a suitable marriage. A number of potential candidates, sons of other hetmen, boyermen, even a few from families wealthy enough to tempt drawing into connections to the hetman line had come and gone. In spite of the advantages of marrying one of their scions into the hetman's family and perhaps producing a son who might become hetman himself, it often took only a single meeting with Maera to dissuade suitors. Not that she was uncomely. She was of medium height with a slender feminine form, lustrous brown hair, a natural grace, and a warm personality, when she showed it. It was that qualification that was a problem, since that warmth was not displayed as often as Culich would have liked, especially with suitors. Word came to Culich more than once of potential suitors returning home to report that the Keelan Hetman's oldest daughter was disrespectful, was condescending, and had a smart mouth. Compounding the problem was that they weren't completely wrong. She *was* smarter than any of them and knew it, and so did they. Despite her efforts, it didn't take long for the men to realize she was their intellectual superior and a woman not able or willing to keep opinions to herself. For those potential suitors she might have liked well enough, it became a familiar pattern: initial interest faded to uneasiness, to coolness, and, finally, to a polite regret they had to leave so soon and how nice it was to meet her. They were never heard from again.

Those were the best cases. There were also men too oblivious to recognize that Maera was not overawed by their masculinity or family station, or they thought the marriage decision was theirs alone. Several had escaped, figuratively, with their lives.

There had been no suitors now for six months. Culich hadn't pressed Maera, given the history, and in spite of himself he depended more and more on her help. He hadn't yet shared one troubling thought, not even with his wife, but he wondered if Maera would *ever* marry. There was no denying—she was different. He blamed himself to a degree. She had always been a precocious child. He had gained satisfaction out of having produced her, and his indulgences had fed her independence. He consoled himself that maybe neither he nor Maera had had a choice. Maybe Maera turned out to be who God intended. He had three other daughters, the next oldest coming to an appropriate age for the first suitors. There would be grandsons, even if not from his eldest child.

***

A polite feminine cough from behind him interrupted Culich's reverie. His attention riveted back to the eleven men at the table looking at him, waiting for him to say . . . what?

Oh yes, first the routine matters before we get to the Narthani.

He cleared his throat and turned in his chair toward Maera, holding out a hand to receive two sheets of paper. "As usual, let's review the last meeting."

In the next hour the men summarized the results of action they were to have taken, then moved on to new items: reviews of crop status, sightings of larger predators shadowing herds of horses (three boyermen from the region agreed to coordinate hunting parties), a landslide blocking the mountain pass to Dornfeld Province for a sixday (dug out from both ends), a renewed request from the Elwyin boyerman for help in building a new abbey complex for their growing population (granted), a missing family from a farm in Wycoff (fruitless intensive search and no answer to what happened), the announcement of an agreed-on marriage of a daughter of Boyerman Funvir to a Hewell Province boyerman's family—on and on, for the next two hours.

Culich's attention drifted as the meeting moved into less pressing items, when once again he was aware of silence. He glanced down at the agenda Maera had outlined and saw that his finger rested on the last item. *Oh yes, finally to the Narthani.*

"As you all know, Boyerman Dornfeld sent a report that one of his fishing boats came on a new Narthani fleet heading to Preddi City. The fishermen ran for our coast, but from their descriptions, the Narthani ships included both warships and cargo vessels. At least some of the vessels had decks crowded with armed men. I'm afraid we must assume the Narthani brought in even more fighting men."

The men shifted uneasily in their chairs and murmured to themselves and one another. Tilston of the Brums District spoke first. "If they are fighting men, do we have any idea if they intend staying? Maybe they're just passing through. Perhaps re-provisioning for a further voyage."

"Possible," said a dubious Culich, "though we should assume not. As the *Word* says, 'Plan for hard times and not the best.' I believe we must assume the Narthani made a permanent increase to their forces here on Caedellium."

"To what purpose?" queried Boyerman Lanthan of the Elwin District. Lanthan already knew Culich's answer. He was one of the boyermen who equally shared Culich's fears about the future intentions of the Narthani.

"Since they have an iron grip on Preddi, and since Selfcell and Eywell seem firmly under their control, we have to continue to consider the possibility the Narthani aren't satisfied with the part of Caedellium they now control. While there's so far been no sign of Narthani action against other clans, we need to be alert to the danger. I'll continue to discuss this with the other hetmen at every opportunity.

"I've asked Vortig Luwis to make another assessment of the clan's strength and to make plans for increased patrols of our northern border with Eywell. He'll report back to us at a future meeting. For now, you all need to be sure of weapons preparation and that every able-bodied man knows how to use them. I know both weapons practice and the patrols take the men away from their work, so do the best you can."

The meeting continued for another two hours, with midday meal served in the room. There were no other major decisions made, but the time allowed every boyerman, representative, and aide to express himself and be listened to, such that by the time the meeting adjourned, all attendees understood the clan's future intentions and were satisfied their own views had been heard.

With the formal conclusion of the meeting, Culich mingled with the other men as they prepared to depart for home, while Kennrick, Luwis, and Maera went over her notes, from which she would prepare the written account of the meeting. Culich was about to leave when he noticed Boyerman Arwin sitting and looking his way.

God's curse on it! I forgot about Belman.

He stopped and berated himself for using God's name in such a manner. Chastised and forgiving himself, he approached the instigator to see what he had to say for himself. In a way, it was a relief to deal with something as irritating as Arwin. At least, it was a problem he could deal with, whereas the Narthani might need a miracle from God to solve.

CHAPTER 14

THE SNARLING GRAEKO

Yozef's plan to find ways to use his chemistry knowledge without getting in trouble gave him a focus, but no solution. A sixday later, he still groped for a practical first introduction. His being pleased with himself to have a plan—any plan—was fading on the evening he looked forward to a session at the Snarling Graeko. He hadn't the faintest clue what a graeko was or why it should be snarling. The sign hanging in front of the pub depicted a creature resembling a cross between a warthog and a hyena. Carnigan had never seen one, didn't know anyone who had ever seen one, and didn't know whether they were real or mythical. All Carnigan knew was the pub had the best beer.

Carnigan always went straight to the same corner table. If the table was occupied, it always became available on Carnigan's approach, the current occupants suddenly finding another table more to their liking.

When Yozef first came to the pub with Carnigan, the two of them drank alone, but over time, a few regular customers joined them, as if seeing that Yozef had survived had emboldened them. On this night that everything changed for Yozef, they were joined by two other regulars, and by the second beer, the three Caedelli told Anyar jokes, some of which Yozef had already heard before, sometimes more than once, sometimes so many times he could have told them from memory. One advantage of the strength of Caedellium beer was that by the second stein, even an old joke was hilarious. Yozef figured he *got* about a third of the jokes, understood the references but didn't get the humor about another third, and had no clue why the other third were amusing.

The three Caedelli started their third stein to Yozef's nursing of his second, when Filtin Fuller, a cheerful man in his mid-twenties sitting next to Yozef, decided it was the turn of the newcomer to contribute.

"Yozef, it's your turn! We've never heard jokes or stories from you. Since you aren't from Caedellium, you must have new ones. Let's hear some!"

"Good idea," declared Carnigan, with a mighty fist to the tabletop. "Let's hear something, Yozef."

Yozef sat frozen for a few seconds before Carnigan urged him again. Jokes? He wasn't good at remembering jokes. And what would be a joke here? It couldn't have any Earth references, and what he knew about the local style of humor wasn't encouraging. What if he told a joke that turned out to be offensive? Yet this wasn't an interview for a guest spot on the *Tonight Show*. Most likely, what would happen was that with the ones he remembered, they either wouldn't get them or wouldn't think they were funny.

The three men looked at him expectantly, quaffing their steins while they waited.

He took a deep breath and launched in. "There's this man in the village working in his shop when suddenly an angel appears before him. Naturally, the man is startled, but, being a devout person, he kneels before the angel and asks why he is so honored. The angel tells him, 'Because you are such a good man, God has granted you a great favor. Unfortunately, there is good news and bad news.' 'Oh, please tell me the good news first,' said the man. 'God knows that when most people pass on from this life, they leave many tasks undone and many people to whom they did not say their last goodbyes. God has granted you to be told one year in advance that your time has come, and that is why I have appeared to you.' 'You mean it's *good* news that I have a year to live?' said the shocked man. 'Well,' said an embarrassed angel, 'the *bad* news is that I've looked for you since a year ago today.'"

Yozef stopped, looked around at the three men, and waited to see the reaction. There were a few seconds of silence; Yozef could almost see the gears turning. Carnigan broke first. He had raised his stein at the punch line and was swallowing when it hit him. The mouthful of beer exited in a fine spray. Fortunately for Yozef, he sat next to Carnigan and the expellant centered on Filtin Fuller, sitting opposite. Carnigan choked for a second on beer that remained in his mouth, then swallowed and roared in laughter. He slammed his stein onto the table, further reducing the beer level within it, and pounded the table with his other hand. The table was sturdy enough to have held the weight of an elephant—which was fortunate. The sprayed-upon Filtin laughed as loudly, although Yozef couldn't be sure whether it was because of the joke or Carnigan's reaction. The third man seemed to lack a fine sense of humor, since he smiled but didn't laugh.

Oh, well, you can't win over everyone in an audience.

Yozef, inordinately pleased with himself, sipped his own stein and waited for Carnigan to regain control. When it happened, it almost cost Yozef serious injury, as the big man slapped him on his back, causing his diaphragm to impact the table edge. Once he could breathe again, he heard Carnigan.

"A good one, Yozef," bellowed Carnigan. "Never heard that one before."

Several neighboring tables had witnessed the explosion of mirth and beer, and two men leaned over and asked Filtin and the other drinking companion what was so amusing, possibly because none of the regular customers had ever seen such a display from Carnigan. Thus did the joke travel among the pub's thirty or so customers within several minutes.

"Another one, Yozef, tell us another one!"

Hey, maybe I have a career here as a comedian. I wonder if there are gigs that pay coin?

By now, most of the customers either stood near their tables or turned at their seats to listen.

"One day I came here to the Snarling Graeko for beer. As I got to the door, there stood Sister Norla." The referenced sister was the "nurse" who was the first person on Anyar Yozef had seen when he awoke at the abbey. The matronly middle-aged sister was an accomplished caregiver, although somewhat prim. On her bad days, and Yozef experienced several when he first arrived, he thought of her as Nurse Ratched from *One Flew Over the Cuckoo's Nest*. He had also heard her comment several times on the evils of too much drinking.

"Naturally, I was surprised to see sister Norla outside of a pub. Then she spoke to me. 'Yozef,' she said, 'beer is an evil that clouds men's minds and strays them from doing better with their lives. At least in your case, you have no family to go without food and clothing when you spend your money in such dens, but both your money and time should be spent elsewhere.'

"'Pardon me, Sister Norla,' I said. 'With all respect, have you ever tasted a beer?'

"'No, never,' the sister asserted.

"'Then how can you know for sure it's evil?'

"The sister thought for a moment, then said, 'You're right, my son. Just to satisfy you, I am willing to try a beer. Naturally, I can't go into the pub myself, but if you would bring me out beer in a cup, I'm willing to try it.'

"So, I went into the pub and asked the owner, 'Could I have a beer in a cup?'

"The owner shook his head in disgust. 'Is Sister Norla *still* outside?'"

Instead of an explosion of laughter, this time it built like an ocean swell that starts low, then grew until it crashed on the beach. Some got the punch line immediately, while others had to think about it, and some had to have it explained. Like the wave, when it fully broke, the pub was fortunate to be constructed of strong timbers. Yozef had assumed Carnigan to be the loudest person in the pub, but his position was bumped down one slot by the pub owner himself, who had come over to hear why so much laughter centered on their table.

When the wave subsided, there were demands for another joke. Yozef obliged with a few more—none with quite the impact. He was thus grateful when other customers offered examples of humor. By the tenth joke of the impromptu comedy club, even old stale stories were hilarious.

Yozef finally finished his second stein and debated a third when the sounds of splintering wood, a loud thud, and a man's scream cut through the noise of simultaneous voices. Yozef jerked his head toward whatever happened and could see a knot of men forming near a keg of beer resting on its side on the floor. The pub's festive mood transformed into panicked voices, and the scream morphed into cries of agony.

Yozef followed his three drinking companions to the knot of men. A keg five feet long and two and a half in diameter lay next to a broken-wheeled cart that must have been transporting the keg. The source of the initial scream and now moans was an elderly man with one leg under the keg.

The pub owner shouted down the turmoil and ordered Carnigan and several of the larger men to help him get the keg off the man writhing on the floor. The keg being too heavy to lift outright, men placed a wooden block under one end of its curved side, and the men heaved on the other end to tilt the keg onto the block. As the men put everything they had into lifting the end of the keg, others pulled the man away. His pinned leg was gruesome. The keg had rolled onto the side of his lower leg, snapping both lower leg bones in several places, since it bent twice in different directions. Yozef could see two sharp ends of shattered bones protruding through the man's pants.

Men shouted and milled about, until the pub owner yelled, "Willager! I saw your wagon down the street! Get it up here! We have to get him to the abbey." A man ran to and through the door—presumably Willager. "Carnigan! I'll get a board, and you and your friend get him on it and out to the wagon."

Friend? Is that me? I'm no medic!

The board appeared, and Carnigan barked at Yozef to help him get the injured man onto it. By then, the man was in shock and only groaned as they slid him onto the board. Carnigan gestured to one end of the board, which Yozef interpreted that he was volunteering as an EMT whether he wanted to or not. Outside was a flatbed wagon drawn by two nondescript horses. They laid him and his board on the bed, climbed on next to him, and the wagon owner, Willager, got the horses and wagon moving at a moderate pace to avoid more jarring than necessary.

Another pub customer rode ahead to alert the abbey, and an open main gate awaited them. They pulled up to the hospital and a waiting wooden gurney attended by two men and a woman. They gently but efficiently transferred the old man to the gurney and wheeled him inside. By this time another wagon arrived with a gray-haired woman who followed the gurney, crying and wringing her hands.

"His wife," someone whispered.

Yozef and Carnigan followed them inside, not with any specific task in mind, but simply trailing behind the flow of people as the victim was moved into a receiving room. There, several medicants appeared in orchestrated movements, reminding Yozef of emergency rooms. By now, Medicant Dyllis had appeared.

"Get him on the table," Dyllis ordered. The gurney crew sat the man on the edge of the table, then were shouldered out of the way as Dyllis and a sister rotated the now unconscious man and laid him down on the wooden surface.

Cadwulf Beynom, the abbot and abbess's older son, appeared at Yozef's side and led him and Carnigan out of the room. "They will take care of him now," he said.

"A nasty break," said Yozef. "I hope they can fix his leg."

Carnigan shook his head. "I would pray so, but from the looks of it, they'll have to take it off. Too much damage. At least, it's a low break, near the foot, so he'll only lose the leg below the knee."

Yozef shuddered. An amputation? What exact level of medicine did they have here? Such details had occurred to him previously, but "thinking" about and "seeing" were different. He found himself imagining needing serious medical care. Such as an amputation. Despite himself, the imagines of blades cutting through his own flesh and sawing bones rose unbidden in his mind.

"If they have to amputate, do they have something for the pain?"

"Only to dull it. The rest he'll have to bear with God's mercy."

Christ! I hope to God I never have an accident here!

"Nothing at all?" choked Yozef. He was pretty sure opiates had been available much earlier than this in Earth's history.

"There are drugs from certain flowers, but those flowers won't grow in Caedellium and need conditions available only in a few mainland realms. The Landolinians charge very high prices for it, but even that source has been cut off since the Narthani blocked all trade between the island and the rest of Anyar. The medicants will do what they can for him. There's nothing we can do here, except pray for him."

The Narthani again. Blocking trade? One more reason to pay more attention to whoever these people are and what they plan for Caedellium. As for growers of the poppies— it sounds like these Landolinians run a cartel. If it was opium poppies or something similar, there are always ways to grow them. Maybe some kind of greenhouse.

Yozef went back to his room. Twenty minutes later, he heard the first screams. There was no doubt who they emanated from and why, and they were audible even in his room a hundred yards from the medical building. Though he tried not to visualize the scene in the operating room, his imagination again betrayed him, as he envisioned the medicants working as quickly as they could to make the agony as short as possible. The screams went on for only a minute or two, then abruptly stopped. Yozef froze in place with the first scream and now found himself soaked in cold sweat. More minutes of quiet passed before he could do more than sit on the side of his bed.

CHAPTER 15

CHEMISTRY

A Proposal

The next day, Yozef stopped the medicant Brother Willer as they left the dining hall.

"Brother Willer, how is the injured man we brought in last night?"

The brother shook his head. "I'm afraid the medicants and our prayers weren't enough. He died while they were taking the leg. Brother Bolwyn said his heart gave out. That's always the danger when someone is older. A younger person might have survived the operation." With that, Willer patted Yozef on the arm and walked away.

Yozef stood frozen in place. The plain but hearty meal lay a lump in his stomach. He walked outside into the cool morning air and leaned his forehead against the cold stone wall to help keep from ejecting the meal.

It was another lesson to him not to forget where he was and to assume nothing. He'd taken for granted Harlie's statement he'd never be sick again. Sickness didn't cover accidents. What if he got injured? Whatever painkillers they had here were scarce or unavailable.

And did they understand about germs? On Earth, asepsis wasn't accepted until around 1860–1870. Harlie had said he'd be immune, but was Harlie right? Or even telling the truth?

Later that night he lay in his bed. Thinking, unfortunately. Thoughts kept returning to unpleasant images. After he'd spent nearly an hour of staring at the dark ceiling, a different thread pushed itself to the front of his consciousness. There was no serious anesthetic. If he could get some of the plants or seeds of the poppy, he could figure out how to grow them in greenhouses. But that was well into the future, if possible at all. He assumed the Landolinians were serious about maintaining a monopoly.

What chemicals could be used? Ether, nitrous oxide, chloroform? Yozef's heart beat faster. He clenched a fist and pounded into the other palm.

"You know . . . ," he mumbled to himself, "I should be able to make all three, given materials and some help."

The next day, instead of joining Carnigan for assigned tasks, Yozef went out to his log, stared through the overhead leaves, and thought serious chemistry for the first time since his arrival.

Of the three chemicals he remembered, nitrous oxide wouldn't work. Production required ammonium nitrate, which had to be synthesized by reacting nitric acid and ammonia, a pretty volatile and dangerous step itself. Then the ammonium nitrate had to be purified and crystallized, then heated to decompose into nitrous oxide and water vapor. Other side products of the reaction had to be removed through various filtering and purifications, which required yet other chemicals likely not available.

The same for chloroform: he needed chlorine gas, which involved electrolysis of a sodium chloride solution, capturing the gasses and purifying the chlorine gas, which was then used to make calcium hypochlorite—bleach.

"Where the hell's Walmart when you needed one?"

He further remembered you then had to react the bleach with methane (CH_4) to get a mixture of the four possible chlorinated compounds (CH_3Cl, CH_2Cl_2, $CHCl_3$, and CCl_4). Chloroform was the third product, the one with three chlorines attached to the carbon. It could be separated by distillation from the others, but Yozef didn't want to get involved with the fourth product—carbon tetrachloride, which he remembered was dangerous, something about liver failure and cancer. The latter might not be a problem for *him*, assuming what Harlie had said about the nanomachines they'd injected into him was true, but what about his workers?

"Nope. Chloroform's out, too."

That left ether. Or, more precisely, diethyl ether. As with the other two chemicals, to his surprise, when he thought about the synthesis of ether he found himself envisioning whole pages of chemistry texts describing ether synthesis and purification.

That's odd I can recall entire pages so clearly. Why couldn't I do this when I took courses?

He could *see* it was a simple reaction of ethanol with sulfuric acid. Heated, but not *too* much. The reaction at 140°C, with alcohol being continuously added to keep it in excess to prevent the reverse reaction of ether back to ethanol.

Not that it was all that easy. *Nasty stuff, if you weren't careful*, he reminded himself. Above 160°C, ether could spontaneously ignite, and even in storage at lower temperatures ignition could occur, due to high vapor pressure.

Yozef could see the page of warnings as if it were right in front of him. The heating would be a bitch. Ether was extremely flammable. Then there was storage—airtight containers in the dark, in small quantities for safety, and add a piece of iron in the bottle to slow peroxide formation, which also had the nasty habit of exploding.

He continued thinking as he paced his room that evening and as he walked the grounds the next day, trying to remember what he could of ether synthesis and crafting how he would broach the subject with the abbot. He had to be very careful. New ideas might be seen as threats to the existing order and attributed to demonic influences or heresy. He knew of consequences that even minor innovations could cause, especially among conservative religious and medical professions. His interview with the abbot had touched on the issue, but he hadn't yet acted on the abbot's advice to come to him first with new knowledge to introduce.

He'd been telling himself he needed to consider all of the ramifications of introducing new knowledge and take action at some point, but knowing himself, he'd likely procrastinate. If the accident at the pub didn't prod him to jump on the potential of anesthetics as an ideal place to start introducing new technology, then when and what would be?

He decided an initial approach to brother Fitham would be the safest test. If Fitham wasn't fazed, then he would try the abbot. On Godsday, the brothers and the sisters were encouraged to mix freely with staff and visitors. The following Godsday evening, Yozef made sure he sat at a table for four with Fitham. The other three did most of the talking during the meal—Yozef waiting for his chance. When the other two finished and excused themselves, Brother Fitham looked across the table at Yozef.

"I noticed how quiet you've been this evening, Yozef. Is there something troubling you?"

Here goes nothing. "Brother Fitham, the man brought in several days ago with the badly injured leg. Something *is* troubling me, and I wonder if you could advise me."

"Certainly, Yozef. Why don't we walk around the grounds? It'll be quiet this time of Godsday, and we'll not be interrupted."

They strolled behind the main buildings and were well into the garden, surrounded by shrubbery and flowers just in the middle of the late season bloom, the last twilight lighting up the few clouds in the sky.

"Brother Fitham—" Yozef said, and the older man placed a frail hand on his shoulder.

"Please, Yozef, call me Petros, or Brother Petros, if you must. I always feel it's better than the 'Brother Fitham' title."

"Thank you . . . Petros. I'm afraid I still don't know what's acceptable behavior and custom here."

"I think you're adjusting well, considering you were ripped from your home and family, all you knew, and thrown on a strange shore, probably never to see your home again. It would hardly be surprising that you'd have a difficult time adjusting, but from what I see, you've done well. The one thing I wonder is whether you have given serious thought to your future? If you're here for the rest of your life, what is it you want and how can we help you find a place with us?"

"I admit I haven't fully adjusted to everything that's happened, but I appreciate all of the kindness and consideration you and the abbey have given me, and I've wished I could repay you all in some way. That's what I wanted to talk with you about."

They moved into a grove of trees sporting lavender blossoms, some of the petals dropping as the earliest bloomers began to fall. He gathered his thoughts and then came to the point.

"About the poor man with the badly injured leg. I could hear him when they started the amputation." Yozef's expression and voice relived the night before.

Petros sighed. "Yes, a terrible injury. The leg hopelessly injured. There was no option except taking it. Otherwise, he surely would have died after suffering for days or sixdays. There's always danger for such procedures. Unfortunately, his age and weak constitution worked against him. However, I assure you the medicants here are as good as any in the province. If they couldn't save him, it's unlikely anyone could have."

"I don't doubt their skill, Petros. What I'm wondering is whether the pain and shock of the surgery killed him and not the injury itself."

"Well . . . yes," said a puzzled brother. "The stress on him was simply too much."

"What if he hadn't felt the surgery? What if he had been unconscious at the time?"

"Then he might have lived. But we only have two ways to produce unconsciousness. One is with drugs, but these are in terribly short supply with the Narthani embargo and are severely rationed. In fact, at the moment we have no supply at all here at the abbey. The medicants are delaying every surgery they can until a new supply comes, but the man couldn't wait.

"The second method is a careful blow to the head. It's a well-tested method, using a small sack of wet sand and a skilled blow to the back of the head to induce unconsciousness. Here again, the man was unfortunate. He'd had a serious head injury when younger, and they feared the blow would kill him. It was a hard decision to try the surgery while he was conscious and hope he could come through with God's grace."

"Petros, you know I was a student. I've spoken with the abbot briefly about this. Our school, er . . . scholasticum, believed in education in many subjects, so the student has basic knowledge in many fields before specializing. My main study was what we called 'chemistry,' the mixing of materials to produce other and different materials."

"Something like our apothecaries?" said Petros.

"Not exactly. Some students specialized to be apothecaries, but chemistry studies how to produce substances that could be used in other skills and trades."

"This sounds like some of what many of our craftsmen do. Their procedures are usually specific to the trade, but am I understanding you were being trained in such procedures for use in many different trades?"

"Something like that, Petros. But more in learning basic skills to create entirely new products not previously known."

"If you don't know what the product is, why would you make it?"

"Perhaps I'm not explaining well, but we believe that by knowing many skills, you could combine them in new ways not previously conceived."

Petros rubbed his trim gray beard. "Well, I suppose I can see some reasoning in that. So, you trained in this 'chemistry'?"

"Yes. And that's what I want to talk with you about. One of the new substances that can be made by mixing two different known substances is called 'ether.'"

"Ether?" said Petros, carefully pronouncing it. "And what is this ether good for?"

"It has many uses, most of which I don't understand or couldn't explain—remember my education wasn't complete. But the one use is that if a person inhales just a few breaths of it, he goes into a deep sleep and will not waken for perhaps an hour or more."

Petros didn't know where Yozef was headed. "I can see it useful if someone cannot get to sleep . . . so I guess it would have its uses."

"No, Petros. Not just a deep sleep. They will be unconscious and not react to *anything* for that time. It's used in surgical procedures the same way as the drugs or blows are used by your medicants. After an hour or more, the person comes awake with no harm, which the blow to the head might cause."

Petros had stopped on the path and turned facing Yozef, his face blank as he considered what he'd just heard. A look of wonder developed. "My God," he whispered, his eyes refocused on Yozef, "and since you're telling me this, does this mean you know how to make this 'ether?'"

"I believe so. I've never made it myself, but I think I remember enough of the steps that it can be done."

"My God," Petros repeated. "We need to talk to Diera, Sistian, and the other medicants of this! They will think it a gift and a sign from God!"

Petros grasped Yozef's left arm in a vise-like grip for someone his age, and, linked together, they hustled to the main courtyard, through the main gate, and along the pebble path to the Beynom's residence outside the complex.

Diera Beynom answered Petros's loud knocking, surprised to see the excited, bent brother pulling on Yozef and by Petros's insistence on seeing her and the abbot "immediately." She led them to a sitting room, while she went to pull Sistian from his reading. It took Petros only a few minutes to lay out to the abbot and the abbess what Yozef told him. As proficient as Yozef had become in the language, he had trouble following the rapid-fire speech of the excited Petros and questions by the abbot and the leading medicant.

Diera turned to Yozef. "You say you know how to make this ether, but have you ever made it yourself and used it?"

"No," said Yozef. "As I told Brother Fitham, ether use wasn't part of my education, but I know how to make it."

"Tell us more about this ether," prompted Diera.

"It's a liquid. If I recall, it smells sweet. It's easy to make in principle, but the exact details would have to be tested. The person to undergo surgery is allowed to breathe it. I think a bag holding some of the ether and held over the nose and mouth would work. For exactly how long, I don't know, but only until the person is unconscious. The doses and how exactly it's used I also don't know, so we'll have to carefully test this. There may be side effects—I don't remember for sure. I do know it can be addictive and harmful if inhaled too much and too often, so it should be carefully controlled. Too much can kill, and that could happen without warning. Maybe it just puts the person into such a deep sleep, he stops breathing. It wasn't my field of study. I remember that it's extremely dangerous to work with. I mean, like, *extremely* flammable, so care has to be taken in making and using it. Oh, and I already said it's highly flammable. Extreme precautions are needed to keep it away from any flame or embers. It can also break down into other compounds that are dangerous, that can explode. I think you need to keep it out of the sun also and probably in a cool place. And very volatile, so it has to be kept in a tightly sealed container, probably glass. It cannot be stored too long, so you would need to make new runs occasionally, even when there is some left from older batches."

Yozef stopped talking, aware he was rattling on. Three different expressions faced him: Petros smiling, Diera hopeful, and Sistian skeptical.

"Yozef, excuse me for asking," Sistian said, "but this is something we've never heard of. You've been recovering from whatever happened to you. It's not unreasonable for us to wonder about what you're saying."

Yozef nodded. "I understand, Abbot. I hope you'll not be offended if I say that your people aren't always aware of what may be common knowledge elsewhere in the world. You and I have discussed this before. Different peoples have not just different customs but can also have different knowledge. I've got the impression that there are things here in Caedellium unknown to my people at home, and the reverse is also true, such as the ether."

"Yozef is right," Diera said to her husband. "When I studied medicine on Landolin those years ago, I learned many things that I brought back to Caedellium. Others had the same experience. It's a problem that our peoples don't share enough knowledge, because of either the distances or willingness. That this ether may be in common usage elsewhere in the world isn't strange."

While the abbot was obviously not convinced, he looked mollified. "What would you need to make some of this ether, Yozef?"

With that simple question, Yozef's isolation from the world outside the abbey ended.

Making Ether

Whatever reservations the abbot had about Yozef's claims of a miracle compound, he had no hesitation in providing Yozef with whatever was needed. By noon the next day, Yozef met with men called to the abbey by the abbot—an apothecary, a metal worker, a glass blower, and a brewer. Each of the four tradesmen owned a shop with workers, and none of the four knew exactly what Yozef expected of them, even after a summary by the abbot and a longer explanation by Yozef. They were there and willing to listen simply because the abbot asked them. Accompanying the brewer was a Preddi refugee who knew of crude batch distillation for a drink favored by the Narthani. He had worked in a shop in Preddi City before he and his family fled from Preddi Province to Eywell and then across the Eywellese border into Keelan.

They needed only two ingredients to produce diethyl ether: pure ethanol and a high enough concentration of sulfuric acid. The ethanol was easy. Though they could have started with wine, the brewer already had gallons of distillate with a higher ethanol content. It was simply a matter of making the brewer and Preddi refugee understand Yozef needed to further distill out alcohol with none of the flavorings or other components of the harsh whiskey they produced.

The acid was harder. Yozef didn't know how concentrated the acid had to be, so they settled for what was available and hoped it would work. It took some time before the apothecary understood that Yozef's sulfuric acid was their "vitriol," a corrosive liquid with various uses and to which the metal worker had access.

In two days they gathered the ingredients, but the distillation equipment took longer. In principle, the apparatus was simple. A glass retort, or reaction vessel, would hold whatever liquid needed to be separated into one or more of its components. A narrow opening at the top of the vessel connected to a vertical glass column. The first try at the equipment they settled on was a column about 18 inches long. Just before the top of the column, a glass sidearm was fused to the column and ran diagonally down to a waiting collection flask.

The sidearm proved a difficult part for the glassblower, because not only did it have to be connected to the vertical column so vapors could enter the sidearm, the sidearm itself needed to be encased in a second tube through which water could be run to cool the vapors. On heating the reaction vessel and the enclosed liquid, the vapors rose in the vertical column to the level of the sidearm. When the vapors entered the sidearm, they were cooled by the water jacket, were condensed back into a liquid, and ran down the sidearm into a waiting receptacle.

They also needed thermometers placed at the top of the vertical column and inside the reaction vessel. To Yozef's chagrin and initial dismay, there were no thermometers. It was a problem he would encounter again and again: each piece of knowledge or technology needing other pieces. It took Yozef several hours to explain to the glass blower that they needed a small reservoir of mercury leading to a fine capillary about a foot long, all sealed in glass. Fortunately, mercury was known and supplied by the metal worker.

How the glass blower managed to make the thermometers, Yozef never asked, but a sixday later the blower showed up with several versions. They were far thicker than thermometers Yozef had used on Earth, and the capillary wider than any he had ever seen. To his relief, when they warmed the bulbous end, the mercury rose in the capillary.

The next problem was the uniqueness of each crude thermometer—different in length and capillary diameter—and none had calibrations. Boiling water and ice—sourced from deep caves in the mountains of northeast Keelan—let them mark 0°C and 100°C on each thermometer. Since the target temperature was 140°C, but not above 160°C, where spontaneous ignition could occur, they needed calibrations higher than 100°C. The only way was to boil liquids that had higher vaporization temperatures. The only available candidate Yozef could dredge out of his memory was olive oil at 300°C. He knew *that* number only because his ex-girlfriend read somewhere that olive oil began smoking at about 240°C, which was a sign of breakdown products that were supposed to be bad for your health. They had been cooking with olive oil then, and Julie wanted to stop. It took some library and Internet research and talking to convince her it was okay. The olive oil would give approximate thermometer calibrations at 240° and 300°, leaving a considerable gap from 100°, but at least they'd have the target temperatures bracketed.

By the vagaries of chance, one of the trees transplanted from Earth was the olive, and a large black version was occasionally served or appeared in dishes. A check with the abbey dining hall confirmed the use of olive oil in cooking.

Yozef and several workers provided by the tradesmen assembled the final distillation test apparatus and were ready to calibrate. Yozef explained they'd assume the mercury rise in a capillary to be linear, and equal increases in temperature would lead to equal rises in the mercury. That no two thermometers were identical meant that every thermometer had to be calibrated separately. They used olive oil to estimate where 140ºC should be on a given thermometer and ran the ether-producing reaction to that point—from a distance and checking the readings behind a shield with a pinhole. If the apparatus didn't explode, they assumed the temperature was no more than 160º.

By this time, only the brewer and the glass blower of the four initial tradesmen remained active in the project. Each supplied materials and labor as requested by the abbot. In the end, it was Filtin Fuller, the glass blower's assistant and occasional drinking companion at the Snarling Graeko, who most quickly grasped Yozef's directions and became de facto leader of the workers. Not that any of the workers fully understood why or what they were doing, but for some reason, Filtin had faith that Yozef probably knew what he was doing. Probably.

A morning finally came for the first runs of ether. Yozef looked at the final apparatus and shook his head. He couldn't believe they were really trying to make ether with this cluster-fuck of a setup. Back home, every safety agency and official on Earth would be screaming at them. He hoped this worked and they didn't kill themselves or anyone else.

Although the reaction called for a continuous addition of ethanol, Yozef settled on self-contained runs of equal starting volumes and stopping the reactions after different reductions in volume. They allowed the products collected from the sidearm to cool, and Yozef smelled the products. Three of five products smelled right for ether.

CHAPTER 16

GUINEA PIGS

Patient Number 1

By midday meal, word spread through the complex, and the afternoon found Yozef, the workers, Petros, Sistian, Diera, and more than a dozen medicants and other abbey staff gathered in an operating room. A coney lay on its back, tied by straps to a board. The rabbit-sized animal filled a similar ecological niche and was the source of some of the unidentified meat in abbey stews. Diera followed what few suggestions Yozef had for the ether application and poured the liquid onto a folded cloth and held it over the coney's nostrils. It squealed, took several gasping breaths, and was unconscious within seconds. The palpable astonishment lasted two minutes, while everyone waited to see whether the coney lived and still breathed.

"It seems the ether puts the coney to sleep," said Diera.

An audible sigh surfaced from the gathering, accompanied by smiles and a few exclamations.

"But does the coney feel pain and would it awaken?" She took a needle and pricked one of the paws between digits, watching for the normal withdrawal reflexes and vocal complaints. The coney never twitched.

"So much for the minor discomfort, but what about serious pain such as a surgical operation might entail?"

"Amputate a leg," said Fitham.

The others looked at him, a little surprised at the cold-blooded suggestion from the elderly brother.

"It's going into the pot anyway one of these nights. Let it help us see if the ether works."

"Yes, Diera," Sistian agreed, "go ahead and take off a leg and sew him up as if it were a person. We'll see how the coney responds."

Diera nodded and left the room for a few minutes, returning with a rolling cart of surgical tools, needles, the local version of catgut for sutures, and cloths for staunching blood. Another medicant assisted. She made a first cut through fur and underlying skin layers at a forepaw joint. The coney didn't respond. She proceeded to cut quickly through the muscles and ligaments, sawed through the thin bone, and sewed a flap of skin over the exposed end of the limb. The coney never twitched, and its chest rose and fell in normal rhythm.

"Blessed by the Almighty God if I don't think it worked like Yozef said it would," she said in awe.

They unstrapped the coney and placed it in a cage with an old blanket on the floor as a cushion, and all retired for the evening. The next morning the coney was awake and moving about the cage, albeit slowly and obviously in discomfort.

Human Patient Number 1

Several of the medicants were eager to use the ether on human patients waiting for surgery. Yozef discouraged the rush, and Diera agreed and enforced that they'd run additional trials on larger animals to test dosages and effects. Subsequent results with goats and yearling cattle showed that a few drops in a leather bag with the end held over the nostrils sufficed to put the animals into a sleep, the depth of which was dependent on how long they applied the ether. Longer and larger doses confirmed it was possible to stop the animal's breathing. After another sixday, Diera agreed they were ready.

The first patient was a pregnant young woman. Diera met with all of the complex's medicants, the abbot, and Yozef. She started off summarizing the situation.

"The child is in breech position. The mother has been in labor for over a day, and we haven't been able to turn the baby head down for normal birth. Prospects for both the mother and the child are grim. We don't see any option, except to remove the baby surgically. Normally, we would use opiates to put the mother to sleep, even though it involves danger to the baby's breathing. We lose about a third of the babies with such a procedure. In this case, we have no opiates and the only option would be to tie the mother to the operating table and remove the child as quickly as possible and sew the mother closed. We expect to lose at least half of the mothers."

Diera paused, reached out, and picked up a small dark glass bottle containing ether. "After extensive discussion among the medicant staff and in consultation with Abbot Sistian, we have offered the option to the woman and her husband to try the ether produced by Yozef. We have warned the family of the risk of an untried procedure, and the husband and the wife have both agreed to try the ether to avoid the alternative."

She looked around the room and continued. "In spite of our discussing this at great length, are there any final comments or thoughts?"

There were none.

"Then let us begin. The patient is in the surgical room next door."

Yozef followed the abbey staff next door to a moaning woman lying with arms and legs strapped to an operating platform. Two female medicants held her hands and wiped sweat and tears from her face. Pain and fear chased each other across her face. The husband waited outside, as was the custom on Caedellium.

Brother Dyllis was to be the lead surgeon, and he and his assistants moved quickly. Everything had been planned, and they didn't delay. Two sections of raised steps had been put together and placed on both sides of the table to allow staff to see the details of the operation. Yozef cringed at the lack of masks and the larger-than-necessary room but didn't see it as the time to bring up aseptic conditions.

He stood on a top step, looking over people's heads and down at the woman. Though the room seemed chill to him, his shirt armpits were soaked, and a cold sweat ran down his neck and back. While all of the tests checked out, this was for real. The assurances from Diera that this was the woman's and the child's best option had not assuaged the voice nagging him that he had facilitated something based on so little experience, and something that could kill one or both of the patients. His breathing was deep and harsh, just short of gasps, as his lungs hyperventilated.

Dyllis removed the cloths covering the woman's swollen abdomen. Another sister swabbed the abdomen with what appeared to be concentrated soapy water. Yozef later learned the cloths and the instruments had been boiled in acidified water. While the woman was being prepped, Dyllis, another brother, and a sister washed their hands and forearms with soap and a basin of evidently water hot enough to give off steam but tolerable to the three medicants.

Sister Varnia held a leather sack serving to deliver the ether, while Brother Bolwyn unstoppered the brown bottle. He shook ether drops into the bag, Varnia closed the opening, rotated the bag several times, then opened it again and placed the opening over the mouth and the nose of the suffering woman. Her eyes widened, as the bag covered much of her face. She took several shallow breaths, gasped as the ether hit her, then closed her eyes. Varnia bent to put one ear to the woman's chest and the other ear to hear the woman's breathing, keeping the bag over the patient's mouth and nose. Dyllis kept a hand on the woman's chest to follow her breathing and motioned for Varnia to remove the bag. Everyone in the room held their collective breaths while they watched the woman. Her chest rose and fell in normal rhythm.

Dyllis continued checking her pulse and breathing. "Everything seems normal at this point. Now we'll check for responses." The classic knee-jerk response was positive, as were iris responses to a light held close. "Now for pain." He took a large needle and did a minor stab to her forearm. No response. Dyllis looked up at the observers and nodded, then repeated the test at several other parts of her anatomy with increasing force.

"No response to the pricks and breathing still normal. We're ready to proceed." He looked at Diera, who nodded assent to continue. Varnia swabbed the woman's abdomen again. Dyllis picked up a scalpel-like instrument and made a quick, shallow, vertical cut in the abdomen. He pulled back to observe whether there was any response. "No response," said Dyllis with more than a little wonder in his voice. "I'll proceed with removing the baby."

Dyllis stepped forward and with a quick and steady hand cut through the abdominal muscles and then the uterus, exposing the placenta. More careful strokes and the baby was exposed, then pulled out from the mother. The umbilical cord was cut and the baby given to another medicant, who carried out the classic swat on the butt while holding the baby by its feet. The collective exhalation of breaths was matched in intensity by the wail of the single small source. While the baby was further stimulated and cleaned, Dyllis applied a gentle pull on the umbilical cord until the placenta came out through the incision, and the mother was sewn closed.

Dyllis again checked the mother's vitals, then announced, "Procedure is complete, mother and baby survived to this point."

Applause and exultations broke out from the audience, followed by multiple conversations and congratulations all around. Yozef was exhausted.

He had never imagined how standing and watching something could be so draining.

The following minutes were still tense, as they waited for the mother to awaken, as well as to see whether either she or her new daughter showed any ill effects. The woman awoke less than twenty minutes after the operation. It took her ten minutes to go from first responsiveness to being awake enough to answer questions. She was in pain, though not exceptional, all things considering.

By the next day, she was eating, was talking freely, and had started nursing. Abbot Sistian held a special ceremony that evening in the cathedral. He had insisted Yozef attend and gave effusive thanks, first to God, of course, then to Yozef.

Patient Number 4

During the next two sixdays, two more surgeries were successful using ether anesthetic. One patient was a tree cutter whose forearm had to be amputated, and a second involved a badly infected wisdom tooth. Yozef didn't see either patient but was called on for a third case. He was with his three full-time workers in a new ether shop, housed in a small building outside Abersford, and was inspecting the latest changes in the procedure. They were about to start a reaction run with a new vessel setup when Brother Alber arrived.

"Yozef, Sister Diera asks you come to the abbey. She has a patient she wants to ask you about."

"A patient? Why does the Abbess want *me?*"

"I'm just the messenger," groused Alber. "I was doing an inventory of the hospital supply room when she came in and asked me to find you."

"Okay, I'll be right with you." Yozef turned to Filtin Fuller, the youngest of his workers and the most innovative. Yozef and Carnigan's sometime drinking companion at the Snarling Graeko was on long-term loan from the glass-blowing shop. "Go ahead with your tests, and I'll be back as soon as I find out what the abbess wants."

A small two-seat cart was outside the shop, its stocky brown work pony untied and waiting patiently. Alber hustled Yozef onto the narrow bench, and they were off as soon as Yozef's rear hit the wood. The cart wasn't intended for the quick pace Alber pressed, and Yozef and his rear were relieved the trip to the hospital was short. Within a treatment room, Abbess Beynom attended a teenage boy of about seventeen years. She looked up as Yozef came in.

"Yozef, thank you for coming so soon. Come look at this." She indicated the patient lying on the table and covered with a cloth. Yozef approached as she pulled down the cloth to expose the lower abdomen. The boy sweated profusely, obviously in pain. The lower right of the abdomen appeared distended and flushed. Diera put her hand lightly on the area, and the boy flinched and groaned even at her light touch. "The skin is hot. Experience indicates the origin of the problem is the . . . ," and Diera used a new Caedelli word.

It must be appendicitis and a new word for my dictionary.

"Are you talking about the small extension of the intestines where it bends here?" He pointed to the boy's lower right abdomen.

"Yes," said a surprised Diera. "You know of this structure?" They exchanged words, and Yozef did his usual categorization and word substitution.

"Yes, it's the appendix and the illness is caused by some obstruction that leads to the death of the tissue," he confirmed.

Diera listened to Yozef's casual comment, raised a questioning eyebrow, nodded, and said, "Our only treatment is to make the patient as comfortable as possible and hope for his recovery. If the pain gets severe enough, we would normally give him small amounts of opiates to help, but since we have none left and since your ether is more a short-term solution to pain, there's nothing more we can do. I asked you to come when it occurred to me your people might have a treatment we don't have."

"There's only one treatment I know of, and that's to remove the appendix."

"Remove it?" said a surprised Abbess. "That carries as much risk as letting the body heal itself, due to the risk of shock from any surgery, from blood loss, and from corruption. I suppose your ether solves much of the first problem, but there are still the other two. And doesn't the appendix perform some function? Many medicants think it has something to do with digestion."

"I don't think blood loss is a problem, Abbess. The loss is minimal when removing the appendix, since there are few blood vessels running directly to it from the larger parts of the intestine." *Thank you, Biology 101.* "As for function, it can be removed without harm . . . as far as my people know." Yozef remembered there was still uncertainty about whether the appendix was an unnecessary vestigial structure or had an immunological role. He didn't want to delve into either possibility, especially since the vestigial option led to dangerous territory. He wasn't ready to say anything about organism development, evolution, and who knew what else, until he understood more of their religion and origin myths.

"If it has no function, why does it exist?"

Yozef shrugged, but Diera's reservations were evident.

"Then there's corruption," she went on.

"Corruption's a problem but can be minimized by aseptic conditions."

"Aseptic? Another of your words I don't know the reference to."

"Well, you know, to prevent bacteria from getting to the incision?"

She frowned, frustrated, "Another word. Bacteria? What's bacteria?"

Whoops. He had to remember to think before speaking. Did they even know of the existence of microorganisms? If they washed their hands, bandages, and instruments before surgery, why wouldn't they know about bacteria?

"Why do you wash or wipe everything involved in surgery?" Yozef asked.

"It started as a custom to signify purifying the body in preparation for asking God's mercy, then came to be seen as helping to reduce corruption. How is not certain, but some believe it also wards off dangerous humors. Whatever the cause, it has a positive effect, and it's standard procedure."

Okay. No knowledge of bacteria. Another place he needed to start introducing new ideas. He wasn't sure whether this was one of those times but plunged ahead, regardless.

Yozef took a deep breath. "Bacteria are tiny animals that are so small, you cannot see them, and they are everywhere. They get into a wound or an incision from surgery, and, once inside the body, they multiply and attack it. There are different kinds, and some cause disease and not just corruption. This process we call 'infections' and is due to the bacteria."

Her demeanor reminded Yozef of parents listening to an outrageous story from a child, perhaps a story the child believed to be true.

"Now, Yozef," she said in a gentle tone, "how can there be animals you can't see?"

"Why not?" he returned. "Consider the balmoth." Yozef had seen pictures of the huge herbivore. Supposedly, there had once been many more of the giants on the island, but numbers had been reduced to small groups in the upland forests. They looked very much like the prehistoric mammal

Paraceratheriums of Earth, extinct there for tens of millions of years. At that moment, the thought occurred to him that the balmoth looked *too* much like the extinct Earth mammal. Could the transplantation from Earth to Anyar have been going on much longer than he thought? He had been assuming the Earth-like animals and plants were brought here only in the last five thousand years.

"Think of the balmoth," he repeated. "Now consider a smaller animal, maybe a large horse. Then one smaller and smaller. What is the smallest known animal?"

Humoring him for the moment, she said, "Well, I guess there are some very small insects. I've seen some so tiny, you only notice them when a dark one moves across a white surface, and only if you're looking right at it at that moment. Brother Wallington knows more about such things. He's made his life study the animals and the plants of Caedellium."

I'll have to talk with this Wallington.

"What if there are animals smaller than those insects? So small your eye can't see them. Just because they're smaller than your eye can detect doesn't mean they aren't there."

Diera hesitated as she considered this reasoning. "Yes, I can see what you say. I had never thought of it that way. It could be a Fallacy of Yodrill."

"A what of who?"

"Yodrill was a scholastic long ago from Melosia. He described a method of logical thinking about any problem. Among his writings are descriptions of common errors in reasoning, still called the Fallacies of Yodrill. What you're saying is that we're making the fallacy of assuming something doesn't exist if we don't see it. This particular fallacy is warned against when one believes a technique is impossible because one hasn't seen it work, or a place doesn't exist because one hasn't been there. The animals too small to see could be another example. That doesn't prove they *do* exist, only that they *could* exist.

"Anyway," Yozef said, "you already do procedures that help with destroying these bacteria, you just need to do even more. For example, the surgeries would best be done in closed rooms that have been vigorously cleaned, where the outside air is not free to bring in more bacteria. The same with too many people in the room. Only those medicants performing the surgery should be present, and all should wear clean clothing and masks, so you won't breathe on any open incisions."

Yozef stopped with his suggestions. Those were all he could remember from TV, movies, and books. He also thought it best not to hit Diera with too much at one time.

CHAPTER 17

IMPACT

Discomforting Hope

Later that evening, Sistian Beynom returned from visiting a nearby village and found his wife sitting on their porch, staring off into the twilight. He climbed the six steps and stood beside her. She continued her faraway gaze, oblivious to his presence.

"Diera?" he asked softly. No response. "Diera!" he said more urgently, now beginning to be concerned. She stirred, her eyes focusing, and noticed him standing next to her.

"Oh, Sistian. I didn't see you come."

"Is everything all right, Diera?"

"All right?" she echoed. "Is everything all right? I think it is. Maybe that's the problem. I think everything is all right, though I'm not sure."

Sistian sat next her and took one of her hands in his. "What's the matter, dear?"

She looked at him, saw his concern, and gave a small and what she hoped was reassuring smile. "It's nothing to worry about. Not as if I'm ill or anything. It's just that I have so many emotions right now, I'm not sure *what* I'm feeling."

"What kind of emotions?"

She smiled wryly, "Confusion, wonder, caution, fear, surprise, hope, excitement."

"About what?"

"About how we help people. How we practice medicine. Are we much better than the primitive tribal shamans in our histories and stories, treating patients with concoctions of herbs and whatnot because of superstitions?"

Sistian frowned. Diera was among the most conscientious medicants he knew, totally committed to helping her patients, and tireless in searching for new medicines and procedures. She fought endless skirmishes, especially with older medicants who resisted changing practices long established, whether or not they seemed efficacious.

"I assume something happened today to suddenly make you doubt your calling."

"Oh, yes. Not only s*omething* happened, but *someone*. Yozef."

"Yozef?" said a startled Sistian. "What happened today involving Yozef?"

Diera described to her husband the patient brought in with the abdominal pain and her calling in Yozef to see if his people knew of any treatment for the conditions.

"And did he know something?"

"Dearest, he not only knew what the problem was, he told me how to cure it, what caused it, and gave an explanation about the general causes of diseases."

Sistian sat back in his chair. "Those are quite astounding assertions. I think you need to tell me more details."

For the next half hour, the abbess did. She recounted Yozef's knowing details of the "appendix," as he called it, and giving a plausible explanation of the pain, of fever, of the consequences without treatment, of the surgical treatment, and of the tiny animals that cause many diseases.

"How do you know what he told you is accurate? He's not a medicant himself."

"Ah, Sistian," his wife murmured, "as usual, you have cut right to the heart of the matter. You're right. Yozef is not a trained medicant. In many ways, he's ignorant of details of treating illness and injuries. That's what is hitting me the most. What he considers common knowledge may be more than all we think we know. And how should that make me feel? Like one of those primitive tribal shamans?"

"Again, how do you know what he told you is true?"

"Because he described how the appendix should be cut out by surgery and what precautions to take. I wonder now at myself, but somehow—how I don't know—I believed everything he told me. It just sounded so *right*. So logical. So explanatory of many things we don't understand." She paused. "So I authorized the surgery he recommended."

"Diera!" exclaimed a shocked Sistian. "Based only on Yozef's statements, you performed surgery and cut out a patient's . . . appendix?"

"Yes. I spoke with Yozef at mid-morning, and we performed the surgery before midday. The patient woke about an hour after the surgery, and he was in less pain than before, even after being cut open, his appendix removed, and being sewn back closed. Before I left the hospital, he asked for food, talked to his family, and wondered how soon he could return home."

Diera looked at her husband. "Sistian, under normal circumstances it would be as if a miracle from God had happened. At least half of the people with this condition die, and the rest undergo agonizing pain and fever for sometimes sixdays. This man wants to go home tomorrow!"

"Isn't that a good thing?"

"Sistian, Yozef dropped this on me with no idea of its importance. It was just a trivial piece of information that was common knowledge with his people. Yet it was unknown to us here on Caedellium, and nothing like anything I'd heard when I was studying in Landolin. Granted, we still need to see if there are any side effects and if any corruption—or infection, as Yozef says—occurs. However, barring those, the patient will be considered cured within days. I then think of all of the patients with this same condition that we . . . I . . . lost over the years because of our ignorance."

"Diera, if all of this is true, I shouldn't have to remind you of all of the patients you'll save in the future."

"I realize that, dear. I honestly do. And I thank God for the knowledge Yozef shares with us. But there's more. Yozef gave an explanation of why patients get worse and often die of this condition."

Diera went on to describe the concept of microscopic creatures that cause both infections and disease.

"Well, this is more your field than mine, and maybe some of the scholastics', but I don't recall ever hearing about such tiny creatures."

"That's because no one has."

"Then how do you know they exist?"

"I don't *know*, but I'm convinced. You've talked with Yozef. You're as good a judge of people as anyone I know, and, frankly, I think I'm not too bad at it either. If anything, he seems naïve but honest. When you talk to him, and he drops these morsels of knowledge on us, it always seems without ulterior motive. It just seems *right* when you have time to think about it. And these 'microorganisms,' as he calls them. First, I've been sitting here thinking about it the last hour or so. It would explain *so* much. And in addition, he doesn't just state their existence, he says how we can fashion a reverse telescope to see them."

"A reverse telescope?"

"Yes. Instead of making things distant, you can make them appear closer. Yozef says by using different-shaped lenses, we can make small things appear larger. He's going to talk to his workmen and set them the task of making what he calls *microscopes*."

Diera sighed. "I also have the intuition Yozef knows much more than he's said so far, and although I need to continue talking with him, I already suspect our practice of medicine is in the process of nothing short of an epic change. Thus, all my emotions. Confusion. Wondering what obvious procedures we've missed and why we have thought our medical knowledge was so advanced. Wonder at what I saw today. Caution that I shouldn't expect too much too soon, since only time confirms how well this new knowledge is put into effect. Surprise that this has hit me so hard. Hope for more knowledge we can help people with. Excitement at what may come. And—fear."

"Fear?"

Diera nodded. "Fear my hopes are too high at the moment. Fear the patient may still die. Fear the appendix we removed is a necessary part of the body or mind, in spite of what Yozef says. Fear there may come such momentous changes that many, including even some of the medicants and the scholastics at St. Sidryn's, will resist and condemn. Fear of exactly who and what is Yozef? The ether, and now this today? What more may come? We want to attribute such things to the grace of God, but could it be a clever ploy of the Evil One? Is this simply a case of Caedellium being so remote from the rest of Anyar that we are backward, or could it be Yozef is an agent of God? If so, to what purpose? Why now?"

Sistian had no answers, nor did he think his wife was asking for them. She was recounting questions without answers. Questions that Sistian would consider many times in the days, months, and years to come.

Dissemination

In the following sixdays, Diera spoke with Yozef almost daily, probing for pieces of information. Yozef willingly offered suggestions, though often had no clues about practical matters, to Diera's awkward gratification that the implementation was still dependent on her and the other medicants. Assuming the knowledge he claimed was accurate, an initially prodigious qualification neutralized the more they talked, Diera's understanding of the functioning of the human body multiplied several-fold. So quickly did her confidence grow that she abandoned her initial reticence to bring in other medicants until she had more evidence about the accuracy of what Yozef was telling her. There was simply too much to think about. She knew she was risking resistance among the older medicants, so the first three she brought in to help were the two younger surgeons, Saoul Dyllis and Arnik Bolwyn, and Wilwin Wallington, the scholastic of the animals and the plants of Caedellium. She felt these three were among the more mentally flexible of the brothers and the sisters. Dyllis was skeptical at first but served as a good counterweight to Diera's and Bolywin's rising enthusiasm. It was brother Wallington who surprised her. While he was diligent in his common duties around the abbey complex, and no one doubted his commitment to his chosen specialty, he was never considered one of the abbey's more illustrious staff members.

Brother Wallington became Yozef's adoring slave, once he was convinced by the first microscopes of the existence of a whole new realm of creatures previously unknown. He was endlessly enthralled by the multifaceted protozoans, while the two medicants were interested in bacteria. Wallington's total acceptance of the concept of invisible-to-the-naked-eye creatures helped convince the other staff at the abbey.

During the following months, Yozef's discussions with Diera introduced an array of new ideas, some of which were adopted immediately, some slated perhaps to the future, and others proved impractical, either technically or because there was no scaffold of current Caedellium knowledge and custom to hang them on. Among those immediately workable, or with some reasonable development, were stethoscopes, Ringers solution, plasma for blood loss and shock, hypodermics, the possibility of blood transfusions (though only considering AB factors, not +/-, so only in emergencies), and cardiopulmonary resuscitation (CPR). The last innovation met with significant trepidation, because it was viewed by many common people and even some medicants as reviving the dead, a power appropriate only for God—or possibly the Evil One, to create his demonic agents.

Once Yozef convinced Diera of the possibility of microorganisms as a cause of corruption, the St. Sidryn's medicants began using Yozef's suggestions about the surgical environment. He also suggested stronger acidic solutions once he remembered that an early antiseptic was carbolic acid, phenol by chemical composition. No Anyar versions of phenol were identifiable, and the easiest source Yozef could remember was the distillation of phenol from coal tar, a process not immediately possible. As substitutes, he suggested acetic acid (vinegar) and boric acid made from the mineral borax, available locally. In neither case could Yozef give advice on concentration, other than low, but Diera didn't seem concerned about figuring out optimal concentrations.

He also championed ethanol. Since it was already being distilled as part of the ether production, source wasn't a problem. He remembered it needed to be 70 percent ethanol in water to kill germs—something to do with attacking cell membranes more efficiently at that concentration, not that he tried to explain cell structure.

He didn't witness the introduction of more stringent asepsis, but from the Beynoms' older son, Cadwulf, Yozef learned details of the storm ignited in getting medicants to change long-established traditions, especially the older medicants and those feeling threatened by an off-islander's strange ideas. In the end, all but the most close-minded medicants admitted that the new aseptic conditions reduced infections, and only one medicant was so stubborn that Diera finally decertified him as a medicant anywhere in the district.

Similar discord occurred in other Keelan Province districts before increased aseptic procedures spread to other provinces. The information dissemination was fueled by Diera sending reports to medicants throughout Keelan who she believed would be most open-minded about this flood of novel procedures and knowledge. From there, the knowledge spread throughout Caedellium, and the reputation and rumors about Yozef Kolsko added to those already circulating about ether.

Yozef tried to be careful with what he revealed to Diera, for fear that too much information would raise worries as to who, or what, he was. Whenever the probing of Diera or the other medicants approached dangerous ground, he feigned ignorance. One strategy he adopted was to pretend some tidbit of knowledge just occurred to him, but that this was all he knew. While this didn't satisfy the more insistent inquisitors, it usually ended a delicate line of probing. The inadvertent side effect, and one to which Yozef was oblivious until it was too late to squash rumors, was that Yozef was literally "hearing" the information, with consequences in times to come.

CHAPTER 18

SUPPLICANT TO TYCOON

In the months since his arrival on Anyar, Yozef had had no expenses. The abbey provided food, clothing, and shelter, and Carnigan paid at the pub. Introducing ether for anesthesia gave Yozef his first independent income.

Abbot Beynom first mentioned charges for the ether. "All of our patients are expected to pay for their treatment, assuming they can afford the payments. If not, the payment is reduced or forgiven. The poppy extract had gotten so expensive that the abbey tried to absorb all of the cost, but that was becoming more difficult even before the Narthani cut off trade. Now, poppy extract is virtually impossible to obtain, no matter the price. It's only reasonable that the cost of the ether should be included in what the patient pays."

The abbot raised an eyebrow at Yozef. "Do you have any thoughts about what the cost should be? It should cover the production and a small income for yourself."

"Sorry, Abbot. I've no idea about Caedellium or Keelan money. I would depend on your advice."

"I wondered about that myself," Sistian smiled. "It's quite simple. There are a few differences among the provinces, but most use the same system as Keelan."

The abbot reached into his desk and withdrew a small clinking sack from which he took out a handful of coins and spread them out on his desktop.

"There are four coins, two silver and two gold. The small silver is one krun, large silver five kruns, small gold twenty kruns, and large gold hundred kruns."

Yozef had seen the coins in the pub but hadn't noticed details until now. The sizes seemed standardized, and each coin had a number stamped on one side and a six-pointed star on the other.

"What do the numbers and symbols stand for?"

Sistian picked up a hundred-krun gold and pointed to the number. "The coins are made in Orosz City, the center of Orosz Province. Clans or individuals can take gold and silver there to be turned into coins. That's to assure all coins are the proper size and weight. The number identifies a specific batch of coins, in case there's a problem." He turned the coin over. "The star is a general symbol of Caedellium. Coins from other parts of Anyar are sometimes used, though people are cautious about using them because we can't be sure of the value of the gold and silver they're made of. A few clans also have their own coins, but Keelan and most clans use the common krun coins made in Orosz City. There are also small copper coins for values less than a small silver one krun coin, but those aren't made in Orosz City."

"What does a krun or a hundred kruns buy?"

"One krun would buy a loaf of bread, a hundred krun a good set of clothes for a common clansman, and an average horse might cost five hundred krun."

"So, Abbot, what would you suggest for the price of the ether?"

Sistian tilted his head up and stroked his beard. "Well, you'll be selling mainly to abbeys in those small dark bottles. From what Diera says, there should be enough in each bottle for at least ten treatments. Let's see . . . I think twenty krun per treatment would be reasonable, which would make it two hundred krun for a bottle." He paused, switching stroking hands. "There're fifteen abbeys in Keelan, so if each one bought one bottle, that would be three thousand krun." He stopped speaking, his eyes widening.

"My word, Yozef. I hadn't realized, but the numbers might get quite high. I'd check with Diera, but our medicant facility is one of the larger, so we would use more bottles than the smaller abbeys. Also, as I remember you saying, the ether goes bad after a few months, so . . . let's say an average of ten bottles per abbey per year." He stopped, eyes widening more. "That's thirty thousand krun a year! And the other provinces will use ether as soon as they hear of it and see it working for themselves!"

The abbot looked at Yozef with a surprised expression. "You're going to become wealthy, unless I'm mistaken, Yozef. Of course, you still have to pay your workers and buy supplies, but still . . . "

Yozef listened to the abbot's estimations and did his own in silence. Even if the abbot overestimated, it sounded as if any issues about supporting himself had just disappeared. His enthusiasm settled as a thought rose up. *The abbey saved and took care of me when I first arrived. Yes, it's part of their calling, but fair is fair.*

And, what about the glassblower and the distiller? They'd been supplying the workers and the materials.

"Abbot Beynom . . . ," he began.

"Please, Yozef, Abbot Sistian is fine, or just Abbot."

"Abbot Sistian, I owe you and your people a great debt for caring for me when I arrived. Then there's the help you gave in convincing the tradesmen to work with me on the ether when they and, let's be honest, even you were uncertain whether I knew what I was talking about. A share of the coin we get from selling the ether needs to go to the tradesmen, and it's only fair you also get a share."

Sistian smiled. "I accept, Yozef. I hesitated to say anything, since it seemed to conflict with the abbey's mandate to serve. I can't take coin myself, but I'm happy to accept it for the abbey."

Thank you, God, prayed the abbot silently. *Once again confirmation of your command we care for our fellows. We cared for the strange man, and, as the* Word *says, "What you give without hesitation will come back to you many-fold."*

"Shall we say," said Sistian, "of the two hundred krun per bottle, the tradesmen will get forty krun and the abbey another forty? You need to talk with the tradesmen to work out paying your workers and buying supplies. Whatever that comes to, I think you'll still keep a good portion of the two hundred krun per bottle."

Thus did Yozef achieve his first income on Anyar. The flow of krun was slow at first, with St. Sidryn's ordering the first bottles. To celebrate that first purchase, Yozef took Carnigan, Cadwulf Beynom, Filtin, and all of his workers to the Snarling Graeko the same night and put the entire purchase price back into the local economy.

Once more he was coinless, though only for a sixday, before an order for two bottles of ether came from the abbey in Clengoth, the district center. Within another sixday, four more orders arrived. As word spread, more orders arrived from more distant abbeys in Keelan, from neighboring Mittack and Gwillamer Provinces, and later from more distant clans. Yozef was at a loss how to fill orders from other provinces, until approached by a traveling trader from Orosz Province. The trader had connections to other traders and proposed he could provide a distribution network for the ether. Yozef consulted Cadwulf and the abbot before accepting the trader's proposal, with relief to be shed of that one task.

At the same time, a second source of income developed. The local brewer, Lunwyn Galfor, produced a crude whiskey from wheat, helped by the escaped Preddi slave whose previous owner had produced alcoholic drinks in Preddi City. Wheat seed was germinated to release enzymes that broke down starch, a natural process that allowed the seedling to access energy stored as starch. By the brewer's steeping the grain as mash for two to three days, the enzymes turned much of the starch into small sugars that could be fermented to produce ethanol. The brewer used a crude copper pot-still to batch distill to produce a liquid that was 25–30 percent ethanol. Based on Yozef's success with ether distillation, the brewer sought Yozef's help in developing a second distillation to increase the ethanol content of his drinks to 40–45 percent, comparable to Earth whiskeys. Yozef's help garnered him a 10 percent share of the profits from whiskey sales within Keelan and exported to other provinces. Although his percentage share was less than with ether, and the price of ethanol per volume was much less than ether, the total volume of sales soon surpassed ether by orders of magnitude. Within two months, Yozef found himself with bags of coins in drawers and under his bed in the abbey room where he still slept.

It was time to find a way to handle the coinage. He procrastinated for several sixdays until he came back to his room one evening to find that a drawer bottom had split under the weight of bags, and coins were scattered across the floor.

By this time, the number of workers in ether and ethanol production had stabilized at five, and he used profits to start development of other products. He was faced with a steady flow of income, increased numbers of workers, and more complex dealings with tradesmen, and keeping it all in order had become a limiting factor in his daily life. Something had to be done.

Though the regular Caedelli lessons with Selmar Beynom had ended months previously, Cadwulf Beynom, the eldest son of Sistian and Diera, had found so many reasons to be around that Yozef suspected the abbot had asked his son to keep an eye on the stranger. Whether to help him or to protect others, Yozef didn't know, although it could be both. The genial Cadwulf was a true convert to the new knowledge Yozef was doling out to the islanders, and whatever the initial impetus of their companionship, it developed into a genuine friendship. The solution came to Yozef's financial organization, or lack thereof, when he complained to Cadwulf as the two were eating the morning meal at the abbey dining hall.

"I'm supposed to be meeting with Pollar Penwick in Abersford today to check out the latest batch of soap." Yozef had been working with a local tradesman who made several products, including soap and candles. "We've several new products coming along, but the number of workers I have to keep track of and the coins coming in and going out are taking up time I need to be in the shops and talking with workers and tradesmen."

Cadwulf chewed on a bread bite as he eyed his strange friend. "I can see where that can be a problem, since you're involved in so many different trades. Maybe I can help. I do much of the accounts for the abbey, and yours can't be any more complicated. Let me have a try at organizing your records." Cadwulf's eyes narrowed at Yozef. "You *do* keep records?"

"Well," hawed Yozef, "at first I just gave the workers their pay weekly and coins to buy supplies when needed. As it got more complicated, I wrote things down on paper. I thought I'd organize when I got the chance, which hasn't happened."

Cadwulf shook his head. "For someone so educated and with so much new knowledge, you can be addled at times."

Yozef bit back the retort "YOU try to get dumped on another planet and see how you manage it!" He didn't utter those words; instead, he forced a smile. "You're right," he said and meant it, berating himself for getting so disorganized.

"Don't let it worry you," laughed Cadwulf, slapping Yozef on the back. "Considering your circumstance, a little addling is understandable. Why don't you go over the details with me, and I'll see if I can organize it all for you?"

"With pleasure. How about right now?"

"I thought you had a meeting with Penwick in Abersford?"

"Shit! That's right. I forgot."

"Addled, as I said."

"How about a couple of hours before evening meal? In my room? That's where I keep most papers."

They met that afternoon, and by mealtime, Cadwulf was Yozef's accountant. In addition, the young Beynom was appalled at the drawers of coins.

"Yozef, you really *do* need a keeper."

Red-faced, Yozef spluttered, "Well, hell, where am I supposed to keep it all? It's coming in faster than I can pay workers and start up new trades, and I'm not spending much on myself."

"Well, you have to do *something*. The abbey is normally safe, but having this much coin sitting in drawers is asking for someone to be tempted beyond his ability to resist. There was a robbery in Abersford last sixday, so it *can* happen here."

"Then where can I put the coin?" Yozef groused. "There are no banks here."

"Banks?"

"I don't know the Caedelli word, but a place to put coin where it'll be safe, which also lends money. A bank."

Cadwulf rubbed a chin just showing the beginnings of a beard. "Bank? We don't have a . . . bank."

"Then where do people keep their coin, and how does someone borrow money?"

"They keep it anywhere they feel is safe. Most people don't have much coin. What they have, they carry or keep where they live, hidden if there's enough to worry about theft. They can also pay tradesmen for future work or purchases, and then the coin is the tradesman's problem. As for borrowing money, you do it from relatives, friends, or tradesmen. Loans are private affairs arranged between individuals, whether they be related or unrelated to each other. Whatever the terms of the loan are by mutual agreement, including what, if any, interest will be added to the loan, and schedules of repayment. Such transactions are registered with the district for mutual protection, especially if the loan's not between relatives or close friends."

Cadwulf paused, giving Yozef a thoughtful look. "To be fair, I suppose I have to acknowledge your circumstance isn't normal. The flow of coin to you has happened so suddenly. Still, *something* needs to be done."

Thus was born the First Bank of Abersford, or B of A, as Yozef couldn't resist referring to it. Cadwulf had jokingly suggested Bank of Yozef. A structure was built into a rock face jutting from the ground just outside the village and in full view of both the village and the abbey. Coinage was stored in a vault carved out of the rock, with frontage and offices merging into the rock face. Coinage flow increased, as did the number of employees, starting with Cadwulf alone and rising to three assistants within a year.

This first primitive bank also changed local custom. A Keelan Clan registrar recorded all important records and transactions in the Abersford area. The man in this role, Willym Forten, owned a clothing shop, with registrar duties carried out in a side room. With the establishment of the bank, overlapping activities and the need to transfer all important bank transactions to the clan registration system led to the registrar spending half of each day at the bank, at a dedicated part of the main room. Local citizens, merchants, and craftsmen arranged loans and could deposit their funds in the bank once convinced it was secure.

The building itself was literally a fortress. It would have taken cannons of significant size to breach the outer walls, not to mention the vault sealed with locking mechanisms built by Abersford metalworkers. Records of all transactions were kept in ledgers, and a duplicate set of ledgers put into the abbey's library storage area. Relevant records were transferred to clan journals and copies sent to the main registrar in the town of Clengoth, the district center.

There were no dedicated guards at the bank, but Cadwulf's assistants were men with varying handicaps from accidents or violent encounters with raiders, clan rivalries, or criminal activity, and all worked armed and were pleased to have employment to support their families. Moreover, the bank was visible from the office of the Abersford magistrate, Denes Vegga, a combination sheriff and local militia leader.

Cadwulf Beynom, Financial Manager and Mathematician

Cadwulf's assumption of accounting duties for Yozef's enterprises and his operating the Bank of Abersford initially perplexed his theophist and medicant parents. They had assumed, practically from the baby's birth, that their precocious child would enter one of the three orders at the abbey. The only decision left for him was which one: theophist, medicant, or scholastic. In Cadwulf's mind, he had long ago dismissed following his father's path. Not that he didn't believe in God, but the theophist life path wasn't for him. As for the medicant option, while he recognized helping others was a noble calling, and he had enormous respect for his mother, his dealing daily with others' body fluids, cutting off limbs, and telling families about loved-ones passing on wasn't going to happen.

That left scholastics. Fortunately for Cadwulf, learning, books, and even lessons were not a chore, but something to look forward to. As an adolescent, he raced through all of the basic studies the abbey's teachers could provide, including extra lessons and projects designed especially for him. Thus, at eighteen Anyar years old (sixteen Earth years), he possessed the broadest knowledge of anyone at the abbey, but no depth of knowledge in any one area, with one exception. He found numbers endlessly interesting. His parents either ignored or misunderstood this fascination with numbers, even the first evidence when a happy four-year-old Cadwulf told them of counting 627 butterflies that day. Sistian and Diera each had the same two reactions—pride that their four-year-old son could count to 627 and confusion over why anyone would bother counting butterflies.

By age thirteen, Cadwulf was led by his love of numbers to do most of the abbey's accounting. For him, counting up columns of numbers was almost a meditation. The solution to Yozef's problem of increasing in- and outflow of funds for workers and projects was a perfect fit for Cadwulf's vocation need. Within a month, Cadwulf's life without focus had changed forever. By then, he was bank manager, was the accountant for Yozef's sundry enterprises, and was helping revolutionize Anyarian mathematics.

The coming of Yozef was a gift from God to Cadwulf. The mathematics on Anyar overlapped most of Earth's classical geometry and elementary algebra and the beginnings of trigonometry and determinants. Cadwulf had absorbed all of the mathematics the abbey's teachers understood and moved beyond them to texts on his own. To go further, he would have to move to another province to one of the two abbeys with mathematics scholastics. That was until Yozef realized mathematics was an obscure-enough field of study on Caedellium that he could risk transferring what he knew.

Although not grounded in theoretical mathematics, Yozef was able to give Cadwulf leads to establish or advance analytic geometry, linear algebra, the rudiments of probability, combinatorics, game theory, infinite series, and both differential and integral calculus. Cadwulf was in ecstasy. Whole new fields of mathematics opened up to him. Granted, while Yozef's knowledge of those fields was limited to the equivalent of the first college course in each, they were either novel to Caedellium and Anyar or a logical coalescence of existing mathematics. What helped was that once again, Yozef found himself able to visualize entire pages of texts from courses he had taken. The explanations, the examples, and the proofs were more than enough to keep Cadwulf busy.

When the day came that Cadwulf asked Yozef to confirm a new extension he had developed of a combinatorics theorem, it convinced Yozef he would make a difference to Anyar.

While pretending to listen to Cadwulf's explanation, Yozef mused, *You know, while the ether helps people, it's the mathematics that will have the biggest long-term impact. Cadwulf is already writing to other Scholastics around Caedellium. Within months, it'll start to be all over the island. And even if the worst happens to the Caedelli from these Narthani, it's likely the new mathematics knowledge will spread to the rest of Anyar. And I did this, no matter what else happens.*

CHAPTER 19

A HOUSE OF HIS OWN

"It's past time you find a place of your own, instead of living in that small room in the abbey complex," chided Cadwulf one day, soon after beginning to organize Yozef's finances.

"I know," said Yozef. "I've thought about it, but with everything else to keep me so busy . . . What he didn't say was that the room served as a sanctuary, a place where he could close the door and feel a degree of peace, as if for those moments he could put all of the months since boarding the United flight out of mind. Cadwulf was right. He needed to move on.

"With all the coin you're accumulating, I assume you'll want a house, probably small to begin with."

"Yes," said Yozef, "but not too far from either the abbey or Abersford, since I spend so much time in both places. I think I'd like it to be not too close to other houses and with a view of the ocean, if possible."

"Why would you want to see the ocean?"

"I find it calming. I see myself sitting on a porch and just relaxing."

"Hmmm," murmured Cadwulf. "I guess everyone's different. When I want to think about something or relax, I like to lie at night and gaze at the stars. Anyway, let me ask around to see what property might be available. Inside Abersford is ruled out, if you don't want to be near others."

In the next three days, Cadwulf identified four available houses and cottages. The third possibility caught Yozef's fancy. The house itself was nothing remarkable—a medium-sized cottage with a thatch roof and three fair-sized rooms with high ceilings. It sat on a small knoll about a mile west of both the village and the abbey and overlooked the ocean a half-mile away. A much smaller, single-roomed hut lay about forty yards away, behind a screen of trees, and the land contained abandoned and overgrown garden plots and several Anyar and Earth fruit trees. There was no information on the original builders and inhabitants or how long it had been unoccupied. Cadwulf suspected it had been empty some time, since the surrounding land was poor for farming—too much slope and too many rocks—although stone fences, rusting tools, and piles of rocks showed someone had made the attempt. There was also a dilapidated barn, but, unlike the two housing structures, the barn was well along the road to kindling.

Cadwulf and Yozef examined the frame, the walls, and the floors of the main cottage and found it solid, though needing a new roof. A dilapidated porch faced the sea, too small for Yozef, who envisioned adding an expansive veranda to sit in every type of weather. From the easterly face of the house, he would see the sunrise over the ocean.

"Well, what do you think of this one?" asked Cadwulf.

"It's the best of the ones you found, although it needs repairs and is a little farther from the village and the abbey than I'd planned. However, it'll do me good to get the exercise. How do I buy the house?" Yozef's growing income provided the funds, but he had no idea of what the land was reasonably worth or how to carry out such transactions.

Cadwulf rubbed his hands together. "The current owner of the land is Heilyn Tregedar, a horse breeder and the owner of an Abersford blacksmithy. The cottage was one of several pieces of land his customers exchanged for horses or blacksmith work. I'll talk with him, and we'll see how many krun he wants for the house and the land. Then we'll get into the bargaining to see what his real price is."

The house, flat land on the knoll crest, a hundred yards of down slope, and upslope covered with trees, all came to 2,300 krun. Tregedar insisted he was being robbed and that he agreed on the price only because he sympathized with Yozef being a castaway, apparently a solid citizen, and a friend of the abbot.

"Sorry, Yozef," said Cadwulf. "The final price was a little high, but I got tired of negotiating with Tregedar and gave in. We should have had father do the bargaining."

"Don't worry," said Yozef. "I appreciate your help and would've paid a lot more if I'd had to talk to Tregedar by myself. Now I'll have to figure out how to repair the house, furnish it, and learn to cook on my own."

Again, Cadwulf provided the solution.

"That's not a problem. Once we deal with the transfer of property at the registrar's office, you'll hire help to take care of the property, since you'll be spending most of your time at work. And you need someone to care for the house and cook. Given how well your enterprises are progressing, you can easily afford a couple of workers, and I think I know just the ones for you."

Thus did Yozef meet Brak and Elian Faughn, a weatherworn couple of sixty-plus years. The husband was short, with a solid body from a lifetime of physical work. He still had most of his hair, but it was gray, along with his beard. Brown eyes bored with the sense of someone proud of his independence and asked for no charity. The wife was a good physical match, though with a more approachable face. Cadwulf brought them to the house, walking with them the mile from the village. Brak eyed the houses and ran off a list of needed repairs, all of which he happened to know exactly how to do. Elian was less obvious, but thought the insides of both structures could be made livable in short order and that they'd be very comfortable in the tiny worker's hut.

After meeting them and giving them a tour of his property, Yozef drew Cadwulf aside.

"What's their story?"

"Story? Why should they have a story?"

"Sorry," said Yozef. "I mean, why do they need a place to stay? I get the impression they are trying not to appear too anxious, but the wife's longing look at the worker's hut makes me think their current conditions aren't good."

"They owned a small farm nearby until about two years ago. When the Narthani began blocking trade, the price of grain went so low many smaller farms had no markets. They had food, of course, but as they got older, they needed more temporary workers, even for their small farm, something they couldn't afford. They finally sold the farm for very little money and moved into town. All of their children live some distance away in Keelan and, I believe, one in Gwillamer. Brak is too stubborn to live with them. He's prickly, especially when the topic is about taking care of himself, but he is as honest as they come and will work to the absolute best of his ability."

"Where are they living now?"

"They have a small lean-to behind the candle works. Brak works part time there when there are tasks needed, and Elian washes clothes."

Cadwulf's statement of the Faughns' situation was so matter-of-fact that Yozef stared at his young friend in consternation.

Yozef was appalled. That was it? An older couple had to sell the farm they'd probably worked most of their lives and raised a family on, then moved into a lean-to and supported themselves by whatever small work they could find?

Clearly, there was no such thing as social security here. The land itself appeared idyllic—green fields of crops, fences, quaint village, abbey complex, ocean setting, and hard-working people. It reminded him of Amish country. He'd have to keep remembering this wasn't colonial New England or the Pennsylvania Dutch country. It was a harsher-cored society, no matter the outward attraction. Any safety net depended on family and charity.

"They seem perfect," Yozef decided. "How much should I pay them?"

"I'd say about thirty krun a sixday."

"So little?" said a surprised Yozef. "Apiece?"

"Oh, no, that's for both."

"How's that enough?"

"That's *more* than enough. They'll have a place to live, and the thirty krun doesn't include food, since Elian will buy and cook for all three of you. All they need is money for clothes and occasional medicant help."

Sounds like goddamn slave labor to me. There's gonna be trouble if they start bowing and calling me master.

"All right. I'll hire them. Let's go tell them."

"Yozef, remember that things are evidently different here than in your homeland. The Faughns expect you to be an employer who expects good work from them. Any hint of feeling sorry for them will be considered an insult, especially by Brak, even if you mean well. Let them set their own pace for work, and I expect you'll have no complaints."

They went back to where the couple stood next to each other, awaiting his decision. They didn't quite touch, though nevertheless gave the sense of clustering together against a difficult world. They had each other and not much else.

"Sen Faughn and Ser Faughn, Cadwulf Beynom speaks highly of you as hard and honest workers. I get a similar impression from meeting you. If it's agreeable to you, I'll hire you to take care of the property. I'll pay you thirty krun a sixday. Both houses need extensive cleaning and repair, both inside and out. My work will keep me in the village and the abbey most of the time, so I will trust you to do all that's necessary to make the property comfortable for me when I'm not at work.

"The small hut is yours to live in. It also needs many repairs. I believe those who work for me do their best work when they have proper places to live, so I expect both the hut and the main cottage to be repaired. Besides the structures, the grounds need work. I would like a garden with fresh vegetables, and the fruit trees need pruning and other tending. I leave the details to your experience, as long as the work gets done."

Elian Faughn beamed at Yozef's words. Brak furrowed his brow and started to say something, but his wife cut him off with a curtsy. "Thank you, Ser Kolsko. We'll be pleased to work for you as hard as we can."

Yozef moved on before the old man could say anything. "Elian will cook, and, in my homeland, it is considered that an employer should eat the same quality of foods as their workers. I don't know the custom here on Caedellium, but I must insist that we follow *my* people's customs. After you move here, I'll give you lists and descriptions of foods from my homeland I would like Elian to do her best to reproduce. It would also be helpful if I understood the customs and the foods of Caedellium better, so I expect Elian also to cook local meals. Any materials and foods we need I'll give you coin for those purchases, and you can return any remaining coins. I won't have time to pay close attention to such details, but I assume you can manage such purchases without me."

Yozef and Cadwulf left them with suspicion in Brak's eyes and a hint of moisture in Elian's. The couple walked hand-in-hand back toward the village, with the promise to return later that day with their belongings and start to work on the property. Yozef was briefly tempted to offer to find a wagon to help them move, then decided they probably didn't have all that much to transfer and wasn't sure how much help to offer and stay within the bounds of their self-respect.

True to their word, when Yozef returned to the property the next afternoon, the Faughns had moved into the hut, and both structures already appeared transformed, debris cleared away, and the inside of the main cottage swept, wiped of dust, and scrubbed.

Christ, marveled Yozef, *they must have only stopped to sleep—I hope.*

Yozef's move took longer. His room at the abbey was cluttered with clothes, books, papers, writing materials, and even a few decorations. He was inclined to move by wagon, but the image of the Faughns walking all of their worldly possessions in one trip made him reticent, so he bought a pack in the village and, during the next two sixdays, gradually made his own move. The decision gave him a chance to discard items he couldn't remember the reason he had them and gave the Faughns time to make the property more pleasant. And that it was. He still had a few things to move when he formally "moved into" the cottage, sleeping there and eating morning and evening meals. By then, the cottage was spotless, if somewhat bare. A new roof was on. Exactly how Brak had done it by himself, Yozef couldn't envision and thought it may be a good thing he *didn't* know. He checked out their hut, ostensibly to be sure his workers had appropriate quarters to maximize their work. He pretended some annoyance that their roof was not as complete as his, and he chastised Brak. This seemed to satisfy the brusque man that the employer wasn't providing charity.

Meals by Elian might not be haute cuisine, though, like most island food, they were hearty and plentiful. He allowed Elian to expose him to some local fare he hadn't experienced before, and he, in turn, let them try dishes from California, or at least those that could be reasonably duplicated on Caedellium. The morning meal, still breakfast to Yozef, was where differences were greatest. Chickens hadn't made the transplantations to Anyar, though ducks had and were a source of eggs. Yozef had never eaten a duck egg, and the first time they seemed a little too gamey, although he got used to the taste. The Anyar version of birds, murvors, provided a second common source of eggs. The ruktor was a kiwi-shaped, flightless, murvor with black and purple feathers and a parrot-like beak for digging roots and cracking nuts. Ruktor eggs were blue-shelled, with a lighter blue interior, and to Yozef, the eggs tasted like something needing disappearance down a disposal. He made several attempts at eating them before giving up and sticking to duck eggs.

As for preparation, eggs were boiled, scrambled, or used as an ingredient in dishes. Fried or poached eggs grossed out the Faughns. Uncooked yolks! Elian made valiant efforts to learn the intricacies of "over-easy," but eventually Yozef, to her relief, took over the preparation on those mornings when such a disgusting dish made the menu.

Other breakfast options to remind Yozef of home included the ubiquitous oatmeal-like porridge, pancakes, and French toast. Pancakes weren't a problem, since they were already common on Caedellium, and were accompanied by butter and fruit preserves, but French toast was a novelty that both Brak and Elian took to with enthusiasm. Yozef was surprised many months later to find that French toast had spread to most of Caedellium.

The cottage became more furnished, as Yozef spotted items he fancied in Abersford shops. Although he wasn't a knick-knack person, the bare walls and surfaces cried out for decorations. A first such addition was when Yozef spotted a colorful shawl in a weaver's shop in Abersford. It was patterned, and the blues and greens seemed to match the ocean view. He tacked it to a bare wall and immediately gave the room more life.

Yozef also couldn't resist a present for Elian but had to figure out how to get away with it, without offending Brak. He complained to the Faughns that during the bargaining, he was "tricked" by the shopkeeper into buying two shawls. The other one was also colorful, with reds and yellows. Those being colors "he" didn't particularly like, and since he didn't want the purchase to go to waste, he insisted that the Faughn's tack it to one of their walls. Brak reluctantly did so, and Yozef suspected Elian thought a treasure had fallen to them. By "coincidence," Yozef had noted Elian wore a tattered red-and-yellow scarf most days.

I actually think I'm starting to accept this new life, Yozef realized one day, as he walked to his shops in Abersford. The cottage had begun to feel like home. He had his routine: breakfast; walking to the village or the abbey, depending on his plans for that day; returning to the evening meal Elian had waiting; and spending occasional evenings at the pubs. He had friends—some, to his surprise, better than any he'd ever had before. He was making a difference and hoped to do more. Life could be worse.

CHAPTER 20

MAERA

Keelan Manor, Caernford

Most days, Culich Keelan and his wife, Breda, talked during their entire morning meal, but not this day. Only the distant sounds of animals and workers on the Keelan Manor grounds broke the silence. This time together was an inviolate routine to their lives, a time for just the two of them. Rarely did they eat mid-day meal together—Culich in meetings or traveling, Breda managing the household and the surrounding estate and attending meetings of her own with clanswomen and others. Evening meal was eaten with the family or, on formal occasions, with clan members, visitors—followed occasionally by more meetings. Morning meal was *their* time. Time to talk of the small things keeping them bound to each other, talk of important family matters, and talk of weighty issues of broader scope. Breda also served as Culich's sounding board for when he needed to unload worries and doubts he couldn't express to anyone else. That he spoke so little this morning told her something weighed on his mind.

Being hetman was a never-ending task few could appreciate without experiencing the weight themselves. It would be different if he felt less responsibility for the sixty thousand clan members. He knew hetmen of other clans who didn't feel the weight, and he thought the well-being of those clans suffered because of it. Culich's father had felt the burden of leadership, and although he had imbued his son and heir with the same mind-set, he also taught that there was a need for time to be yourself, to admit doubts, if he had them, and for those moments not to be the *hetman*. These morning meals were one such time. Usually.

Breda was patient. After twenty-five years of marriage, she knew he had something important to discuss, something he was not comfortable with, something he would get to in his own time.

She watched him with a slight smile when he glanced up from finishing his latest biscuit lathered with butter, and his thoughtful expression morphed into a grin.

"Yes, yes. Something we need to talk about."

"I assumed so. Either that, or you lost your voice overnight."

He laughed. "No, I managed to keep it." The laughter fled. "It's about Maera. I've been thinking about her again, and . . . "

Breda's face became somber to match her husband's. "You think it's time for her to marry."

"Yes. We haven't pushed her. I'd hoped she would come around to it by herself. Lately, I wondered whether she ever would."

Breda nodded sadly. "I know. I've felt the same. Even though she's said nothing to me, I think she still hasn't come to grips with both how unhappy she became at the thought of marrying Folant and how she harbors guilt about feeling relief at his accidental death."

Culich sighed. "Folant wasn't a *bad* man. Maybe they would have worked it out."

"Maybe," said a dubious Breda. "Oh, I agree he wasn't bad or evil, but I'm afraid Maera holds fantasies about marriage. Likely at least somewhat our fault."

"Our fault?" exclaimed a startled Culich. "How?"

"Dear, she had us as her model."

Culich was silent for a moment, then nodded. "Yes, you might be right. I guess I never thought of it that way. We were so lucky. Inter-clan conflicts seemed to be a thing of the past, and the Narthani were still many years away. My father didn't think a political marriage necessary when it came my time, and he had no objections to my marrying the daughter of one of his own boyermen. It's easy to forget how marriages for our families are so often political affairs."

"Maera knows the responsibilities," said Breda. "We raised her so she knew a marriage might be arranged to benefit the clan, and she knows we would try to make a match with the potential for a degree of happiness."

Culich shook his head. "I thought we succeeded with Folant. Marriage to the second son of Hulwyin Mittack would mean she might never be the wife of the Mittack hetman, but it would be of appropriate station. It would help keep our clan's connections close to an allied clan, and, of course, one of their sons would be in line as a possible heir to Keelan. Plus, Folant seemed like a likable sort."

"I'm afraid, dear, we never know what will go on between two people until they are put together. Folant may have been honorable and solid, but he didn't see Maera as a person outside of himself and his belief in her expected roles. I know he didn't listen to her. Maera always saw the two of us discussing issues, and she assumed it would be the same in her marriage. Unfortunately, Folant didn't see it that way. During one of her visits to Mittack, he told her to stay out of Mittack clan business, because she was a woman and not even from Mittack."

"That's not only stupid, but it makes me angry," said Culich. "Any husband of Maera's would be lucky to have her. But that was then, and this is now. She's twenty-three. She engaged late as it was, at twenty-one. I would never try to force her to be with someone she doesn't approve of, but she's aware of her obligations. Nothing has changed. We all know a hetman's family has duties to the clan that don't always mesh with personal desires, but we do what we must."

Culich reached out and held his wife's hand, his grip tight. "And then there's the Narthani. While we can't tell the future, I fear for the coming years. Questions about the Keelan succession are uncertainties the clan can't afford."

He paused, then continued. "I see three paths forward. We give her more time, we accept the possibility she never marries, or we talk with her that it's time."

Breda nodded. "As much as I hate the thought of forcing her to marry, I wonder whether it wouldn't be best for her. I fear her sinking into a shell and turning into a tired, bitter, solitary woman. The problem remains, who would she marry?"

Culich sighed. "Yes, and there we return. A marriage of similar status to Folant's might not happen. There aren't many similar candidates who are unmarried, unless it's someone much younger. The facts are that her age, her previous engagement, and she herself all work against her. I'm sorry to admit it, but most men prefer a more pliable wife, and Maera was never one not to give an opinion. She'll be smarter and more educated than any husband."

"What about forgetting the political marriage between clan families? What about within Keelan?"

"Who would it be?" asked Culich. "Knowing Maera, I'm afraid she's stubborn enough not to marry someone without advantage for the clan, even if she likes him, and I'd hate to frame it as simply producing candidates for the heir. At this point, I would be amenable to any marriage that made her happy, but let's admit it, my dear, our family has such solid clan support that there's no advantage to a marriage within the clan. That leaves outside of the clan, and we're back to *who*?"

Breda nodded. "Also, I worry about her leaving the clan. If her marriage was cheerless, and she didn't have the familiar around her, it would break my heart to know she would live an unhappy life."

Culich was silent, having no solution.

Breda cleared her throat. "What about getting her out of here to travel more? She has always been interested in helping me with activities with widows and orphans and has even occasionally wondered whether, if she weren't a Keelander, she might have joined one of the orders. On her own, she's dabbled in medicant texts and probably knows almost as much as medicants in training. She's also something of a scholastic in her own right in Caedellium history, stories, and folklore. Could we arrange for her to visit some of the scholasticums in other clans? Maybe she would meet a kindred soul there who might be appropriate."

Culich rubbed his nose as he considered his wife's suggestion. "Perhaps. I confess I sometimes feel guilty about how much I've come to depend on her as an advisor. Even in Keelan, though, it can be a problem having a young woman giving advice heeded as much as that given by the graybeards. If I hadn't tolerated . . . no, let's be honest . . . *encouraged* her scholastic interest, she would have found a more acceptable role."

Breda shook her head and laid a hand on his forearm. "No, Culich, she is who she is. We talk about duty to the clan, and the benefit of her helping you is important. We shouldn't judge ourselves too harshly if her helping is both good for the clan and makes her feel useful."

Culich grunted and abruptly pushed his plate away. "So we accept, but where does that leave us with Maera?"

Breda sighed. "Maybe we continue to do what we are already doing, nothing, for now. Your first choice. We can also look for ways to let her travel away from Caernford. Then, wait longer and see whether Maera, God, or circumstances somehow solves the problem."

Maera and Anarynd

The object of the discussion at the hetman's morning meal at that moment finished a spiced bread roll and washed it down with kava in her own quarters of the Keelan manor. Maera noticed neither the roll nor the kava as they were consumed. Her attention focused on the disarray of papers spread out on the table. Sometimes she ate with one or more of her three younger sisters. On Godsday morning, her parents expected all of them to eat together before riding their surrey to St. Tomo's Abbey for the morning service in Caernford. Many days, Maera ate alone. Not that she preferred it, but it was easier at times, particularly when she was absorbed in her readings, reports for her father, or correspondence. Today it was all three.

She finished editing a summary of her observations from her father's last district boyermen meeting, and her ink-stained fingers pushed the completed report aside, to copy the final version later in the morning.

Next, she opened a book on the Keelan Clan history, written a hundred years ago, about what was known or what lore believed to be true about the early days of the clan's founding. She was a third of the way through the book, and the dryness of events and names made it hard for her to focus for too long. Today she waded through ten pages, as resolved, then replaced the page marker and closed the book.

She saved the best for last: a letter from Anarynd. Maera twirled strands of her long brown hair through her left forefinger, as she read the letter for the fourth time. A smile played across her lips, as she imaged Anarynd's latest stories and thoughts about her suitors. With blonde hair, an eye-catching figure, and a little-girl-wonder face, Anarynd had drawn male attention since she'd entered puberty. Though her male relatives kept men who were *too* interested well away, Anarynd was not reticent about enjoying the attention. What was new in this letter was more detail than usual about one specific suitor, a district boyerman's eldest son from northern Moreland Province. Maera noticed herself frowning at where this new suitor was from. If Anarynd married and moved farther north, Maera would see her even less often. Maera chided herself. The important thing was that Ana, as Maera called her, became happy in a marriage. If it meant she and Maera were farther apart, that was a trivial consideration. Maera knew that was what she was "supposed" to think, and she honestly hoped only happiness for her best friend, but still . . . *Ana, please don't move farther away!*

Maera smiled at herself, folded the letter, walked to a cabinet, and placed the letter in the box holding all of Ana's other letters. As she returned to the table, she saw herself in a mirror. She stopped for a moment. She and Ana might seem like two improbable friends. As attractive and vivacious as Ana was, Maera saw herself as a contrast. Ana always took great care about her clothes and appearance. The young woman in the mirror wore her usual plain smock, this one a purple shade—a deliberate choice, since it helped hide new ink spots—a pair of long stockings, and uncombed hair tied into a ponytail to keep it out of the way. Then there were the shoeless feet. Maera had preferred going shoeless as long as she could remember. Her parents and the family's station discouraged her being shoeless in public, but when in her own quarters and sometimes in other parts of the family manor, she indulged in being barefoot, if temperatures allowed.

She looked at a bookcase holding her timepiece, an expensive gift from her parents on her twelfth birthday. Time to make the eldest daughter of the Keelan hetman presentable to the world. She washed as much of the ink from her hands as possible, combed her hair and braided it to lay atop her head, changed into a sleeveless full dress with a white undershirt, and donned thin stockings of delicate cloth and well-crafted everyday women's shoes of the finest gurnel leather.

She was ready to play her roles: dutiful daughter of the hetman, benefactress of orphanages and hospitals, scribe and unofficial advisor to the hetman, and . . . *what?* The mirror showed her ready. She saw an average young woman of undistinguished appearance, a little slenderer than most, perhaps shorter than average, and a serious look.

Her thoughts went back to Ana. The first time they'd met was when Maera visited Ana's family in Moreland Province. It was the custom among the clan leaders' families for children to go on extended visits to other clans. The plan was to help keep the clans' future leaders and their wives, in the case of female children, from becoming too insular and to identify potential future marriage partners. How much this helped reduce inter-clan conflicts was uncertain, but the custom was long-standing. Maera's visit that year had been to the family of Brym Moreland, first cousin to the Moreland Clan Hetman, Gwynfor Moreland. Brym was, in theory, sixth in line to be heir to the Moreland Hetman position, meaning it unlikely he or his family would ever be any closer to the succession, but high enough in the Moreland clan to be a proper site for a visit by a Keelan daughter. Under other circumstances, the visit would have been with the hetman's family itself, but Culich Keelan and Gwynfor Moreland detested each other, so all parties were satisfied with Maera visiting a secondary branch of the Morelands.

That was how she met Ana—Anarynd Moreland—second daughter of Brym and Gwenda Moreland. Maera was fourteen and Anarynd thirteen. Maera was shorter and slenderer than Anarynd, and they were so different in personalities and interests, it was to general surprise that they developed into steadfast friends. An outside analysis might have speculated the reason was that they complemented areas where each girl thought herself lacking. Anarynd had always been doted on because of her appearance, and she took her attractiveness for granted, whereas Maera had never seen herself as other than ordinary. In reverse, the young Maera always seemed to know she was smarter than anyone else, although contact with scholastic brothers and sisters at abbeys caused her to revise that opinion to "smarter than almost anyone else." In contrast, Anarynd was never praised for being clever, and by the time the two girls first met, Maera was reading texts most adults couldn't manage, while Anarynd could hardly read. Education of family girls would never have occurred to Ana's father or mother as something either desired or useful. Both girls were willful but in different degrees and manners. Anarynd pleaded or pouted to get her way, while Maera resorted to stubbornness and arguing. They were so different and so perfect for each other.

At first, the two girls had little interest in the other. Everything changed the day of the year's Harvest Festival. The local Moreland version drew from the surrounding twenty miles. Several thousand people engaged in activities scheduled and unscheduled, religious thanksgiving and prayers for the coming harvest, food of all varieties, physical contests for the men, home crafts for the women, games for the young, dancing in the evening, and less respectable activities in darker corners late at night. Anarynd and Maera accompanied Anarynd's mother and aunts on a tour of the activities, when Maera spotted a group of early teen boys shooting crossbows at improvised targets. Maera asked whether she could watch the boys shoot, and Gwenda Moreland assented, after telling Anarynd to go with Maera so she wouldn't get lost in the crowd or be subjected to inappropriate behavior by any males not aware of Maera's standing. Although Anarynd was annoyed at having to shepherd the odd Maera, she was pleased to be out of her mother's view and to have the opportunity to practice flirting.

After a few minutes watching, Maera's mouth twisted in disdain. "Most of them can't shoot worth anything. I'm better than any of them."

"You've shot a crossbow before?" asked a startled Anarynd.

Maera glared sideways at Anarynd. "Well . . . yeah," as if the answer was obvious.

"I never have," Anarynd confessed.

Maera turned to face Anarynd. "Why not?"

"It's . . . just not something women do."

"Why not?"

"Because."

"Pretty lame reason, if you ask me. Have you ever *wanted* to try it?"

"I've never thought about it. It's just one of those things that men do and women don't."

"That's not the way it is in Keelan."

"All women in Keelan do things like crossbow shooting?" asked an astounded Anarynd.

Maera hesitated. "No. Not all. But any who want to, can."

Anarynd looked back at the boys occupied with their contests. "I wouldn't mind trying. Maybe sometime we could sneak out of our estate and go off into the woods to try it," whispered Anarynd, as if hatching a conspiracy.

"Why wait? There's plenty of crossbows right here and targets all set up."

"With the boys," said Anarynd in a sly voice. "Hmmm . . . that could be fun talking the boys into letting us."

Maera looked at Anarynd and asked—already expecting the answer, "And how would you go about getting them to let you try?"

"Oh, they're just boys."

With a coy smile, Anarynd transformed into a young seductress, sashaying over to the cluster of boys. They parted like water before a gale, hovering just out of touch. Maera followed. She couldn't hear whatever Anarynd said to the boys, but within seconds, one of the older ones was showing her how to hold the crossbow. She fired, and the crossbow quarrel arched high above the targets.

Maera choked back her thought. *Merciful God, I hope Anarynd doesn't skewer some person or animal wherever the quarrel lands.*

Instantly, a second boy handed another cocked crossbow to Anarynd. The next five minutes or more, Anarynd fired many a quarrel without coming close to a target, not that any of the boys noticed. Finally, she turned to Maera, "Do you want to try it?"

The closest boys noticed Maera for the first time, with an irritated look she interpreted as, *Why would we be interested in her?*

Maera flushed, angry at the boys, at Anarynd's act, and at the world in general. "Well, I couldn't be worse at it than you," she snarled.

Anarynd turned red. "Okay, Miss Smart Mouth, let's see what you can do." She handed Maera the last loaded crossbow.

A rustle of discontent rolled through the gathered boys, and the tight cluster that had been around Anarynd expanded, as the level of interest waned.

Maera took the crossbow, eyed the target forty yards away, and raised the stock to her shoulder. She looked over the quarrel at the target and pulled the trigger. *Twang!* sang the string as the quarrel leaped out in a flat trajectory and buried itself within six inches of the bull's-eye. The stunned silence was deafening, followed by exclamations.

"God above, did you see that?"

"What luck. She didn't even aim."

"Whoa, nice shot."

"Why are we letting girls shoot?" another said, along with similar and less polite comments.

Anarynd stared at Maera for a moment. "I guess you *have* done this before."

Maera held the bow out to the boy who had originally handed it to Anarynd. "Not a bad bow, but shoots a little to the left."

"Try it again," said the impressed boy, to the disgust of the boy standing next to him, who looked like a family relation.

"Hell, that was just a lucky shot," said the second boy.

Peeved again, Maera stood the bow on its point, pulled out the cocking lever, and pumped to recock the string. The first boy handed her another quarrel, which she slotted into the bow stock and notched it to the string. With a smooth motion, she raised the bow and sent the second quarrel three inches from the bull's-eye. Proof that the first shot was not a fluke reanimated the group of boys, and during the next fifteen minutes, Maera sent further quarrels into the center of various targets. Several of the older boys tried, without success, to match her marksmanship. By then, the group had split into the boys who disassociated themselves from a female competing with them and those who admired her skill. The latter group wanted to discuss the merits of various bow styles, pull-strengths, and quarrel lengths and asked whether she had done any hunting. The episode ended with Anarynd's mother and coterie finding them and swooping them away from such unseemly activity.

Later that night, after the evening meal and after socializing to the limit of her boredom, Maera lay in bed. She'd just closed her eyes when there was a knock at her door. Anarynd let herself in, crossed to the bed, and sat. A surprised Maera sat up.

"Maera . . . no one listens to me." Anarynd's voice bespoke a resigned sadness.

At first, Maera was uncertain what to say, though she wondered why the girl was telling her this. The silence dragged on.

"Uh. . . what do you mean no one listens?"

"Oh, they listen, but they don't *listen*."

"You mean they hear the words but not the meaning?"

Anarynd nodded. "To my parents, I exist, but only to do what they expect. My brothers treat me as a sister who should know her place. Iwun, my younger brother, and I are near in age and played together when we were younger. He listened then, but everything changed a year ago when he began spending more time with older boys and our father and our older brother."

"Learning the way he was *supposed* to treat you, I bet."

"Yesterday, the boys at the bow range, they listened to me only because of how I look and how I flirted with them. I could have been saying *anything*, and they wouldn't have noticed or cared."

"You knew that would happen before we went over to them."

"It's what I do. It's the only way I can get people to listen!" Anarynd exclaimed.

Maera sighed. This wasn't how she'd planned on spending her sleep time, but Anarynd obviously needed to talk, something Maera too often missed in her own life. She knew her parents loved her, but somehow she never talked to them as much as she wished she could. To turn away someone else in need didn't seem "right."

Anarynd continued, "They listened to you yesterday. You didn't flirt with them. You showed them you could do something as well as them or better."

"Some were okay with it, but some left," Maera said with a grimace.

"But many *did* listen," insisted Anarynd. "I wish I was more like you. That I could make people listen to me."

"I don't know if you can *make* people listen as much as *want* to listen," Maera said.

"How do I do that?"

"What can you offer them except your looks?"

Anarynd was silent for moments, then shook her head. "Nothing I can think of."

"Then maybe that's the problem. You need to have things to say and show you can do things. Do you read much?"

"Read?" echoed the other girl. "I don't read much."

"Well, what *do* you read?"

Anarynd flushed. "I already said I don't read much."

Oh, Graceful God, she can't read!

"Anarynd . . . you can't read, or at least not much at all, can you?"

The blonde's face reddened more, and she shook her head to confirm. "It's not considered necessary for a woman to read, as long as she knows how to take care of her husband and family. Is it different in Keelan?"

"Yes. Not all girls go to school as long as the boys, but that's the choice of the family and the girl."

"Girls don't go to school at all in Moreland. I know a few words that my brother Iwun taught me. He would come home from school and want to show me what he'd learned that day. I wasn't interested most of the time. Then he stopped sharing with me."

"That's something you need to do—learn to read."

"How? My family wouldn't let me go to school, and if they did, I'd be with six-year-old boys. Mother can't read, and father and my brothers wouldn't think it worth their time to teach me."

"*I'll* teach you," asserted an annoyed Maera, before she took the time to think about it. "I'm here for another month. How much do you know? The letters? Any words at all?"

"Iwun taught me the letters, and I know the words for some things like animals, food, places, and peoples' names."

"Good. You aren't starting from nothing. I think if we work very hard the next month, you might be able to read simple texts. Then, when I've returned home, we can write letters to each other for you to practice. I can also talk to my teachers and family and send you books as your reading gets better."

"Do you really think I could learn?"

"You're not dumb, Anarynd, just stupid for letting other people tell you who you can be."

As if I'm all that different. I'm put into roles, but at least I have more freedom than this blonde blank spot.

"Oh, thank you, Maera!" exclaimed Anarynd, wrapping her arms around Maera tightly and squeezing. "I'll work really, really hard. You'll see."

Anarynd released Maera and pulled back to look her in the eye. "We mustn't let anyone know. I'm sure my family wouldn't approve. We'll have to find ways to be alone."

Maera was already planning ahead. "Neither of us has any particular duties or activities, so no one should notice if we spend time together and away from others. Going for walks, for example. Once we're out of sight, we can work on reading." Maera was in full conspirator mode. If she had to endure this visit, she might as well play at deceiving adults.

"We'll need quills, ink, and paper . . . and take care not to get the ink on ourselves or, if we do, wash it off before someone else sees it. We can also 'play' in our rooms during the day and work on reading after the others go to bed."

Maera paused. She was about to tell Anarynd something she had never told another person.

"Anarynd, you say you wish you were more like me in being sure of myself and making people listen to me. Today, I wished I was more like you in some ways."

"More like me? Why?"

"I don't have many friends, and boys don't seem interested in me. I don't say I want them to ogle me all the time, but I'm not attractive and don't know how to talk with them. Maybe you can help me."

"Of course! It'll be fun teaching you. And don't tell me you're not pretty enough. You just have to use what you have."

And thus was born a conspiracy between two pubescent girls. Maera would teach Anarynd to read and be more assertive and, in return, get lessons in dress, rudimentary makeup, flirting, and playing on male egos. To Anarynd's discouragement, Maera learned the first two well enough, but the flirting and talking herself down to a male's level never took hold. For Anarynd, it was two years before her father realized she had learned to read. Although she was never going to be a scholar at Maera's level, the ability to read not only expanded her horizons, it slowly imbued her with enough confidence to assert her own wishes on occasion and when it was important enough. Even this level of independence didn't sit well with her father, but their eventual semi-truce involved Anarynd following his wishes on small matters, in exchange for more freedom to follow her interests. The big things, by mutual consent, they tried to avoid.

Over the years, the two girls each spent several sixdays a year visiting the other. The visits of Anarynd to Maera were longer, because the Morelands eventually figured out the source of the changed behavior of their once-docile daughter and only reluctantly allowed Maera's visits.

In addition to the visits, they wrote to each other once a sixday. The letters conveyed all of the things girls, and then young women, talk about to their best friends: what they were feeling, Anarynd's lessons, Maera's studies. Then, as they got older, they wrote about looking ahead to when they would marry—more eagerly in Anarynd's case than Maera's. Their paths, which had casually come together, would stay intertwined during the rest of their lives, albeit with episodes of both joy and despair.

CHAPTER 21

KEELAN JUSTICE

Cadwulf's news of a robbery in Abersford made Yozef realize he was ignorant about the Keelan justice system, which could be dangerous. He could violate a law and not know it, and what would happen if he did? Since he was already pumping Cadwulf for tidbits about Caedellium and Keelan society, history, and customs, why not add the functioning of their legal system?

He broached the idea with his young friend and employee the next day.

"Yozef, the current external adjudicator just arrived in Abersford for a justice session. Court will begin tomorrow, if you'd like to watch. This is the perfect way for you to see how the law functions here. I could come with you and explain what's happening."

"Tomorrow? I told Filtin I'd work with him on the new distillery setups. I guess that can wait a few days. Where are proceedings held?"

"In the cathedral. Anyone who wishes can observe, and the cathedral is the only gathering space near Abersford of sufficient size."

"Will there really be that many attending?" Yozef asked in surprise.

"Not usually. It depends on the individual cases. The list is posted to all nearby villages, so the size of the crowd will vary, depending on the case, who is involved, how entertaining it might be, how many witnesses, or whether it involves people who are relatives or someone you either like or dislike. Of course, some people come just because it's one of the more exciting things to happen in the Abersford area."

By arrangement, they met at the abbey complex main gate the next day. People were walking from the village, and there were horses and wagons tied to stakes outside the abbey walls. Once inside the cathedral, they found two spots at the end of the eighth row of pews. Perhaps three hundred people sat in the eight-hundred-capacity space, when a man in black and white livery walked down the center aisle, turned to face the audience, and pounded a heavy staff on the floor three times.

"All present heed the justice of Keelan. All present heed their roles in this proceeding. All present acknowledge the justice that protects the people." The man pounded his staff three times more. From a side door appeared three men dressed in black-and-white checkered robes. The men filed to a table set on the first level above the audience. In front of them, with backs to the audience, were a set of chairs filled with men and a few women.

"What is the significance of the black-and-white robes?" Yozef whispered to Cadwulf.

"It's supposed to symbolize even-handedness. The judges should not come to any predetermined conclusions until they hear the charges and evidence."

From where they sat, Yozef at first couldn't discern the faces of the three judges, but once they turned and took their seats, he could see that the one on his right was the abbot.

"You recognize Father. On the left is Longnor Vorwich, boyerman of our district, containing Abersford and St. Sidryn's. Vorwich lives fifteen miles away near the town of Clengoth, which serves as the district center."

"Are abbots always judges?"

"Not always. One judge is a citizen of high regard from the area. For this year, Father was proposed by Vorwich and approved by village chiefs and mayors. I think it's the third or fourth time he's had this year-long duty."

Yozef didn't recognize the white-haired, vigorous-looking man. "Who's the man in the middle?"

"That's Scholastic Adris Carys. He's the adjudicator and is a scholastic from St. Tomo's Abbey in Caernford. He's an expert in the law and previous cases. While normally he would be addressed as Brother Carys, for these proceedings he is Adjudicator Carys. He will preside and advise Father and Boyerman Vorwich on law and precedence, and all three vote on each case. He oversees all cases in Keelan. Most of the time, the three men will agree on the verdict. When one judge disagrees with the other two, those cases are referred three times a year to Caernford, where the case will be presented again with Hetman Keelan becoming a fourth judge. In that case, if the disagreement is 2 to 2, the case is dismissed. If 3 to 1, then the decision of the three is determinative."

"Are the three judges always men?"

Cadwulf turned to Yozef. "Well . . . yes, of course."

Of course? Women's rights had quite a ways to go here.

Yozef filed this information away and sat back to take in the first case. Carys called two men to stand before the judges. A dispute originated over a cow claimed to have been stolen by one of the men. The other man claimed it had been a sale. The case sped to a conclusion after the judges asked to see the bill of sale for the cow. The accused said he had forgotten to get a written bill and had no witnesses to the sale. The cow in question was characteristic enough that several witnesses agreed the cow in possession of the accused had been the same cow owned by the accuser. There were no other witnesses.

It was over in less than ten minutes. Adjudicator Carys consulted briefly with Sistian and Vorwich, then announced, "The verdict is that there being no other witnesses or evidence, it cannot be concluded for certain that the cow was stolen. Therefore, the accused is not considered guilty of theft. However, since the supposed sale was not registered with the local registrar or witnessed, and since original ownership of the cow is supported by several witnesses, the accused is required to deliver the cow or one of approximately equal value to the accuser. If a different cow, the value will be determined by the local magistrate."

Yozef whispered to Cadwulf, "So, if the cow was actually sold, the original owner gets the cow back because the buyer didn't have proof of sale, and the owner keeps the money paid for the cow?"

Cadwulf looked disgusted. "The accuser has done this before and likely is lying about the sale, but the law is clear. You must have proof of sale, either written or witnessed. Otherwise, it's not recognized. The buyer in this case was foolish to deal with the seller."

"Next case," announced the adjudicator.

A man and a woman rose and came before the judges. They stood well apart, with a rugged-looking man in his mid-thirties standing between them.

"The man in the middle is Magistrate Denes Vegga. He enforces laws around the Abersford area and serves to support the court."

The sheriff, Yozef assigned the title.

The woman's right arm was in a splint, she had several bruises on her face, one eye was swollen shut, and she limped when she rose to stand. Boyerman Vorwich read from a paper in front of him. "Hulda Camrin accuses her husband, Yuslir, of beating her and their two children repeatedly and asks for justice." He stopped reading and addressed the husband, "What do you say to these charges, Ser Camrin?"

"Your 'onor, I only beat 'er when she deserves it. A man 'as to keep order in his 'ouse, and she is lazy and doesn't do 'er duties in cookin', caring for the 'ouse, and our bed. As for the kids, she spoils 'em and tries to turn them 'gainst me. I then 'as no choice but to beat 'em."

Yozef leaned right and whispered in Cadwulf's ear. "Am I hearing right? The man seems to speak differently than everyone else."

Cadwulf kept his eyes on the proceedings, using a hand to direct a mumble back to Yozef. "He's from Nyvaks Province on the far north Caedellium. You can tell them by how they don't pronounce some first letters, like most other clans."

It was Adjudicator Carys who rejoined the defendant, "Granted that a man has the right to maintain order in his family by reasonable means, the question before this court is whether the punishments given were justified or not."

So much for women's lib, Yozef thought. *I assume there're going to be quite of few more differences in the justice system here compared to the U.S.*

Carys turned to the abbot. "Abbot Beynom, you have a report on experiences with this family?"

"Yes," said the abbot, casting a stern eye at the husband. "Ser Camrin has been admonished numerous times in the past about excessive violence against his family. I and several other brothers have counseled him repeatedly. He has appeared twice before this court on similar charges. In those cases, the accusations were brought by medicants who had treated his wife or children for beatings. In neither case would the wife admit her husband had beat her. She said she 'fell.' It was believed by all she was lying, either because she was afraid or still didn't want to get him in trouble."

No prohibition for hearsay evidence or opinion instead of facts.

Carys addressed the wife. "Sen Camrin, on the current treatment by the medicants you told them, and then later Magistrate Denes, that your injuries were caused by a beating from your husband. Do you still assert this as fact?"

The wife edged next to Magistrate Vegga and looked around him at her husband. Then she took several deep breaths. "I do, Ser. He's just beat me too much. I'm afraid he's goin' to hurt the children even more. Gettin' worse all the time. I don't want to be married to him no more."

The husband flushed, glared at her, and started to say something, until Vegga barked, "No talking until the adjudicator asks you a question!"

And no objections from the defense—not that he has his own advocate.

The adjudicator continued talking to the wife. "In two previous instances, you have testified that your injuries resulted from your own accidents and not beatings by your husband. Do you still say the same?"

The wife's face took on a defensive and somewhat fearful look. "Your Honor . . . I . . . was scar'd. He'd threatened to beat me and the kids worse if I said anything. What was I to do?"

"What you were to do is tell the truth. You deliberately lied to the court at those times."

Carys consulted the paper in front of him. "I see here that the witnesses include the medicants who treated Sen Camrin this time and in the previous instances, several people who have seen Ser Camrin strike his wife in public, and Abbess Beynom, who testifies her observations on both the husband and wife in this case."

So, self-incrimination and conflicts of interest with witnesses are also okay. Perry Mason would not be happy.

"Ser Camrin, are there witnesses to show you do not regularly beat your wife?"

Yozef almost choked. *It's the old joke. "When did you stop beating your wife?"*

"I already said, I only beat 'er when she needs it! It's my right and duty as 'er 'usband."

The adjudicator looked at his assistant. "Let the record show the accused has no witnesses."

A sullen Ser Camrin glared at the judges, then shot another dangerous look at his wife.

The three judges conferred among themselves for four to five minutes, then turned back to the audience.

The adjudicator wrote something on paper in front of him, cleared his throat, and spoke to the accused, the accuser, and the rest of the attendees.

"It is determined that Yuslir Camrin has continued to abuse his wife and children, despite repeated counseling and warnings. From witness statements and the record, we see no reason to think Ser Camrin would stop this behavior if given more chances to change. Therefore, we have no choice but to consider him a habitual abuser of this family. To protect that family, this court now dissolves the marriage between Yuslir Camrin and his wife, Hulda Camrin. Ser Camrin is never to have contact with his former wife or children again."

Well, it simplifies custody battles or visitation rights.

"To assure that this does not happen, Ser Camrin is banished from the Abersford area for the rest of his life. Sen Camrin is ordered to move nowhere where her ex-husband lives, if she wishes to remain under the protection of this court, unless she remarries and is therefore under her new husband's protection."

The man turned red and shouted, "I've spent ten years workin' that farm! All the work I've put into it and I'm to be sent 'way with nothin! It ain't fair!"

"We recognize that the farm inherited by Hulda Camrin from her family was significantly improved by Yuslir Camrin," Boyerman Vorwich answered. "Therefore, it is reasonable for him to receive compensation. It is ruled that ownership of the farm, which was transferred to Yuslir when he married Hulda, is to be transferred back to Hulda. To compensate Yuslir, Hulda is ordered to give Yuslir one quarter of the farm's value, either in coin or deed to land equivalent to that value. The local registrar will work out the details with Hulda and Yuslir."

Camrin visibly relaxed. Yozef whispered, "This Camrin man doesn't appear as worried about the decision as I thought he would be. Am I missing something?"

Cadwulf whispered back, "He's not from this area originally, so he has no other family ties here. He'll move elsewhere with some coin in his pocket and experience at successful farming, so he shouldn't have any problem finding a farm widow willing to marry him."

"I don't understand. Why would any woman want to marry him after this?"

"I'll explain later."

Finished with the basic verdict, the adjudicator addressed both the ex-husband and the ex-wife, one after the other.

"Hulda Camrin, by your own admission you lied to two different courts in the past. While we appreciate the conditions and fears that led to you lying, no court can permit deliberate lies. That you admitted to those lies is mitigation but does not excuse lying. You are therefore sentenced to three lashes."

The wife turned white and started crying. She was led away by several women.

"Kind of harsh, wasn't that?" said Yozef, a little louder than he intended—loud enough that several people turned to him, and it brought a sharp gaze from the abbot.

"Shh," whispered Cadwulf. "The judges had no choice. To lie to the judges is considered a serious offense. In this case, three lashes are considered a mild punishment, and the person giving the lashes will make them more symbolic than painful."

"Yuslir Camrin," intoned Carys, "we cannot be sure whether you are too sadistic or too stupid to understand your own actions. In either case, it is determined that a strong lesson be given in hopes of changing your future behavior. You are therefore sentenced to be taken to the village square and ten lashes to be administered before sundown this day."

Camrin protested loudly, to no avail. As Magistrate Vegga led him away, the adjudicator had a last word. "Be also aware, Yuslir Camrin, that you are required to report to the district registrar where you go in Keelan Province. Details of this judgment will be sent to that district, and any further offenses committed by you will be weighed, along with this verdict. Depending on severity, future offenses could involve banishment from the province. Next case."

"He may well move to a different province," murmured Cadwulf.

"So, the record of this doesn't go to the other provinces?"

"No. Many clans are very strong in maintaining independence and won't pay attention to any such records coming from Keelan. Mittack and Gwillamer and maybe a few others might, but Moreland and the northern clans wouldn't care what happened here."

A number of lesser cases were called, heard, and disposed of in rapid order as the day wore on. There were no such things as continuances in Caedellium justice. The final case of the day was the most serious. It was a compound situation that on Earth would require two separate trials. Cadwulf whispered a running account of who was who, what he knew of them, where they lived, and some details on how the judges might view the case.

It started with a teenage girl, maybe seventeen Anyar years (fifteen on Earth, Yozef reminded himself), claiming she had been raped by a neighbor's twenty-two-year-old son. There were no witnesses, and the girl did not make the accusation until she knew she was pregnant. The case got more complicated when one of her brothers accosted the accused, and, during a fight, the accused was stabbed to death by the brother. Of this part, there were multiple witnesses that the brother had instigated the fight and had pulled a knife, when he started getting the worst of it. The case then had to resolve multiple issues. Because the accused rapist was dead, that charge was resolved. However, by custom and law, a rapist and his family could be responsible for helping support the child.

"The person and his family are responsible for the actions of the person, such as regarding any money to compensate a victim or their family," Cadwulf whispered to Yozef.

The second decision concerned the brother. There was no doubt he believed his sister and in anger had sought the accused. There also was no doubt he had started the fight and had drawn the knife and stabbed the other man. Two issues needed determination. One was whether the brother and his family were liable for blood-money—payment to the deceased's family for loss of a family member. The second was how to evaluate the killing and pass judgment on the brother.

Again, Yozef noted a huge difference with the Caedellium justice system. Judgment was quick, compared to back on Earth. After hearing all of the evidence, the three judges huddled together on the platform for twenty minutes before the adjudicator announced their unanimous decision.

"As is there is no confirming evidence a rape occurred or that the child was fathered by the deceased, and since no accusation was made for some months, no penalties or obligations are directly assigned to the family of the accused rapist. As for the killing of the accused, Kellum Mellwyin is confirmed guilty of the death. No evidence of malice before the accusation of rape was presented, and given the nature of the accusation, we believe it reasonable that the death occurred during a time of reduced judgment. Nevertheless, a killing did occur. Whether or not the accused rapist actually committed the act, it is still the prerogative of Keelan justice to deal with the accusation, and there is no justification for either initiating the fight that led to a death or justification for pulling a knife simply because the initiator of the fight began to lose. It is therefore judged Kellum Mellwyin is ordered to pay the family of the deceased thirty thousand krun, with the method and timing of payment to be submitted to the local registrar within one month. Kellum Mellwyin is also placed on probation for the next ten years. The case is settled. Next case."

"The 30,000 krun is judged to be what the dead man would have earned for his family in ten years," said Cadwulf. "Mellwyin won't have the krun himself, so his family will pay the judgment."

"What if they can't pay?"

"Then Magistrate Vegga and the registrar decide on what the family *can* afford. That could include family members working for the victim's family for no pay for a length of time."

"What does probation mean?" asked Yozef.

"If he commits another serious act of violence within those ten years, he might be banished from Caedellium. If it's a premeditated act, or the act is serious enough, he could be sold to Frangel slavers and the coin given to victims or their families. Normally, those with such sentences are held in confinement in Preddi, awaiting the slavers who come about every five or six months and collect all those condemned to either banishment or slavery. Since the Narthani stopped all ships except their own from coming to Caedellium, such people are being held in Orosz City until a solution is found. Some have been there for several years."

"So this is not normal ... to keep them imprisoned here in Caedellium?"

Cadwulf frowned. "Why would we keep them imprisoned? They'd be a burden on the community. They are punished by fines, whippings, or probation or sent away from Caedellium, either as exiles or slaves, depending the severity of their crimes."

"So there's no death penalty on Caedellium?"

"Only for the most heinous crimes, where the person is judged so dangerous that even sentencing him to slavery or banishment off Caedellium would place others in future danger. It happens rarely, but I know of two such cases in Keelan Provence during my lifetime."

"What about an appeal? Can the accused, if found liable or guilty, try to have the decision changed?"

"The adjudicator's assistant," Cadwulf indicated a man sitting to one side of the judges table, "will write a report of the facts of the case and the judges' decision. The report goes to the Keelan hetman, Culich Keelan, in Caernford. The accused and his family can write to the hetman at the same time to give reasons the sentence should be changed. Most of the time the hetman won't change the verdict. He might reduce the penalties, but he never increases them."

During Cadwulf's explanation, the day's session ended, the three judges filed out, and the spectators began to leave. Yozef had numerous questions.

"Cadwulf, if you have no other plans for evening meal, I'd like to talk about what we saw here today. Could you join me at my house? Elian always cooks more than enough."

"A pleasure. I had no plans, other than eating with my family. Give me a moment to tell Father not to expect me this evening."

Cadwulf left Yozef standing alone and returned a few minutes later.

As they walked the mile to the house, Yozef recounted the day's cases to check whether he understood the proceedings and details of Keelan law and whether there were differences with those of other districts. That is, what was general to Caedellium and specific to Keelan?

"Cadwulf, when you said this Camrin fellow will likely find another farm woman to marry him, you said you'd explain later."

Cadwulf grunted. "Oh, yeah. Well, it's that there are often more women wanting husbands than there are available men."

More women? Yozef thought. On Earth, there were about 105 male babies for every 100 females. He remembered something about the speculation that male babies were more susceptible to diseases and male adults died more from hunting or fighting—some kind of evolutionary compensation to even out the sexes during the reproductive ages. However, somewhere around thirty to forty years, it evened out and from then on, there were more women than men. *Why would the sex ratio of births be different here than on Earth?*

"There are more female babies?"

"Yes, something like ninety-six boys to every hundred girls. I forget the exact numbers. It's thought the different ratio is God's plan to assure there should be equal numbers of men and women later in life, since women can die in childbirth. I was never convinced of this reasoning, because men die in accidents more often than women. There also used to be many more men who die in clan fighting than happens now, but I don't see how God planned for that."

Well, if it's God's doing, he has different plans for Earth and Anyar. One thing's for sure—at least one of the theories to explain the sex ratio differences is wrong.

"So, with a shortage of available men, I assume that since Ser Camrin is gone now, the odds aren't good for the woman to find another husband, if she wants one?"

"Yes," said Cadwulf. "One might think an unmarried adult woman owning a small farm would have many suitors. The problem is many-fold for her. She's already been married and has two children, which are negative factors for some men and families. Also, farms aren't as valuable as before, since the Narthani won't allow shipping of our grains to the mainlands. And finally, most men are already married. As you might expect, the unmarried men tend not to be of the most desirable types."

"Such as Yuslir Camrin?"

"Such as him, or simply not a man whom a woman might risk tying herself to, because when they marry, he becomes the owner of all of her property. Some women prefer to remain unmarried, rather than take the risk. On the other hand, when an appropriate man is available, the competition among women can be fierce."

"Available? Like widowed or a newcomer?"

Cadwulf nodded. "Or from a dissolved marriage, if the woman couldn't be lived with or if there's reason to believe she's infertile, and the husband wants children. The husband can petition and be granted a cancellation of the marriage; then all of her original property reverts to her, so the man must be very serious about wanting children, or he has property of his own."

Yozef shook his head. "I think the woman today, Hulda Camrin, will have a hard time. She'll have three-quarters of her original farm, no husband, and two children to care for. From the details we heard, I assume the husband did all, or most, of the farm work."

"That's a problem for her. If the farm had been larger and more productive, they might have had several workers. But since it's a smaller farm and no other workers, it's difficult to see how she'll keep it."

"You said the farms are not as valuable as in the past, so she might not get much coin if she's forced to sell."

"A bad situation for her," agreed Cadwulf. "In that case, she'll need to find family members to take in her and the children. The option should work for her, since the family is obligated toward the children, and she'll come with some coin from selling the farm.

"However, not all farm women are in such a difficult situation. Did you notice the woman sitting on the other end of our bench?"

"No. There were a lot of people, and I was paying attention to the cases."

"I'll point her out to you, if we see her sometime. She owns a medium-sized farm about ten miles north. She's in her late twenties or early thirties and a widow. Her husband died several years ago after an accident on their farm. In her case, she's successful in running the farm, because it's big and productive enough to have several workers and since there were no children. She's something of an exception, both because of her circumstances and since she's known to be both strong minded and bodied."

They sat on the steps, facing the ocean. The moon Aedan was just rising from the ocean horizon. The other moon, Haedan, would appear much later that night, if Yozef remembered the pattern of their cycles.

"I assume she has the same problem finding a new husband?"

Cadwulf laughed. "Yes, the same problem of too few men she would want to marry, and I doubt she's interested in giving up ownership of the farm. She's quite used to running the farm by herself."

They rose and entered the house. Elian had somehow known there was a guest and had set an extra place at his table. Yozef often ate with the older couple, at first to their discomfort, but tonight they had already eaten. Brak was nowhere to be seen, and Elian served them, set an open bottle of phila wine on the table, and excused herself for the evening. Conversation lagged, as they focused on roast coney, potatoes, a chard-like vegetable Yozef had come to like, the wine, and a version of sourdough bread Yozef and Elian had been experimenting with. As they finished the last of the coney, Yozef brought up the topic they had been discussing on the way from the abbey.

"Cadwulf, doesn't the excess of women over men cause problems? Not just for the women themselves, but for the entire clan and society? What happens to an unmarried woman?"

"If she has no property and can't work to support herself, then her family is responsible for her. Otherwise, the local abbey or village tries to find her a place, especially if there are children. Obviously, being married is best. In some clans, though, the shortage of men has been worse, due to conflict within or between clans. When that happens, some clans, particularly the northern ones, have customs that help the problem by allowing husbands two wives. More in rare cases, but usually just two."

Yozef was surprised. "Does that also occur in Keelan?"

"While it's not disallowed by either *The Word of God* or Keelan customs, our clan has traditionally frowned on the practice, although there are a few exceptions. I can think of only three examples I know of, and none in Abersford. In some of the provinces, the man must get approval from his local abbey or boyerman to take a second wife, depending on the customs and laws of the province, and the first wife has to approve sincerely. It's usually not allowed for the husband to pressure the wife into agreeing, although I understand this occurs more in the northern clans."

"Well," said Yozef, "I can see the logic as a solution to excess women, but it's a brave or foolish man to have even two wives, much less more than two."

Cadwulf smiled. "Yes, the obvious problems of two women in the same house." His face took on a more serious demeanor. "Not to mention the ability to commit to the marriage equally and as deeply as the *Word* instructs. Then there's the obligation to care for all children resulting from the marriage. More wives mean more children. That's the primary responsibility of marriage—the children."

"In the last case today, what if the man accused of rape hadn't been killed?"

"If there was confirming evidence or a confession to the rape, then he'd be held responsible for the rape and care of the child."

"What if the judges didn't decide there was proof of rape, and the child was his? He could claim the girl consented?"

"It's the same. If there was proof or admission that the child was his, then he'd be responsible for helping support the child. If no such proof, then the judges would rule he had no obligation."

The classic "he said, she said" problem. There are no DNA tests here.

"And if the girl was considered too young to give consent?"

"Too young?" questioned Cadwulf. "What does that matter?"

Oh, boy.

"Could she not be considered a child herself and not of age and maturity for such a decision?"

"All persons, of whatever age, can make decisions. The younger they are, the more their age is taken into consideration in handling the consequences of such decisions. She and her family shouldn't have put her in a situation where rape could occur."

Zounds! We're not in Kansas anymore.

CHAPTER 22

THE BULDORIANS

Preddi City

Okan Akuyun was two hours into the current stack of paperwork when interrupted by a knock at his office door. From the rhythm and strength of the four raps, he recognized it was the tall, solid, and dangerous-looking Major Perem Saljurk, long-time aide and unofficial bodyguard.

"Come, Perem," he said and laid down his quill. The door opened, and the officer strode across the floor and handed Akuyun a dispatch with the seal broken. Akuyun had no secrets from Saljurk, and the aide read most dispatches before deciding whether they needed to be delivered immediately or could wait.

"From Admiral Kalcan, General. A picket sloop came on a group of Buldorian ships and is escorting them to Rocklyn."

Right on time, thought Akuyun. Captain Adalan was as efficient as he'd judged. They'd arrived as agreed, five months to the day. He opened the dispatch and read, while the major waited. Seven Buldorian ships, their usual design, each with sixteen 15-pounder cannons. No one of the Buldorian ships was a danger to a Narthon frigate, but a pack like this could be dangerous to a larger warship caught alone.

Kalcan estimated the Buldorian ships would reach the abandoned Preddi fishing village by early evening and assumed they'd anchor well offshore before any of them docked the next morning.

"Thank you, Perem. Please send the admiral an acknowledgment and request he accompany me to Rocklyn first light tomorrow."

"Yes, sir, and I'll arrange a carriage and escort."

"Make that two carriages. I'll be returning the next day, but the admiral or some of the staff going with us may stay longer."

Akuyun watched his aide leave. There was definitely an advantage to having someone like Perem, who'd been with him so long he could anticipate.

They would ride in relative comfort, instead of on horseback, himself preferring the carriage option, since his riding skills had atrophied once he rose in the Narthani hierarchy. Also, he knew the admiral detested horses.

One more step on the path. Akuyun mentally checked off a milestone. Once they got the Buldorians settled, they could move along. Within a year, with good fortune, they could finish their objectives here. When this assignment was completed, Grand Marshal Turket hinted a successful conclusion would impress the High Command enough to pull him back to Narthon. There, he anticipated a rise in rank and assignment to either a field position or a regional command over a conquered territory. Akuyun wasn't in love with war, but after years of administrative work dealing with political and civilian issues on Caedellium, a field position would be a welcomed change. His current rank was equivalent to a division commander, so a promotion to the field would likely be as second-in-command in a corps at a major front. Command of a reserve corps or facing a lesser enemy was also possible. Any would suit him.

He turned in his swivel chair and pulled one of several cords hanging from the ceiling. Elsewhere in the headquarters, the other end of the cord rang a small bell. Within seconds, a runner appeared in front of his desk, as he finished a short note.

"Take this to my wife."

The soldier took the paper, saluted, and ran off. Rabia would pack an overnight valise for him, since he would spend the night in Rocklyn. He didn't fancy riding even in a comfortable carriage the sixty-mile round trip in one day.

Next, he wrote a memo to his senior commanders to alert them that the Buldorians had arrived. There was nothing for them to do at the moment, but he assiduously kept his immediate subordinates apprised of everything relevant. He turned and pulled a different cord. This time, a clerk came in.

"Copy this memo and send copies, except the last paragraph, to Commanders Zulfa, Metin, Erdelin, and Ketin. Send the complete copy to Assessor Hizer." The added words "invited" Hizer to accompany himself and Kalcan to Rocklyn. The assessor wasn't formally a subordinate, so Akuyun couldn't order him to accompany them. The Buldorians would coordinate with the Narthani navy, and Hizer would provide intelligence on targets for the Buldorian raids.

Rocklyn, Fishing Village, Preddi Province

The three Narthani leaders left Preddi City at first light. The morning sun vanished behind a weather front that blew in, and light rain began falling halfway to Rocklyn. Heavier rain didn't come until they were within a few miles of the village; otherwise, the dirt roads would have turned to mud. As it was, they made the thirty-mile trip in four hours. Akuyun used the time to go over every detail of the mission plans and the Buldorians' role. Not that either Kalcan or Hizer didn't already know everything, but Akuyun never missed an opportunity to reinforce every man's position and duties. Even so, they talked it out within two hours, followed by an hour of conversation about home and families. The final hour was quiet, as they crested a low hill and saw the fishing village.

"There they are," noted Hizer, pointing to three Buldorian vessels docked at the village harbor, while the other four anchored two to three hundred yards offshore.

"And there *we* are," responded Kalcan.

Two Narthani sloops and three frigates were anchored seaward of the Buldorian ships, ostensibly to provide protection when the Buldorian crews were ashore, but also reminding the Buldorians in whose waters they sailed.

The village itself consisted of two dozen structures assumed to be meeting houses, warehouses, shops, and homes of more prominent Preddi. Surrounding this cluster were forty to fifty smaller houses and huts, enough for an original population of four hundred. Though the village citizens had avoided most of the harsher consequences of the Narthani conquest, the last three hundred had been forcibly moved to allow the village to serve as the isolated base of operations for the Buldorians.

The two carriages and fifty Narthani cavalry escort covered the last mile to the village and stopped at one of the larger structures, where a Narthon banner flew from the roof and where several soldiers waited for the new arrivals. Major Saljurk dismounted from his horse, spoke with an awaiting junior officer, and came back to Akuyun's carriage.

"The Buldorian commander is at the dock. Shall I send for him right away?"

"No," said Akuyun, "tell him we'll meet him here in an hour. That'll give us a chance to stretch our bones after the trip and get something to eat."

Exactly one hour later, Major Saljurk ushered Musfar Adalan into a room where Akuyun, Kalcan, and Hizer waited. Akuyun smiled and rose to greet the Buldorian commander. The smile was genuine, since he appreciated punctuality and sensed it boded well for these mercenaries' coming performance. However, the smile was the closest they came to contact—clasping of hands or arms was reserved for close associates, not between a Narthani general and Buldorian raiders.

"I'm pleased to see you, Captain Adalan, and right on time, as we agreed. I take this to mean a good start to our relationship. I hope your voyage here went well."

"Thank you, General. Yes, everything was smooth. No weather or other problems, and all seven ships and crews are ready to begin."

"Fine, fine. And you *will* begin soon, but after spending a couple of days meeting with Assessor Hizer." Akuyun used an arm to indicate the man sitting next to him. "He is in overall charge of information gathering and will be selecting targets and coordinating the raids. Also, Admiral Kalcan will want to inspect your ships, and you'll be meeting with him to go over coordinating naval issues."

Adalan was a master at concealing his thoughts, a talent that served him well to hide his exasperation. *By all the Gods that might be, these Narthani loved to hear themselves talk!* He thought they just liked to be sure everyone else knew they were in command. Not that the Buldorian commander didn't appreciate good intelligence information, but he had dealt with the Narthani before and anticipated being told the same information over and over and over.

Patience, Musfar. They're paying for your time by setting this up for us, so you shouldn't complain too much.

"No problem, General. I look forward to our meetings." To the facile lie, he added a flamboyant gesture touching forehead, lips, and chin, assuring himself the Narthani didn't realize the order of touching was reverse a standard Buldorian gesture of respect and indicated the target should do something quite rude with the member between his legs.

Akuyun was thorough in everything he did. There were three ex-Buldorians among the tradesmen brought in to resettle Caedellium, one of whom was a clever and fervent convert to the Narthon Empire and a willing tutor in the more relevant Buldorian customs.

The general's pleasant demeanor never wavered. *So, our good captain tells me to go fuck myself,* Akuyun thought, amused, though he showed no emotion. *Never mind. As long as he does what we brought them here for, I don't care what he thinks to himself or what he thinks he's slipping past me.*

"Then, if it's agreeable, let's begin the briefings right away. I'm sure you and your men are eager to start."

Adalan barely managed to hide his surprise. He had been prepared for the Narthani to blather on. He recognized a different kind of Narthani than he'd dealt with before. This one was not one to be underestimated. While it didn't quite rise to the level of worry, the Buldorian wasn't as sure as he had been moments earlier that the Narthani didn't know he had been insulted.

"In that case, General, I need to send for my captains, if we are to begin immediately. Shall we reconvene in half an hour?"

First Target

It was near sunset when Hizer and Kalcan finished summarizing what they believed the Buldorians needed to know about Caedellium, including general topography, clan structure, types of weapons, most likely defenses the raiders would face, and enough detail of the coast and the nearby waters to begin. Sets of maps had been distributed, and the Buldorians asked many questions. Adalan, his second-in-command cousin, and the other ship's captains were attentive to every detail. Akuyun was satisfied the mercenaries knew their business.

Hizer ended the briefings. "And that, gentlemen, is our overview for you. Now, I'm sure you're interested in the first target we've selected."

Saljurk handed each Buldorian another map showing an expanded view of a section of the islands making up Seaborn Province off the northwest coast of Caedellium. A settlement was prominently marked.

"This is your first target, the fishing village of Nollagen on the southernmost island of Seaborn Province. The population is about 400, and, as far as we know, the Seaborn Clan doesn't maintain a regular militia or security force of any kind. They believe their isolation and relative poverty protect them from such needs."

Hizer paused, as he noticed frowns from several of the Buldorian captains. "I realize this is not as attractive a target as you were expecting or as attractive as future targets, but we chose this one for the first raid. Resistance should be minimal for a force your size. Other settlements are far enough distant to minimize help arriving before you finish with the village, and news of the raid will take time to reach the other clans, meaning you should be able to carry out another raid or two before other clans are warned."

Not all of the captains appeared mollified, but Adalan accepted the arguments. Not that he thought there would be a problem with going directly to a richer target, but he agreed with the Narthani that careful preparation was never unnecessary. If everything worked as expected, there would be opportunities for better spoils.

Admiral Kalcan took over the meeting and went over surveys of the coast around Nollagen, using the maps to point out beaches, reefs, coves, inland terrain, and other details his sloops had gathered from a year of careful patrols and mappings. The degree of detail alerted Musfar.

"Pardon, Admiral. I don't see how you got such impressive details simply by observing from offshore."

It was Hizer who answered. "That's because the Admiral's data is supplemented with observations on shore. You don't need to know other details."

While Adalan would have liked to learn more, he was satisfied. Obviously, the Narthani had agents in place within the Seaborn Clan and therefore likely among all of the clans. They might be genuine Narthani spies or paid Caedelli. Either way, he was reassured the information being given him had multiple sources.

Hizer continued, addressing Adalan. "We would like you to think about what you've heard these last hours and propose how you would carry out the raid on Nollagen. Let's meet again tomorrow at mid-morning to go over your plan."

Nollagen, Fishing Village, Seaborn Province

Senwina Kardyl roused from her sleep. Their small house was dark, but noise got through her dreams. A tone overlaid with distress. Still half asleep, she automatically reached out to the cradle beside her bed where six-month-old Onyla slept. The baby hadn't stirred. Senwina tucked her arm back under the blanket and rolled toward her husband's warmth, when she heard shouts. Many shouts. The walls of their home were thick stone to keep out the rain and dampness endemic to this part of southern Seaborn Province, so she couldn't make out the words being yelled, but there were many voices.

She rose to one elbow and turned up the whale oil lantern on the table next to their bed. The lit lantern was a luxury they permitted themselves when they had their first child. Now fully awake and trying to understand what she was hearing, she sat up.

"Kort," she whispered, so to not wake the baby or their five-year-old son, Allyr. Kort didn't respond. She put a hand on his shoulder and rocked him. "Kort," she repeated, louder. He grunted. She shook him hard with both hands and yelled, "Kort! Wake up! Something's happening in the village!"

"Wha . . . ?" her husband croaked.

"KORT!! SOMETHING'S HAPPENING IN THE VILLAGE!"

Kort's eyes flashed open with her fourth and loudest prompt. He sat up, listened for a moment, threw off the covers, and ran to the main door. "I'll see what's happening." He could hear yelling and other noises, even through their walls. His first thought was a fire, the only occasion in his lifetime he'd experienced similar turmoil.

Senwina remained sitting up in bed, watching through the bedroom door into the main room and a view to her husband opening the outer door. Instead of the darkness expected, she could see reflections of fire on the door and the jamb. The faint noise changed to ferocious pandemonium when the door opened. Yelling in Caedelli and some other language, screams, cries, clashes, animals joining in. Kort stood frozen for several seconds, then slammed the door shut, jammed the wooden locking arm into its brackets, and turned toward the bedroom. Even in the low light, she could see the fear in his eyes.

"Get the children and go out the back door!"

She stared, frozen, as he ran into Allyr's bedroom. Then she threw off the covers, jumped to her feet, and grabbed Onyla from her cradle.

A moment later, he appeared in the bedroom doorway, carrying their son in his arms. He ran to her, grabbed an arm, and pulled her out of the bedroom, dragging them toward the back door.

"People are attacking the village!" he choked out. "Many of them. They're everywhere!"

Someone tried to open the front door and then pounded on the heavy wood—the sound of an ax. They could hear wood splitting.

"Go!" he yelled to her, setting Allyr down and shoving him into her. "Run into the woods and keep running! Don't look back! Run for your lives!"

"Kort! You're coming, too?" she cried, the baby in her left arm, her right hand gripping Allyr's small one.

"I'll be right behind you, now *run*!!" He opened the back door and looked out into the darkness. Their house was on the edge of the village, so there were no more structures between them and the woods fifty yards away. He pushed her out the door. She stumbled toward the darkness of the woods, when she thought she heard Kort say, "Take care of the children." She turned in time to see Kort close the door. In that last moment, her mind noted that he appeared to be holding his fisherman's knife. Then she ran, barefoot, clad in only her nightshirt, clutching Onyla and pulling Allyr behind her. She was too afraid to cry or feel the rocks bruising and cutting her feet, focusing only on the woods and holding her children. She was within a few yards of the first trees when a hand shoved her in the back. She lost hold of Allyr, as she fell and twisted to avoid landing on the baby.

Flames covered the entire village, reaching thirty feet above the main buildings, illuminating everything within the line of sight for a mile in all directions, including the smoke billowing upward and drifting from the onshore breeze. Musfar Adalan waited on the main dock. He hadn't led the assault and wouldn't come ashore on subsequent raids, but for this first one he wanted to get a feel for the island and its peoples. His men had rowed straight to the dock from their ships anchored offshore. There had been no watch by the villagers, no one to alert what was to come, no defensive positions, no general alarm, no organized resistance once his men burst into the village itself. Only the cries from the Caedelli met his men, as they plundered from structure to structure. Adalan was pleased it had gone quickly, but not pleased with the disorder of his men once they realized they faced little opposition. It wouldn't always be this easy. There would be measures taken to ensure discipline was maintained.

Still, he had to admit the Narthani information was accurate. He watched as the four wounded and one dead of his men were loaded on a longboat and rowed to a waiting ship. One of the wounded told Adalan he had been injured by a single villager, who had also injured a second raider and killed a third. The wounded man begrudgingly admitted that the villager, wielding a wicked fisherman's knife, had put up a ferocious fight in a house's darkness before dying of a dozen wounds. Adalan took the account to heart. This village may have fallen easily, but that didn't mean the islanders couldn't fight.

His men set fire to the buildings nearest the dock, having saved those for last. Several longboats of booty had already been to the ships and returned to shore. Now it was time for the last of the captives and his men. A line of the former were led to the boats, a dozen at a time, linked to thirty-foot sections of rope by nooses tightened around their necks. They were females and boys of three to seven years—the age limit for male captives. Some of the captives were too shocked to show expressions; others were crying, all stumbling along. At the end of this rope was a woman holding a baby and a small boy clinging to her leg. She would bring a good price. Still young, comely enough, and obviously fertile. If she was lucky, a buyer would take all three. Otherwise, she might never see the children again after the auction, especially the boy.

Yes, it had gone well enough, Adalan thought, but they'd need to go over the raid in detail before the next one. They wouldn't all be this easy.

CHAPTER 23

EARTH FADES

Forgetting

The summer moved toward fall. The contrasting green of Earth and the darker foliage of Anyar became more distinct, as leaves turned shades anticipating colors to come. Scattered yellows to reds of Earth and blues and purples of Anyar already graced the higher elevations.

Yozef nestled under several blankets, out of which poked his face to take in the cool air coming from the open window. One eye opened to note the morning light, then closed again. He turned and stretched under the covers, feeling . . . good. He drifted in and out of sleep for the next hour, coming awake enough to know he was too comfortable to get up yet and then drifting under again. He had to get up. There were things to do. Things he *wanted* to do. Things he was *eager* to do, which was . . . odd, he thought. He couldn't remember ever being this eager at Berkeley. The effort pulled up other memories of his previous life. He could picture Julie's voice, her face, her body, her smell. Her favorite stuffed animal—a bear, saved from childhood—was named . . . what? He couldn't recall the name. His forehead wrinkled.

Why can't I remember the damn name? I saw the bear every day, and we joked about a third tenant in our apartment. We carried on conversations with it, as if it were another person. What was its name?

He searched other memories: family, school, television, Berkeley, books. English! It had been an Anyar year since he'd heard anyone speak English, except for talking to himself. He still carried on audible English conversations with himself but found speaking Caedelli easier and easier. The initial need to translate everything through English was fading. The periods of remembering were also less frequent. Snuggled under the covers, he realized he hadn't thought about Earth for several days.

Earth? Why did I think "Earth" instead of "home?" I should have thought, "Thinking about home."

He mulled this for several minutes. Earth. Anyar. Home.

Home wasn't Berkeley or his parents' house where he was raised or even Earth. It was . . . wasn't. Then where? Here in Caedellium? He didn't know. There was a sense of having lost something he hadn't been aware of possessing, overlaid with the sense of the need to find something he couldn't quite identify.

Sounds coming from another room diverted his thoughts. His attention shifted to his nose. Biscuits and bacon. *Elian in the kitchen making breakfast.* Sourdough biscuits that could have come from his mother's kitchen. A not-quite-bacon smoked meat made from a wild herbivore—a slothin. His stomach growled. Confusion set aside for the moment, he rose and dressed. Life went on. Breakfast and then head to the shops.

Fair Practices

The months whirled past Yozef. The ether business had taken off, with orders coming in from a dozen provinces and ether production handled by the workshop crew with minimal oversight by Yozef. He stopped in occasionally to check whether they were maintaining safety procedures. The men acted skeptical of his early warnings, until their cavalier attitude to Yozef's safety obsession tempered after a lesson in the explosive potential of ether. Fortunately, singed hair, missing eyebrows, red skin, and moderate shop repairs were the extent of the event.

Freed from constant attention to ether and ethanol production, Yozef's attention had shifted to soap. The single Abersford soap maker, Pollar Penwick, produced a single bar soap used for both body and clothes. The bar cleaned but was harsh and gave Yozef a mild rash if he rubbed himself too hard. Penwick's initial skepticism that there would be markets for different soaps converted to enthusiasm with the demand for the first two products. By the time Yozef was ready to move on to other projects, the soap maker was producing other bars, liquid soaps, soaps better for clothes, and harsher versions for industrial-level cleaning. Not all products were well received by the citizen of Abersford and surroundings, but enough were that orders increased each sixday.

The soap maker expanded into a small factory set outside Abersford and near the new spirits production facility in an area Yozef now called his "industrial park." He wasn't interested in following the soap business and was happy to have better soaps for himself and a cut of new profits—content to let Penwick reap most of the benefits. Months passed, and he assumed all proceeded well in the soap world, until Cadwulf noticed several wagons loading at the soap factory late one night and then moving with deliberate stealth down the road toward Gwillamer Province. Exactly what Cadwulf was doing in the middle of the night in the village Yozef never asked, but he suspected it involved one of the village's young females. Whatever the cause of his presence, Cadwulf shared with Yozef his suspicion that not all records of soap shipments were accurate.

Over Penwick's protests, Yozef insisted Cadwulf examine mandated operation records, which confirmed his suspicions. Penwick had recorded only half of the soap production, as required by their partnership.

Yozef, with Cadwulf and Carnigan beside him—Carnigan, in case they needed intimidation or security—confronted Penwick. After first denying any impropriety, he admitted the obvious, though instead of being apologetic, the shameless Penwick told Yozef that since they had no written agreement filed with the district registrar he was under no obligation to share anything with Yozef, and that Yozef should be grateful he was getting *any* share of the new business at all. Although customs and laws of Keelan were on the side of the soap maker, who had counted on Yozef's reputation for being mild-mannered, the brazenness turned out to be a monumental mistake.

"You mean he gets away with cheating me!" Yozef ranted after the meeting with Penwick.

"I'm sorry, Yozef, but it's not considered cheating, since you didn't follow the requirement to register such agreements. Everyone will see Penwick as untrustworthy, but they'd see you as stupid for not protecting yourself."

"And how about yourself?" Carnigan dug at Cadwulf, who blushed.

"Carnigan's right. It's also my fault. You were handling the soap making, and I was so involved with the bank, I assumed you remembered the lessons about registering all transactions. I'm sorry, Yozef, blame also has to rest on me."

Yozef took several deep breaths. "All right. I screwed up, and you didn't help, Cadwulf, but the result is that Penwick gets away with stealing, or whatever else you call it?"

"Sorry again, Yozef," Cadwulf said. "But yes, that's the way it is."

Yozef's fiery anger abated into cold fury. "So be it. I have enough money to live well, but I hate being screwed over by a dickhead. If I couldn't get Penwick to give me my agreed-on share, I'll take *all* of his business."

Yozef spent the next three hours querying Cadwulf, then Filtin Fuller and brewer Galfor on Keelan business customs. Caedellium had no history with excessive monopolies. The deliberate undercutting of competition to drive them out of business was not yet so serious an issue on Caedellium as to need intervention by a district boyerman or the clan hetman. By the same time the next day, Yozef had hired away half of the workers in the soap factory, bought a building, and arranged for construction of all of the needed facilities for making soaps. Within two sixdays, they were operational and selling soap at half the price it cost to make, with Yozef easily absorbing the losses from his ether and ethanol income. Within another two sixdays, Penwick failed to secure intervention by the abbot, the district boyerman, and a final appeal to the Keelan Hetman. Two sixdays later, the soap maker attempted to meet to apologize and repay the debt. Yozef ignored the overture. A month later, the soap maker closed his shop, sold all of his holdings in Abersford, and moved to Adris Province to start a new soap business. Before he left, Yozef sent him a letter explaining that he would consider their original arrangement still active in Adris. Yozef would get his originally agreed-on share, and as long as that happened, he wouldn't repeat driving Penwick out of business no matter where he moved on Caedellium.

As for the soap workers, all ended up working for Yozef's soap factory at higher pay than before. The senior worker, one of the first to jump to Yozef, was given a share to manage the business, and even then, Yozef's share of the profits was more than with Penwick.

Cadwulf and Carnigan saw to it that details of the soap maker's fate widely circulated. The lesson learned by the Abersford soap maker was hard, and the episode became incorporated into descriptions of the strange man who had washed up on a Caedellium beach. A mild-mannered man of average appearance, except for unusual light-bluish-gray eyes. An honest man, generous to workers, teller of jokes—and ruthless if crossed.

Harvest Festival

Days grew shorter, temperatures lowered, and foliage peaked in a kaleidoscope of color. Yozef stood mesmerized, facing the forested hills north of Abersford. He'd thought New England in the fall was spectacular the one time he'd visited at the right time. But *THIS!*

The End-of-Harvest Festival fell on a perfect day. Wispy clouds set off a bright midday sun and a blue sky. Only the occasional tinge of coolness in the breeze foretold of the coming winter and shortening days. The two-day event bustled and sprawled across a large field between Abersford and the abbey. All work stopped for those two days, and half of Yozef's workers had failed to show up for work the day before to prepare for various events and competitions. Now, Yozef stood among the throng attending the opening ceremony speeches, most mercifully short.

He estimated well over a thousand people stood listening, and even more busied themselves elsewhere on the grounds—several times more people than the entire population of Abersford and the abbey. He wondered how many miles away some of them had come from?

With the festival officially open, Yozef dispersed with the others to sample the offerings of the tents and the stands set up across acres in all directions. Much of the festival resembled a rural fair in the United States or a 4H gathering, showing off prize animals, holding competitions for sizes of vegetables and animals, and displaying pumpkin-like gourds, leather, metal, and wood crafts. The festival featured tradesman stands, gambling, foot races, and other activities Yozef never identified.

The sounds of the festival beat on his eardrums: people talking, animals vocalizing, and everywhere music from all quarters and a myriad combination of instruments and voices, individuals and groups, all lively. Yozef wandered among the crowd, stopping at a craft table here, a food judging there, and lingering near music that caught his ear. Some performances seemed planned and others spontaneous, with performers claiming an open space to sing or play. It was Yozef's first exposure to the full range of Caedellium instruments: drums and stringed instruments of all sizes and sounds, wind and brass horns, and instruments of whose categorization he was uncertain. The bagpipe-like performances he moved past quickly, then stopped in wonderment before what resembled a kazoo quintet. The five small, bulbous instruments were each of slightly different shape, with sounds reminiscent of oboes and flutes.

Yozef turned away from the kazoo performance and spied Cadwulf waving to him through the human stream.

"Yozef, I wondered if I'd find you here somewhere. How are you enjoying all this?"

"Quite an impressive assortment of displays. Is the festival always this large?"

"This is normal. It's tame right now and best for families. After sundown, it gets rowdier when the women and the children go home, and the men drink more. It used to be worse, but when I was about six years old, Hetman Keelan ordered that no alcohol be served at festivals until sundown. Since then, more people attend and stay longer. At the time it wasn't the most popular ruling from the hetman, though now most see it worked for the best."

"Is there any recommended order to what I should try to see?"

"No. I'll walk with you awhile and answer any questions."

The two of them started down a row of leather-goods displays, when they became three after finding Filtin Fuller examining a leather vest and haggling with the maker. When Cadwulf called out, Filtin dropped the vest back on the table, said something to the disappointed tradesman, and wove his way to where they waited.

"Where's the family, Filtin?" asked Cadwulf.

"Nerlin and the children are off looking at coneys, colts, and the food preserve exhibits and contests. I have leave to do anything else and meet back with them in two bells."

Cadwulf gave Filtin a sardonic grin. "So your wife decides what you can do?"

"My wife is a wise woman. She knows how bored I am with those parts of festivals she finds most interesting, so she doesn't drag me to them. She also knows I'll be in a better mood for later when the children get tired."

"A wise woman indeed," laughed Yozef. By now, Filtin was close to being an indispensable worker and was also a friend. Besides being Yozef's chief equipment designer and craftsman, Filtin was a sometimes drinking companion and someone around whom Yozef's mood always seemed to lift, possibly because Filtin's bright complexion, short red beard, and round face, when combined with a habitually optimistic disposition, reminded Yozef of a Christmas ornament.

"Filtin, Cadwulf is educating me on Caedellium harvest festivals. How about joining us to add to my enlightenment?"

"Glad to . . . until I'm summoned back by the wife."

In the next hour, Yozef learned to distinguish the three breeds of milk cows, how to estimate the weight of an ox, how a roasted merkon (mussel-like) tasted (bad), and that the muddleton berry jam prepared by Filtin's wife was the best in the district (Yozef couldn't tell the difference, so he lied). Cadwulf seemed to have little interest in the fair itself, but his two compatriots noticed his roving eye whenever they passed young women.

Yozef elbowed Filtin. "I don't know why Cadwulf even pretends to do anything else besides fishing for girls."

"Fishing for girls? Hah! I'll remember that one." Then, addressing the younger man, he asked, "Any bites today?"

Cadwulf smiled good-naturedly, "A few nibbles. A good fisherman knows how to be patient."

"What about you, Yozef?" queried Filtin. "You're of marriageable age, becoming a wealthy man, and person of note in Abersford. Any women catching your eye? Or should I ask if you've already been fishing, and there are catches you haven't told us about?"

The question hovered around Yozef's consciousness for several steps, then coalesced, and he froze. The other two men continued several steps, oblivious to their diminished number before missing him, then stopped and looked back.

Women. Sex. He'd been here nine months, a full Anyar year, and he hardly remembered thinking about sex. How could that be? Had the Watchers done something to him during the "repair job"? A chill trickled down his arms and back, not only at the thought of a life without sex, but of what else they might have done to him.

"Yozef?" asked Cadwulf. "Are you all right?"

He stared at the others. "I just realized I haven't thought about women that way the whole time I've been on Caedellium," he said in a tone both wondering and worrying. "That doesn't seem natural."

"It's not!" said a concerned Filtin, as he and Cadwulf stepped back to where Yozef still stood. "A grown man has his normal needs. Uh . . . you say you haven't thought about women that way, but . . . uh . . . surely, you must have noticed being 'aroused.' Maybe when asleep or daydreaming?"

"Aroused? What—? Oh, you mean an erection. Not that I remember."

"Not at all?" blurted Cadwulf. "I guess the shock of being washed up here and knowing you'd never see your homeland again might have something to do with it. Maybe you should see the medicants about it?"

"Somehow I don't see myself discussing my sex life with Brother Dyllis or Sister Diera."

"Doesn't have to be those two. Brother Alber would be understanding, and no one thinks he'd tell of your confidence," offered Cadwulf.

"Why go to the medicants when you've two perfectly good advisors right next to you?" chortled Filtin.

"Practical advice we might give," said Cadwulf dryly, "but if there are medical problems, he needs to see the medicants."

"He can always do that later, after seeing if our advice helps. Right here and now is the perfect opportunity to survey the women of Abersford and see if any gives Yozef a 'rise' in interest."

Both Filtin and Cadwulf laughed. Yozef was less amused.

"Now, now, Filtin," said Cadwulf, "it's important to let Yozef know which women might be available. We don't want our mysterious friend and employer to get into trouble with the magistrates or irate husbands and family members."

For the next half hour, they alternated between experiencing exhibits and a running commentary on the names, attributes, and availability of Abersford women. At first, Yozef cringed at the degree of detail, although it was all done with good humor, and the ribald nature of the comments paired with an unmistakable undertone of respect.

"Cania Narberth. Now there's a good-looking woman," whispered Filtin, as they passed a black-haired woman in her late twenties. "Too bad she had to get married. She and I had some times."

"Before he was married," added Cadwulf.

Filtin continued his running travelogue, as they passed a teenage girl with long auburn hair. "Ah, one of Gerrael Horsham's daughters. Elwin is her name or something close to it. A little young yet, but in another year or two our young Cadwulf will sniff around her."

Cadwulf laughed. "No, in this case. It's best to avoid complications with more than one woman in the same family."

"You dog," laughed Filtin, "I assume that refers to the oldest daughter, Rhawna?"

Cadwulf sniffed. "An honorable man does not discuss such details among common louts such as yourself."

"I'll have you know I am *not* a common lout," declared Filtin. "It takes effort to stay an *uncommon* one!"

Although Yozef told them he had not had thoughts of women, meaning sex, since he arrived, what he realized was that he had not *consciously* had such thoughts. He *had* been noticing females more lately, though he hadn't realized how much until minutes ago. As it always seemed here, realization of one issue raised more questions and problems.

Trying to sound nonchalant, he asked, "Exactly what *are* the customs here on Caedellium, as far as men and women are concerned?"

"I assume you don't mean how they dress different," replied Cadwulf with a mischievous grin.

"He means how do they *undress*," ribbed Filtin. "Or more to the point, how does a man get a woman to lie back and spread her legs."

Yozef's face heated. "I mean, if they're attracted to each other, what are the customs here? What's considered appropriate behavior?"

"Appropriate behavior?" said Filtin. "That all depends on who you ask."

"True," Cadwulf conceded. "The *Word* sanctions the union of husband and wife but is not clear on non-husband and non-wife. You can get the theophists to argue endlessly over the issue without coming to a consensus. What the *Word* emphasizes is the responsibility to care for any children that result."

Filtin's jovial expression became more serious, as he listened to Cadwulf's words. "And it must be that the woman is both of a reasonable age and willing."

Cadwulf nodded. "Definitions and customs vary. What is defined as 'appropriate age'? Parents will believe it's several years older than the girl does. There's also some sense that a person is less respectable if he or she is *too* frequent or public in relationships with the other sex. On the other hand, it's a fairly common custom for two such persons to acknowledge the relationship in front of others, in case a child results. That way, there is evidence of fatherhood, if necessary."

"That sounds better than what really goes on," Filtin qualified. "Too often, there's some reason not to want to be public, such as embarrassment or the perceived objections of family or friends. Not to mention that opportunity and urges might not fit with planning or rational thought."

"True," said Cadwulf, "which is why, whether fair or not, the burden falls more on the woman to be sure of circumstances and intentions. Especially since she needs to know her monthly bleeding cycle. Unless she's too much a simpleton, she knows that the chances of getting with child are greatest the sixdays around her time."

"That gives her at about four sixdays each month when it's safe, if she wants to avoid getting pregnant," said Filtin.

Hmmm . . . considered Yozef. *That's interesting.* The larger of the two moons here had a thirty-six-day orbit pattern. The month divisions were matched on the same cycle, and women here must have their ovulation cycles synchronized with the moons, as on Earth, except here it was thirty-six days, instead of twenty-eight. So, for maybe two-thirds of each month, a woman here could have intercourse with a lower risk of pregnancy, assuming she was regular and kept accurate track.

I wonder what this means for customs on extramarital sex?

Before he could ask, Filtin answered.

"Mothers teach daughters to be aware once they start their monthly bleedings, but when she reaches her full size, she's considered an adult and responsible in this matter."

"That coincides with reaching what's considered the usual marriageable age of seventeen," added Cadwulf.

Seventeen? Yozef did a quick conversion. That was about fifteen years on Earth.

"So, if I understand, when she's of marriageable age she might start to engage in sex. Are there any restrictions for age or position of the man?"

Cadwulf shrugged. "While it's not considered good behavior for a man *too* much older to have relations with a much younger woman, that's her responsibility."

The two Caedelli continued with Yozef's sex education class for several more minutes. Yozef listened carefully. It was evident relations were condoned outside of marriage.

"Ah . . . is there any problem with . . . ah . . . illnesses passed between a man and a woman when they have sex?"

"Diseases?" queried Filtin. "Why would there be? Sex between men and women is natural. Why would God design diseases to prevent it?"

"Oh, just wondering," said Yozef. *So, no STDs came along with the transplantation from Earth. I wonder whether that was planned or a side effect of sampling from small, isolated populations? Of course, with those nanomachines or whatever, that wouldn't supposedly be a problem for me, anyway.*

"What about relations between two people who are already married to others?"

Filtin grunted. "That's different."

Cadwulf agreed solemnly. "There might be room for different interpretations of women and men outside of marriage, but the *Word* is very specific once you're married. To violate the marriage bed is a major sin."

Filtin nodded agreement. "And for even the less observing people of the *Word*, there're the practical implications. Inheritance goes through children of the couple. Children from infidelity can be excluded from inheritance. Husbands can divorce their wives if the women have been unfaithful."

"In theory," said Cadwulf. "Though if most of the property was originally the wife's, it reverts to her, so husbands might be hesitant to divorce in those cases and just take it out on the wife by beating her. Another option is to accuse the other man of infringing on the marriage and ask for a monetary penalty. That requires making it all public, shaming everyone involved, and having proof a magistrate will accept."

"Can a wife divorce a husband for his being unfaithful?"

Filtin looked surprised. "The wife divorcing the husband? That rarely ever happens."

"Except for cases like you saw in the justice session," Cadwulf chimed in. "You must understand that if a wife wants a divorce, unless there are extenuating circumstances, the children and the property of the couple go with the father and his family, if the father demands it. This means that if there are legitimate children, the wife might only ask for divorce if the husband didn't want the children or any property that once belonged to her. Otherwise, she'd have to go back to her family with no children and no possessions, except her clothing."

"And you don't see this system as putting more burden on the woman than on the man?" queried a disgusted Yozef.

Filtin raised an eyebrow. Though he didn't say anything, Yozef interpreted the expression as, *"What are you talking about?"* Cadwulf seemed to consider this a novel idea, although he simply said this was the custom.

By now, they'd made almost a complete circuit of the fair and stopped, as they considered what to do next. A stocky woman walked by, nodded to the two Caedelli, and bestowed a longer smile and look at Yozef. He found his gaze lingering as she walked away. Did her hips swing a little more than necessary or was it his imagination? And she wasn't so much stocky as sturdy, with well-shaped calves and arms. She looked about thirty, with brownish hair somewhat bleached looking, he assumed from the sun, since her face showed weathering with only the beginnings of lines that would deepen with age.

Filtin elbowed Yozef back to attention. "Well, I see you're not *totally* oblivious to women. Actually, that one might be a good candidate for you."

Cadwulf frowned reproachfully at the other man but grudgingly agreed.

"She looks familiar," said Yozef. "Who is she, and why would she be a *candidate,* if I was so interested?"

"Her name is Bronwyn Linton," said Cadwulf. "She sat on the opposite end of our pew during the justice proceedings last week. I mentioned her to you. She owns a good-sized farm north of Abersford."

"And she's a widow," Filtin piped up.

"Her husband died about two years ago in an accident on their farm."

"And she's a widow," repeated Filtin, "who hasn't bedded a man in those two years, if the rumors are true."

"She's attractive enough, and if she owns a good farm, I'd expect there'd be *many* men interested in her," said Yozef.

"Remember our talking about the shortage of men," countered Cadwulf. "She's a strong woman with good common sense, and there aren't that many possibilities for her once you rule out married men. I'm not surprised she gave you a good look. The one exception to a woman's property transferring to a new husband is if they register that agreement. She almost certainly knows who you are, the mysterious stranger who is becoming wealthy and is unmarried. Therefore, she knows there's more chance she could keep ownership of the farm if you married."

At that moment, Filtin's wife with two children in tow interrupted the lesson in Caedellium mating customs. With his free time expired, the family went off to find a midday meal at the food shops. Cadwulf also excused himself, and Yozef found himself alone again, but now thinking about the day, about women, and what he could do to make an impact by using his knowledge of chemistry.

Is This Home?

Yozef walked back to his house as the sun set. It had been a good day. Maybe it was time he admitted this was home. Here and now. Not Berkeley, the United States, or even Earth. Here. Anyar. Caedellium. Abersford. It wasn't the life he would have chosen, and he'd always miss what he'd lost, but here he made a difference. He had friends better than any he'd ever had on Earth. He was changing the trajectory of Anyar's future by the knowledge he introduced, even if no one here realized it now or perhaps ever would in his lifetime.

He could see the lights from his house. Elian would have evening meal ready. She had relaxed around him enough to mother him, and even Brak was almost jovial—at times. He would sleep solidly this night, then rise in the morning to fill his day with interesting projects. It was a good life.

CHAPTER 24

A WORLD BEYOND ABERSFORD

Yozef accepted himself as introspective. Not that he didn't enjoy fellowship, but there were always times he needed solitude to settle his mind and emotions. His time on Anyar had focused on the abbey complex, then expanded to Abersford and its immediate surroundings, including his cottage. When he felt the urge for more isolation, he walked the coast and country west of Abersford.

The territory was unpopulated, he assumed due to the rough terrain and lack of roads. At first, he would hike a few miles or more along the coast and inland. During his initial wanderings, he found a cove with a picturesque beach a hundred yards wide. At lower tides, the rocks at the opening of the cove absorbed most of the waves' power, but during high tides, major surf broke onshore. The combination of gentle low and the more vigorous high tides resulted in the sand being kept within the cove, but every day the beach had a different contour. Rising from the shore, a gentle grassy slope ended two hundred yards at a tree line of mixed Anyar and Earth species.

The first time he stood at the high-tide mark, Yozef decided it was perfect. He guessed the distance at about three miles from Abersford and the abbey; otherwise, he'd have wanted a house right there up against the trees, close enough to hear the surf, but not too close to the sound or spray. While hiking back to Abersford, he decided to investigate how to purchase the land and build a small retreat house.

He frequently returned to the same cove, though as he explored more, he rode a horse. His horse. Carnigan had selected a small gray gelding, assured Yozef a child could ride it, and gave him rudimentary riding lessons—enough to keep Yozef on the horse's back most of the time.

"Why did you name the horse Seabiscuit?" Carnigan asked the first time Yozef cursed the unoffending animal after falling off.

"It's the name of a famous horse back where I came from," Yozef groused.

Even Yozef had to admit Carnigan was right. Seabiscuit was probably the mellowest horse on the island, making him just within Yozef's ability to ride. The first few trips from the house to and from the abbey or village were major adventures, and only later did he ride Seabiscuit to venture farther afield during his wanderings west of Abersford.

Inland, he discovered the charm and mystery of a multitude of small valleys, dales, ravines with widely varying terrain, rock formations, and flora. It was farther along the coast where he stumbled on the resources for his next enterprise.

Two sixdays after the Harvest Festival, Yozef extended his wanderings along the beaches and cliffs beyond his cove and came upon what he ended up calling Birdshit Bay. In retrospect, it wasn't a bay at all, maybe an inlet or a fiord, except the enclosing hills were lower than his vision of a real fiord. Whatever it was called, a mile-long finger of water intruded from the coast inland. Rocky cliffs framed the quarter-mile-wide and deep central channel, and at the mouth of the inlet and out to sea sat rock formations up to a hundred yards across. At first glance, the flat surfaces of the cliff tops and offshore formations appeared chalk-like. Only after closer examination did he realize the whitish rock was guano. A cursory survey suggested that twenty- to forty-foot-deep solidified guano covered the offshore formations, while those on the cliff tops were up to eight feet thick.

The source of the guano was no mystery; the rocks and the skies teemed with a menagerie of flying creatures, birds from Earth and Anyarian murvors. The murvors appeared to be birds from a distance, but up close, they had more reptilian-like heads and longer, thinner feathers. Both features indicated a separate evolutionary history to the same niches as Earth's birds.

Wherever they evolved, the flying creatures seem to get along with one another. Obviously, they all contributed to the guano, but most of the deposits must be from the murvors, assuming he was right that birds and humans had arrived on Anyar about the same time, only a few thousand years ago.

Yozef walked the length of the inlet along the cliff tops until he reached the end, swarms of flying creatures swirling around him the whole length, while he thought of fertilizer. Guano contained all of the major nutrients for plants—nitrogen, phosphate, and potassium. *Christ! There must be enough guano in this one spot to supply most of the entire island's fertilizer needs for decades, if not longer.* He wondered whether the islanders already used it for their crops. He'd have to check when he got back. If they didn't, maybe this was his next project.

A second use for the guano occurred to him only when he was in sight of his house and a stray thought included the Narthani. *Gunpowder!* The main ingredient was potassium nitrate. It was usually sourced from mineral deposits but could be isolated from excrement, such as manure piles and guano. Yes, he remembered. Potassium nitrate could be extracted from bird guano by a series of filtering and precipitations, but bat guano was a better source. The South in the U.S. Civil War used guano from bat caves as a major resource in making gunpowder.

He didn't know whether the Caedelli made their own powder or imported it, but if these Narthani were a big enough threat, more sources of gunpowder might be important. He'd need to check about both fertilizer and gunpowder.

His inquiries confirmed that guano deposits were common to the coasts of Caedellium, but its use as fertilizer was unknown.

Not really a surprise, mused Yozef. With so much fertile land and the island relatively underpopulated, there was no pressure to increase yields over what they already produced.

As for the farmers using guano to fertilize, the obvious question was "Why would the Caedellium farmers care if they could increase their crop yields?" The Narthani embargo of trade resulted in the island's farmers producing more than there were markets for.

But this won't last, Yozef figured. Eventually, trade would start again, and increased yields from fertilizer would pay off. It wouldn't be of any use right away, but fertilizer was a good long-term investment, even if years from now. He'd also need to investigate whether there was a market for gunpowder.

To pursue fertilizer production, he needed an action plan. First was to find out how to buy or lease the land from the current owner. Then, hire workers to mine enough guano to test, and find farmers willing to find out how much of this fertilizer to apply, how many times to apply, and when in the growing season to apply it. Increased yields might not tempt farmers to cooperate, so he might have to pay farmers for the use of their land and aid in the experiments. Depending on the cooperation of the farmers, he might also need to hire someone to manage the tests, both to keep accurate records and to make sure the farmers didn't do anything to invalidate the outcomes.

Filtin Fuller confirmed Yozef's supposition that inquiries into property ownership of land needed to be through the clan's registrar system. However, the relevant records and changes in ownership had to come at the district registrar's office in Clengoth, the district seat fifteen miles east. Not having his aged Volkswagen Rabbit at hand, Yozef's next problem was getting to Clengoth and back. Although his horsemanship had improved, he didn't see himself riding Seabiscuit thirty miles.

There being no formal transportation systems on Caedellium, that left Yozef walking or finding a wagon heading his way and willing to take passengers. He didn't mind the idea of a good hike, but not in both directions.

The solution came in the form of an abbey wagon taking a patient to Clengoth. A man visiting Abersford had broken his leg. Brother Alber was returning the man home by wagon, with the patient's horse tied behind. The man, being moderately prosperous in whatever was his trade, was paying the abbey for both his treatment and the ride home and was displeased when informed it would be a working wagon and not a carriage. He was also disgruntled to learn his paid-for transportation included sharing the ride with other passengers. His complaint to the abbot was futile, and he endured the trip alternately sullen and wincing at the harder bounces. However, the abbey provided him with a straw mattress to lie on, whereas Yozef and the other five passengers sat on burlap bags containing something round and not quite hard. It turned out that two of the passengers had the same destination as Yozef—one man was going to register a major land transaction involving a disputed inheritance, and the other was the part-time local agent of the registrar himself and carried a satchel of papers of everyday matters to copy at the district's main registrar's office. The other passengers were a woman visiting family and a young man who told Yozef he traveled to Hewell Province to a scholasticum well-known for apothecary training.

The trip to Clengoth took two and a half hours. After leaving the low hills around Abersford, they rode into the central valley of the Keelan Province and passed farms separated by scattered groves of trees. It was the longest trip Yozef had made since waking on Anyar. He would have enjoyed the experience and the views more, if he hadn't had to constantly maintain a semblance of balance while jostling on his assigned bag. Once at Clengoth, he followed the two men with registrar business to the office, then roamed the town for an hour until he figured the others had finished.

Clengoth was large enough to be considered a town. He estimated three thousand citizens, compared to Abersford's nine hundred or so. What Clengoth also had was a significant business district with far more variety and a number of shops. Mixed in with smaller shops were a few with up to twenty-five workers, enough to be considered small factories.

In addition to the local main abbey they passed on the outskirts of Clengoth, there were several smaller abbeys in the town, and by their bells he knew when it was time to find his way back to the registrar's office. Inside sat two desks where clerks worked with other customers. Several straight-back chairs lined against the front wall near the door, and two chairs were occupied, Yozef assumed, by people waiting for a free clerk. He sat on a chair and daydreamed until interrupted.

"Next," said a clerk, who impatiently waved him to the now-empty chair facing the desk.

"What matter?" barked the clerk.

"I'm interested in buying two pieces of land near Abersford, but no one there knows who is the owner of the land. I'm told that information would be kept here."

"That's correct. You'll have to tell me exactly where this land is. Did you get a map showing the location from the Abersford registrar agent?"

Yozef hadn't but reached into the leather portfolio he carried and withdrew several sheets of paper, each of which unfolded twice to reveal hand-drawn maps about eighteen inches square. The clerk looked at the top one, then back at Yozef with a little more interest and respect than moments earlier.

"Not from the local agent," Yozef apologized. "I didn't know about getting maps from him. I drew the maps myself. Here is a rough map of the Abersford area, and the land I'm inquiring about is west along the coast." His finger traced from Abersford to his cove and to where Birdshit Bay cut into the shoreline. He then moved to the second, more detailed sheet, which showed only the two plots and the immediate surrounding land and shore. A heavy line squared around the cove where he dreamed of a house, and two miles farther west other lines followed the contours of the inlet a few hundred yards inland and included the rock formations within the inlet and offshore. "And these are the two pieces of land I'm interested in purchasing, but I need to find the owner."

The clerk managed a smile, without cracking his face. "Excellent maps, Ser. As good as the ones the Abersford agent would have given you. If only more people understood the importance of good records and maps, it would make my job much easier. Let me see whether our maps correspond to yours. If they do, then I should be able to determine ownership."

The clerk rose and went through a door into the rear of the building. Since the room with the two clerks was only a fraction of the total building, Yozef suspected that where the clerk disappeared included a record repository. Sure enough, a few minutes later the clerk returned with a two-by-three-foot bound ledger and three rolls of large paper. He checked the label on one roll, then spread it onto his desk. It was a map of the Abersford area. Even looking at it upside-down from across the desk, Yozef could recognize details of the coastline and markings of the abbey and Abersford. The writings on the map were in three colors—the red and blue ink the first he'd seen, other than the ubiquitous black.

The black ink divided the land into large sections with blue or red numbers. Offering no explanation, the clerk mumbled to himself as he examined the map. Yozef divined that the blue referenced the owner, and red meant there were many smaller parcels, and a scroll with more detail was needed. Yozef's and the official maps were compared to satisfy the clerk that Yozef's maps were reasonably drawn, then another roll showed the regions containing Yozef's two sites of interest. The first thing Yozef noted was that most of the region fell within a single marked parcel, with smaller parcels ending only a mile or so from Abersford.

This means no one owns the land I'm interested in? That doesn't seem likely. Someone owns everything.

The clerk examined the official map closely and compared it to Yozef's, then looked up. "It appears this is undeveloped land, according to our records. This usually means the terrain is unsuited to common uses, such as farming, and no minerals worth mining have been found there. You have examined the land carefully?"

"Very carefully," answered Yozef.

"Did you find any signs of present or past occupation or human activity?"

Yozef shook his head. "Nothing I could see. A few game trails, but no sign anyone has been there recently."

The clerk nodded and spoke in the rote cadence of someone who has said the exact words innumerable times and was hardly aware of what he was saying.

Sounds like the McDonald's worker telling a customer, "Thank you for eating at McDonald's and have a nice day," in one breath.

"Then we can register you as the temporary owner, subject to your showing improvements and use of the land within one year, no other claimants to the land appearing, and continued use yearly thereafter. Any lapse in use of the land, and it reverts to the clan."

At first, Yozef wasn't sure he knew what the clerk was saying. When he didn't respond after a few moments, the clerk looked up, annoyed.

"Sorry," Yozef said. "I'm new to Caedellium and not familiar with the laws and customs. Do you mean this land doesn't belong to anyone?"

"It belongs to the clan until someone registers its use and continues that use," the clerk said in a tone implying, *"As any dolt knows."*

"So … I don't have to buy the land?"

"You can't *buy* unused land, because it belongs to the clan. If no one else is using the land, you can try to make something of it. If you do, then the land is yours as long as it's being used by you or your heirs. The same applies to anyone you might sell the land to." *You, double dolt,* being unspoken.

It was logical, once he thought about it. The island was still underpopulated for its resources. The system worked well now because as the population grew, people could expand into empty land that the government, the clan, or whatever, kept in trust until that time. It might work well until all usable land was taken up, and then they'd have a problem adjusting to a permanent ownership system.

"In that case, I'd like to register to use these two parcels of land."

The clerk opened a drawer and pulled out two forms.

I'll be damned. Honest to God forms. God knows how far I am from Earth and still forms!

It was a piece of paper with print and lines and boxes to fill in. Yozef had read printed books at the abbey but had assumed they were all imported. The form the clerk handed him had obviously been printed here on the island, since some of the information asked for was specific to Caedellium. It wasn't a long form, but one section asked about the intentions for the property. He wrote "to build a house" for the parcel at the small cove and "mining" for the inlet parcel. The clerk took both forms and, to Yozef's surprise, didn't ask the two obvious questions: "Why would anyone build a house on useless land where there are no roads?" and "Why would you be mining on beaches and offshore rocks?" Evidently, once the form was filled in, the bureaucratic attention span ended there, just as on Earth.

Yozef filled out the forms, signed them, and handed them back to the clerk, who cautioned, "Be sure to place stone markers with the parcel number chiseled in them. The borders you specified are straight enough to need markers only at the corners and shoreline. You will need to have the local registrar agent inspect the sites and the markers in the next three months to confirm the marker locations."

With those final instructions, the clerk counter-signed and stamped the form with a seal, collected twenty krun per parcel, informed Yozef that a local magistrate would check on the requirements for usage in a year, and gave Yozef a "deed" spelling out the exact locations and condition. Yozef walked out of the office with the deeds secured in his satchel, the proud owner of two parcels, as long as he worked or used the land.

The Anyar sun was still high enough in the clear sky for Yozef to estimate he had five to six hours of daylight left. Based on his partial tour of the town and some directions given by the registrar clerk, he visited shops and bought a backpack, several vials of red and blue ink, some bread and cheese, two comfortable pairs of shoes for everyday wear, and a flagon of wine. He packed it all and headed back to Abersford, walking. The wagon was going back the next day, but he didn't want to wait. He looked forward to the walk back, so he could see the countryside from a level, non-bouncing position. His rear appreciated the plan.

The fifteen miles took him six hours. By the time he got home, the last light had faded, travel complaints had long ago shifted from his butt to his feet, and the bread, the cheese, and the wine were only memories.

CHAPTER 25

IGNITION

An Abbey Burns

Musfar Adalan chafed while waiting for word from his cousin Adel, who'd led the men ashore on their first mainland Caedellium raid. He understood that his place was to remain with the seven ships anchored offshore. The first raid had been an exception, but his days of always leading from the front were over. His responsibility was to keep control of the ships and respond if the raid went badly. He didn't doubt his men understood this, though the emotional part of him wanted to be ashore, leading his men, as when he was younger.

Their first raid on the fishing village on the archipelago of small islands making up the Seaborn Province to the northwest of Caedellium had gone smoothly, but this was different. Seaborn was isolated, sparsely populated, and unsuspecting. This time, the target was an abbey complex in Pewitt Province, less than a hundred sea miles from Seaborn. There was always the chance that word of the Seaborn raid had reached the main island, and his men would walk into prepared defenses. Pewitt was also more populated, meaning help could come faster if they were warned.

The Narthani had been their usual annoying selves, making arrogant assurances their information about the Pewitt abbey was accurate. Musfar knew they were sincere and respected the competence of the Narthani pigs, but sending men ashore was nothing to take lightly, especially since most of the men were from his own clan. Many were blood relatives, one of whom Musfar could see in the longboat, rowing back from the shore. Kiltar Adalan was his eighteen-year-old nephew, the son of one of his many younger brothers. This was Kiltar's first action, and he served as Adel's aide and runner, meaning the youth would be bringing word on the progress of the raid.

The longboat rowers stowed their oars and secured the boat against the ship's hull. Kiltar raced up the rope ladder as only an eighteen-year-old could, and Musfar smiled at the memories of when he could do the same.

"Uncle . . . er . . . Captain," stumbled Kiltar, "I'm to report the raid went off as planned. The abbey is ours, and the raiding party is finishing looting and setting the abbey afire. Sub-Captain Adalan says it will take several boat trips to move everything to the ships."

While Musfar welcomed the oral report, he already knew the raid had gone well. The boat delivering Kiltar and Adel's message was piled with sacks and boxes he assumed were plunder, and crewmen busied lifting a dozen bound Caedelli aboard ship. Eight were young women and the rest children between three and seven years. All would be slaves, either kept by officers as part of their shares or sent to slave markets. None would ever set foot on their home soil again.

"Casualties?" asked Musfar.

"Three dead," Kiltar reported, "and seven wounded, one severe. Sub-Captain Adalan says they will be on the next boat out."

"Good report, Kiltar." Musfar slapped his nephew on the back. "Get your boat unloaded and back to the shore with you. Tell Sub-Captain Adalan I'll move around the cape and closer to shore to speed up the transfers. Off with you now."

Kiltar vanished over the side, shouting at the crewman to hurry with unloading.

The boy was full of himself now and bursting with energy, but he'd learn it wouldn't always be this easy. Adel would look after him until he had enough experience to keep a clear head.

Musfar turned to a signalman standing nearby. "Host signal flags for all ships to follow us." The raiding party had put ashore two miles around a rocky cape hiding the ships, while men moved overland to surprise the abbey. Concealment was no longer necessary.

He next turned to a senior sailor in charge of cargo. "Get the prisoners secure in the lower hold, and remind the men to leave the women alone for now. There'll be time for them later when we're loaded and heading back to Preddi waters." Women destined for the slave markets would bring higher prices if pregnant, and during the voyage home, the ships' crews would do their best to bring about that condition.

Well, well, Musfar mused to himself. *The Narthani information was good, again. Maybe this is all going to work out as well as I hoped.* Whatever the Narthani plans for Caedellium, he needed to sail in their wake until it was time to leave. Of course, that was the problem—*when* to leave.

Boyermen Meeting, Caernford, Keelan Province

Culich pulled out a paper leaf with a neat outline prepared by Maera. "Major item today is the reports of attacks on Caedellium coasts. So far, we know a Seaborn village and a Pewitt abbey were sacked by seagoing raiders. There's no confirmation, though evidence points to Buldorians. They come in on five to ten ships, land several hundred men, loot the village, abbey, or both, and take prisoners—usually women and children—undoubtedly to be sold as slaves. They then burn everything they can and are gone before help can arrive. St. Bodwydell's Abbey in Pewitt was burned to the ground, along with the scholasticum and library, and all brothers and sisters killed, as well as several hundred villagers who initially tried to fight and then surrendered."

Cries of shock and anger rose from the Keelan boyermen before Culich was halfway through the report.

"There have also been sightings of Eywellese and Selfcellese encroaching into Stent and Moreland Provinces, and similar reports from our Dornfeld district bordering Eywell. Sometimes it's only a few men, but one incursion involved several hundred Eywellese into Moreland. As soon as trespassers are discovered and locals gather, they ride back to their own provinces. So far, there's been no major fighting, although several small skirmishes happened in Moreland.

"There are also unconfirmed reports of small numbers of unknown men spotted in the ridges above the Dillagon pass." The pass led from the main part of Keelan through the Dillagon Mountains to the Dornfeld district on the shore of the Gulf of Witlow and opposite Preddi Province across the gulf.

"How about the Narthani?" asked the Yorm district boyerman.

"Nothing so far," said Vortig Luwis, Culich's military advisor, if the clan had had such a title, "but does anyone think the Eywellese and the Selfcellese would be doing this without the knowledge of the Narthani?"

"Luwis is right," said Culich. "This is all but certain under the Narthani."

"And similar with the Seaborn raids," said Luwis. "As with the land incursions, it has to be with Narthani knowledge and planning. The Buldorians wouldn't dare dip their toes into what the Narthani consider their waters unless the Narthani approved."

"And worse," said Culich, "the Narthani may think their control of Selfcell and Eywell is firm enough that this is the first step toward other provinces."

The expressions around the room confirmed that most of the boyermen had had the same thoughts.

"Then what are we to do?" grated the Wycoff District boyerman.

"That's what we're here to discuss today," said Culich. "For one thing, we need to increase patrols in the northern districts and the Dornfeld to Nylamir pass. I've also asked Vortig Luwis to look into setting up coastal watch stations to catch signs of Buldorian ships."

"While that's all well and good," said the Nylamir boyerman, "we already have a good third of our men on such patrols. What about crops, trades?"

"Believe me, I understand your concern." Culich went to the wall with a map of Keelan and the neighboring provinces. "You can see the problem. We have three coasts, as well as our border with Eywell. The coasts are the most vulnerable. I believe we can rule out raids along the Funwir Coast in eastern Keelan. The only coastal settlement is the district seat. The population size and the terrain make it a difficult target. Plus, it's protected by offshore shoals at that part of the entrance to the Gulf of Normot.

"Dornfeld is the only Keelan settlement on the western coast, across from Preddi on the Gulf of Witlow. Thankfully, Dornfeld's natural defenses make it an unlikely target, at least for now. More likely is our southern coast. There are several villages and two abbeys the Buldorians may see as attractive targets.

"As far as land incursions, there are the Dornfeld and Nylamir districts bordering Eywell Province. The more central districts are in no immediate danger, but they'll have to provide assistance to Dornfeld and Nylamir."

Culich continued, "Those not in immediate danger must worry about your own harvests and trades, but that's the price to be paid in helping fellow clansmen. Vortig and I have discussed this, and districts will contribute about equal percentages of their men to the patrols. Those not in immediate danger are to help those who are. We'll have to work out something where distances to patrol areas require too much travel. I'll want all of your input, but in some cases it may involve relays. For example, if Elywin contributes to Dornfeld patrols, then men from Brums might help with harvests or other major work in Elywin. As I say, we'll work out the details.

"The rotation of men to those districts in our northwest borders will continue from the other districts. We've had no major incidents in Keelan, but let's not relax our vigilance. I also expect each of you to maintain the training programs for men of fighting age and condition." He stopped when the last words brought several frowns. "I assure you, I appreciate how this affects your districts by having men more and more occupied away from their normal work, but you're all aware it's something we have to tolerate in case the Narthani turn our way. We have to assume they have spies in Keelan, and maybe our preparedness might even discourage them from raiding us."

This comment brought nods of agreement, though no less unhappiness with what was necessary.

Discussion. Objections. Digressions. On and on, it continued for three hours until every person was finished with his input, and all agreed to the general plan. It took two hours more than Culich thought necessary. He would have preferred to cut off the discussion and just tell the boyermen, "This is the way it will be," but part of their loyalty to his family was due to believing the hetman valued their input.

Finally, it was the Shamir boyerman who restated the paramount question: "Is this or is it not part of a Narthani move on other provinces?"

"Some of the other hetmen believe Moreland the likeliest target, though there's no way to be sure. I suspect Moreland myself, since this is where most incursions are happening and has involved the largest numbers of men."

Culich rose and walked to the Caedellium map on the wall. "Look at the map. Taking Moreland would be a dagger into the heart of the island, and all other provinces would be in danger."

"That could be a feint," argued the worried Yorm District boyerman. "With their navy, they could attack anywhere."

"True," Culich allowed, "but we can only do what we can do. We all realize that if there's a major Narthani move on other provinces, we'll need all the clans involved. However, as you know, getting clans to work together is problematic at best."

"More like trying to scale an unclimbable mountain," said a disgusted Yorm.

There was general laughter, though not of humor—rather, laughter at a task with little probability of success.

"Keelan is in better shape than many other clans," said Culich, "thanks to our alliance with Mittack and Gwillamer. I've kept you aware of our discussions with the Hewell and Adris clans about joining the alliance. Hewell will join, though they were in no hurry, since there was no urgency, until now. Adris would like to join, but there's no direct land connection, so it isn't clear how their joining the Alliance would work. Still, I believe it worth pursuing.

"Orosz is sympathetic to our views of the Narthani danger, but since the clan Conclave site is within Orosz, Hetman Orosz believes they need to maintain the appearance of neutrality in inter-clan conflicts. Similarly, the Stent and Bultecki clans are aware of the danger, though the problem there is distance and coordination."

"What about Moreland?" asked the Wycoff boyerman. The sour look on his face made it obvious he already knew the answer.

"Hetman Moreland has assured all that Moreland will repulse any Eywellese or Narthani attack on his clan and province." Culich managed the words with a straight face. The antipathy between the two hetmen was well-known.

Luwis spat a curse. "That ass is living proof of the dangers of primogeniture. God's pity on the people of Moreland Clan."

"Now, now," snarled the Nylamir boyerman, "let's instead pray God has mercy and arranges a tragic accident."

Culich grimaced. "I keep hoping Hetman Moreland isn't as stupid as he seems, and at some point he'll realize the dangerous position of his clan. If our worst fears are realized, and Moreland is attacked, we and other clans will need to come to Moreland's aid, no matter our opinion of Hetman Moreland."

Though the thought of doing anything to help Moreland didn't sit well with the boyermen or Culich, they all recognized the necessity.

"What about Stent Province?" asked Longnor Vorwich, boyerman of the Caedell district where Abersford and St. Sidryn's were located. Hetman Welman Stent was highly regarded, and his clan was thought by Keelanders to be one of the better functioning on Caedellium. It was commonly believed that if the Stent Province wasn't on the opposite side of Caedellium, they'd be part of the Tri-Clan Alliance.

Culich shook his head. "Stent's a possible target. We think Moreland is more likely, but Stent would be the next probable victim. Unfortunately for Stent, they don't have close cooperative relations with their neighboring clans. Bultecki and Vandinke might help, but so far Pawell and Swavebroke assume that since they're far enough away from the Narthani, it's not their problem."

"Assholes!" was one of the milder comments from several boyermen.

"I'll be going to Orosz City for a hetmen meeting next sixday," Culich continued. "We'll continue working to convince more hetmen about the seriousness of the Narthani situation at every opportunity. Though more of the hetmen are coming around, we can only pray the Narthani give us enough time for all the clans to wake up."

With that comment, Culich moved on to more mundane matters that in other circumstances would have occupied the entire meeting.

After the boyermen left, Culich sat alone at the table until Maera changed seats to sit beside him.

"Any questions for your notes, Maera?" She would write a detailed account of the meeting, including actions each of the boyerman had committed to.

"No, Father. I have it all. I'll write it up for your review by this evening."

"How do you think they're all dealing with worries about the Narthani?"

Most of the boyermen would have been surprised, if not angry, to have their performance reviewed by a woman, even if she *was* the hetman's daughter.

"All will do their duties." She paused and then, with a noticeable lightness to her voice, said, "Even Arwin."

Belman Kulvin was boyerman of the Arwin district of Southeast Keelan and chafed at having his people helping other districts and out from under his view. Culich considered Kulvin the least among the Keelan boyermen.

"If a crisis develops, as I fear, I may have to find a new Arwin boyerman," Culich said. "So far, he hasn't given me enough excuse. Maybe he'll surprise me someday."

Culich laughed in spite of himself. It wasn't appropriate for him to be critical of one of his boyerman with another person, but Maera was not "another person."

He changed the subject. "You've seen all the reports coming out of Moreland. What do you think?"

She was blunt as always. "They'll try to take Moreland. Besides being in a central location, the Narthani aren't going to find a stupider hetman bordering the land they already control. When is uncertain, but most of their attention is pointed that way. It's just a matter of time. If I had to guess, I'd say within a year, two at most."

He grunted in disappointment, having hoped she would argue with his same assessment. He also knew she worried about Anarynd Moreland.

"Which makes all the more important the outcome of the next conclave I called at Orosz City," Culich said. "There has to be a way to make more of the other clans understand what's happening."

"Do you really expect such recognition at this meeting, Father?"

"This is more a meeting out of duty and hope, rather than one with optimism. I'm obliged to try, though." Culich's face drew down into discouragement. "Since it's not an All-Clan Conclave, it's up to each clan whether it comes at all, and even if it does, who will represent it. The best I hope for is for two-thirds of the clans to be there and as many as half of the hetmen. My expectation is somewhat lower."

"A great Caedellium philosopher once said that all a man can do is his best," said Maera.

Culich smiled. It was something he himself was fond of saying. "Obviously, a great thinker."

"Obviously," replied Maera innocently.

Preddi City, Narthani Headquarters

General Akuyun scanned the new report he had just received and laid it on his desk. "Well, Morfred, everything seems to have gone well on the Buldorians' first mainland raid."

Admiral Morfred Kalcan sat relaxed by the window overlooking the harbor. "Yes, I give those Buldorian scum credit. When it comes to raiding unsuspecting islanders, they're efficient enough for our purposes. I admit, they surprised me with their discipline. They're already agitating to move on the next target."

"Where do you and Hizer plan the next raid?"

"Two raids on the same province within a few days of each other, either Swavebroke or Pewell Provinces. We'll see how the clans react to a double hit so near each other in time. After that, if things continue to go well, we'll jump around the island to different provinces.

"As we've discussed, we're saving the three southern provinces for later. If any clans are going to give the Buldorians major problems, it'll be those, particularly Keelan Province."

CHAPTER 26

FERTILIZER

Production

Yozef's discovery of the guano deposits occupied his mind after returning to Abersford from Clengoth. The next morning, he went straight to the ether shop. He found Filtin Fuller working on a new distillation apparatus. The amiable man smiled and hummed to himself.

Yozef shook his head. Was Filtin *ever* in a bad mood? Being too cheerful could be just as irritating as being always dour.

"Filtin, are you always happy?"

"Happy?" queried Filtin. "What's not to be happy about?"

"Never mind. Can you stop for a moment? There's something I'd like to talk with you about."

Filtin put down a distillation column he was inspecting, "Sure. What about?"

"Let's go outside," said Yozef. "It's quieter there."

They left the shop, and Yozef led him to the shade of a tree.

"Filtin, I have two new projects and wanted to ask if you could be in charge of one of them." Yozef outlined ideas for both his retreat house and guano mining. Filtin listened, then shook his head when Yozef finished.

"I don't think it's a good idea for me to get involved, Yozef."

"Why is that?" asked a surprised Yozef. Where was Filtin's usual enthusiasm for anything new?

"For one thing, I'm already so busy with the distillation and other equipment projects that I would have to stop working here before taking on other major tasks. Also, anyone who took my place in ongoing projects wouldn't be familiar with the problems, and progress would slow. You're also looking for someone more senior. The person in charge needs to have not only authority but also the respect of workers in different crafts. I'm too young for the role."

Shit. He's right. Yozef hadn't thought this through. If not Filtin, then who?

"Do you have any recommendation of who would be appropriate?"

Filtin's perpetual smile got even wider. "My father, Dyfeld Fuller. He's one of the most respected craftsman in the district and works with wood and combining wood with glass and metal. He's worked with glassblowers and metal workers for years, and they all know and respect him. He's also worked with most of the carpenters in designing and building houses and other structures. His furniture is well known throughout Caedellium. You must have seen some of his pieces in the abbey or in businesses and houses in Abersford."

"If you don't mind my asking, Filtin, why don't you work with your father? That's normally how things seem to work here on Caedellium."

"Oh, I've worked with Father for as long as I can remember, but I wanted to get some different experience, and glass blowing was the only other trade in Abersford I hadn't worked at. I expect I'll go back with Father and someday take over his shop when he can no longer work. Right now, I'm having too much fun working with you."

"Sounds like he might be the person, Filtin. Can you arrange a meeting with him?"

"I'll stop by his house tonight and let you know tomorrow."

When Yozef arrived at the distillation shop the next morning, Filtin waited with another man, who gave an initial impression of being an old and worn lifelong laborer—stocky, heavy shoulders, thick arms, and large hands, gnarled and scarred with decades of heavy work, one finger missing, a lined face, graying hair and beard, a limp, and a noticeable resemblance to Filtin.

"Yozef, this is my father, Dyfeld Fuller."

They exchanged greetings. Dyfeld's gravelly voice matched his appearance. However, the initial impressions vanished when Dyfeld spoke. His son had already primed him with the outlines of Yozef's two projects. He jumped right into asking questions, as if assuming whether he would work for Yozef was his decision alone. It wasn't arrogance as much as a master craftsman confident in his skills and with enough other work not to *need* these projects. Within five minutes, the two men were going over Yozef's maps and rough sketches, with Dyfeld pointing out issues that hadn't occurred to Yozef and suggesting solutions.

Dyfeld immediately grasped the potential of guano fertilizer, compared to the skepticism of his son and Cadwulf. He also saw it as the simplest task.

"As far as I understand it, Ser Kolsko, at first you will only need a few dozen sacks of the bird shit deposits crushed to a fine powder. Those you intend on using to test out whether the powder can increase crop yields. I wonder, though, if you need that many sacks. From what you describe, two or three sacks would be enough to test."

Yozef thought it interesting that Dyfeld caught that. No wool on his brain, even if he looked like a common laborer. Yozef didn't need to tell anyone he'd eventually experiment with extracting potassium nitrate for gunpowder—if he got around to it.

"True, Ser Fuller. However, as long as we're doing this, I'd like to be sure I have a sufficient supply."

Dyfeld shrugged. "It's your coin. If it works as you think it will, then we'd need to expand the work. In that case, I see two issues." Dyfeld went back to the map of the inlet. "As for the extractions, there's no reason to pulverize the shit deposits on site. Since it has to be hauled here anyway, all it will take is to break it up the into small-enough pieces to load into sacks for pack-horses to carry and bring it back here, where we can do the crushing. Once it is known that the fertilizer works, and you want to increase extraction, then we can think about more efficient ways to do the crushing, either doing it on site or bringing it here in wagons.

"The second issue is that you'll need to show use of the land to satisfy the registration of ownership. The registrar did explain the usage provision, didn't he?"

"Yes. I have to show the land is being used for some purpose."

"That shouldn't be a problem. You say there's no proper road or path to this site, so, if necessary, we'll simply hack out a pack horse trail for now. We should also build a small encampment for workers to sleep and eat, and provide some minimal evidence of land improvement. If major extractions are to occur, we can build a regular road for wagons getting in and out. No point doing that, though, until we see whether it's worthwhile. If your fertilizer idea doesn't work, then you'd best just let the land revert to the clan."

By now, Yozef had forgotten that this was supposed to be an interview to see whether he would consider hiring Dyfeld. Instead, Yozef had been told that Dyfeld would *let* himself be hired, and they continued with the planning.

"The little house you want is something else. It's not just a small house you'll need. I assume you'll get there by horse, so you'll need a barn as well, plus an outhouse appropriately distant from the house. The house itself looks like you want one different than most houses, what with so many windows and some of them quite large. There's no way we can get either lumber or glass there by pack animal, so we'll need a minimal road. I can have one of my assistants check out possible routes, but we may be able to use beach sections, combined with new roadbeds where necessary. While this will add to the costs, if you expand the fertilizer extraction, we'd only have to improve the existing road for heavier wagons and extend the road on to the mining site."

Dyfeld stopped and, with the hand missing the third finger, pulled over the sketch of the house. "I'll have suggestions on the house design after we've talked more about the features you want."

Testing

Dyfeld Fuller's speed and efficiency caught Yozef by surprise when, eight days later, a wagon holding twenty sacks of crushed murvor guano waited at the distillation shop. No arrangements for testing on farms had been made. He knew nothing about how much was needed per acre. He did remember Julie chastising him for giving one of her orchids too much plant food, something about excess nitrogen burning the leaves. Different terrain might also vary the amount of fertilizer needed.

There was also the problem of the seasons. He worried about the cooler weather after the Harvest Festival and whether he'd have to wait months for the next growing season to begin, but Dyfeld said no.

"The main crops won't go in for another three or four months, although there are always cool weather crops some farms plant. My brother used to farm until his death, and he'd plant crops that grew until the weather got too cold and then sit dormant until temperatures were warmer to finish growing and maturing. And it depends on the farm. If the location is right, it's possible to grow something year round. I'm not sure what's growing now, but check with the local farmers."

Yozef set Cadwulf to the task of contacting farmers to see whether any were interested. Not unexpectedly, few were, with variations on the same themes.

"Murvor shit on my fields? Nonsense!"

"My family has always farmed the same way for generations. There's no reason to change."

"Are you a farmer? I didn't think so. Who are you to advise us how to grow crops?"

"Why would I want to increase yields? We are having trouble selling or using the crops we already get before they spoil."

It was the latter excuse that led to the solution. If farmers were having difficulty selling their crops, they could be paid to carry out Yozef's experiments. However, the attitudes of many farmers worried him. Could he trust them to do what was necessary to validate the tests? He needed a farm that followed directions and kept accurate records, and he'd need to check progress and compliance, either doing the checking himself or training someone to do it.

"What about that farm woman you told me about at the festival?" said Yozef. "A widow owning and running a medium-sized and productive farm."

"Who? I don't … oh, wait. You mean Bronwyn Linton? The one who eyed you?"

"I don't know that she *eyed* me."

"She did. And if I recall, there was eyeing in return." Cadwulf's face took on a leer. "Are you sure it's only to test your fertilizer that makes you suggest her? Maybe some other fertilization occurs to you?"

Yozef flushed. "Nonsense. I'm just trying to find farmers who will work with me."

His young associate and friend relented with the teasing. "You may be right about her being easier to work with. Her reputation is that she's practical, works hard herself, demands the same of her workers, and is fair and honest."

The next day they rode the ten miles to the Linton farm, located on a river valley bottom. The farm had dark soil, and lush foliage separated fields of crops. Yozef's nose pulled in rich odors of damp soil and growth. Newly planted fields had sprouts of a grassy crop and other fields with broader leafed plants. Cadwulf recognized winter wheat and turnips. The fields appeared well tended, the fences and several out-buildings in good repair, and the farm house had been painted in the not-too-distant past. A middle-aged man came out of a barn as they rode up.

"Good day, Ser," said Cadwulf. "I'm Cadwulf Beynom and this is Yozef Kolsko. We're here to talk with Bronwyn Linton."

"She's in the north field," the man answered, walking away with evidently no intention of either going for Linton or telling them the location of the north field.

Cadwulf wasn't perturbed and called to the man's back.

"If you could direct us to where she is, we would be appreciative."

The answer was a jerk of his head, presumably meaning the field was in that direction.

Cadwulf thanked him more than Yozef thought deserving. He had to keep reminding himself that people weren't so much rude as brusque—a reasonably neutral brusqueness and not the abrasiveness of some New Yorkers or the deliberate, feigned superiority of the French.

They tied their horses to a rail in front of the house and walked in the indicated direction. Sure enough, when they got around the house, they could see a figure in a field, plucking wheat shoots from the ground, chewing on them, and then spitting them out and moving on.

"She's checking for moisture in the leaves," said Cadwulf. Yozef didn't know why that was important and didn't ask.

When the woman saw them, she gave a slight wave and moved to where they waited just off the field. As she got closer, Yozef recognized the woman from the fair, dressed more workmanlike today. His previous impression was stocky, bordering on plump, but perhaps it had been the clothes. Sturdy she was, but without much excess weight, probably attributable to regular farm work. Her face and arms were browned from the sun. She'd wrinkle before forty, given this much tanning. Her bare arms looked strong, as did what he could see of her legs, as her skirt swirled around her calves. But of her femininity, there was no doubt. The curve of hips below her waist and swells under her top-shirt made that clear. Her brown hair was braided into a bun, and a straw farmer's hat provided shade to her face.

"Ser Beynom, welcome to my farm." Though she addressed Cadwulf, her eyes never left Yozef. "And I take it this is the mysterious Yozef Kolsko whom everyone talks about." She smiled.

"Guilty as charged, Sen Linton," said Yozef, smiling back.

Her eyebrows rose at his offhand remark, then she looked at Cadwulf. "And to what do I owe your visit?"

In the next half hour, Yozef described his interest in running test plots with the powdered guano fertilizer and what he hoped to find out about efficacy and application amounts. Sen Linton quickly agreed with the potential but confirmed no immediate advantage to increased yields.

"I already use about half of my crops for animal feed. The other half I sell for island consumption at lower prices than before."

"I noticed there were more cattle and horses than I expected as we rode in today," Yozef remarked. "I thought you only farmed crops."

"Normally, yes," said Linton. "But since the crops don't keep that long, I'm raising more animals than usual, since they keep longer. Many farmers are doing the same."

A longer shelf-life. Yozef approved. *Very smart and thinking long term.*

"There's no problem with helping you with your tests of this new fertilizer, Ser Kolsko. We already spread manure on the fields, but there's never enough. Having another fertilizer source would be useful, *if* this idea of yours works. As for your paying me to do these tests, what if instead we agree that should the fertilizer work as well as you think, and if the conditions for selling improve in the future, that you'll sell me all the fertilizer I need at half the going price?"

Yozef was about to say, "Done deal," when Cadwulf jumped in.

"Half price for how long, Sen Linton? Surely not indefinitely. Shall we say for five years?"

Her eyes glinted, and the corners of her mouth suggested good humor. "Five years hardly makes it worth my time. I couldn't possibly agree for less than twenty years."

Ten minutes later and with protestations of being robbed from both sides and how much they were conceding, Linton and Cadwulf agreed on eight years of reduced price once trade off Caedellium resumed, if the guano worked.

The basic deal settled, they proceeded to details. Yozef explained they'd need multiple plots to vary the amount and number of guano applications. Since he had no idea of the proper amounts, they settled on the initial test with four different amounts of guano, one and two applications, two different sites, and a control plot of no application at each site for a total of eighteen plots per crop. Yozef was encouraged that he didn't have to explain the need for the control plots.

What crops to use was the next question? Yozef had thought of wheat, but Bronwyn suggested that barley and turnips were better cool weather crops. Though she had already finished the current plantings, there were several fields being left fallow she could use for the tests. Bronwyn suggested the square plots be a sixteenth of an acre, about fifty-two square feet along each side.

The business concluded, Bronwyn invited them to stay for evening meal, but both Cadwulf and Yozef were due to eat with Cadwulf's parents that evening and gave their thanks for the invitation. Based on Linton's estimate of the time needed to set up the test plots, Yozef said he would return in one sixday with sacks of fertilizer.

CHAPTER 27

A CLOSE ENCOUNTER

A sixday later Yozef returned to the Linton farm with a wagon holding enough bags of powdered guano for the trials, plus extra. One of his workers drove the wagon, with Yozef as passenger and Seabiscuit tied behind. Linton saw them coming up the road to the farm and met them at the house.

"The wagon will return to Abersford once we've unloaded the sacks," he explained. "I'll ride back after checking the plots you've prepared and see the first applications."

Linton nodded. "Then we'd better get to it." She climbed onto the wagon bed and began handing sacks to the two men to transfer them to a farm cart with a pony hitched to it. She wore similar working clothes as on his previous visit, although her shirt was untied several inches lower than before. Yozef caught a brief glimpse of considerable breast the first time she bent to hand down a sack. He averted his eyes, but they betrayed him on the next two sacks. The views were impressive.

Yozef and his worker had gotten a later start from Abersford than planned and had arrived in early afternoon. As a consequence, by the time he and Linton finished with checking the first set of plots, observing the applications, and checking her record keeping, the sun was setting behind the eastern hills.

It had been an awkward day for Yozef. He couldn't resist positioning himself to catch further glimpses down Linton's shirt whenever she leaned over. Yet at the hint of a nipple, which elicited unmistakable stirrings, he steeled himself to avert his eyes during the last hour of work.

His face had a sheen of sweat, and his heart thumped as they finished the final plot, only partly due to exertion.

"That's the last one, Sen Linton. I'll be riding back to Abersford now. I'll come and check back here next sixday."

"Ser Kolsko, you'd be returning in the dark, and since you're not familiar with these roads and by your own admission are not the most experienced rider, perhaps it would be best if you spent the night here and returned in the morning. I'd be pleased to offer you hospitality for evening meal and the use of the extra bedroom."

Yozef wasn't sure but suspected a hint of anticipation in her offer. He wondered whether there was the same in his acceptance.

They washed up after the day's work. He expected a washbowl and maybe some soap, but she directed him behind the house to a small enclosure containing a tub of water, soap, and a drying cloth. The water was ambient temperature, meaning on the chilly side, but by now he was accustomed, or resigned, to only occasional hot water. He'd brought a change of clothing, not knowing what and how much work he would do at the farm, and when he entered the house, he was greeted by a similarly scrubbed and reclothed Bronwyn Linton.

Where's the other tub? In the house?

It had to exist, since her hair was still damp and she didn't seem to exude the natural odors most working Caedelli carried with them after a full day. Her work clothes had been replaced by slippers and a red dress with a more than suggestive plunging neck. Bras were unknown on Caedellium, and the sleeveless, form-fitting dress left little to the imagination.

Dinner combined the efforts of Linton and an older woman who excused herself and exited when the meal was ready. While waiting, Linton served Yozef a pre-dining aperitif. The first swallow burned on the way down.

Christ! This stuff'll take paint off a wall. Probably a home brew of some kind.

After his throat recovered or perhaps was anesthetized, he rather enjoyed the glow and the mellow feeling. He also saw through a door into another room, where glimpses of cloth hanging off a table, wicker baskets, and a cot suggested the spare room where he would spend the night.

Dinner was a typical Caedellium repast of roast beef, turnips, whole-grain heavy bread, and a yellow-tinged sweet wine whose origin he couldn't identify. Conversation was scintillating—prospects for this year's crops, expectations on the fertilizer tests, the weather, how nasty were the Narthani, and a gossip about Abersford society. Yozef learned that Linton had inherited the farm from her parents, was married for two years before her husband died in accident, had had one child stillborn, and had a sister living nearby.

For his part, Yozef recited his rote summary of his own family and the mystery of arriving on Caedellium. As far as he knew, he held up his end of the conversation, although between the alcohol and views of cleavage he wasn't sure. The meal and wine finished, the conversation lagging, he sat back and pushed his chair away from the table.

"Thank you, Sen Linton. I enjoyed the meal and your company. If your other bedroom is ready, I'm tired from the trip and our work and will retire for the evening."

"Ser Kolsko, the extra bedroom is used as my sewing room and is so crowded with my work I'm afraid it might not be comfortable for you." She rose from her chair, stepped out of her slippers, and slipped the top of her dress from her shoulders. Her breasts sagged from their fullness, the nipples pointing outward and erect. "I'm sure you'll be more comfortable in my room." She turned and walked toward the rear of the house.

Yozef's eyes fixed on her breasts swinging when she turned and then the view of her hips swaying as she walked away barefoot. He stood frozen. While the moment wasn't a total surprise, neither was it anticipated. Filtin had clued him in that unmarried Caedellium adults were free within cultural restrictions in matters of sex, but this was more upfront than he expected. If he followed her, did this mean a commitment? Was he really interested in her this way?

The questions were ignored by his feet and his groin. She lay naked on a bed. Flickering candles gave a warm, subdued glow to the room, and his pants tightened at the contrast of light and shadows across her skin. The parts of his brain still functioning noted the sturdy, definitely feminine body, the armpit hair, the thatch covering her mons, and her breasts settling downward as she supported herself on her left elbow and held out the other arm.

The only sound, if he had noticed, was both of their heavy breathing. His clothing cascaded around his feet, his erection pointing skyward. As he moved to the bed, she rolled back and spread and raised her knees. There was no foreplay. He mounted her, and she grasped him with her legs. There was an immediate rhythm to his thrusts and her hips. When he came quickly, she kept her clasp of him for several minutes. It was an urgent coupling, not lovemaking. They didn't speak. When he lay next to her, he could hear the slowing of their breathing, the sounds of the house, and the occasional animal sound from outside.

Now what do I do? Say something? Go to sleep? Thank her for the quick roll and retire back to the supposedly crowded guest room?

The answer came half an hour later when she explored his groin. Though her hands were rough, other parts of her were soft. This time, it took longer. His basic urge slaked, Yozef held himself back until she came with a series of gasping cries and a four-limbed attempt to compress his torso. The aftermath of this second round came quickly. When he was released and rolled off her, she grunted, he thought in satisfaction, turned on her side, and was asleep within moments. He reciprocated.

The next morning, he awoke to an empty bed and the day's light just coming in the bedroom window. He lay wondering, again, about his next move. No answer appearing to him, he rose, dressed, and went to the kitchen from which emanated bakery aromas. Linton held an iron pan full of biscuits above the wood stove, holding the handle with a heavy cloth. She saw him, smiled, and waved to a chair.

"Sit down, Ser Kolsko. A day's work is waiting for me and travel for you."

He took a seat at the sturdy table, on which sat a jar of butter, plates, knives, and a bowl of pilla fruit, tangerines, and apples.

He wondered where the tangerines came from, *Shouldn't they be ripening at a different time of year? And why tangerines here, but not oranges?*

Linton plopped the plate of hot biscuits onto the table, along with two large mugs of kava, and his overnight tryst partner sat opposite him and dug in. He followed suit in short order.

"Are you sure you need to return to Abersford today, Ser Kolsko, or might you stay another day and night so we can plan more . . . fertilizer tests?"

"I think . . . Bronwyn . . . that after last night we can use our first names."

"Thank you . . . Yozef. I didn't want to appear too forward."

Christ! Too forward! After last night? If that wasn't being forward, I'm in dire danger if she ever gets aggressive.

"I think my shops and workers can get along without me for another day," he assured her.

His curiosity about what he'd be doing this additional day was answered as soon as they finished the biscuits and most of the fruit. This was a work day, and for Bronwyn that meant *work*. They spent time on more planning of the test plots, and, together with one of her workmen, they laid out the final plots with stakes. By noon, everything was ready for the fertilizer. He continued taking copious notes and diagrams and impressed on her the absolute requirement to follow every step of the planting, the fertilizer regime, and the records for all plots, if the results were to be valid. She listened carefully and didn't comment on his redundant entreaties, but he ended confident she would adhere to the instructions.

They ate a lunch of dry sausage, cheese, and bread, a standard Caedellium midday meal, with the other workers. The rest of the day Yozef learned more than he needed to know about repairing barn stalls, plowing, and catching, killing, and plucking a goose. She didn't direct him to do these tasks; it was what she was doing, and he followed along, helping as he could. This was a working farm without a husband. He suspected it flourished both because of the good location and soil, and because of her work habits. It was near dusk when the workday ended, and they returned to the house. Yozef's back ached, and he had several new blisters. He was in better shape than ever in his life, but this day he'd used different muscles and in different motions than usual, and they let him know their disapproval. He wouldn't have minded eating and going straight to sleep, though he rightly suspected Bronwyn had other plans.

Once gutted and plucked, the goose had been put in a version of a deep-pit, brick-lined roaster set-up near the house. When Bronwyn had done this, he had no idea, because the woman from the night before hadn't appeared this day.

The grease-laden bird was delicious, and the two of them finished it, along with a fresh loaf of bread, a bowl of dark olives, and another flagon of the sweetish wine. The post-meal proceedings followed, similar to the previous night, with the difference that they engaged in only one round before sleep, compensated for when they both awoke the next morning.

Morning meal was her version of the Caedellium porridge—this one a combination of wheat and something like amaranth, laced with nut bits and what looked and tasted like raisins.

"Yozef, Godsday is two days from now. I can plan on being in Abersford to attend the abbey services . . . if you have no other plans." Bronwyn looked at him expectantly.

"No, Bronwyn. No other plans. I look forward to your company at the service and hospitality at my house." *And the bedroom later.*

She appeared at the abbey complex just before the Godsday service began. Yozef had attended many services, but he wasn't a regular. It had been left open whether he would accompany her to the service or meet later. By default, he met her in front of the cathedral when she rode up on a bay mare. He had seen side-saddles here for women, but Bronwyn rode astride with a pantaloons-style skirt encasing her legs. Once she dismounted, a curtain of cloth held behind her while riding was wrapped around her legs to appear as a skirt, the pantaloons hidden beneath.

They entered the cathedral together and sat together in the middle of the pew rows. Yozef felt every eye following them, even if they weren't. However, some were, and among the raised eyebrows included those of Cadwulf and Filtin, followed by a friendly smile from the former and a leer from the latter, which drew a sharp elbow from Filtin's wife.

Yozef often worked part of every Godsday, but he and Bronwyn spent the day in his cottage, mainly in the bedroom. He told the Faughns he wouldn't need Elian to prepare meals that day, a task Bronwyn took on.

The low afternoon sun shone through a window onto Bronwyn sleeping from their last coupling. It was the first time he'd seen her unclothed in full light. When he first arrived on Caedellium, women's armpit and leg hair was disconcerting, but by now it seemed normal, and it was the idea of shaving that seemed odd. Bronwyn's hair was only a shade darker than her parts tanned by the sun, the hairs on her calves becoming sparse above the knees. Not that the hair mattered. Yozef found other of her parts to keep his attention.

CHAPTER 28

NOT TO BE

Advice

They followed the same pattern the next four sixdays—Yozef arriving at Bronwyn's farm in time for evening meal, staying two nights, and returning to Abersford the second morning— Bronwyn coming to his house the evening before Godsday and returning the morning after Godsday.

Neither spoke of commitment. He liked Bronwyn. She was honest, hard-working, and level-headed, all traits he would expect of a single woman running a large farm. He wasn't sure of her view of him, but she clearly respected him as a prominent Abersford figure. They satisfied a mutual need, his part being hard to fake and her enthusiasm unquestioned. However, they had little else in common, except for one possible complication.

What if she gets pregnant? Contraception certainly wasn't on my mind that first night, but as far as I know, there's no such thing here. It might even be forbidden to try to prevent pregnancy, what with the way they emphasize caring for children. Well, shit. What should I do?

The time spent with Bronwyn impacted Yozef's various enterprises. Several projects languished by his diversion a good part of each sixday, and workers were becoming impatient for decisions and directions.

As sixdays passed, the advantages and doubts about their relationship weighed more and more on Yozef. Did Bronwyn think this was leading to a long-term commitment, even marriage? What would be her response when she realized it wouldn't happen? At times, he felt he was taking advantage of her, but he knew that was a holdover from how he might have viewed things back on Earth. Customs were different on Caedellium, and she'd started the affair, with his acquiescence. These uncertainties led him to seek out someone who had previously offered advice, Filtin.

The opportunity to get Filtin alone came after being shown his crew's latest distillation column, a multi-jointed one some eight feet tall with a maze of connecting piping. After the inspection and progress report, the other workers left for a mid-morning kava break, leaving Yozef and Filtin alone.

"Somehow, Yozef, I don't believe the distillation equipment is what you needed to talk with me about."

"No. It's not about business. I need the advice of a friend."

Filtin's cheerful manner took on a more serious tone. "What is it, Yozef? How can I help?"

"It's Bronwyn."

"Ah. I've wondered how that's going. You two aren't starting to argue, are you?"

"No, no. Not that. I'm just worrying about what she expects of this and if I'm in trouble with Caedellium customs and laws in such matters. I'm wondering whether what we've been doing is taken to mean the intention for something long term."

"Has she spoken of this?"

"No, not a word."

"How long have you two been bedding? And how often?"

"Over a month, and four nights a sixday."

Filtin grunted. "Four nights? I thought you seemed a little more tired some days than before, and everyone has talked about how you're seldom around the shops." Filtin thought for a moment, then asked bluntly, "What are your intentions? It sounds like you're thinking about when it'll end."

"There's nothing long term, as far as I'm concerned. I respect Bronwyn. She's doing an admirable job running her farm, and she's honest as could be. But our paths are just too different. It has to end sometime, although I don't have any idea when. I'm also concerned about what if a child comes from this? If that happens, what commitment would that put on me?"

"The child part is easy," said Filtin. "Everyone knows the two of you are bedding, so if a child comes, you'll be acknowledged as the father by everyone and the law. What that means is that you'll be expected to assist raising of the child. If you don't marry her, which I hear you'd not want to do, then she'd raise the child, and you'd provide support both for the child and her lost time in working the farm. The provision could be in coin, providing a worker for the farm, or some other arrangement that either the two of you'd agree on or would be determined by a magistrate, if you couldn't agree. From knowing you and from what I know of Bronwyn, I wouldn't anticipate it going to the magistrate."

"So there'd be no requirement for me to marry her?"

"Why would there be? She's a grown woman. A widow who owns her own farm. You're a grown man with businesses of your own. What the two of you do in bed is your own concern, as long as any child is cared for." After a moment, Filtin added, "Something you might consider is that it might not entirely be your overwhelming charm and sexual appeal she's interested in. A child might have been part of her intention."

Yozef stirred, startled. He'd considered the possibility of a child, but not that it might be Bronwyn's deliberate plan.

"Why hasn't she said anything? I just said a moment ago how honest she is, but if she's planned this from the beginning, that's deceitful."

Filtin shook his head. "Not necessarily. She knows you're not from Caedellium, but she might assume you understand the customs better than you do. I take it she was forthright inviting you to her bed."

Yozef nodded.

"I suggest you simply *ask* her. Remember, she's unmarried, and the farm has been in her family for generations. If she doesn't have children, there'll be no one to pass it on to and no one to care for her in her old age. Then there's the need most women have for children."

"If she has such a need, why not find another husband? I would expect she's a prime candidate for marriage."

"She would be, if there were more unmarried men."

Then it came back to Yozef, what Cadwulf told him after the trial of the Camrin man for abusing his family, and the poor prospects for the wife to remarry once the court dissolved the marriage.

Yozef ran a hand through his hair, as he considered his situation.

"I'm not sure how I think about any of this. Back home, before I came to Caedellium, my wife was with child. I lost both of them, and now there's the possibility of a child here that I wouldn't raise."

Okay, so Julie and I weren't married yet, but we were going to be, and there was the child I don't even know if exists.

Filtin's expression was sympathetic. "I'm sorry about your family, Yozef. You've never said anything about them, and I guess I'd assumed you weren't married."

"It's just that I've been adjusting to the reality of never seeing them, and now there could be a child here."

"Maybe it would be God's gift to you to replace the child you lost. It's up to you to decide what you want to do, Yozef, just as it is Bronwyn's decision to do whatever she wants. Again, I'd advise talking to her about all this. Openness is always best."

The Conversation

The suggested conversation took place the next evening when Yozef made his sixday trip to the farm. A stew was simmering, according to Bronwyn needing another half hour to finish. He thought they should have the conversation before eating and heading to the bedroom. Yozef took a deep breath and leaped.

"Bronwyn, can we sit and talk?"

She turned from cleaning a dish and looked at him with a raised eyebrow at his serious tone. Wiping her hands on an apron, she sat opposite him at the table.

"Bronwyn, you know I come from a different land than Caedellium."

She nodded.

"The customs in my homeland aren't the same as they are here. That means sometimes there can be misunderstandings between me and people here on the island. I try to understand the customs here, but often I'm not sure whether my understanding is correct."

She sat back a little in her chair, as if thinking she knew where Yozef was heading.

"My people would say that two such as ourselves should both understand what is happening between them. I'd like to be sure that's true for us."

Bronwyn tilted her head to one side with a puzzled look. "What's happening between us? We're bedding, and I hope to get with child. What's not to understand?"

Well, shit. That answers that.

"I just wanted to be sure there was no misunderstanding. In my land, having a child places a strong responsibility on both parents to care for the child."

"As it does here," said the still puzzled woman. "I'll admit, I first thought you might be a possible husband, but we're too different. This farm is my life, and I won't leave it. For you, your shops and experiments and all the other things you do are your place. If a child comes, you're an honorable man and of means, so I've no doubt you'll be generous in providing for it."

So, I guess I'm the rich sperm donor. It wasn't a score for his ego, but he could see the rationale from this culture's point of view.

Bronwyn crossed her arms. "Although we share beds for now, I assume it will end. Is that what you're telling me, that you wish the bedding to end?"

"No." *Maybe.* "I was just concerned about you and the possibility of a child."

"It seems this is the only way I'll have a child, since marriage isn't likely."

"Haven't there been men interested in you, and you in them?"

"Very few. Those who wanted to marry me either I wouldn't have or they were mainly interested in getting control of the farm."

"How did you first meet your husband?"

"We grew up on neighboring farms. His family had three boys and mine were three girls. There were few other farms in the area at that time. My sisters and I grew up with those three boys, the only other children we'd see for months at a time. One of the boys, Cynwin, I wanted to marry, but my sister Dellia got a commitment from him first." Bronwyn laughed. "If I didn't love Dellia so dearly, I'd have hated her. The next son was Murdrew. He was my second choice and, truth be told, just as reliable as his older brother. So I married him."

"Did the other son also marry your other sister?"

"No. He died in a horse fall while taking part in a search for Eywellese intruders in northern Keelan. My other sister married and lives near Caernford, which is just as well, since I could never stand her. Dellia and Cynwin live a mile from here. When our parents died, the land was divided among their three daughters. Luvolia sold her section without even asking whether Dellia and I could somehow buy it—the bitch. Dellia and Cynwin have three children already." The last words were wistful. "I love visiting them and the children, but every time I see them, I'm reminded of being childless."

Yozef thought for a moment, then said, "It's not just you who has this problem. It seems to be an issue throughout Keelan Province and maybe all of Caedellium."

Bronwyn nodded sadly. Neither spoke for several minutes, each in a private world. Yozef mulled over Bronwyn's dilemma, forgetting for a moment his relationship with her, when a stray thought coalesced in his mind.

"Looking at it from the perspective of the entire island, and given the trends, there may be one obvious solution, although a difficult one. If there are too many women for the number of men, some men could have more than one wife."

Bronwyn shifted uncomfortably in her chair. "I've heard of that happening elsewhere, but what does the *Word* say?"

"As explained to me, the *Word* doesn't forbid it but demands husband and wife treat each other with love and respect, and of course, the primary responsibility is to care for children. Such marriages don't seem to happen often here in Keelan, though supposedly it's a more common practice in other provinces."

Bronwyn shook her head and had a sour expression. "What woman wants to share a house and a husband with another woman? I certainly would never agree to that."

"I didn't say it was a good solution, just a possible one. Back to ourselves, and just to help me be sure I understand everything, our bedding will continue as long as we both want it. If a child results, you'll raise the child, and I'll provide support, but we don't expect a long-term relationship between the two of us?"

"Of course, that's understood." She stood up and moved to the stove. "I believe the stew is ready, so we can eat," she said matter-of-factly.

So much for a big dramatic scene. And how about the nice weather today? It made for comfortable fence mending and manure shoveling.

But a child? He hadn't been sold on Julie and he having one so soon, and now this. He was confused. Maybe nothing would happen. She had been married several years and had only gotten pregnant once, so it might not happen with him.

End of the Affair

They continued as before and never spoke about the topic again, but during the next five sixdays, the nights they spent together decreased from four nights a sixday to three, then two, and finally Yozef arrived at the farm after they hadn't seen each other for a complete sixday. A cart hitched to two horses was tied to the front rail. As he rode up, Bronwyn came out the house to meet him.

Her face was serene. "Please come inside, Yozef, I have something to tell you and some people for you to meet." She took his hand and led him inside. A man and a woman about Bronwyn's age sat in the main room. The woman looked like a chunkier version of Bronwyn.

"Yozef, this is my sister Dellia and her husband, Cynwin. As I told you, they live nearby."

Yozef nodded, said a greeting to them both, and clasped an offered forearm with Cynwin.

The four of them sat in a circle, Bronwyn opposite Yozef, Dellia and Cynwin flanking Bronwyn. His fleeting thought was that he faced a threesome.

"Yozef, I thought about what you said about marriages with more than one wife. At first, the idea seemed impossible, but the more I thought, the less impossible it seemed. Then, three days ago I went to my sister, and we talked."

Dellia's and Bronwyn's hands reached out to each other as if magnetized. Dellia smiled softly at her sister.

"Dellia spoke with Cynwin, and the three of us have agreed with what you said. We are to be married. Dellia, Cynwin, and me."

Dellia spoke for the first time. "Bronwyn and I have always loved each other dearly, even as young children. As happy as I've been married to Cynwin, I've missed her every day. When Bronwyn spoke to me about this, it seemed the right thing to do."

Cynwin reached from the other side of Bronwyn and took her other hand. "Two wives are not something I ever thought of. Certainly not with a wife as good as Dellia, but we both love Bronwyn. And Dellia's right, the more the three of us talked about this, the more natural it seemed. Dellia will have her sister with her. There will be more children and more parents to raise them. There's also the farms. Both ours and Bronwyn's are good farms, and by joining them together, it'll be easier to tend the sum than both by themselves."

From their body language, Yozef had already suspected what he had just been told. He sat quiet and ambivalent, though relieved that the inevitable end to the affair was easy for him and good for Bronwyn.

"Yozef," said Bronwyn, "there's something else. I'm with child. I suspected as much the last two sixdays when my time passed and I didn't have the bleeding. Now there're other signs, so I'm sure."

Yozef sat immobile, his mind churning over the possible having become real. What did he feel? What should he be saying?

"We'll raise the child in our new family, and it will have many brothers and sisters. It'll also have four parents, since we hope you'll always be part of the child's family and our friend."

They talked for another hour, mainly about the anticipation of the three, how Yozef would see the child as often as he liked, and Yozef pretending to take all of this in stride, while part of him watched the four of them like a disembodied observer. He remembered little of what he said in that hour, but whatever it was, the other three took it well. When he left to return to Abersford, a hundred yards from the house he turned from his saddle to look back. Three figures stood on the porch, arm in arm and waving. He waved and urged Seabiscuit into a grove of elms, as the farm disappeared from view. The road was dark most of the way, with enough light from the larger moon and the stars to let him and Seabiscuit stay on the road. There was little wind, all wildlife had settled in for the night, and everything was quiet, except for hooves on the dirt road. It took an hour and a half to get back to his house in Abersford. It was the loneliest hour and a half of his life.

CHAPTER 29

COULD BE WORSE

Avoiding Deja Vu

Yozef lapsed into a funk. He had thought the relationship with Bronwyn was only physical, but once it ended, emotional ties lingered.

No one asked, but his increased presence and the absence of Bronwyn told everyone he was once again solitary. As a palliative, he plunged with a vengeance back into projects delayed by the time diverted on the affair. Within a month, he slipped back into his life before Bronwyn. He spent most days in his shops, attended lectures at St. Sidryn's, had talks and walks with Cadwulf, Sistian, Diera, and others at the abbey complex, drank beers with Carnigan and Filtin at the Snarling Graeko, and, to his initial consternation, deflected overtures from more widows.

Though his months with Bronwyn had awakened dormant physiologies, he was ambivalent about taking advantage of the obvious interest of three different Abersford widows. Ironically, the urge to go slow was reinforced by a failure to follow through with this reticence. Buna Keller was a widow and the owner of a clothing shop in Abersford that made pants, shirts, and a coat more to Yozef's liking than the local styles. He would stand as the shop owner took his measurements. One such visit was for a formal suit of clothing, appropriate for meetings with the more prosperous merchants and higher-level officials.

Keller and her assistants had measured him in the past and kept records, but on this visit she insisted more accurate and newer measurements were needed, which should best be done in the back room. On this particular day, it had been two months since he and Bronwyn had last bedded. The seamstress wore a dress with bare shoulders and a plunging neckline. She was all business, taking the measurements from waist up, but when she moved to lower regions, her hands dallied and casually contacted parts that, to his embarrassment, reacted. Instead of her being offended, he erroneously thought she hadn't noticed or ignored his condition. A subsequent invitation arrived by letter from Buna to attend a small dinner gathering of several prominent tradesmen, shop owners, and their wives. It was his first social occasion with most of the guests, and he enjoyed the business-oriented conversation as an opportunity to search for other potential enterprises. In spite of his hesitancy in becoming involved again so soon, the next morning he awoke in bed next to Buna. He remembered all of the details of how he'd ended up there and what had occurred. What he couldn't remember was what had happened to his resolve after the third glass of wine.

Indecisive about getting involved again so soon, by default Yozef found himself at Buna's house the next two nights. Relief came when he found her not interested in a child; she was past childbearing age and had two grown children. What she did have was a libido. Straightforward sex was simple, except he didn't *like* her. She could be abrasive, they were a personality mismatch, and she had more hair than Yozef—and not just on her head. He was relieved when on the last morning, she told him not to come to her house again. She found him too *different* from Caedellium men. Although he was curious about the difference, he wasn't curious enough to risk losing a quick exit. From that point, Yozef swore to himself, yet again, to keep his nether parts under better control.

Paper

The episode with Buna had been short enough not to impact his focus on new projects. The ether, ethanol, and soap enterprises required little ongoing input from him. He knew he fussed, and although his staff didn't say it, their opinions were obvious: *Please go away and let us do our jobs.*

He needed new projects. The first new idea came to him while strolling among the village shops, and he came upon a stall selling writing paper. A customer could buy single sheets or tied packets of twenty, either a light-yellowish-brown rough texture or a smoother, whiter paper. The former was the only paper made in Abersford, while whiter, more expensive paper came from a larger papermaker in Caernford, the Keelan capitol. Yozef knew the basic procedure for making paper. Almost anything containing fibers would work, including cotton, cloth, straw, wood, and flax. The material was chopped as small as possible, then suspended in water and a screen passed through the mixture to catch pieces and fibers on the screen. Once dried, a single sheet of paper was peeled away and could be cut to different sizes and written on. Those were the basics, as confirmed to Yozef by Ser Myrfild, the man manning the paper stall, who also happened to be the Abersford paper maker. Yozef never learned his first name.

Over beers that evening, Yozef proposed new types of papers and Myrfild alternated telling him why it wouldn't work and being enthused about novel ideas and products. By the end of the evening, they agreed to form the Abersford Paper Factory. Novel products included whiter papers than yet produced on Caedellium, colored papers, and poster-board for announcements. All found limited markets—enough to justify continued production, steady incomes, and market interest in other provinces. However, the jackpot products had nothing to do with literacy or communication and were afterthoughts from Yozef. While Myrfild was initially dubious that anyone would actually pay hard-earned coinage for such products, Yozef insisted, later annoyingly proud of himself for the brainstorms. Myrfild was amazed when, within two sixdays, orders poured in for toilet paper and sanitary napkins. The toilet paper immediately started taking the place of the customary moss or, when necessary, leaves, grass, old rags, hands, or nothing. The market was obvious—every human on Caedellium had bowel movements. Use of the new option started slowly, then spread to other provinces within a month.

Faster to be accepted were sanitary napkins. Existing custom used cloth fragments, when available. Yozef's first models were made from either wood pulp or cotton. A red-faced Yozef endured an awkward meeting with Sister Diera, where he explained their use. The abbess was initially perplexed but smiled at Yozef's embarrassment and offered advice on size and took samples to be tried by several younger women. Although the responses from the women contacted by Diera were positive, Yozef and Myrfild were astonished when requests for the product started within days—first as a trickle and then a flood, from within Abersford, then the district, the rest of Keelan, and other provinces. The demand was relentless, in spite of husbands and fathers not seeing the same value as did women in spending coin on such an item. Myrfild hired more workers, expanded into a vacant building, and commented they might consider finding papermakers in other provinces interested in partnering. Yozef never explained why he called the napkins "kotex."

Kerosene

The second major new project originated from Yozef's forgetfulness. One evening, he worked on updating his English-Caedelli dictionary. He planned to write for an hour. One advantage of the short affair with Buna Keller was that he now knew the Caedelli words for most male and female body parts that he hadn't found the opportunity, or nerve, to ask anyone else. He suspected the querying and Buna's rejection were connected—a twofer. It was time to add those new words to the dictionary. He wasn't sure when he would have other opportunities to either hear or use the words.

He was working on the breast area when his whale-oil lamp went out. The sudden darkness startled him, until he remembered he should have checked the oil level. He knew there was more oil somewhere on the property, but he had no idea where and didn't want to wake Brak or Elian.

Wait a minute! Whale oil? People on Earth only used whale oil until they killed most of the whales and then went to kerosene and vegetable oil lanterns.

Yozef didn't know what local plants might produce oils, but kerosene he *did* know about.

Petroleum. Kerosene was a major fractional distillation product of crude oil. It could be produced from coal, which was abundant on Caedellium, though petroleum was more efficient—if there was a source. He remembered that crude kerosene had been produced from petroleum in limited amounts for thousands of years on Earth, but its common production and use for lighting didn't exist until the 1850s.

The next day he wrote down all he remembered about petroleum and its fractional distillation. They were already distilling ether and ethanol, so how hard could it be to modify the procedure for petroleum?

Much harder, it turned out, yet not impossible.

First, they needed to find a source of petroleum on Caedellium. When Cadwulf proved no help, the two of them asked around the abbey and the village and found a tradesman who knew of the black, sticky substance used for caulking ships and waterproofing. He pointed them to a Gwillamese trader named Linwyr, who knew of several places on Caedellium where oil seeped into pools above ground. None of these petroleum seeps were nearby in Keelan Province, though just across the border in Gwillamer Province was a region avoided by farmers because of the prevalence of the noxious pools.

Yozef paid Linwyr one hundred krun to show him, Cadwulf, and Filtin the pools. On horseback, they followed the road into Gwillamer from Abersford, about twenty-four miles to where they left the main road and wound their horses into a marshy area a few miles from the sea. It was the longest horseback ride Yozef had made, and for the last few miles, he couldn't get out of his mind the joke line "'Fifty Days in the Saddle' by Major Assburns." He now appreciated the reference more, though the humor was lost in his present condition.

They smelled the pools before they saw them.

"Thank you, God or whomever!" Yozef exclaimed in English, as he gingerly dismounted next to an odious-looking pool with a skim of water covering the seep. Sulfurous odors came and went with the breeze off the water. The pool was both encouraging and discouraging. Encouraging, in that it existed at all, showing that surface petroleum did exist on Caedellium; discouraging, in that the pool was only three feet in diameter. Linwyr assured him that larger pools were nearby.

"I'm walking for a while to rest Seabiscuit," Yozef asserted. Cadwulf objected, Carnigan smirked, and Linwyr grunted. They walked, Yozef slightly bowlegged at first.

They found several small pools in the next hour, and Yozef was about to give up when they hit pay dirt. Before them, in a shallow valley, lay a crude oil seep a hundred yards across.

"This is more like it," said Yozef, kneeling down to inspect the crude. While any grade of petroleum could be used, the heavier grades would be useless in the foreseeable future, given the available level of technology and infrastructure. Yozef stirred the crude with a dead tree branch and got below the surface layer.

"Good, good," he said. "This will work fine." It looked like what was called "light-sweet" grade on Earth. If he was right, there'd be less of the heavier, more difficult to work with fractions and a high percentage of the lighter molecules. Benzene would come off early, and they could let it blow away—no worry about the Environmental Protection Agency (EPA) rules here. Then, 30 to 50 percent of the total would distill off as kerosene.

They probed the seep and found an average depth of three feet at six feet from the edge. Assuming the depth increased toward the center of the pool and the depression, there was enough petroleum to supply production until they found out whether kerosene would succeed as a product. If it did, they might have to drill, though it wasn't something to worry about, yet.

"Linwyr," questioned Yozef, "would it be a problem in either buying this land here in Gwillamer or in taking the crude?"

"We'd have to check with the local district center," said the trader, "but I don't think there will be any problem. Customs and laws in Gwillamer are similar to Keelan. Give me a couple of days, and I should be able to find out. Of course, my time is valuable, and who knows what unexpected problems might occur."

After some dickering, it was agreed Linwyr would receive a percentage of profits from the Gwillamer petroleum. Yozef figured that giving Linwyr a small share in any profits, in exchange for his dealing with the Gwillamese, better ensured Linwyr's dedication to the project than salary. Approval to take the oil came the next sixday, details about which Yozef never inquired, as long as the petroleum was available.

With paperwork in hand that Linwyr said authorized them to collect unlimited petroleum, the next two steps were how to get the oil to where it could be processed and distilled. Logistically, setting up the distillation at the source would have been more efficient, but at the beginning it would have to be in Abersford, where there were already shops and workmen. Yozef put Linwyr in charge of getting the petroleum to Abersford, and Filtin with working out the distillation.

Linwyr's solution to getting the oil from the Gwillamer pools to Abersford was simple. A wooden tanker wagon was built that would hold twelve hundred gallons. The bed of the wagon was a wooden box with no lid, the crude also serving as caulking for the wood. Once full, the top of the bed was covered with canvas to keep out dust and critters. How Linwyr got the oil from the pools to the box Yozef never asked. A six-horse team pulled the wagon, and once it arrived in Abersford, the wagon was rolled over a basin dug into the ground and lined with brick, a "cork" built into the bottom of the wagon bed was knocked out, and the crude drained into the basin. The cork was then replaced, and wagon returned to Gwillamer for another load. Yozef cringed, as he watched the first load empty into the basin, and wondered how much seeped into the ground and the water table. Again, no EPA. However, if this took off, they'd have to make other arrangements.

Filtin's task was by far the hardest. The fundamental principle was the same as with ether and ethanol, yet the details weren't minor. Yozef knew that on Earth, a typical refinery had combinations of huge metal fractional distillation and cracking towers to break down the larger petroleum polymers into smaller chains being distilled continuously, with fractions removed and additional feedstock added as needed, a process for which Yozef didn't understand the underlying engineering, except for its being too complex a technology for Caedellium. Obviously, they were going to work on smaller amounts than Earth refineries did, and they'd have to use batch distillation. He remembered references to Arabic devices similar to pot stills used for making whiskey, essentially bulbous vessels that could be many feet in diameter. This approach to distillation was cruder than they were using for ether and ethanol but was more amenable to larger amounts. Then there was the residual crude once the kerosene fraction was removed, which he directed Filtin to store in deep pits, in case they eventually got around to using it for asphalt in road paving. He left the details of handling the crude and the residues to Filtin.

And figure it out Filtin did, although it took two months, three moderate accidents, turnover in workers coinciding with rebuilding a demolished first petroleum workshop, and some considerable coin. The first Anyar petroleum fractional distillation succeeded in a run producing ten gallons of kerosene. The twenty-foot-tall bronze column Filtin designed looked like something out of a metal junkyard, but it worked.

Yozef waited until they knew the kerosene could be produced before moving to the next step—what to burn it in? The test to see whether existing whale oil lamps would also use kerosene was conducted outdoors and with all witnesses at a distance, so no permanent damage resulted from the first test. Consultation with a local lamp maker and a promise of rights to produce the new lamp type gave them a functioning kerosene lamp within another sixday after tweaking existing whale oil lamp designs.

Acceptance of the new lamps benefited from Yozef's access to standard Earth marketing strategies: free samples, demonstrations, and product placement. Evening demonstrations at the abbey and Abersford let the populace compare light from the traditional whale oil lamps to the new kerosene. Then the first batch of lamps, along with a supply of kerosene, was loaned to anyone who wanted to try them out on a three-day trial before passing the lamps on to other interested denizens. Overnight, orders began coming in, and by the next month Filtin was working on larger fractionation columns, Linwyr was building more and bigger wagons, and the lamp maker switched most of his production to kerosene lanterns.

The village of Abersford was in the middle of minor industrial and population booms. The ether, ethanol, soap, paper, and now kerosene and lanterns had long ago absorbed all available and competent workers, and additional ones were coming from surrounding villages up to twenty miles away. To avoid overloading the local community and to aid distribution, Yozef started "franchising out" production, first to the district seat at Clengoth, then to the clan center at Caernford, and later to other provinces. He left the details to Cadwulf, who hired two more assistants to handle the formalities.

Yozef's reputation as a tycoon rose even higher. Silver and gold coins gravitated to him exponentially.

A Plan

His enterprises flourished, but never far from Yozef's consciousness were thoughts of, *What "exactly" am I doing here on Anyar?* Earth was still out there . . . somewhere. The Watchers studied humans, and he found himself glancing at the sky and wondering whether they were looking at him at that moment. Not that he would ever know, assuming Harlie told the truth about non-intervention.

The patient who had died during an amputation had jolted him into teaching the Caedelli how to make ether, and that had led to ethanol and distillation as a basic procedure, kerosene production, soaps, and different papers. He didn't doubt there would be more. Ideas were constantly bubbling up, some to be discarded as too impractical, some for further consideration, and others many decades or lifetimes away from implementation.

Still, when he surveyed his time on Anyar, he had made a difference: useful products, simple technologies, rudimentary medical-related knowledge, and introducing novel branches of mathematics to Cadwulf. All to the good, so why a longing for more? In his old life, living with Julie, contemplating leaving graduate school for a safe job and a comfortable lifestyle had been the extent of his ambitions. He had been satisfied then, but now . . .

By local standards, he was becoming wealthy and would only get richer. Did he have any other purpose, except to live out his life as best he could? Not that such a future was all bad, considering his circumstances, but he was angry. Angry at the Watchers, angry at the fates, angry at—God? Even if he couldn't assign blame, there was a need to "show" that he mattered, that his existence left a mark. Such thoughts were confusing, since they'd have been alien to Earth's Joseph Colsco.

One inescapable fact of his existence on Anyar was Bronwyn's coming child. What kind of future would it have? What if he married and had more children? What would be their and their descendants' future? What of all of the peoples of Anyar? There must be hundreds of millions to low billions. If the people of Anyar had the knowledge lying available in his brain, the planet's technology would leap ahead centuries. What if the Watchers were not neutral observers? He had only the word of Harlie that they'd had no hand in transplanting humans.

He worried. What if the Watchers or whoever had done this someday returned? If they showed up in two hundred years, would they expect to find Anyar with the technology of Earth 1900–1950? If the Anyarians could be pushed ahead, maybe they'd have the ability to stand on their own against whatever came. For that to happen, Yozef would have to both attempt to transfer his science and technology knowledge *and* have it accepted. He had made changes, yet most of those would have come on their own within a century or more, assuming they didn't already exist elsewhere on Anyar. In his focus on himself and the here and now, he could easily forget there was the rest of the planet beyond Caedellium, and who knew what level of technology might exist elsewhere? He knew of the Narthani, having gotten an earful from both Carnigan and the abbot, but were the Caedelli views parochial? Maybe the Narthani were a better vehicle for what he knew. And what of other realms that might be more advanced?

These thoughts monopolized Yozef for an entire day. He walked from his house to Abersford, then to the abbey, back to his house, along the shore to his cove, to Birdshit Bay, and back to his house. By twilight, he had walked more than twenty miles without eating or drinking since morning meal. His throat was parched, his stomach ate at his backbone, and his feet protested blisters, but none of the complainants were noticed.

When he got back to his cottage, he had decided on a goal to underlie everything else for the rest of his life. When he'd first arrived on Caedellium, he'd feared introducing new ideas. Now, his position and reputation were solid enough that the risk of introducing new knowledge was acceptable, as long as he took care.

He envisioned three objectives. First, continue pushing his various projects and staying alert for new opportunities. Most important were not the novel products themselves, but the techniques and the technology adopted by workers and getting those workers to think in new directions. In addition, products generated coinage—life's blood for change.

Second, push more basic scientific knowledge beyond the medical and biological ideas he had shared with Diera and the scholastics. He had so far been circumspect on what he shared, not knowing what they could absorb without triggering countervailing reactions. Their current level could not absorb cell structure, DNA, RNA, antibiotics, and the associated chemistry, genetic engineering, molecular biology, genetics as applied to plant and animal breeding—along with another topic that could be tricky: the evolution of organisms. It was only a matter of time before the people of Anyar recognized two lines of organisms on Anyar, and humans belonged to the line that couldn't have evolved on this planet.

He had already changed the course of Anyarian mathematics, yet he hadn't touched the physical sciences—physics, astronomy, geology, and whatever else he could remember. He would have to introduce knowledge step by step, trying to remember the stages in Earth's scientific history, so the new concepts could be accepted and integrated.

The third objective was long term, mostly to be used beyond his lifetime. He would write down as much as he could remember about *everything*. One set of books for the sciences and a second series on how he came to Anyar, the Watchers, and as much of the history of Earth as he could recall. He would develop a plan to keep the second set of books concealed until some indefinite future, likely well beyond his own lifetime. Anyone reading them too soon would judge him insane. But one day, there needed to be a record to let the people of Anyar know about Earth and the Watchers. And not incidentally, he admitted to himself, to know about Joseph Colsco, a.k.a. Yozef Kolsko.

He stood on his veranda, smelling the evening meal being prepared by Elian, watching birds and murvors sail over the surf. Having a life-long plan, albeit one for which he didn't know the outcome, gave him a feeling of focus. He would dedicate himself to knowledge transfer in the confidence it would spread to all of Anyar. It would be his purpose in life and his legacy, a path for the rest of his life, a life of purpose here in Abersford. He sat back and looked at the ocean. He felt calmer than he had since his arrival—naked on the beach not too far away.

A cruel God would smile. A beneficent God would be sympathetic.

Yozef Is Happy?

The next evening, Yozef celebrated his newfound commitment to his future by walking to Abersford after eating with the Faughns. He peeked into the Snarling Graeko, and, sure enough, Carnigan sat at his table against the wall, alone.

A jovial Yozef plopped himself on a bench opposite Carnigan.

"What are you so cheery about?" Carnigan grated to an oblivious Yozef, who had decided many months ago that most of the time the grating was just the natural tenor of Carnigan's voice. He wasn't ready to crush your skull. Most of the time. When he was in a bad mood, his voice got softer—*that* was the time to make a hasty exit.

"Oh, just in a good mood tonight. Who else would I want to share my good humor with, except Carnigan Puvey?"

Carnigan's response was a grunt and a renewed focus on the half-full beer stein. He picked it up and downed it in one long draught. By magic, a woman appeared with two new full steins. Yozef was about to thank her for anticipating his order when she said, "Ev'ning, Ser Kolsko. Will yuh be hav' y'r usual?"

"Ah . . . yes, thank you," he answered. Yozef's mood shifted to concern. Carnigan was a prodigious drinker, but usually a few beers put him into as openly a good mood as he was likely to get.

He kept a watchful eye on Carnigan, until the woman returned with a third stein for their table. He then sipped. Sipped again. Again. Then jumped in.

"Carnigan," he ventured, "is there some problem? You seem . . . troubled tonight."

Carnigan was quiet at first, then took a smaller quaff from one of his steins.

"Sometimes our lives go in directions we never dreamed of. One thinks he knows his place in the world and what's in the future . . . then everything changes, and everything he expected is gone." Carnigan looked up from his beer at Yozef, a melancholy expression on his ruddy face. "Does that ever occur to you, Yozef?"

Yozef was thunderstruck by the question.

Carnigan saw the expression on Yozef's face and slammed a giant fist on the table. "God's curse on me, Yozef! If there's anyone on Caedellium who's been jerked from his life path, it must be you! My apologies for wallowing."

"Nonsense, Carnigan," reassured Yozef. "All of us have this feeling from time to time. Granted, some more than others, and I guess I'm one of those others. What about you, though? What is it?"

Yozef could see the hand holding the metal stein tighten, and he half held his breath, wondering if Carnigan was going to crush the vessel without realizing it. Then the hand relaxed, and the owner sat back against the wall. "It's the day."

"The day? Something happened today?"

"No. The date," he whispered. "This date every year. It was on this date that my life changed. On this date, I realized I wasn't a good person."

"Could you tell me what happened?"

"No," Carnigan replied in the soft tone, signaling it was time to end this discussion thread.

Yozef decided to try another tactic to maybe improve Carnigan's mood. He'd let Carnigan rib him about the brief affair with Buna.

Whoops, Yozef thought. *Wait a minute. Carnigan isn't married. He lives in the abbey, and I've never seen or heard of him in relation to a woman. That's unusual among the Caedelli, what with their attitudes toward sex and the shortage of men.*

Granted, Carnigan wasn't the most personable of men. Still—something involving women? Or a woman? Best to avoid the topic.

Yozef spent the next half hour rambling about progress on his various projects, news and rumors about the Narthani, the weather, and anything else he could think of, trawling for any topic that might bring up a spark of interest from Carnigan. He was about to give it up when he hit pay dirt.

"Filtin tells me he had another run-in with his mother-in-law. Or, as Filtin refers to her, 'the old witch.'" Yozef's attention spiked when he thought he saw a hint of Carnigan's mouth turning up at the corner. The referenced older woman was notorious throughout Abersford for making caustic remarks at the slightest perceived provocation. However, Filtin insisted she needed no provocation, and it was her nature that anything coming out of her mouth was required to be nasty. Her looks were a good match to her personality. She had straggly gray hair, seldom washed, and had bad teeth. Her rheumy eyes reminded Yozef alternately of a snake or a wolverine, and her breath could melt metal. All in all, a charming person. Anyone would have questioned the wisdom of Filtin not having serious reservations about marrying a daughter of this harridan, yet to the surprise of all, the daughter was nothing like the mother. Nerlin Fuller was, from all accounts, mild-mannered, was liked by all, adored

Filtin, and was a conscientious mother. Filtin half-jokingly speculated one evening that Nerlin had the perfect model of whom *not* to be.

Encouraged by Carnigan's reaction, Yozef attempted humor. "That reminds me of a joke about a woman, possibly someone like Filtin's mother-in-law. It seems she was one of three old women who died and arrived in the afterlife at the same time. When they get there, God says, 'We only have one rule here: don't step on the ducks!'

"The three women agree, though they don't understand why ducks are so important, and they enter Heaven. Sure enough, there are ducks all over the place. It is virtually impossible not to step on a duck, and although they do their best to avoid them, the first woman accidentally steps on one.

"Well, along comes God with the most unpleasant man the first woman has ever seen. God chains them together and says, 'Your punishment for stepping on a duck is to spend eternity chained to this man!'

"The next day, the second woman accidentally steps on a duck, and along comes God again with an extremely unpleasant-looking man. He chains them together with the same admonition as for the first woman.

"The third woman has watched all of this and is determined *not* to be chained for all eternity to an unpleasant man like the other two women, so she steps extraordinarily carefully wherever she goes. She manages to go months without stepping on any ducks. Then one day, God comes up to her with the most handsome man she has ever laid eyes on—tall, dark hair, and muscular. God chains them together without saying a word and walks away.

"The happy woman says to her dream man, 'I wonder what I did to deserve being chained to you for all of eternity?'

"'I don't know about you,' the man says, 'but I stepped on a duck!'"

There was no reaction for some seconds, then the first cracks appeared in granite, like an avalanche that started slowly and then accelerated as an irresistible force. Fortunately, unlike the first time Yozef had cribbed a joke from Earth and told it as a novel one on Anyar, Carnigan didn't have a mouthful of beer. Yozef was spared an evening shower. And he was fortunate that he had moved his chair back slightly in anticipation at the first signs of motion and thus wasn't bounced by the edge of the heavy table when both of Carnigan's fists pounded the defenseless wood.

Other patrons stopped their own activities, as heads rotated toward the volcanic outburst. Then, recognizing Yozef, people spread the word that one of Yozef's story sessions might be in the offering. The evening's sparse distribution of patrons flowed around Yozef and Carnigan's table, forming a U-shape against the wall.

If Carnigan at first noticed the gathering, he gave no sign until his laughter subsided. Then he looked around with his usual angry expression and sighed. "Can't a man be left in peace with his dark moods anymore?"

"What are friends for, if not to save friends from themselves?" Yozef assured him. "Which reminds me of a story . . . " and he was off and running with more plagiarized jokes from Earth, many of which fell on deaf ears, since the context was lost, but enough of which hit universal themes and references to maintain his reputation as a major wit.

The pub was nearly empty when Yozef decided it was past time to head home. The problem with that intent was that once he stood, moving in a straight line proved troublesome. Still, considering the amount of strong beer he'd consumed, his brain idly wondered why he was even standing. Carnigan, evidently possessing an infinite capacity for beer, steadied Yozef and walked him the mile to his house.

It had been a good evening. As he dozed off in his bed, Yozef thought that everything considered, it wasn't a bad life. He had friends. The affair with Bronwyn had ended, though with good memories and no real regrets. The affair with Buna had ended, which was the important fact. He was making a difference. He was well-known and respected, and he thought he had a plan to focus his life. Despite all that had happened to him, it could be a lot worse.

CHAPTER 30

THE RAID

Buldorian Ship, *Warrior's Pride*

Musfar Adalan was a contented man. From the aftcastle of his flagship, he could see all five of his ships. Granted, they weren't *real* warships, with heavy cannon and three- to four-foot bulwarks, but their 15-pounder cannon would subdue any lumbering merchant ship, and they were agile and fast enough to outrun anything they couldn't outgun. He'd brought seven ships with him to Caedellium. Two ships had sailed home laden with spoils: gold, silver, jewelry, fine rugs and cloth, slaves, and whatever goods and trinkets caught his men's fancy and for which there was room in the ship's holds. The *Scourge from Buldor* left three months ago and returned the day before the rest of his ships left for the current raid. He would have liked to have the sixth ship along, but rudder problems and other repairs would have delayed the raid by several days, something neither he nor the Narthani desired. The seventh ship, the *Bravado*, had left for Buldor ten days ago, also stuffed high with booty, but with orders not to return. Adalan trusted his sixth sense, and it told him their time in these waters ran short.

Adalan didn't think of himself as a pirate by trade but as more of an "opportunist," ready to take advantage of *opportunities*. Sometimes those involved pirating, but, depending on circumstances, he and his men dabbled in the slave trade, smuggling, raids, and mercenary work when the remuneration was appealing. It was a version of the latter two activities that engaged them on this day and had for the last several months, raiding the Caedellium coast under the patronage of the Narthani. Dealing with the Narthani was dangerous, yet he accepted the risks for the spoils he and his men had amassed.

While Adalan was not privy to the exact reasons the Narthani had come to him, instead of using their own formidable navy, it would have taken someone far less sagacious in the ways of the world not to assume it was because the Narthani wanted a plausible degree of deniability. Adalan knew the current arrangement would end whenever it suited the Narthani, but that would be in the future, and Adalan dealt with the *now*.

This would be their fourteenth raid. For Adalan, the results had assuaged his initial caution. The Narthani gathered intelligence and picked rich, vulnerable targets with meticulous efficiency. Twelve of the first thirteen raids were successful, with minimal losses. In one case, Abel Adalan, Musfar's cousin and second-in-command, had withdrawn before a complete sack, due to indications of reinforcements arriving and where the final holdout positions were judged too strong to be overcome for the expected return. Only one of the earlier raids was aborted on discovering the Stent Province abbey defended by two hundred Stentese men fortuitously gathered for a muster drill unanticipated by the Narthani. The accompanying Narthani liaison excoriated them in both cases, but General Akuyun, the Narthani commander, accepted Musfar's explanations as reasonable.

To Adalan's thinking, there were two downsides to the arrangement. One was that he knew the time would come when the Narthani no longer needed deniability. Before that day, Adalan planned that he and his men should slip away, in case the Narthani severed their relationship on other than friendly terms.

The second downside was that several Narthani officers always accompanied the raids. They didn't go ashore, only observed and offered advice, which Adalan neither needed nor wanted. On the first raids, the lead Narthani was tolerable. No such luck on this raid. The three new Narthani stood on the forecastle, the leader using a telescope to examine the shoreline and talking to the other two, one of whom took notes.

The Narthani leader was an older, blocky man whose main skill was to confirm the worst stereotypes of the Narthani—arrogant, condescending, and eyes like a Drilmarian zernik, the goat-sized omnivore renowned for being stupid, prolific, vicious, and making parts of the Drilmar continent essentially uninhabitable. Musfar hoped someday that someone would exterminate both the zerniks and the Narthani.

"Look at those asses, Musfar," said Abel Adalan. "Strutting around and acting like they have any idea how to sail a ship or carry out a raid."

Musfar turned to his cousin and second-in-command. "Now, now, Abel, you mustn't show such disrespect for our benefactors. They have made all of us exceedingly rich the last few months. When we return home, both we and our clan will be among the greats of Buldor."

"They're still asses."

Musfar sighed. "Yes, Abel, they *are* asses, but they're *our* asses for now."

The two cousins laughed loud enough to draw disapproving looks from the three Narthani on the other end of the vessel. Musfar gave them a respectful bow and waved. "I will bow and scrape before even these asses for the loot we've already accumulated, but my cousin, I feel it may be time for our sails to catch the winds homeward."

"My thoughts as well. As our illustrious grandfather has said to us many times, 'It's good to be greedy, just not *too* greedy.'"

Musfar looked at the other ships in line behind *Warrior's Pride*. All five vessels were abuzz with activity, as crews unsheathed and prepared to lower longboats to be filled with the armed men waiting on and below deck. The normal ships' crew complements were around 350 men for the five ships. However, for shore raids, more men were needed, and months earlier Adalan had sent back to Buldor for another 100 clansmen and 170 men from another clan of Buldor. Though Musfar's clan considered the Benhoudi to be little better than dogs, they were available, since the poorer clans always looked to hire out their men to supplement their own activities.

The raid this day involved 400 men ashore, 250 of Musfar's Benkarsta clansmen, and the 150 Benhoudi, leaving skeleton Benkarsta crews on the ships. Although it wasn't spoken openly, all, including the Benhoudi, knew that the Benhoudi would get the more dangerous assignments on raids. Still, the potential for loot was so great, and their clan so poor, the Benhoudi leader considered the risks acceptable. So far, this calculation had proven profitable for all, even for the Benhoudi, who would return home among their clan's wealthiest members, having so far lost only 20 of their original 170.

Abel Adalan, as Musfar's second-in-command, would lead the raiding party. The two men went into the command cabin, where a map of Abersford and the abbey area was pinned to a wall.

"I've looked over your plan for the raid, Abel, and I see no obvious changes to make."

Abel traced lines of planned movements with a forefinger. "You'll get us within about two hundred yards of shore, assuming the information from the Narthani agent is accurate, and the bottom is as deep as they say," he commented, unknowingly pointing to the same beach where Yozef had been found.

"We'll anchor offshore and immediately lower all shipboard longboats, while we pull in those we're towing." The Buldorian vessels didn't have room on deck for enough longboats to contain all of the men heading to shore, and hawsers connected more boats to the ships. On earlier raids, they put the men ashore several miles from the target, believing it gave better chances to approach undetected. Since then, they had changed their approach tactic and at first light drove the ships as close to shore as they could, then rushed ashore before the locals had time to react.

Abel's finger rested on the abbey, as he continued his review. "Four hundred men, two hundred and fifty of ours and the hundred and fifty Benhoudi. As usual, I'll try to keep the Benhoudi in the forefront, if there's major resistance. I'll be with the main group of three hundred hitting the abbey, since that's where the major resistance should concentrate and where the Narthani information tells us the best booty is located. It's also where large numbers of the villagers will go for safety, so there should be many women and children inside.

"The other hundred of our men will sweep through the village, making quick plunder of cartable valuables and potential slaves—the sweep to be finished within thirty minutes and all booty returned to the ships. The remaining men of that group are then to reinforce the abbey looting if necessary.

"The main body of three hundred men will move on the abbey, as soon as ashore and organized. Speed and coordination are essential. The information from the Narthani and a look with our telescope confirm the wall around the abbey is only seven to eight feet tall. Assuming the other information is correct, most of the fighting men will be absent, partly due to our feints on the other villages down the coast two days ago and partly from Narthani assurances that another portion of the fighting men will be absent.

"It bothers me, as it always does, that we're proceeding based on information we didn't gather or confirm ourselves. So far, though, I have to give reluctant credit to the reliability of the Narthani intelligence," grumbled a resigned Abel. "Assuming, once again, the information is accurate, the locals shouldn't be able to stop a simultaneous assault at multiple points on the wall." Abel pointed to three 'X's on the map. "We'll attack the abbey complex wall at these three points in hundred man groups. First, two groups, each of seventy-five Benhoudi and twenty-five of our men, will attack about halfway between the main gate and the two corners—we assume the gate will be closed and barred. Either or both groups should be able to get over the wall and engage the locals. The wall next to the gate, and the gate itself are twelve feet tall, so ignoring the gate area and going directly over the eight-foot wall is easier. Once we're inside, we should be able to overwhelm the defenders. It's getting over the wall where most of our losses will happen.

"The third group of one hundred of our own men will wait for the first two groups to launch their attacks, then hit the western wall of the abbey complex. Most defenders should be involved with the first two group, so the third group might get inside the walls untouched or might not even be needed, but just in case . . ."

Musfar approved. His cousin had earned his position. He was fearless as necessary in battle, yet his real value was his planning and cool thinking. Musfar knew of too many Buldorian men wasted because of stupid leaders. He took it as a matter of pride that his men suffered as few casualties as they did when balanced with the volume of booty this expedition had garnered. No small part of that success was the result of Abel's careful planning and attention to detail. This might be the last trip with Abel as his second. He was due for a command, and Musfar would support him if he chose to go out next time as a commander. He'd miss him.

"If all goes as expected," Abel went on, "we should be back at the beach within two to three hours. If there's either more resistance or more booty than expected, I'll balance time and booty potential. Whatever happens, I don't expect the raid to take longer than four hours at the most."

The two men returned to the deck and squinted to shore as their ship sailed toward the beach. Within ten minutes, they'd be anchored and the first men scrambling into the longboats.

"Good luck and good hunting," said Musfar, and they clasped forearms.

Alert!

The sun peeked above the eastern mountaintops on a typical morning on the southwest coast of Keelan Province. Scattered white clouds hinted at a clear day. The slight onshore breeze brought in the usual sea freshness. A morning haze still lay on the fields, and the same atmospherics allowed the haze hovering over the ocean to just start to clear with the sun's first rays.

Sistian and Diera Beynom finished morning meal—both late this morning for their duties, but they were in charge of their respective orders at St. Sidryn's, and no one begrudged their luxury of occasionally lingering at morning meal.

Abersford's fighting men were organized into Thirds of fifty men each. Carnigan Puvey and Denes Vegga belonged to the one Third currently in Abersford. A second Third of the local levy was, "by chance," on a scheduled patrol duty, this time farther north than usual. Eywellese riders had crossed several times into the northern districts, and Hetman Keelan had ordered increased patrols. Those fifty Abersford men were seventy miles away and a day out of semaphore or courier contact.

The final Third of the Abersford men spent the previous night thirty miles west at a Gwillamer Province coastal village that had spotted sea raider ships unloading men several miles farther west. No attack had yet occurred, but the local Gwillamer boyerman had invoked the Tri-Clan Alliance agreement, and Abersford, being the closest Keelan settlement, was obliged to respond. Denes Vegga, the local magistrate, the overall supervisor of the Thirds, and the direct commander of one of the three, vociferously objected to leaving the area with so few men. A rider carried Gwillamer's request to Langnor Vorwich, the district boyerman, who reluctantly ruled the request had to be honored and promised to start additional men moving toward Abersford the next morning. The village and the abbey would only be short fighting men for a few hours.

Both Carnigan and Vegga were already at work—Carnigan helping a village smithy repair an iron railing at the abbey hospital, and Vegga at the local authority office, preparing to ride out accompanying the registrar to a farm delinquent in taxes. The farm itself was productive enough to pay the taxes, even in these times, yet the owner managed always to be late. The farmer was also a disagreeable character, and the registrar agent asked Vegga to accompany him.

Halla Bower had just walked her oldest child, Manwyn, to the village school. At six years old, he would attend the small local school for another three to four years before she and her husband decided whether to send him to the abbey school, where older children could further their education beyond that needed for most trades. Her husband worked in his father's leather shop, and although he knew he would someday inherit the shop, he didn't intend for his son to be obligated from birth to take over the business. Halla loved her husband for this attitude, for the consideration he always showed his family and other people, and just because she loved him.

After returning home, Halla put down Manwyn's sister. At eighteen months, the toddler was getting a little big for Halla to carry too long. As usual, it would be a busy day for Halla. Clothes to wash, clothes to mend, their vegetable garden to tend, turnips past ready to pull and store in their root cellar, a return trip to the school to collect Manwyn after the midday bell, and tending to the girl. The toddler was walking and running, sort of, and would soon start training to use the outhouse. If that training took hold in the next few months, then Halla would have a six-months' respite; she hadn't told her husband about another child on the way.

Yozef Kolsko had risen with only a slight hangover from the night's pub session and had eaten a morning meal with Elian. Brak had eaten earlier and had been at work around the property before light. Yozef didn't see the need for the elderly man to rise so early and work so hard, but his suggestions met with disapproving looks from the proud older man, and Yozef dropped the subject. Elian wasn't as regimented as Brak. While she saw no need to rise as early as her husband, Yozef's sleeping well past sunrise seemed decadent. However, since she wasn't always hungry when she rose, and since she perceived that Yozef didn't always wish to eat alone, many days she waited, and they ate together. Over the months, Yozef learned what he thought must be every detail of her life and Brak's, the past and current lives of their four children, and the preferred methods of preserving local products and cooking the traditional Caedellium dishes. Despite his hearing most of it multiple times, somehow the gentle nature and kindness of the older woman and her pleasures at what seemed to Yozef a hard life never bored him. It was meditative and a lesson for finding life's positives.

Today, Yozef was due to meet with Cadwulf to go over his total finances; then Filtin had another of his ideas about improving the petroleum distillation. Most of Filtin's ideas proved impractical at the moment, others impractical now but perhaps someday implementable, and occasionally one was truly innovative, including several ideas that helped narrow the curve between kerosene production and demand.

After the morning meal, Yozef started off on the walk into Abersford. Brak thought he should ride, both because of his stature as a prominent citizen and because of his abysmal horsemanship. "How yuh expect to get better if yuh don't do it?" Yozef declined most days, unless he had appointments. The walk didn't take long, and he needed the exercise. It gave him a chance to think, and he still didn't like horses or trust his horsemanship, even with Seabiscuit.

Yonkel Miron loved roaming the beaches near Abersford. Not every day, but often. By planning, he left home early for school, so he could detour half an hour along the shore. He bragged he had the best seashell collection in the district and occasionally found an intact and rare enough shell to sell for a few krun in the village. Then there was always the chance he would find something mysterious washed up. After all, had it not been *he* who first found Yozef Kolsko—the strange man who washed up on their beach naked and within a year turned into an important figure and for whom Yonkel's father and older brothers worked in the lantern-making shop, or *factory*, as Yozef called it?

His father kept telling Yonkel he should call Yozef by his formal title—Ser Kolsko. Yonkel always replied that Yozef himself had given permission to use his first name, and "You wouldn't want to chance offending Yozef, would you?"

Yonkel attended the abbey school this year. Yozef had spoken with Yonkel's father about how the boy was smart, and in the future there'd be many good-paying jobs and professions that required more education than was traditional on Caedellium. The father had been hesitant, but a family gathering decided that the pay from Kolsko's various businesses had put the extended family in such a good financial position, and since Kolsko had taken a personal interest in Yonkel, that the boy could attend more schooling. Yonkel overheard Yozef telling one abbey brother that in a few years, Yonkel might be a candidate for a scholasticum—whatever that was.

He took off his shoes to walk in the surf without ruining them, something his otherwise tolerant mother would be angry about for months. The spent water running up the sand swirled around his feet as he moved along, eyes sweeping back and forth for signs of shells worth collecting. The morning mist still hung over the beach and the sea, just now lifting in patches. The gulls and the murvors flew back and forth, scolding him when he came upon a cluster of them on the sand.

He had just inspected a glitter in the sand, which turned out to be only a fragment and not a buried complete shell. He shifted his pack containing his shoes and schoolbooks, when he raised up and faced out to sea. There, through a break in the mist, he saw a line of sailing ships right offshore, the first one only a few hundred yards from the beach. As he watched, startled, he could see the first ship drop anchor and a frenzy of activity on a deck crowded with armed men. The first longboat started to be lowered, and the second vessel likewise dropped anchor. Shoes, schoolbooks, and papers forgotten as the pack dropped onto the surf, Yonkel Miron ran toward the abbey as fast as his eight-year-old legs would permit.

Yonkel might have been the first to see the Buldorian ships, but Brother Alber gave the alarm. He happened to be in the cathedral bell tower. There had been signs of a leak in the cathedral roof the last time it rained on Godsday, and the abbot asked him to see if he could find the source. From the openings in the tower, he could look down on much of the cathedral roof. He hoped to spot a broken or misaligned tile or anything out of place, the alternative being to go out on the roof and inspect each tile, one at a time. He had done this before and left that option as a last resort. Thus, while he focused downward toward the roof, the motion of a distant figure running toward the abbey caught his attention. From there, his eyes elevated only slightly to take in the beach and the sea half a mile away. First, he saw the scattered breaking of the morning mist, then his brain registered five ships, sails gathered, and anchored.

He stared for a full minute, while his mind ran through options. Trading ships? He didn't think so. The Narthani had blocked all trade, and even if they hadn't, traders seldom came directly to Abersford, instead of the clan's port facilities at Salford. Ships seeking cover from a storm? What storm and what cover did this part of the coast provide? Caedellium ships? Certainly not from Keelan or any nearby provinces. Preddi had had vessels, but the Narthani controlled Preddi now. Could these ships be Narthani? It was the Narthani option that finally triggered a reaction. Warnings had been sent from the hetman and reinforced by Abbot Beynom. A raiding party!

The main bell was rung by using a thick rope attached by a block-and-tackle arrangement, the bell itself weighing several tons. Alber couldn't ring the bell from atop the tower. He would have to climb down the stairway to reach the end of the ringing rope. Several brothers and sisters gaped at Brother Alber sliding down the rope, using his cassock to grip and protect his hands from rope burns, his bare legs and private parts on display as he descended the four stories in a few seconds. When he hit the block-and-tackle setup, he lost his grip and dropped the last ten feet to the stone floor. His ankle broke, but he didn't notice and jumped to his feet, grabbed the lower end of the rope, and rang the bell. One ring signaled each hour. Three rings repeated with breaks assembled the people for worship on Godsday, accompanied ceremonies such as weddings, announced visiting dignitaries such as the hetman, or called a general gathering of all people within hearing. Continuous ringing meant imminent danger. No one living in Abersford had ever heard the continuous ringing, but all knew the meaning. Armed men were to gather at the abbey, citizens living far enough away to escape inland, and those living close to the abbey to run to its protection.

Denes Vegga and the registrar were just leaving the registrar's office to ride out to the tax-delinquent farmer when the peals started. They both froze in place through the first dozen peals. Then, "Hallon! Get on your horse and wait while I see what's happening!"

Denes raced back into the two-story building and up to the roof, where he had a view of the coast. As soon as he saw the ships, he shouted and waved to the mounted registrar and yelled out, "Clengoth! Ride for help! It's a raid!"

The district headquarters was fifteen miles away. Help would be dispatched from there, and a semaphore message sent on to the province capital at Caernford. Unfortunately, the first help would be three or more hours away. They were on their own until then.

Denes raced back down the stairs, mounted his waiting horse, and galloped toward the abbey, where he would organize the defense.

The abbey appeared chaotic at first glance. Word of the ships as the explanation for the bell ringing spread quickly. Sistian and Diera had drilled the abbey's staff for just such an event. They knew the abbey would become a receptacle for a flood of refugees fleeing from the village and the surrounding countryside. If the worst came, the defense would be here, at the abbey complex with its main stone walls. Given news of other raids, that defense would be to the death. No surrender contemplated, no matter what.

Carnigan moved without waiting for confirmation. He knew his immediate task and set out within seconds of the fourth peal. He was to assist the armorer in opening the block building that served as the area's armory. The armorer had a key to the building, as did Denes Vegga. By chance, the armorer was one of the men called to respond to the request for assistance from the Gwillamese under raid threat and hadn't given Carnigan the key before leaving. Vegga wasn't at the abbey at the moment. Carnigan solved the problem his usual way—he grabbed a ball-peen hammer as he ran to the armory. He took one second to smash the lock on the door. *Gonna need new locks*, he thought inanely, as he flung open the door. Men would bring their own weapons, and the armory served as a reserve. Racks of muskets, crossbows, and spears of various lengths and blade shapes, along with a mélange of swords, axes, and knives, made up the accumulated stockpile of weapons discarded, inherited extras, and only God knew from what other sources. Carnigan didn't know who would use what weapon. That was Vegga's problem—his was to move the arms to the courtyard for distribution.

Halla Bower still rested from carrying the toddler to and from Manwyn's school when the peals began. Her breath caught, and her heart seemed to stop as the peals continued. What was she supposed to do? She and her husband had spoken of it only briefly, since neither believed it would happen. Her husband would be on his way to the abbey and the gathering of his third group of Abersford's fighting men. Manwyn would be watched after by the teachers at the village school. She couldn't remember whether the students would flee inland or go to the abbey. There was nothing she could do for Manwyn, and she'd have to trust the teachers. She was supposed to take their other child to the abbey as the safest place. She grabbed the protesting toddler, who had just found a favorite ball under the table, and ran out of their house toward the road to the abbey, all tiredness from their previous trip forgotten.

Yozef was partway to Abersford when the peals started. He walked another fifty yards before his brain woke up, with the help of people running or riding toward the abbey. He remembered the talk of the possibility of Narthani or other raiders attacking the village, but it had seemed a theoretical discussion. Whatever it was, the answers lay at the abbey, now a third of a mile away. He joined the flow of runners.

Confusion at Sea

Musfar Adalan was *not* happy. The two-hundred-yard clearance reported by the Narthani for anchoring offshore turned out to be more than three hundred yards. *Warrior's Pride* narrowly missed ramming onto barely submerged rocks, and Musfar ordered anchoring short of their goal. The three Narthani officers were impervious to his glares, and Buldorian curses leveled at the Narthani fell on uncomprehending ears.

Adel Adalan was even less happy. *He* was the one going ashore to command the raid. Not only were they farther off the beach, but several lines became snarled as they attempted to lower the longboats. They had carried out this maneuver a hundred times in raids and training, but it didn't help this day. They'd be a good fifteen minutes later ashore than his plan called for.

CHAPTER 31

PANIC AND PREPARATION

Denes and Yozef arrived at the abbey within seconds of each other, with Denes's horse coming within inches of knocking Yozef down as they both hit the main gate. That's where the two men's actions differed. Denes knew exactly what he must do—create order out of the chaos and prepare to defend the abbey. Yozef had no idea what he was supposed to do. In fact, now that he was there, his immediate thought was that he wanted to be somewhere else. Anyplace else. What good was he going to be? Lacking a task or any idea of what to do, he instinctively followed Denes.

The available armed men gathered in the center of the courtyard, surrounding Denes and the abbot. Yozef edged closer through the group to better hear.

"How bad is it?" asked a grim abbot.

"Bad. Very bad," replied an even grimmer Denes. "At full fighting men strength, we could hold off a raiding party of this size. That was what the defense plan was designed for. Unfortunately, we are not at full strength. One Third is away on a scheduled patrol in northern Keelan. Even with them gone, we should have been able to hold, but now a second Third is away to Gwillamer."

"What does that mean for us now?"

Denes shook his head. "We can't hold with fifty men. This is a nightmare. If we'd known we'd have so few men, it would've been better for all of the people to run or ride as far inland as fast as they could. Most would've gotten out of reach of the raiders. We told them to come here because this was the safest place. Instead, it's turning into a trap," Denes ended bitterly.

"We have the walls," protested the desperate abbot.

"The walls are not tall enough!" Denes snarled. "I've told you and the district boyerman that several times! They'll come right at them. If I was them,

I'd fake at the main gate to force us to defend it and then attack the walls in at least two places. With the few men we have, the raiders will take casualties and then be over the wall, and it'll be the end for us."

Yozef elbowed his way near the two men in time to hear the last exchanges. They couldn't defend the walls with the number of men available? Denes was saying the raiders would overwhelm the defenders on the wall?

Oh, shit! What am I doing here?

He'd come all this way from Earth and made a life here, and now to die during a pirate raid?!

How about a fucking break now and then!!

Yozef cast around over the heads of the gathered men, looking for a way out. They were in the courtyard between the main gate and the cathedral. The hospital building and one of the residence buildings flanked the courtyard, with the main gate and wall forming the fourth side. Then ... he had an idea, and without thought, he said in normal voice, "Don't fight them on the walls."

No one paid any attention. He stepped closer to Denes and Sistian and yelled, "Don't fight them on the walls!"

The two men stopped facing each other and turned to Yozef. Sistian's expression was blank, because he didn't understand what Yozef had said.

Denes snapped, "What did you say?"

Yozef swallowed and tucked his shaking hands under his armpits. "If you can't hold them off at the walls and they'll come over, let them in the courtyard."

"Quiet, Yozef," Sistian admonished. "Let Denes—"

"Shut up!" Denes growled at the abbot, who jerked his head back, not used to being so ordered.

Denes swiveled his head from the front gate at the courtyard to Yozef, to the courtyard. He licked his lips. "It's risky. There isn't much time to get ready, but it may be our only chance."

"What are you talking about?" asked the bewildered abbot.

Denes grabbed the abbot's arm and leaned closer to him. "If we can't keep them outside the walls, our one chance might be to make the courtyard a trap. Turn the trap for us into a trap for them. We lure them here, so they're clustered together while *we* surround *them*. Then we can fight them from all sides, while they can't use all of their weapons at the same time. It'll help balance their number advantage."

"Let them in the gate!" Sistian shrieked. "That's insane! How can we not hold them at the walls, then let them inside the complex?!"

"Not inside the complex, inside our trap."

"But—"

"I'm in charge, Abbot. We have to do something, and it's my decision." With that, Denes quit paying attention to the abbot, who stood white-faced and confused when Denes turned again to Yozef.

"We'll give a good account of ourselves, but they'll still probably win. We just don't have enough men."

Yozef's mind was split. One part wanted to run and not stand and give advice he had no qualifications to give, but the part controlling his babbling was ascendant. "Maybe not fighting out in the open, but there are plenty of people here who can fight behind barricades."

Denes whirled back to the abbot. "Abbot, you and your staff get all the oldest people and children into the farthest and most secure rooms in the basements. Then everyone able enough to stand and fight in place, get to the courtyard."

The abbot stood and stared glassy-eyed at Denes.

"NOW, ABBOT!!" Denes screamed.

Sistian blinked twice, then hitched his cassock and took off running, yelling for other brothers and sisters.

Denes shouted for the clustered men to shut up and listen. "If we try to hold the walls, they'll break through easily. Even if every adult, man and woman, joins us on the wall, there's too much of the wall to defend and react to their attacking at different places. Once they're over the wall in even one place, it'll be over. We need to get them where they're at a disadvantage.

"Here's what we'll do—build a continuous barricade around the edges of the courtyard, then leave the main gate open and let them pour through. They might not be able to resist if they see we haven't closed the gate. When they enter the courtyard, we can fire at them from behind the barricade. If they reach the barricade, they'll have to climb over and be vulnerable."

"What if they don't take the bait?" asked a rough-looking man toward the rear of the group.

"Then we're back to defending the walls as best we can, with everyone who can hold a weapon," Denes replied grimly. "I think we're dead in that case. We're also dead if we try to lure them into a trap and they don't take the bait. We're dead if they take the bait, and we can't hold them in the trap. The only way we're not dead is if the trap works and we hold them, so that's what we'll do."

Neither the questioner nor any of the other men were happy with Denes's reply, but no one offered another option.

"Filtin, Seflux, Wilfwin—" Denes named seven or eight men, "split up everyone and go into the building and bring out everything that moves and might provide some protection. Build a barricade in front of all the buildings. Grab every able-bodied adult to do the same. Gather everything. Tables, chests of drawers, chairs, boxes, pews from the cathedral, beds, mattresses—anything. Carnigan, you take ten men and head for the barns. There are wagons and carts there. Bring hay bales and anything else useful. Once the wagons are unloaded, turn them on their sides as part of the barricade. And Carnigan, is the armory open?"

Carnigan nodded toward the steps of the cathedral, where lay piles of weapons. "Most of the weapons are there."

"Send people to bring the rest out and tools from the garden sheds and barns, anything that can be used as a weapon."

Denes stopped speaking. The men stared at him, some waiting for more instructions, some confused by the plan, and some stunned at the events.

"NOW, PEOPLE!!" Denes screamed again. "WE MIGHT ONLY HAVE FIFTEEN TO TWENTY MINUTES BEFORE THEY GET HERE!!"

The cluster of fifty men exploded, men running in all directions, leaving only Denes and Yozef. "Stay with me," said Denes and ran to the southern wall, climbed a ladder onto the rampart, and pointed a small telescope seaward.

Yozef, his heart racing, throat constricted, hands trembling, stumbled after Denes, thinking, *Oh shit, oh shit, oh shit.*

"Sons of whores, may dogs eat the balls of the Gods—" Abel Adalan ran through every curse he knew in three languages. He and his foul humor stood on a large sand dune, as the next longboat loads of men jumped into the surf and moved up the beach. His anger resulted from his view of longboats loading the last men off the ships, men who were supposed to be ashore already. It would be another ten minutes before those final boats reached the beach.

The Benhoudi were the problem. Despite their previous experience on successful raids, they simply weren't as skillful or disciplined as his own men.

He then used some of the same curses on himself for not having the Benhoudi loaded first.

Abel rejected starting inland without the full complement of men. The plan that had been drilled into the men involved all four hundred fighters. To change now would only cause more confusion. Narth's damnation on the Benhoudi! The delay would give the islanders more time to prepare and was liable to cost them more casualties, yet from the looks of the village and the abbey, the pickings were too rich to pass up. All he could do was send the hundred men assigned to sweep the village on ahead and wait to move on the abbey when all of the Benhoudi were ashore.

From the abbey wall rampart Denes could see a body of men, he estimated eighty to a hundred, trotting toward the village. Scattered Keelanders still ran and rode for the abbey or headed inland. He hoped everyone would be out of the village when the raiders arrived, though he feared there would be stragglers—people who, because of age, illness, sleep, stupidity, or whatever, would still be in the village. There was nothing to be done about them. He had to focus on the hundreds within the abbey complex.

"What about the people in Abersford?" Yozef asked. "Aren't they coming for the abbey?"

"They'll come," Denes said in a flat tone. "Those who can. Many who don't will flee inland. Hundreds more."

Yozef's shirt was soaked in cold sweat. *So what the fuck am I doing here?*

Panic fed his urge to run and hide, but there was a detached part of him, as if he had two minds. It was the second one that came to Denes's support.

Yozef put a hand on Denes's shoulder. "You said yourself what the most likely outcomes are, and this was the only one you believe has a chance."

"What if they don't take the bait? I'm taking a terrible risk with everyone's lives if they don't," Denes choked, his commanding demeanor gone. He didn't notice Yozef.

They both were silent for a moment, then Yozef said, "Lure them toward the gate. Give them something to chase."

Denes whirled and leaped off the rampart six feet to the ground, then raced off, yelling at someone. Yozef scrambled down the ladder and followed.

Denes was talking to a group of men, one of whom was Cadwulf. "I need a few men to give the raiders someone to chase into the courtyard. They'll need to fire at the raiders as they come close to the abbey, then run back, but close enough to let the raiders be right behind."

The grim men looked at one another. What Denes asked would get some or all who volunteered killed. All of the men raised a hand, including Cadwulf.

"Not men," blurted Yozef. "Have them chase women."

Several of the men glared at Yozef and started to protest, but Denes spoke first. "Better! They won't fire at women they want as captives. Better yet if they are young and healthy looking."

"They need to be fast and not panic," cautioned Yozef.

"Cadwulf," ordered Denes, "be quick and try to find about ten young women willing to do this and who you think can run fast enough to get back inside the walls before the raiders catch them."

Cadwulf nodded, gave Yozef a troubled glance, and ran off.

By now, the barricades were taking shape. People of all ages and sexes carried and dragged furniture, pews, boxes of who knew what, chests, beds, tables, chairs, and everything movable out of the buildings, stacked them on top of previous objects, or dropped them for others to position, then raced back for more. Carnigan drove a flatbed wagon up to a large gap in the developing barricades, jumped onto the bed, and threw off bales of hay that must have weighed a couple hundred pounds each. Men and women dragged the bales to plug holes in the barricade.

Once the wagon was empty, Carnigan untied the horses, letting their reins fall to the ground. Being well trained and used to working with people, the horses stood in place even with the surrounding turmoil. With some help, Carnigan pushed the wagon onto its side to take its place in the forming barrier. Carnigan then led the two horses to another gap, pulled out a large-bladed knife, and slit both their throats. The bodies collapsed where they had stood and, like the bales and wagon, became part of the barricade.

Yozef joined those pulling pews from the cathedral. They were solid wood, about twelve feet long, a perfect size for the barricade, and two people of moderate strength could carry them. Yozef and another man formed a "team" and had just finished placing their fifth pew when someone shouted, "No more pews!"

Sweat rolled off Yozef's face from both exertion and fear. He looked around for the first time in perhaps fifteen minutes. The results were impressive. Ugly, but impressive for the available time. A three-sided barricade about forty yards along each side faced the main gate. It was a jumble of objects that would slow anyone trying to climb over. In most places, the barricade was four to five feet high, but there were still obvious low spots and even a few outright gaps.

Another yell came, this time from someone on top of the rampart by the main gate. "Here they come!"

The second of silence at the news was followed by chaotic cries and a sense of impending panic, until Denes, the more senior of the fighting men, and some of the abbey staff shouted and shoved people into position. Yozef followed Denes back to the rampart. They could see a large body of raiders coming into view a quarter mile away.

"Three groups of about a hundred men each," Denes said. "Probably means they're planning to hit us at three places."

Yozef could have sworn there were three or four times that many—all armed with a hodge-podge of muskets, swords, spears, and various bladed weapons. They paused as they cleared the shrubbery along the road and began to spread out.

"There!" said Denes, nodding toward a group of villagers just emerging from the tree-lined road from the abbey to Abersford. There were about fifteen of them, mainly women, two of whom carried babies. Three men held spears and helped the women run.

Yozef recognized Cadwulf. He was one of the decoy men. Several of the women looked young and were scantily dressed, as if surprised by the alarm and hadn't had time to put on clothes. One woman was naked from the waist up. Even from his distance, he could see her breasts bouncing as she ran. The cries of fear and for help were audible. Occasionally, one of the women fell, and a man helped her to her feet to run again.

Phony falls? Yozef suspected. *Nice job, Cadwulf, but don't overdo it.*

There were also several individuals or couples at various distances from the abbey. None of these were part of the lure, and some wouldn't make it to the gate.

The leader of the Benhoudi, Omir Abulli, was ambivalent as he followed Abelan's orders. He and his men had profited greatly from this venture. When they returned home, they'd be honored for the booty they brought back and have stories to tell for generations. It had also cost them a sixth of their men. The Benkarsta leaders always sent Benhoudi men into the exposed parts of the raids, and too often Adalan's men had found themselves picking over what Benkarsta clansmen left after skimming off the best.

Neither of the Benkarsta leaders had shared their plans with Abulli, but he believed this might be the last raid before returning home. Subtle changes in tone and topics from the two Adalans made Abulli think this was the last chance for major spoils.

Abulli led the group of a hundred men assigned to attack the right section of the wall and was as surprised as Adalan to see the abbey gate still open and islanders running for safety. He sensed the rise in anticipation in his men as they saw a group of women, some partially clothed, trying to make it to the gate. He saw Adalan staring at the open gate and knew what was going through the Benkarsta leader's mind—should they rush the gate? Then flags signaled to disperse for the attack as previously planned. Adalan was ignoring the gate! A rush of anger colored Abulli's face.

Maybe the gate would get closed before they could reach it, or, if not secured, maybe they could fight their way through. It was a chance for fewer losses than fighting over the walls. The possibility of this being the last raid, the overbearing attitudes of the Benkarsta, and the chance he saw for his men to be first at the spoils on this raid coalesced into a decision. He turned to face the men in his group, raised his sword, and waited until his men in the second front wall group saw his raised sword. Then he pointed his sword at the gate and screamed, "For the Benhoudi! All Benhoudi, follow me!" And took off at a run, straight for the gate.

With little hesitation, most of his men from both groups followed him. A few who hesitated joined in once they saw most of their clansmen racing to the gate. The fewer numbers of Benkarsta men lingered seconds longer, then half of them followed.

Abel Adalan saw his carefully considered and drilled plan evaporate in seconds. He slashed his sword in front of himself, as if to decapitate the Benhoudi leader. *Gods curse the Benhoudi dogs!* The plan was now for shit. Or was it? He forced calm on himself. Maybe the Benhoudi could get into the abbey grounds using the main gate. Even if the gate closed first, they might still have enough presence of mind to regroup and carry out the wall assaults. The third group of a hundred was deploying as planned to breach the western wall, while most of the islanders concentrated on the frontal attacks. This third group consisted of his own clansmen, who, unlike the Benhoudi, were disciplined and held to their orders. He waved to the leader of that group to continue as planned, then had subordinates gather the Benkarsta men who had been part of the frontal assault groups but had not followed the Benhoudi. Those he kept with him, as he moved closer to observe the action.

Once again on the rampart, Denes had a hand on Yozef's forearm as they watched the raiders. His fingers dug into Yozef's flesh. Most of the raiders in the two groups facing the abbey front wall had broken from their original trajectory and were now charging directly at the gate, Denes's grip squeezed harder and almost brought Yozef to his knees.

"By merciful God! By whatever gods, they're taking the bait!" Denes burst out.

He turned back toward the courtyard. Most of the people watched him with eyes fearful, resolute, or defiant. "It worked! Here they come. No one fire until I do! Do you understand? No one fire until I do! Watch the fighting men near you, if you're uncertain. Do what they do!"

The frozen figures exploded into action, racing to positions, climbing over the barricade if they were in the courtyard, grabbing for available weapons, and older and younger islanders came out of the cathedral and other buildings from where they had been sent for safety. There was no safety. All knew it. They would live or die at the barricade.

Denes jumped off the rampart onto the courtyard ground, Yozef following, and Denes ran to the open gate, shouting for Carnigan. The large man was fast for his size and nearly trampled several people in reaching Denes.

"Keep Yozef with you. Alive, if possible."

Well, that's reassuring, a part of Yozef's mind noted.

Carnigan grabbed Yozef's arm and ran back to a large gap in the barricade facing the main gate. Yozef barely kept his feet under him to prevent Carnigan from dragging him. Carnigan took up a musket leaning against the inside of the barricade. Next to it was a second musket, the battle axe that Yozef doubted he could lift off the ground, a dented and rusty shield, and several spears of different lengths.

Yozef looked up and down the line of islanders standing behind this part of the barricade. Too few men of fighting age interspersed with older and young men, women, and even children. He thought he glimpsed eight-year-old Yonkel Miron holding a rusty sword and looking anticipatory, as if this were a game or part of some legend. Muskets and crossbows were brought to the ready. More people poured from the buildings, many without weapons, because there were no more available, ready to pick up weapons of those who fell. The abbot ran partway into the courtyard. He held a spear in one hand and traced gestures in the air in front of himself, praying and calling on God for strength, then tore back to the barricade.

I hope, Yozef prayed. *God, I hope it works!*

"Can you fire a musket?" graveled Carnigan at Yozef, who stared back as if Carnigan had asked him to speak in some different language. "Yozef!" Carnigan bellowed. "Can you fire one of these?"

Yozef shook his head. He'd never touched a firearm of any kind, much less a musket.

Carnigan picked up one of the shorter spears and shoved it at Yozef. "Take this. Stick anyone who gets by me. Try not to stick *me*."

Yozef held the wooden shaft with both hands. The six-foot spear ended in a narrow, wicked-looking blade that gleamed in the morning sun just now shining over the main wall. He shivered, his breath coming in gasps, as he gripped the shaft with both hands held against his body. A thought rose like a hand reaching for safety, a thought he had not had for many months.

Let this be all a dream! A nightmare! I'll wake up back home!

That all of this had been an elaborate fantasy was momentarily more plausible. He had been a chemistry major at the University of California at Berkeley. An alien spaceship had destroyed the plane he was flying in, saved him, then dumped him on another planet with humans put there by parties unknown. And now he held a spear and was about to take part in a battle where most likely he and everyone else around him would be killed?

Maybe I am crazy, and all of this is merely some complex illusion. Please let that be it!

His plea ended before it could paralyze him further, when Cadwulf and the bait party reached the gate. Yozef saw Denes say something to Cadwulf and the others. Yozef could now see the women up closer. They were all young—nineteen to twenty-two years old (fifteen to nineteen Earth years). All breathed hard, both from the run and from fear. Several had tears streaming from their eyes. Two women discarded bundles of clothing masquerading as babies, as they ran to the barricade. In one of those inane thoughts that appears at inappropriate times, Yozef predicted that the girl with the generous breasts would have back problems when she got older and had children. All such thoughts were ended by sheer terror, as the first of the raiders came through the gate.

CHAPTER 32

THE BATTLE FOR ST. SIDRYN'S

To the Death

"We're going to make it!" Omir Abulli exulted, as he neared the gate. Not that anyone heard him over the din of almost two hundred men running, the beat of their feet on the earth, the clanking of metal from armor and weapons, and the shouts of defiance as they neared the abbey's main gate—still open! The islander rats were stupid to worry about saving too many of their people! All that much easier for the raiders! Now, even if they tried to close the heavy gate, it'd be too late.

Abulli led the initial charge at the gate, but by now half of his men had passed him, as they all raced to get inside the abbey walls. If he had wanted, he could have stayed closer to the front, but while he needed to be *seen* as leading his men, he didn't have to be in the forefront. He let a few more pass to save his wind and put himself in a less exposed position for first contact. His scars and reputation dismissed the need to demonstrate his bravery, and being leader also meant not foolishly exposing himself.

His focus on the gate and the walls caused him to almost trip over an old couple huddled on the ground. The woman knelt with her head on her knees and her arms covering her head, the gray-bearded man draped across her as if to protect her. A rusty sword lay nearby. Abulli leaped aside and slashed at the man, cursing and yelling, "We'll deal with you later!" as he continued on.

He couldn't see beyond the opening in the wall; too many of his men were between him and the last of the fleeing islanders. He kept glancing at the abbey masonry wall, watching for the first flash of muskets. Still no firing by the islanders. Were they so timid to be mounting no defense at all?

The first of his men passed through the open gate. *Still* no firing. His elation ebbed, as instinct surfaced. Alarm flags hoisted, but there was no stopping. By the time he reached the gate, sixty of his men were already inside the walls. He needed to get to the front to see what was going on!

The first raiders rushing through the gate focused only on the islander women being chased, with only yards between the fastest raider and the slowest woman. It took several seconds for the foremost Buldorians to recognize what they found in the courtyard. Instead of a chaotic panic of islanders and an abbey open for looting, on three sides they faced the hastily constructed barricades, with heads and torsos of men and women facing them. Some of the Buldorians tried to stop, and a few recognized the danger and would have retreated, if not for the press of men behind them pouring through the gate.

Denes agonized over each flaw in their desperate plan. As each flaw passed without disaster, the next took its place. Thus, the worry that the raiders wouldn't take the bait was replaced by the fear that they'd recognize the trap and stop outside the walls, which in turn was replaced by the possibility that only a few raiders would pass through the gate before they recognized the trap and retreated or warned the others. Hope surged when the first raiders stopped in the middle of the courtyard. It was the best of all actions for the Keelanders and the worst of all for the raiders. The raiders still coming into the courtyard saw only the backs of their countrymen. Seven endless seconds elapsed between when the first raider entered the courtyard and when Denes fired his musket.

Omir Abulli could see the movement of his men slowed. Why? As he pushed through his men, he heard a single musket firing, then a flurry of muskets from three sides. He felt the whisk and sharp whine of a musket ball pass his ear.

The mass of men blocking his view thinned as men fell. In a glance, he took in their wounds from musket balls and crossbow quarrels. His elation at breaching the abbey walls disappeared in shock when he saw the barricade and the islanders. Many were older men and women, some frantically trying to reload muskets, and others holding spears and swords. A fractional second glance behind him showed more men still coming through the gate. To stand still was death. To retreat back through the gate would be chaotic, as the islanders shot at their backs. His years of experience told him their best chance was to attack and break through the barricade. The islanders were short real fighting men, so once his men engaged face-to-face, they would prevail.

These recognitions, calculations, and the resulting decision lasted no more than two seconds. Abulli rushed to the front, knocking aside shocked men and leaping over bodies of dead and wounded, raised his sword, and screamed, "Shoot at them, you idiots, then drop your muskets and draw your blades. To me, for the glory of the Benhoudi!" He turned and charged a gap in the barricade, assuming correctly that his men would follow.

Denes had fired his musket at the closest raider. The ball hit the raider in mid-chest and knocked him on his back, unmoving. All of the other muskets and crossbows followed Denes. It wasn't a simultaneous volley, but a rolling firing that lasted three to four seconds. Sixty-nine muskets and thirty-one crossbows sent their projectiles into the mass of raiders. Twenty shots went into the ground or over the heads of their targets. Ten projectiles, nine musket balls and a single quarrel somehow passed through the raider mass without hitting flesh. One musket ball found the throat of an unarmed Abersford woman peering over the barricade on the opposite side from the ball's origin. The other seventy projectiles hit raiders. Seven raiders were hit more than once. One unlucky raider was hit four times by musket balls and once by a quarrel. Of the fifty-three raiders struck in the first volley, forty-five of the hits were fatal or incapacitating.

Denes saw a grizzled raider shout, gesture with his sword, and lead a charge straight at himself, Carnigan, a cowering Yozef, and the opening in the barricade.

A second, smaller rolling volley followed from those barricade's defenders having a second loaded musket, pistol, or crossbow at hand. Another thirteen raiders went down.

Yozef crouched behind the edge of the opening of the barricade. He had a perfect view to see what appeared to be an unstoppable mass of savage men screaming bloodlust and charging straight at *him*. His imagination envisioned blades lopping off his limbs or his head or cleaving him in half. Carnigan, Denes, and three other men filled the gap. One man went down without a sound, landing next to Yozef, a hole just above his right eye, both eyes staring skyward and blood running into the earth under his head. Yozef's stomach contracted as if prepping to retch. He wanted to run. He wanted *to live*! More than anything, he wanted to drop the spear and run for the back of the abbey complex. There were other gates, or he could drop on the other side of the wall from a rampart. He could go somewhere else in Caedellium and start over. Or go to the Narthani and convince them of his worth and maybe end up more secure and honored than here on this primitive island. He wanted to be *anywhere* else but here at this moment.

He didn't know why he didn't run. Maybe because he didn't know *where* to run. Maybe because no matter how terrified he was, he couldn't leave his friends. Carnigan. Cadwulf. The abbot and the abbess who had cared for him. His workers and their families. Brak and Elian. Dour Denes, who pretended to ignore Yozef most of the time but listened when it counted.

Even if he wanted to run, his legs didn't feel strong enough to take him there. So he crouched, both hands locked to the spear shaft.

Abulli felt his men behind him. They had a chance, though perhaps he didn't, as he faced the enormous islander in the middle of the gap. He snarled, voiced an appeal and an acceptance at the same time to whatever gods there were, and swung his sword.

Carnigan deflected the sword of the first raider to reach the gap with the shield on his left arm and, with the same twisting motion, brought the battle axe down onto a shoulder at the base of the swordsman's neck. A shower of blood sprayed six feet and washed over Yozef. Within seconds, a melee engulfed the entire forty-foot section of barricade—defenders fighting for their lives against the wave of raiders.

Several raiders leaped over lower spots in the barricade to land in the midst of Keelanders. The raiders died quickly, though not before hewing down men and women.

The most desperate action centered at the gap. The tip of the raider assault followed their fallen leader. All that stopped them was that the gap was too small for the number of raiders wanting to hit it at the same time. A flurry of swords, axes, and spears held the gap long enough for defenders to flow in that direction.

A man next to Carnigan went down, a slash across his sword arm causing him to drop his weapon, and a second raider stabbed him in the belly. A white-haired man rushed to fill the place of the fallen man but went down himself from a pistol shot.

Another pistol shot glanced off Carnigan's old shield, briefly staggering him. The deflected ball smacked into Yozef's leg. He cried out but was too terrified to check for a wound. Carnigan stepped forward again, a new dent in his shield, as more raiders pushed forward.

Yozef was barely conscious of glancing down the line and seeing islanders fend off raiders who tried to climb over the barricade. Here and there, vicious exchanges started and ended within seconds. The brutal fact was that a blade fight with minimal protection tended to be short, one opponent or the other going down quickly. For the raiders, if they dispatched one islander, another took his place. If an old man fell, a teenage boy or girl was there with a spear, a sword, or even a pitchfork to stick any raider occupied with a defender.

Denes yelled, fending off raiders and yelling instructions at the same time. Not having the brute power of Carnigan, he made up for it with speed and form. His sword never stopped slashing, warding off other blades, and stabbing. Raider bodies mounded in front of the gap.

Yozef edged away from the barricade, though he never remembered moving from where he was crouching. Carnigan fended off several raiders by swinging his axe in mighty swaths. No raider was willing to come too close, but neither was the axe wielder able to concentrate on any one attacker. One raider slipped to one side of Carnigan, when a woman who had rushed to fill a space vacated by a wounded man went down from a spear. Carnigan could not turn to face the threat to his side, fully occupied with those to his front. The raider raised his sword to slash at Carnigan, and, without thinking, Yozef lunged forward and stabbed at the raider. His spear-point hit the raider's leather armor just under the armpit and buried the blade into exposed, vulnerable flesh. The raider screamed and dropped his sword, blood streaming down his side, and turned a shocked face toward Yozef. Their eyes locked. Yozef stood frozen. Another defender slashed at the wounded raider, opening the side of his neck and severing an artery. The raider fell without a sound.

Seeing the raider he'd stabbed fall jolted Yozef. He had no idea how to handle any weapon, but he could stab with the spear he held in a death grip. He made no attempt to face a raider on his own, but two more times he came to the aid of defenders in trouble with raiders. His stab attempts did no damage, but both times it forced the man to divert effort to avoid Yozef's feeble efforts, and the other defenders made good the distraction.

There was no time to reload firearms. After the initial volleys, it was all steel against steel, and steel into flesh. Underneath the yells of defiance, the screams of the wounded, and the clashes of metal, there was the scything of blades through air in their search for blood. *Sss . . . Sst . . . SsT . . . Ssssst.* The sound and intensity varying with a blade's shape and size and changing tone when metal found flesh or other metal. Somehow Yozef heard every *Ssst*, and every one seemed aimed at him.

What saved the defenders from being overwhelmed was the raiders initially charging a single point in the barricade. They were in one another's way, instead of bringing all of their men to bear on the villagers at the same instance. By the time the raiders spread outward on both sides of the gap to climb the barricade, it had given the defenders farther away time to run to the points of attack.

The fighting was vicious but brief. Raiders died in front of the barricade, on it as they tried to climb over, or amid villagers on the other side. Of the 175 raiders who followed Omir Abulli's order to charge into the gate, 153 entered the courtyard. Of these, 45 fell dead or were wounded in the first volley and 13 in the second. The remaining 95 raiders rallied to Abulli's call and charged the barricade section in front of the cathedral.

The entire Battle of St. Sidryn's, as it came to be named, took fewer than five minutes, from the instant the first raider entered the courtyard until the last of the surviving raiders fled back through the gate. Later, Yozef recollected that the battle had lasted hours.

The villagers and the abbey staff stared, stunned, at the courtyard. Bodies carpeted the blood-covered cobblestone. A few portions of the barricade had fallen or been pulled down, mostly the side facing the gate and including the gap. Bodies of both raiders and defenders lay inside the barricade in several places. No raider was standing, but many were wounded and unable to flee with their comrades. The disbelief that they'd survived held the villagers for almost a minute, then the moans and screams of the wounded from both sides brought them back from wherever their minds had gone. A roar of hatred swelled, and the defenders poured over the barricades to finish those who had intended to destroy their world.

Yozef saw one raider sitting on the ground, one leg nearly severed at the knee, wildly swinging his sword to ward off three women with spears and a pitchfork. They didn't kill him immediately, but danced around him and kept him trying to watch all three, pulling their stabs enough for the blades or prongs to pierce flesh but not deep enough to be fatal. Finally, either from loss of blood or fatalism, he gave up and dropped his sword. One young woman Yozef recognized as part of the decoy group, still bare from the waist up, stood in front of the raider, shook her breasts at him, and yelled, "Take a look, you asshole! These are the last tits you'll ever see!" and drove her spear into his throat.

Most raiders were dispatched quickly. The islanders weren't interested in prisoners.

Yozef turned to Denes. "Denes, we need a few prisoners to question." Denes looked at him but didn't respond.

"Denes! Prisoners can tell you who these people are, where they come from, and how many more there might be!"

Denes's eyes focused on Yozef's for the first time, as his mind processed what Yozef had said. He then strode out into the courtyard and yelled out something. Whatever he said, two of the men stood guard over a small knot of wounded raiders, while the rest were sent to whatever god or afterlife they believed in.

Yozef's legs gave out, and he dropped to the ground before he realized the paving stones were smeared with blood. He jumped back to his feet, looking down at himself. His arms were covered in dirt, sweat, and drying blood from the raider Carnigan had axed. Yozef felt his pants wet. He had peed himself. Carnigan walked over to Yozef, grabbed him by the scruff of his neck, and marched him over to a water trough.

"Happens to many the first time," he grunted, just before dunking Yozef completely into the water. Then he jerked Yozef back, stood him upright, and left him there. Yozef was now wet everywhere, evidence of his weak bladder obscured.

The St. Sidryn's medicants dropped their weapons, for all able bodies had been part of the defense, picked up their medical bags, and began tending the wounded. Considering the number of defender bodies, the casualties of the defenders were relatively few. That fact was of little consolation to those few. The dead themselves no longer cared, but their families either knew or would soon know. Injuries varied from abrasions and bruises that would heal on their own to wounds that required staunching and stitching, to a few truly hideous wounds. One man was missing half of his lower jaw. Several had deep slashes that might have reached internal organs. A man missing an arm below the elbow moaned, as medicants carried him inside. And others. Yozef wandered around, thinking to himself that he wanted to help, but mainly just moving and doing *something*, instead of thinking and recollecting what had just happened and how close he'd come to dying.

Yozef had dropped the old spear. His leg ached where the spent round had struck. His head spun. He was about to look for Denes and Carnigan, and when he turned, right under his feet sprawled the body of a young boy. A gash gaped across his chest, probably by a raider axe, since the wound cleaved halfway through the small chest. The boy's eyes gazed wide, sightless at the sky, a surprised look on his face. It was Yonkel Miron. Yozef stared disbelieving, hoping somehow he was wrong. He sank to his knees, putting a hand on the boy's bare leg already growing cold. Yonkel would never attend the abbey scholasticum for which Yozef thought he had potential. The boy's curiosity, boundless energy, and potential were gone. Yozef's mouth tasted bile at the pointlessness.

When once again aware of his surroundings, Yozef realized that other people knelt around Yonkel. Yozef had never sensed them come. It was Yonkel's family. He recognized the parents, a sister, other children who must be siblings, cousins, and several adults—aunts, uncles, and grandparents. Most cried. They must have waited for Yozef to return to the world, for once he made eye contact, the father patted him on the shoulder, and weeping women wrapped Yonkel's body in a cloak and laid it on a cloth. The men then picked up the corners, and the family walked out of the gate with their sad burden.

While Yozef knelt beside Yonkel, Denes, the abbot, and several other men climbed the rampart to look seaward. It had been half an hour since the last raider fled the courtyard. There were other raider groups, the one that had deployed for a possible assault on the abbey side wall, and the group that had first gone to the village. If they chose, the raiders could make another try at the abbey, but Denes didn't think they would.

"Doubtful," he told the abbot. "These are not Narthani, although I suspect they are in the employ of the Narthani. These are pirates, raiders, general free-booters. They aren't out for conquest, only gold and slaves. They won't shed blood if it's not in their interest. The Narthani might try again after their losses, but not these people."

He was right. The different raider groups gathered out of musket range and then headed toward the shore. Denes and the others watched, as they loaded onto their longboats and rowed to the waiting five ships.

Homeward Bound

Musfar Adalan watched the raid from the aftcastle of his flagship, using a powerful telescope made in one of the Iraquiniks. It had cost enough that he almost didn't buy it, but it had proved its worth many a time. The edge of the village and the abbey complex were visible upslope from the beach. Although from a mile he couldn't resolve details, he observed enough to know something had gone wrong. Instead of the assault on the abbey following Abel's plan, a number of men had gone straight for the main gate—which even from this distance looked open. Something *could* have made Abel change the plan at the last moment, but Musfar doubted it. Abel was meticulous in planning and loath to change, unless necessary. More likely, Abel lost control of the Benhoudi.

As men poured through the abbey main gate, he saw a group of men headed toward the side wall of the complex, according to plan, then stop as Musfar heard faint musket fire—two volleys. There was no way the Benhoudi would be firing musket volleys in this situation; it had to be the islanders. Three or four minutes later, a small group ran from the abbey back toward the main body, far fewer than had entered the main gate. Obviously, most of his men were still inside, and the speed of the runners and the lack of new musket fire likely meant no more men would be coming out. The carefully planned raid had collapsed.

The group of men sweeping the village joined the remaining men nearer the abbey; then a few minutes later the entire mass headed to the beach. There was only one explanation. The attack on the abbey had cost so many men that Abel decided it was not worth continuing. Either there were more men inside the abbey complex than the Narthani had told them, or Abel believed the defenders too well positioned to be defeated without unacceptable losses.

Musfar turned to the grizzled man at his side, a veteran of many years and innumerable raids and a trusted clan member. "Memur, get two good men and find something here on the aftcastle they can appear to be doing."

The man's eyes narrowed, as he translated the meaning of Musfar's words.

The three Narthani officers watched the action ashore with a lesser telescope and reacted when the raiding party started back to the beach. The leader, followed by the other two, stormed across the deck and climbed to where Musfar pretended to observe the shore.

"What's the meaning of this!" raged the Narthani. "Your men are coming back without taking the abbey!"

"I can only assume the raid didn't go as planned and the commander on shore decided to abort and return to the ships."

"There's still time to take the abbey as planned. You must go ashore yourself and order your men back!"

"I don't 'must' have to do anything. We're here to carry out raids that are supposed to be easy with the information you provide us. Mostly, it has worked well; this time it didn't. I'm not in this to lose more men than the return justifies. You should be happy that this is only the second raid that has *not* gone well." Memur returned with two crewmembers, and they busied themselves with redoing knots on ropes tied to the gunwale.

The Narthani leader turned red, gritted his teeth, and moved near Musfar so that he smelled the other's breath. "You will do as you are told, or you will answer to General Akuyun when we return."

Actually, Musfar knew Akuyun was smart and rational, not like this idiot. Who did he think he was to make such threats, with only three of them on a ship of Musfar's men?

"My pardon, now that you've shown me the necessary action, I will carry it out immediately." In one quick motion, Musfar pulled his dirk and drove it into the Narthani's diaphragm. The man's face registered shock. Musfar jerked the dirk back out and grabbed the man's hair, turned his head, and slit his throat.

Before the other two Narthani reacted, one's head was crushed under a belaying pin, and the other Narthani took another dirk into a kidney. The third wasn't quite dead when all three were unceremoniously dumped overboard.

"Thank you," Musfar complimented his men. He always believed in making sure efficient actions were appreciated. By this time, several of the ship's crew had seen what happened and came running with weapons drawn. Musfar held up a hand to indicate all was well.

"What was that all about?" asked one sword wielder.

"It seems the raid today did not go well, and Abel is bringing the men back. Our Narthani employers thought we should continue the raid until taking the abbey, evidently no matter the cost. I respectfully disagreed."

One officer spit over the side to indicate his opinion of the Narthani. "I assume this means we'll *not* be staying in these waters?"

"No," said Musfar with a humorless smile. "After due consideration, I think it's time we returned home."

Fifteen minutes later, the first longboat rowed alongside, and Abel Adalan climbed to where Musfar waited on deck.

"Cursed Benhoudi got suckered into charging the open gate, instead of following the plan," he reported. "It was a trap. Most of them were killed. It was such a total disaster, I decided that either there were more islanders than the Narthani had told us about, or the islanders somehow knew we were coming. Either way, I decided the risk to our men too great to continue." Abel stopped his brief report and looked at his commander and cousin for signs of approval or reproach.

"What of our illustrious Benhoudi? How many of them are left? And is Abulli among them?"

"Maybe thirty. Unfortunately, no Abulli."

"Unfortunate, indeed. I would have liked to hang him in front of his men for disobeying orders. Oh, well, one can't have everything."

Abel glanced around. "Am I missing something, or is there an absence of our Narthani friends?"

"They were so dismayed at today's events that they decided to swim back to Preddi City. I hope they'll arrive in due fashion. However, we won't be able to confirm this, since as soon as all the men are aboard, we'll go directly to our base camp at Rocklyn, pick up our other ship, load the remaining booty from previous raids and the provisions we set aside for just this eventuality, and set sail for Buldor."

The Battle of St. Sidryn's was over.

CHAPTER 33

AFTERMATH

Surveying the Damage

The courtyard fighting lasted minutes, and surprisingly, given the ferocity, there were few Keelan casualties: eleven dead and twenty-three seriously wounded.

"Well," mused Yozef aloud, as his eyes followed the last wounded being taken inside the hospital, "at least this is the place to be wounded, if it *has* to happen to you. God. Imagine if the wounded were hours or even days away from the medicants."

While many of the wounds were not immediately life threatening, gruesome results from musket and blade battles were inevitable. Ether was used to quiet victims, while gashes and stab wounds were cleaned, debrided, and sewn closed, and limbs too damaged, amputated. Yozef later learned the medicants used ether to end the suffering of three victims with terminal wounds.

He felt numb as he helped clean up the courtyard. Wagons were brought to the front gate and bodies of the Buldorians stacked onto wagon beds after being stripped of weapons and any useful armor. Yozef couldn't bring himself to help with the bodies but tried to help gather equipment being saved. This effort lasted until he picked up a sword and found the handle coated with half-dried blood, presumably the owner's, since the blade was unmarred. He dropped the sword and stared at reddish brownish globs and stains on his hand. His gorge rose, as he staggered to the water trough, then furiously shook his hand in the water and rubbed it against the trough wood, not wanting to touch it with his other hand. When he couldn't see any more of the raider's blood, he bolted from the courtyard and lurched out a side gate toward his house. Instead of following the worn and winding path, he aimed straight for home, cutting through brush and trees. Halfway there, his legs gave out, and he sat on a bed of dead leaves under the trees, gasping for breath and shaking.

The sun was up, the morning mist gone, and under the forest canopy he could feel the usual breeze off the ocean. The filtered sunlight made dancing spots on the dry leaves, as their living brethren quivered above. Time passed, while he calmed himself and processed the events. Now what should he do? The planned tasks of the day seemed so trivial. Go home? For what? And the people? What of the people here he knew? Were any of them among the casualties? Carnigan was okay. He saw Filtin helping the wounded. What about Cadwulf? Going down the list brought up the image of Yonkel. Yozef's eyes watered, but this time he felt mad. Mad at whoever had so savagely taken the boy's life, mad at the raider's people, mad at the Caedelli for not protecting the weak, mad at the Watchers for putting him here, mad at the universe, and so mad at a rock he sat next to, he picked it up and hurled it into the brush.

He was unaware of time passing. Finally, he rose, walked back to the abbey complex, and reentered through the same side gate he'd used to flee the carnage site. Would anyone notice he'd left? Would anyone care? People scurried about, attending to various tasks. In the courtyard, the last of the bodies were still being gathered, the stacks of raider weapons and armor piled to one side, and Caedelli working to dismantle the barricade. Many horsemen milled outside the main gate, and a cluster of men huddled near the center of the courtyard. He recognized the abbot, Denes, and a man he thought was Longnor Vorwich, boyerman of this district.

He joined the others as they dismantled the barricade, not knowing where most of the parts originated and looking for something he recognized. A dozen or more men concentrated on the cathedral pews, and he found himself on one end of a pew with another man at the opposite end. About half of the pews were already back in place. Brother Fitham directed their placement, his left arm held to his side by a bloody cloth wrapping, his face pale but determined. Yozef hadn't realized he was covered in sweat until the coolness inside the cathedral brought on a chill. When they set the pew down, the man on the other end turned. It was Cadwulf.

"Yozef!" the young man exclaimed. "I didn't see you after the fight! I was worried."

"I've been around. Helping where I could." *Peeing myself and almost puking.*

"You're all right, though? I saw you next to Carnigan, then lost sight of you."

Yozef was quiet, as they walked back out for another pew. In the noon sunlight, Yozef's chill faded. They pulled another pew off a line of hay bales.

"How many were killed?" he asked in a detached voice.

"Too many," Cadwulf replied grimly. "It's fortunate there weren't more." Cadwulf recited names, most of which Yozef didn't recognize. He did know Yonkel, one of his kerosene lantern workers, and an abbey brother he knew of only by name and appearance, a short, balding man who worked with the livestock. The brother had always given Yozef a friendly smile when they passed each other. The smile was gone forever, and Yozef wondered idly if the animals would notice they had a new attendant.

He frowned, angry at himself. *What was the brother's name? Christ! I don't even know what his name was!*

He shook himself. "How about the raiders?"

"Looked like at least eighty bodies. Damn their souls to eternal damnation!"

"Where are the bodies going? I saw them being put into wagons."

"Out to the refuse pits. They'll be burned down to ash and buried with the rest of the garbage."

Yozef imagined what served as the garbage dump about a mile farther inland, a natural dry gully where locals dumped refuse, and which accounted for the relative lack of the general odors and decay he had expected from a seventeenth- or eighteenth-century-level settlement. The image of raider bodies being dumped into the gully and then set afire brought up photos of World War II concentration camps, though in this case the image was accompanied by satisfaction.

"Did Denes question any wounded raiders? Who are they, and why did they do this?"

"Buldorians," spat Cadwulf. Yozef's expression was blank. "Buldorians," repeated Cadwulf. "From a small country on the Ganolar continent. Pirates, slavers, and anything else you can imagine. One of them confirmed the Narthani were behind it."

"Any more information from them?"

"That was all we needed."

There must be more, thought Yozef. Maybe the Caedelli didn't recognize the value of any small pieces of information. "Where are the prisoners now?" he asked.

"Dumped with the others, of course."

Yozef swallowed. So much for further interrogations.

"Yozef, what's wrong with your leg?"

"My leg?"

"You're limping, and that's blood on your pants."

Yozef looked down. His clothes had dried after Carnigan's dunking, but now something soaked the right leg of the pants below his knee. "I don't . . . " He didn't finish before a pain washed over him and he collapsed to the ground. "Agh! What's goin' on?"

Cadwulf helped roll up the pants leg. Yozef's fingers poked through two holes in the cloth, and he almost fainted when his shin was exposed. A two-inch furrow gouged across his white skin, blood caked across half of the lower leg, more blood seeping from the wound.

"You're shot!"

"Oh, fuck!" Yozef slipped into English, then back to Caedelli. "It was a ricochet off Carnigan's shield. I thought it just hit me and bounced off."

"You didn't feel this?"

"No. Not till just now."

"Well, it needs to be cleaned and sewn up. I'll help you into the hospital. Doesn't look serious, but you'll have a good scar."

Report to Boyerman Vorwich

The rider Denes Vegga dispatched for help nearly killed his horse in getting to Clengoth. Boyerman Vorwich himself and fifty men were on the road back to the abbey within fifteen minutes. Another hundred men followed thirty minutes later. They had no way to know the fighting at St. Sidryn's Abbey was over before the first group left Clengoth. When they arrived at the abbey, it had been only three hours since the first sighting of the Buldorian ships and two hours since the raiders were back aboard and gone.

Vorwich shook his head at the pile of Buldorian weapons. "I still can hardly believe the miracle that you fought them off with so few men."

Sistian took a deep breath and turned his head skyward. "A miracle it may well be, Longnor. If it was, then I will need to pray thanksgiving for many an hour. When it was all happening, everything was a blur."

"What on Anyar's name made you think to let them into the complex, instead of defending the walls? It worked, but it's insane," queried a grizzled, burly man in the boyerman's party.

"It *was* insane, but somehow it succeeded, thanks to Denes Vegga here."

Vorwich regarded Denes with a nod of approval and raised questioning eyebrows.

Denes was discomfited. "Oh ... I agree. To the insanity. But it wasn't my idea. Remember, Abbot, Yozef suggested it."

Sistian's face was blank for a moment, and then his eyes widened when he remembered the chaotic scene in the courtyard as they prepared for the raiders. "Yes, now I remember. Where in God's creation did Yozef come up with the idea?"

"I don't know, but I'm glad he did. It was a boon from God that he thought of it."

"Or God whispered it to him," murmured Cadwulf, who had been listening from the outer circle of the gathering.

Sistian threw his eldest son a sharp look, frowned, and took on a more thoughtful expression.

"Yozef?" asked Vorwich. "Who's this Yozef?"

Sistian grimaced—or grinned. "Yozef Kolsko. The stranger who washed up on the beach here not two years ago. I've written you about him several times."

Vorwich's eyebrows rose. "The stranger who's been introducing all these new products? The same one?"

"The same," said Denes.

"Hmm . . . ," responded Vorwich. "And now he's some kind of warrior, too?"

"Well," said Denes, "certainly not a fighter. He made the suggestion and tried to help during the fighting, but from what little I saw, I doubt he'd ever held a weapon in his hands before today."

"Then how is it he understood enough to make the wild suggestion to let the Buldorians into the abbey? And now that I think about it, what made you listen to him?"

Denes grunted. "I think you'd have to be around Yozef to understand. After all of the new ideas that seem to come from him, it's given him the status of someone to be listened to. I only paid scant attention to him before, but when he said to let the Buldorians inside the walls, it was like a light went off in my head. After today, I'm sure I'll find myself listening carefully to *anything* he says."

"Denes is right. There's no doubt he's someone to listen to," said Sistian. "A little strange he might be, and I'll admit I still have reservations about where he came from and some of his ideas, but I can't deny he's brought major changes to Abersford. I'm sure even in Clengoth, you've seen the effect he's having."

"I know, I know," said Vorwich. "The ether and the new lanterns are impressive. I wasn't so sure about some of the others, but my wife and daughters assure me the . . . ah . . . personal products have given him considerable status among the women of Clengoth. I've also heard complaints from some of our craftsmen about this Kolsko ruining their trades with all these innovations."

Sistian nodded. "I can see the argument, but Yozef has been a boon to Abersford workmen, and he's extraordinarily generous in putting coin into works that benefit all."

"Yes," said Vorwich grudgingly, "I've heard several of the workshops in Clengoth are using his tools and techniques. It's those who cling to their traditional methods who complain the loudest."

"Believe me, I understand . . . and Diera even more so. There are still a few district medicants who resist the new treatments, including ether, and one brother at St. Sidryn's still suspects Yozef is somehow an agent of the Evil One."

"That seems doubtful, given those for whom the ether is considered a God-send, and if he really did help save Abersford and St. Sidryn's from the Buldorians. I would have to say that gives him considerable credit to draw on."

The boyerman looked around again at the courtyard. Only remnants of the barricade remained. His gaze touched the piles of raider weapons and armor, the pools and swatches of drying blood on the courtyard ground—and shook his head. "However you did it, you all deserve my respect."

He turned again to Sistian and Denes. "What's the final butcher's bill?"

The abbot's lips pursed, and his jaws clenched. Then he sighed and forced himself to relax. "I know it could have been far, far worse, but we have fifteen dead, about twenty-three serious wounds, a couple of whom might not live, and perhaps thirty lesser injuries."

"How many dead Buldorians?"

Sistian looked at Denes. "I'm told one hundred thirty-three bodies," answered Denes with a satisfied snarl.

"My God. A hundred and thirty-three dead Buldorians and only fifteen or more dead Keelanders," summarized the amazed Vorwich.

"Only eleven of our dead were here at the abbey," said Denes. "The other four were villagers who didn't leave in time—one too ill to walk, two older citizens who either didn't want to leave or physically couldn't leave in time, and one younger man who his friends think was sleeping off a drunk."

"Even more amazing," said Vorwich. "The actual fighting to result in one hundred thirty-three to eleven dead, and the Buldorians all experienced fighting men. *I'm* willing to believe it a miracle from God."

"Oh, I assure you, there will be many a prayer of thanksgiving this day and for years to come," declared the abbot. "This will be a day Abersford remembers for many lifetimes."

Vorwich motioned to one of his men to come forward. The man carried a leather pouch across one shoulder and reached into it for quill, ink, and paper he then handed to his boyerman. "I need to send a rider back to Clengoth to semaphore on to Hetman Keelan the general situation. I'm sure he's hard to be around right now, and he and Vortig Luwis must have started preparing more men to head this way. He needs to know the situation is stabilized, and there's no assistance needed at the present time.

"Abbot, I know you're busy with everything here, but as soon as you can, write a detailed report of everything that happened. Both you and Denes write separate reports to get different perspectives. Although I don't think there's any chance the Buldorians will return. However, just in case, the fifty men I brought with me will stay the next two days, until your other men return from Gwillamer and patrol. The rider carrying the message for the hetman should meet the additional men coming from Clengoth. I'll include instructions for them to turn back. I'm assuming you have enough medical help for the wounded, but let me know if there's anything I can do to get more help."

As If Nothing Had Happened

For several more hours, Yozef sat on a stone curb, watching people moving about. His leg throbbed from his wound and the stitches. He relived the minutes of the battle a hundred times. It was late afternoon by the time he recognized signals from his body. His muscles ached, his throat was parched, and his stomach growled to remind him that despite what had transpired, he was still alive and had not eaten or drunk anything since the morning meal.

It was a slow walk to the cottage, aided by a forked tree branch serving as a makeshift crutch. Seeing the cottage exactly as he had left it that morning seemed . . . wrong, as if the intervening time might have been either another dream or a nightmare.

Elian sat on the porch. As soon he rounded the hillock a hundred yards from the cottage, she rose and went inside. When he approached, Brak appeared in the doorway of the barn he had built to replace the original dilapidated one. He held a pitchfork in one hand, the other arm bandaged and tied to his side. Brak gave him a curt nod and disappeared back into the barn.

He entered the cottage. It smelled of freshly baked bread and a meaty stew. The table was set for one.

"Is Brak all right?" Yozef asked. "His arm is bandaged."

"A minor cut from the abbey this morning. The medicants treated it, and we came back here."

"Is he working in the barn with an injury?"

"There's work to do," Elian said matter-of-factly. "He's not one to let needed work be put off."

Not even if wounded in a life-or-death fight that morning?

"Sit and eat," Elian said. "I bet you haven't eaten anything since morning meal."

She never asked about his limp or the condition of his pants leg.

Yozef sat. Elian set a bowl of stew, a covered loaf of warm bread, and a flask of phila wine in front of him, then stood there to be sure he ate. He looked at the food . . . at the older woman . . . at the food . . . and ate.

He thought he had caught a glimpse of her at the abbey this morning. She and Brak must have moved as fast as their aging bodies would let them get to the abbey before the raiders, taken part in the defense, then come back here for Brak to work and Elian to bake fresh bread.

Who were these people?

Caernford, Hetman Keelan's Manor

Culich Keelan couldn't sit. He had been on his feet for ten hours, ever since first word of the raid on Abersford and St. Sidryn's had arrived from Clengoth via semaphore. His bad knee ached, and Breda gave up trying to get him to sit. Maera didn't try; she knew it was futile and was surprised her father didn't wait for news at the semaphore station in Caernford, instead of at the Keelan Manor.

The men in the main hall also waited for news, but most sat. Word had spread throughout Caernford, and those with families and friends at Abersford, along with those simply concerned, milled by the hundreds around the semaphore station just outside the clan's capitol.

For the fifth time, Culich asked the same question. "Pedr, Vortig . . . you're sure we shouldn't be sending men to Clengoth?"

For the fifth time, Vortig gave the same answer. "Not from the reports we've had so far. Boyerman Vorwich dispatched a hundred and fifty men. They should be at St. Sidryn's by now, although even they are likely too late to make any difference. If the pattern is the same as raids on other clans, the raiders are gone within a few hours. All we can do is wait and hope for the best."

For the fifth time, the answer did nothing for the hetman's mood.

Maera and Breda watched the latest exchange from a doorway to the main hall.

"I wish your father would get off that bad knee of his," Breda said. "What good does it do to aggravate it?"

"Speaking of Father sitting, what about you, Mother? I can't remember seeing you not standing."

Breda wrung her hands. "Oh, Maera. I still have trouble even conceiving of this. St. Sidryn's! I can't help but imagine Sistian and Diera killed and the abbey burned! That's what happened to other abbeys attacked the last few months. Somehow I didn't believe it could happen in Keelan."

"I know how you feel. I knew it was possible, but *knowing* something is possible is nowhere near the *reality* when it happens. There's still hope. The abbey is some distance from the shore, and people might have had time to flee inland."

Breda shook her head at the attempt to assuage her fears. "Do you really think Sistian would abandon the abbey or Diera, if there was even one patient in the hospital?"

Maera was quiet for several seconds, then morosely shook her head. "No. They'd both stay at the abbey. All we can do now is await word and pray they fought the raiders off."

"Which is what I have been doing all day. I only hope God is listening."

Both women jerked their heads toward the front of the house when they heard a horse gallop up, then neigh as if being brought up short by its rider.

Then voices—many voices from the others waiting on the front veranda. Culich and the other men poured out from the main hall and through the front door, Maera and Breda merging with the men.

A messenger from the semaphore station leaped off his horse and bounded up the front stairs, as Culich rushed out the door. The hetman grabbed the message without saying a word or looking at the messenger. He glanced over the message, visibly relaxed, and then read it again slower. People held their breath. Culich let the hand holding the message fall to his side. Pedr Kennrick snatched it without asking and started reading, as the hetman spoke.

"The raiders were beaten off and have left. St. Sidryn's and Abersford suffered minimal damage and casualties. No further assistance is required, according to Boyerman Vorwich."

The sounds of multiple lungs letting out air was audible, followed by a cacophony of exclamations and questions.

"How—? Other information—? Thank the Merciful God! How many casualties—?" On and on it went.

Culich raised both arms to quiet the gathering. "There's no other information in the message. Boyerman Vorwich says he'll pass on more as it comes to him. There's no way to know when more will come, so it's best we return to whatever we were doing until we hear more later today or tomorrow."

The request to disperse was fulfilled, although it took a half hour of small groups talking and Culich meeting with Kennrick and Luwis before he could finally sit.

After the Keelan family was alone again, all six members knelt at the small altar in the manor's great room and gave thanks for the deliverance of Abersford and St. Sidryn's.

Abersford, Service of Thanksgiving

The day after the raid, word spread that in four days, Godsday, a special service for those slain in the raid and for deliverance of the rest of the people would be held in the cathedral. The time was later than normal for a Godsday service to allow those more distant to travel. And they came: every soul in Abersford and the abbey who could move, people from farms, mines, and settlements as far away as Clengoth, including Boyerman Vorwich and his entire family. Visitors traveling through the empty countryside and nearby hamlets would wonder what had happened to the people. They'd have learned the answer if they reached St. Sidryn's Abbey and viewed horses, carts, wagons, and carriages staked for hundreds of yards around the main wall, and they may or may not have been able to pack themselves into the cathedral. The normal seating capacity of 800 was extended to 1,300 with temporary benches, chairs, cushions, boxes, and anything else that could support a person, with more people crammed into the pews than usual. Another almost 300 souls stood at the back and sides, on walkways two, three, and four stories around the chamber and a final hundred or more sat on the floor of the altar area normally reserved for the brothers and the sisters.

Yozef found the cathedral packed. He squeezed into the main hall, content to find a place among the throng standing to one side, when Brother Fitham appeared, grasped his right elbow, and dragged him to a front pew, where Denes held a space for him.

He had attended many services since his arrival, and this one started out with the standard call to worship and a series of traditional calls and responses between Abbot Sistian and the people. The difference came when Sistian, instead of launching into a sermon, recounted their deliverance from the Buldorians. Naturally, primary thanks were given to God, then the abbot named names: the fallen, the dead, and the seriously wounded; those who had lured the Buldorians to the open gate; Denes Vegga, for organizing the defense; and Yozef, for his insights into defending the abbey. Yozef dreaded the attention. He had been so afraid. Four days since the raid and he still shook and his throat constricted whenever he let his mind linger over that morning.

"And thank you, Merciful God, for Yozef Kolsko," the abbot intoned, "the stranger who came to us in need, who became part of our community, who brought so many betterments, and who has been the implement of God's grace on our day of danger."

Yozef cringed. He'd only made a suggestion that had popped into his head! He'd wet himself! He didn't want everyone looking at him as a hero.

No one knew it, but the abbot's reference to Yozef being "an implement of God's grace" would linger in people's minds.

CHAPTER 34

NOT OVER

Preddi City

Okan Akuyun dismounted, gave the reins to a guard, and was halfway to the headquarters entrance when stopped by Admiral Kalcan's voice.

"General, a moment of your time, please." Akuyun turned to the naval commander walking briskly toward him.

"Yes, Admiral. Come on up to my office." The two men entered the outer foyer. Guards came to attention, as did other staff, as they climbed the staircase into Akuyun's office.

"So, Morfred, what has you excited this morning?" Once alone, Akuyun often used first names with his immediate subordinates and allowed them the same privilege. While such familiarity was not universal among the Narthani, Akuyun believed it helped them believe in his trust and confidence.

"The Buldorians, Okan. They were due back from the raid on the Keelan abbey by yesterday at the latest, possibly sooner since the distance is so short. There's been no sign of them. This morning I sent a sloop to the Buldorians' base at Rocklyn. They should be back late today or tomorrow. In addition, another sloop reported back today after finishing a routine sweep along that part of the Caedellium coast. They were some distance offshore, but the captain reported that the abbey and the nearby village appeared intact. The Buldorians had orders to burn anything they couldn't carry off, but the captain saw no indication of fires. The last time we had contact with Captain Adalan and his ships was when they left four days ago for the raid."

"I assume there continues to be no sign of any other warships around the island, except ours? No one else the Buldorians could have run afoul of?"

"No. So the question is, where *are* the Buldorians?"

"Your conclusion?"

Kalcan shrugged. "I expect they decided their association with us had reached an end, and they sailed for home."

"Well, I suppose that simplifies how to end our relationship," Akuyun grimaced. "We are about to move into the next phase anyway, so this won't change our plans."

"I agree. We suspected the Buldorians would do this eventually. What about Major Nertof and his two aides?"

"Ah, our redoubtable Major Nertof. It seems unlikely the Buldorians would take them home to Buldor, so I surmise our liaison men came to an unfortunate end."

"That would be my guess," agreed Kalcan. "Too bad the Empire loses such a capable and well-connected officer."

Both men smiled. Nertof was from an important Narthani family but had been considered incompetent by superiors in his previous and current assignments. Only his family connections had protected him. Even worse than his incompetence was his delusion of his own superiority and resentment at not having advanced faster.

"What an unfortunate coincidence the Buldorians ran for home on the first mission Major Nertof served as liaison," Kalcan commented, with a raised eyebrow and tweak to his lips.

"Yes, a tragedy. I'll write a report extolling the major and his contributions to the mission. He'll be remembered as having fallen in service to the Empire."

"Naturally, we'll want to exact revenge against the Buldorians," Kalcan said cryptically.

"Naturally. And you're already looking for their ships. Unfortunately, the ocean is wide, and our mission here takes priority. We'll give assurances we're on the lookout for these particular Buldorians."

Kalcan smiled and nodded. Without words, the communication was clear: they were well rid of Nertof and his two junior officers and would think no more about them.

That point settled, Akuyun sat at his desk and motioned for Kalcan to seat himself. "Now, I assume the navy is ready to take the Buldorians' place in future raids and to support our direct ground operations? Get with Hizer and decide on targets using our own forces. I'd like to renew raids in about two or three sixdays."

Kalcan nodded. "Shouldn't be a problem. I'll leave a message for the assessor."

Keelan Manor, Caernford

Boyerman Vorwich had used the Clengoth/Caernford semaphore line to relay raid updates to Hetman Keelan as fast as details were known. Even the fastest semaphore station crews could only transmit the equivalent of six complete pages of text a day. As a consequence, for two days, the limited capacity of the semaphore line was preempted from more routine communications, including news of friends and relatives. The commandeering of the semaphore lines from Caernford to the rest of Caedellium lasted an entire sixday with messages among the clan hetmen.

"The reports from St. Sidryn's are thorough, but I want firsthand accounts," Culich said to Kennrick and Vortig. "Let's get Abbot Beynom and Vegga here as soon as possible." Thus, three days later Denes Vegga and Sistian Beynom, accompanied by Boyerman Vorwich, answered the summons to Caernford and spent an entire day with their hetman, along with Kennrick and Luwis, going over the events in excruciating detail. Denes then returned to Abersford, while Sistian remained for more discussions, one topic of which was Yozef Kolsko.

"The new knowledge he's given us is already amazing, but he'll often say something without realizing the impact. For example, when we first talked about the lack of poppy extract, I explained that poppies only grew under conditions found in Eastern Landolin. He stated there was no reason they couldn't be grown anywhere by making the right conditions inside an enclosed area. He called it a 'greenhouse,' a small building with windows all around the sides and roof so the sunlight can get in. The light passes through glass to allow plants to grow. It also warms the inside of the structure. The warmth can escape out through the glass in the other direction, but as he describes it, the energy of the sun passing in is more than the warmth that passes out. By adjusting various factors, it should be possible to grow the plants here on Caedellium, if we obtained plants or seeds."

"Do you believe these greenhouses would work as he claims?" asked Culich.

"It's one of those things that just *sounds* right when you hear Yozef's explanation. Combined with the success of some of his other ideas, I'm inclined to think it would work."

"Then there's the problem of getting plants or seeds from Landolin," said Culich. "They impose the death penalty on anyone trying to smuggle out any plants or seeds."

The abbot nodded. "There *is* that. However, I'm sure a hetman of your influence, ingenuity, and wealth could find ways around such annoyances."

"Hah!" barked Culich. "Flattery will get you nowhere. I'm shocked, absolutely shocked that an abbot of your stature could conceive of such nefarious deeds."

The two gray-bearded men shared a laugh. They had grown up together as boys in Caernford. Although the abbot had moved to different positions over the years, they remained friends, exchanged regular letters, and met whenever the opportunity lent itself.

"Pardon my saying so, Sistian, but this stranger of yours sounds too good to be true. If this keeps up, there are going to be fears he's either a demon familiar or belief he's an archangel sent from God to deliver Caedellium."

The abbot sat back in his chair and sighed. "Don't think I haven't thought long and hard about those very points, Culich. I must admit to being leery of all of this at first. The *Word* warns us the Evil One can tempt in ways that seduce us into believing our actions are meant for good." He paused. "However, I've observed Yozef for almost two years now, and several other brothers and sisters have discussed him with me. We all agree we detect no evil in the man. Not that I'm sure he's told us the entire story of how he got to Caedellium. As for being an archangel, I think I can rule that out. He's quite human."

"Well, then," said Culich, "if he's not a demon familiar or some agent of the Evil One, and he's not an archangel, what is he? A spy or an agent of the Narthani or some other power outside of Caedellium?"

"I don't see how the knowledge he's already passed to us would help any agency with designs toward Caedellium. I think his basic story is true, that he's from a distant land that has knowledge that has not reached Caedellium. That he was a student still involved in his studies. That he was taken from his land against his will, perhaps in a manner he doesn't fully understand. That he had a long bout of both loneliness and some despair when he arrived here, since he believes he'll never see his home again, and that he harbors no animosity toward us. In fact, I believe he feels an obligation to us for the help we gave him. I also believe he's accepted whatever fate brought him to Caedellium and has become a real member of the Abersford community. Having said all that, I also believe he knows more about how he got here than he's told us."

"How should we view this reticence to reveal all?"

"With a degree of caution, but still make use of what he knows. While I can't be certain what he doesn't tell us could be harmful, my sense is that what he's not telling us is more personal, perhaps something about himself he doesn't want to share. If so, it likely doesn't pose a threat."

Culich was thoughtful. "Knowing you as long as I have, I expect you have some recommendations for me."

Sistian smiled. "Of course, my Hetman."

"And those are . . . ?"

"I recommend you meet him yourself. I've given you my impressions, but yours would be from a different perspective. You've dealt with different ranges of human interactions than I have, at least from the political standpoint. I'm interested in your assessment of him. That's one recommendation. Second is that while these pieces of knowledge he drops on us are giving us extraordinary advances in medicine, trades, and agriculture, I also wonder whether it might apply to other areas, perhaps even military."

Culich's eyebrows arched. "Military? You mean like the mainland realms that keep large numbers of men permanently armed and fight large-scale battles?"

"Yes. Like the Narthani. We haven't done this on Caedellium, thank Merciful God, but we know from writings and reports that it's common elsewhere on Anyar. It's only logical to believe there are formal studies on managing such fighting."

"Do you believe this Yozef Kolsko has military training and experience?"

"He's given no such indication, and I once steered a conversation in that direction. I asked if he had been in any battles, and he said he had not and hadn't been part of his people's military. That confirmed his people had a military and indirectly suggests they were involved in these large battles. When I asked why he hadn't served, he said they had a professional military drawn from their citizens, and most people don't serve or receive training."

"Then I wouldn't see how he might have useful military information, except that the idea for defending St. Sidryn's came from him."

"Yes," said Sistian, "there's that. He's told us how his people's education is long and broad, so maybe his military knowledge is only from study."

"Well, I trust your instincts, Sistian. Arrange for this Kolsko to visit Caernford, and I'll meet with him."

Sistian hesitated. *Forgive me, God, for the little lie I'm about to speak.* Any Keelander would heed Culich's "request" without hesitation, but Yozef was not from Keelan, and Sistian wasn't sure he'd come just because the Keelan hetman asked him to. He didn't want Culich's first interaction with Yozef to start off wrong.

"Actually, I wondered that since it's coming the time for your yearly tour around the province, if you could manage to stop over a night or two at Abersford. I'm not sure Yozef is ready to leave where he is as yet, and I'd rather not force him to change his routine. I know the attack shocked him, perhaps in ways I'm not sure about, so it might be best if he stays where he is for now."

"Then it'll have to wait for a month or more. I'm postponing my inspection of the province. There's a conclave called at Orosz City to discuss the Narthani threat." Culich paused for a moment, stroking his beard in a manner the abbot knew indicated he had a new thought and was running it through his mind before sharing it. After a few more moments, Culich said, "Although *I* can't go immediately, what about sending Maera? She's wanted to visit St. Sidryn's for some time, because it's been several years since she's been there. I've put her off because I value her help so much, but she can't accompany me to the conclave, and this would be a good time for her to spend a month at the abbey."

A smile warmed Sistian's face. "We're always happy to have a visit from Maera. Diera especially will be pleased. However, I still believe you will need to assess Yozef personally."

"Of course, but Maera will have more time than I could spend, so her examination of this Kolsko character might be in more depth. I'll speak to Maera, and I'm sure there'll be no problem."

Sistian nodded with a thoughtful expression.

Culich recognized the look. "Something else about this Kolsko?"

"Something I wasn't planning to mention at the time, to allow you to see for yourself. Since it'll be a while until you meet Yozef, I'm now thinking I should mention it to you, and you can decide whether to pass it on to Maera."

Sistian rose from his chair, walked to the window, and looked out over the manor grounds. Culich was patient, knowing Sistian was gathering his thoughts.

After several minutes, the abbot turned back to Culich. "It's not just pieces of knowledge, like the ether. I'm hearing from farmers he's given them ideas on increasing yields and warding off plant diseases, and tradesmen on new products and techniques, even more than the innovations you know about. Then there are the medical issues. Yozef knows little of how to treat patients and seems ignorant of basic facts. Yet the medicants tell me he's answered questions about the human body that have always puzzled them. Also, he seems to have knowledge that even when they are convinced it's true, they can't understand how the knowledge was developed, nor can Yozef explain it. I've heard it said several times it's almost as if someone is whispering knowledge into his ear."

"Someone?" asked Culich, sensing where this was going.

The abbot smiled. "Yes, the someone being . . . God? I'm afraid I inadvertently contributed to the rumors when I spoke at our service of thanksgiving at St. Sidryn's."

"And this would make him . . . what?"

"I think you know the answer. A Septarsh. One who is directly inspired by God. The *Word* describes the Septarshi as men in touch with God like no others. Sometimes God whispers in their ear, sometimes in their dreams, or sometimes they simply know something without knowing how."

"Not an Avatar?" said the skeptical Culich.

"No. I'm not even beginning to think of Yozef as an Avatar, a descent of God into human form. That's too close to blasphemy."

"So, what do *you* think?"

Sistian shook his head. "This is not something I would commit to. Not yet."

Culich's eyebrows rose. Sistian's response meant he was leaving the question open, a major sign of the seriousness with which he took the issue. "So you think it's possible?"

"Possible? Yes. Nothing in *The Word of God* or *The Commentaries* says all of the Septarshi have already lived. There are eleven recognized. The last Septarsh was over a hundred years ago. Each has differed from the others, but all are associated with major changes, sometimes with holy writings, sometimes with conflicts, and sometimes with gifts of knowledge. But all were acknowledged as Septarshi, either during their lives or after their deaths, and all were considered as God's response to prayers for help or directing the people onto correct paths."

"It sounds like Yozef fits the qualification of gifts of knowledge. What about writings and military?"

"I don't see Yozef as creating new Holy Scriptures. I believe him to be a good man but firmly rooted in the world and not interested in theological issues. Military? As I said, I don't know. He doesn't fit what I'd expect out of a military leader, and I get the sense his view of how conflicts are pursued is very different from ours, if for no other reason than Caedellium has had no history of wars like the mainlands have had. I again advise your drawing him out on this topic to see whether there's anything to help with the Narthani."

"And, of course," prompted Culich, "the Narthani would qualify as the threat that God is sending Yozef as an answer to prayers?"

"That *would* be the more common folks' interpretation."

Culich was dubious. "I must say, this bothers me. Men regularly claim to commune with God, usually because they're either mad or charlatans."

"Yes, but *usually* is the main word. Septarshi may be rare, but the *Word* and *The Commentaries* acknowledge their existence."

"You and I have spoken about the possibility that Rhaedri Brison in Orosz Province might be eventually acknowledged as a Septarsh, because of his commentaries on the *Word*. As infrequent as they seem to be, isn't having two alive at the same time hard to believe?"

Sistian smiled. "Not being privy to God's plans, I'd hesitate to offer any opinion on the matter. Brison has been working on new commentaries to the *Word* for thirty years at St. Wyan's Abbey in Orosz City. Any elevation of Brison would be based on his writings. There's no reason to think God couldn't arrange a Septarsh with other talents."

Culich chuckled. "Meaning I shouldn't give advice to God?"

"You'll do what you think best," Sistian said with a pious twinkle.

"What does Kolsko think of all this?"

"I don't believe he's aware of it. I've neither seen nor heard indication of such."

"What do you think his response will be once he *does* become aware?"

"I suspect he'll be appalled. Truth be told, I'm not sure he believes in the existence of God."

"Then how can he be a Septarsh?"

"Nothing in the *Word* says a Septarsh must be a believer. He only has to be in communion with God, whether he knows it or not. We commonly think of the Septarshi as archangels, carrying out commands they hear directly from

God, but all a Septarsh has to do is carry out God's will, irrespective of how he gets the direction."

"Well," said Culich, "I'll be skeptical. Then again, I suppose so will you. Keep an eye on him, and we'll see what Maera reports back. When I get back from Orosz City, and there's time, we can think again about arranging for me to see for myself."

Veil of the Future

Two sixdays later, Culich Keelan sat alone in his study amid papers strewn across his desk. Semaphore messages from other provinces reported incursions and small raids into their territories bordering the Narthani client provinces, Selfcell and Eywell. Suspected sightings of Eywellese occurred in Northern Keelan. Raids erupted along the coasts throughout Caedellium, now by the Narthani themselves. There were details on the attack on Abersford and St. Sidryn's, along with Maera's transcription of his notes from a hetmen conclave in Orosz City, chronicling his discouragement at failing to convince more of the other hetmen of the seriousness of the Narthani threat.

His right shoulder blade had a knife of pain in it, he knew from tension. He avoided looking himself in the eye when before a mirror these days, too afraid to see the fear he hid even from Breda. When he was alone like this, it was the worst. It was then that he closed out externals and looked deeply into how he saw the play of the future. Every instinct he had said the Narthani meant to enslave the entire island, and he discerned no path to stop them. Even if it might not happen in his lifetime, this didn't provide solace. The weight of his ancestors and the entire Keelan Clan was crushing.

***

Okan Akuyun's mood contrasted with Hetman Keelan's. Akuyun was cheerful. He engaged in friendly conversations with both immediate subordinates and common troops. Rabia and the children all teased him on his relaxed manner at home, and he found himself noting minor things like a sunrise, the passing of seasons on this beautiful island, and the pleasure of reviewing the progress of the newest Narthani civilian colonists. He even found time to read Landolin poetry, something he would never confess to any other Narthani, besides Rabia.

Everything was going according to plan. All of the assigned troops were in place. Granted, they had been of poor quality when they arrived, but continuous training had them rounding into shape for what was necessary to accomplish the Caedellium mission. The attempts to confuse the Caedelli and prevent them from uniting was ongoing and impossible to evaluate with any certainty, but the Buldorian and Narthani raids, the secret contacts with several clans, and the placement of agents throughout the island had all proceeded as planned.

Now it was time to ratchet up the pressure on the Caedelli before launching the final phase. It was only a matter of time before they integrated the island into the Narthon Empire. Akuyun was not a cruel man. He would prefer that all of the Caedelli lived to serve Narthon, but serve they would, even if by no longer existing.

***

While Culich Keelan and Okan Akuyun both foresaw future paths, one dark and one beckoning, Joseph Colsco, aka Yozef Kolsko, had no such clarity. He sat on the porch of his house, the Faughns long asleep. The sounds of the night were similar to Earth's but different. A breeze wafted across his face. The scents were similar to Earth, though not *of* Earth.

The stars were bright on this clear night, as they would be on Earth, yet not the same stars. There were no recognizable constellations as seen from Earth. Did the Caedelli have constellations? If not here, elsewhere on Anyar? He wondered whether he could even see any star here that was also visible from Earth. Harlie, the disembodied voice that had been his only contact with the aliens whose vessel collided with his flight near Denver, had never answered his queries about Anyar's location. It could be within sight of Sol or tens of thousands of light-years across the Galaxy.

Were the Watchers, or whoever they were, up there looking down at Anyar . . . at Caedellium . . . at him? Was this just someplace where they dumped him and went on their way again? Would anyone ever know what happened to him? No, he decided. No one would know. At least, not in his lifetime. His journals could someday let it be known. But now . . .

He stood and paced the porch slowly, back and forth, his footsteps helping anchor the feeling that he was *here* and *now*. Once again, everything had changed. On Earth, he had been satisfied with a predictable future. Then he'd been ripped away and left on Anyar. He'd been here almost two years. Anyar years. He'd struggled to accept and adjust. And he had. He had begun to think he knew the direction of his life here: satisfied and predictable, once again, as it had been on Earth. Now . . . ? *What was* predictable?

The Narthani and the Buldorians were a reality of this world. He could easily have been killed at the abbey, and who knew what might yet happen? The Narthani weren't going away. They'd be back, and if what he heard was accurate, it sounded like soon. And it wasn't just him. He *did* care for these people. They were rough in many ways but basically honest and appreciative of the lives they had. Even the Faughns, with all of their struggles, had a pride of self. The Narthani might destroy all of that.

He stopped pacing and took a deep breath. There must be more he could do to help, both for himself and the Caedelli. Some knowledge he could dredge out of his enhanced memory. *God! I might have to accept that this life may never be safe and predictable.* It wasn't a comforting realization, but it somehow eased the confusion of his thoughts and kindled a determination to face reality.

Yes, he had to give all of this much more thought. But not tonight. He entered the cottage, walked to the bedroom, and climbed under the covers. His last thought before drifting off was that whatever came, he would have to face it.

END OF BOOK 1

Major Characters

Abulli, Omir. Buldorian mercenary from different clan than the Adalans.

Adalan, Abel. Buldorian mercenary. Second-in-command to cousin Musfar Adalan.

Adalan, Musfar. Commander of Buldorian mercenaries.

Akuyun, Okan. Commander of Narthani mission to conquer Caedellium.

Akuyun, Rabia. Wife of Okan.

Balcan, Mamduk. Narthani religious prelate.

Beynom, Cadwulf. Student. Son of Diera and Sistian. Friend and employee of Yozef.

Beynom, Diera. A medicant. Abbess of St. Sidryn's abbey. Wife of Sistian.

Beynom, Sistian. A theophist. Abbot of St. Sidryn's abbey. Husband of Diera.

Bolwyn, Elton. A medicant at St. Sidryn's abbey.

Dyllis, Saoul. A medicant at St. Sidryn's abbey.

Erdelin, Memas. Narthani colonel.

Faughns, Brak and Elian. Elderly home staff couple of Yozef.

Fitham, Petros. Elderly theophist at St. Sidryn's abbey.

Fuller, Filtin. Skilled worker and friend to Yozef.

Gwillamer, Cadoc. Hetman of Gwillamer Clan.

Harlie. Name given by Yozef to alien artificial intelligence created to interact with Yozef.

Hizer, Sadek. Narthani Assessor reporting direct to Narthani High Command.

Kalcan, Morfred. Narthani naval commander.

Keelan, Breda. Wife of Culich. Mother of Maera.

Keelan, Culich. Hetman of Clan Keelan. Father of Maera.

Keelan, Maera. Eldest daughter of Culich and Breda.

Kennrick, Pedr. Advisor to Hetman Culich Keelan.

Ketin, Erkan. Narthani colonel.

Kolsko, Yozef (a.k.a. Joseph Colsco). California chemistry graduate student who boards an ill-fated flight to a conference and meets an unimagined future.

Linton, Bronwyn. Widow owner of farm near Abersford.

Metin, Nuthrat. Narthani colonel.

Miron, Yonkel. Abersford boy who first discovers Yozef lying on the beach.

Moreland, Anarynd (a.k.a. Ana). Friend of Maera Keelan. Distantly related to Moreland Clan hetman.

Moreland, Brym. Father of Anarynd. Cousin to Moreland hetman.

Moreland, Gynfor. Hetman of Moreland Clan.

Puvey, Carnigan. Physically imposing member of abbey staff. Friend of Yozef.

Tuzere, Nizam. Narthani civilian administrator.

Vegga, Denes. Magistrate and sheriff-equivalent in town of Abersford. Commander of Abersford fighting levy.

Luwis, Vortig. Advisor to Hetman Culich Keelan.

Vorwich, Longnor. Keelan Clan boyerman (district chief) of Abersford and St. Sidryn's area.

Watchers. Name given by Yozef to alien creators of Harlie and whose spaceship destroyed Yozef's flight to Chicago.

Zulfa, Aivacs. Commander of Narthani troops on Caedellium.

THE PEN AND THE SWORD

Book 2 of Destiny's Crucible

Joseph Colsco, aka Yosef Kolsko, was abandoned naked on a human inhabited planet after aliens observing Earth had accidently collided with his passenger airliner. Although rescued and injuries healed, his knowledge of his rescuers prevented his return to his previous life. After the initial shock and adjustments, he envisioned his new life would be busy with introducing as much science and innovations from Earth as the society of Caedellium could absorb. While it wasn't the life of his choosing, he foresaw a peaceful existence.

He was wrong.

Large swaths of the planet Anyar were racked with wars between Narthon, a people believing their destiny was to rule the entire planet, and neighboring realms. The violence had bypassed the island of Caedellium—fortuitously placed distant enough from fighting that the island's people believed themselves unaffected by events elsewhere. Their complacency and Joseph's naivete were shattered by Narthani facilitated raids on Caedellium's coasts.

Joseph survived a desperate fight but realized his life and those of people he had come to like were in grave danger from an overwhelming military force. Every advantage possible was needed if they were to survive. He would search his memory for technology and lessons of Earth's history.

His life was about to take another unimaginable turn.

ABOUT THE AUTHOR

Olan Thorensen is a pen name. Olan is a long-time science fiction fan (emphasis on 'long') who has jumped into independent publication with all its pitfalls and unknowns. He thinks all colors go together: clash, what clash? A fan of Dilbert, Non Sequitur, Peanuts (even if old strips), and still thinks the end of The Far Side was a tragedy. In his youth, served in the US Special Forces (Vietnam:SOG). Has a Phd in Genetics, around 200 science publications as author and co-author, and is a Fellow of the American Association for the Advancement of Science (AAAS). Lives in the Blue Ridge country of Virginia. Thinks it's totally cool someone can read his stories and enjoy them. Loves fireflies, thunderstorms, is eclectic in music, and thinks four seasons are better than one. His web page is olanthorensen.com and hopes his books sell enough he can afford a better web site, better maps, and faster publication. All input from readers is appreciated.

Please email me with any comments at olanthorensen@gmail.com or through my web site at olanthorensen.com where downloadable color maps of Anyar are available. I promise to read all emails, though I won't be able to answer personally every one. Also, if you enjoyed the story, please leave a comment/review on appropriate venues, such as Amazon and Goodreads. Readers wishing to be on a mail list for news of new releases should email me.

Made in United States
North Haven, CT
11 December 2023

45516518R00183